Anne Atkins is an actor as well as a writer. Brought up in Cambridge, where she attended the Perse School for Girls from time to time, she received her education from the Cambridge Footlights. After school she went to Paris, to attend the Decroux School of Mime and to study the harp under Solange Renié. She then went to Brasenose College, Oxford, celebrated her marriage and went on to attend the Webber Douglas Academy of Dramatic Art.

Her husband is a vicar, and they live in Fulham with their four children and various chickens, bees, cats and doves, but sadly no horses. Her hobbies include the school run and doing other people's piano practice.

Her first work, *Split Image*, a book challenging traditional relationships between the sexes, was published in 1987 by Hodder & Stoughton. Her first work of fiction, *The Lost Child*, was published in 1994, followed by *On Our Own* two years later. Both novels are available from Sceptre.

A Fine and Private Place

Anne Atkins

FLAME
Hodder & Stoughton

Copyright © 1998 by Anne Atkins

First published in 1998 by Hodder and Stoughton
A division of Hodder Headline PLC
First published in paperback in 1999 by Hodder and Stoughton
A Flame Paperback

A CIP catalogue record for this title is available
from the British Library

ISBN 0 340 67221 8

Typeset by Palimpsest Book Production Limited,
Polmont, Stirlingshire
Printed and bound in Great Britain by
Clays Ltd, St Ives PLC, Bungay, Suffolk

Hodder and Stoughton
A division of Hodder Headline PLC
338 Euston Road
London NW1 3BH

My beloved is mine, and I am his: he is . . . chiefest
among ten thousand.
Until the day break, and the shadows flee away, turn,
my beloved, and be thou like a roe or a young hart upon
the mountains . . .

The Song of Songs

ACKNOWLEDGEMENTS

Thank you to Dr Jane Sequeira, Professor Susan Greenfield, and Dr David Vaux, for their pathology expertise. To Jane's husband, Jonathan Ruffer, for his advice on guns. To Perry Southall, herself the victim of a persistent stalker, and her family for their help and hospitality. To Graham and Margaret Scott-Brown for the welcome and friendship they gave me in Pokhara, many years ago, and for their advice since, and that of their daughter Anna. To Jamie Mackay, and all his colleagues, including Coroner Peter McCormack, for continual help on police procedure, and particularly to Ken Talbot for his framing of the perfect crime, and apologies for the shock he received when he thought I'd committed it. To Steve Midgely, psychiatrist, for his insights into the criminal mind. And to Sue Fletcher, my editor, for her tireless patience.

He went into his small kitchen to fill the kettle. His window framed a beautiful late spring day. Birds dipped and laughed in the branches outside. The water from the cold tap splashed on his hands and drummed in his ears as the kettle filled. In time, he thought idly, in time to a different drummer. Where was that from? Somewhere in his childhood; he remembered somebody repeating it sometime in his childhood. Not his mother. One of the others, he thought without obvious bitterness. He opened the fridge for the milk, and took out a chocolate fudge cake in a Cellophane wrapper. It always started like this, very quietly and gently, without his noticing it. He continued to get his tea ready without any apparent awareness that it was beginning again, that the needle was on the same old track.

The kettle growled on the heat. He took a grubby tray from next to the oven and put it on the table. The noise from the kettle seeped gently over the other, unnatural, silent noise, like oil over troubled water. He put a mug, a knife, a carton of milk and the cake on the tray. He would have his tea in the sitting room. There was a television programme he wanted to see in twenty minutes or so. He liked to behave as though he would still be there to watch it. The noise grew.

It wasn't really a noise. No ear heard it. No soundwaves moved. But if he had to describe it that was the nearest he would get: a silent insistent hammering of distant kettle drums. The other kettle was just about to boil. Automatically he poured the boiling water over the tea bag in his mug. He was becoming less aware of his actions, numb, wrapped in a distancing haze. The drumbeat was beginning to drown the other sounds around him. He cut himself a slice of cake, broke off a mouthful, and ate it before picking up the tray to take into the other room. He tasted nothing. He seemed to be behaving normally. A face looking in at the window would have seen nothing strange. The churning panic was invisible.

Occasionally, when he was still at school, he had wondered whether to tell someone. There was once a teacher who might have helped. Sometimes the pain was so great he couldn't understand why he hadn't. But now there was no one. She had never listened to him in his life. He would never have told her.

He went into the other room and sat down. By now he was only dimly aware of the television, as a dreamlike interference in the background. He neither trembled nor dropped anything. Very carefully, he ate his cake. He drank his tea. Silently, something was gathering strength, like water building up behind a dam. Soon he would go out. By the time he left the flat he would barely notice the front door or the key or whether or not he was putting on his coat. Already the noise was so loud that the room seemed to breathe in and out. Not that he saw anything unusual, any more than he heard a sound, but the overall impression nonetheless was that the walls beat like an enormous heart all around him.

And all the time the noise, the throbbing on and on, the thrashing of the world in and out around him, continued louder and louder, growing, embracing everybody and everything, until it was all over. Yet nobody else was aware of it. No one else heard it. Nobody would have seen anything odd at all.

2

It was not a suitable day to die.

The weather was glorious – which was lucky, really, seeing as it was the day of the Fair. As early as seven, when I woke, the sky was achingly clean, the moon still smiling, shy and transparent, the morning star just beginning to twinkle out of sight. A few snags of cloud far away, over Cambridge. For the rest quite endless, deep blue, and empty. Except for the bird song. The bird song was deafening. I don't know why it should have been louder that day, 3 May, than any other; I can't remember hearing them sing like that since I was a child, almost. Starlings, no doubt, coming home to England and putting the world to rights.

The morning had that hazy distance which seriously hot days often have almost before they have begun. The horizon was breathing a quiet, misty threat. The pool still had the chill of spring on it.

I cleaned my teeth briskly, splashed soap and water over my face, and went to see if Sara wanted to join me for a swim. She tends to sleep with her curtains drawn, so her room was shadowy, her teenager's mess sprawling everywhere, the thin cotton of the curtains blowing in the sunny breeze and a trickle of Bach oozing softly from her CD player. Had it been playing all night? Or had she woken earlier and turned it on? Hard to tell, but she seemed asleep now, with nothing but a tangled web of hair showing on her pillow. I pulled the curtains back slightly to let more sunlight in, and left her in peace.

I'm not sure whether I've started in the right place. I've thought about it so often, wondering whether to write an account of what happened, that I hadn't stopped to think when the story really begins. The third of May is surely the middle. I picked it, I suppose, because it's the day our lives changed, the pivot on which the story turns.

And yet that's not true either. It was only the climax really: from one point of view one could see it as the end of everything – of a story which started years ago, before this summer, before we went away, even, perhaps, before we had children. In a way it started that afternoon in Christ Church Meadows, when David astonished me, and possibly himself as well, by kissing me suddenly by the banks of the Isis, just before his research supervisor came jogging round the path like a jelly squeezed precariously into a grey tracksuit.

'I suppose I'd better ask you to marry me,' he laughed, after Dr Bullen had disappeared around the bend of the river again. I stared at him as if he were mad. It was such an extraordinarily old-fashioned thing to say. I suppose there always was something profoundly out of date about David: the chivalry, the restraint, the essential gentlemanliness.

That day was another which I shall never forget as long as I live – the day I fell in love. The air itself, even the leaves on the trees seemed to have changed colour. It was as if one had previously lived life on rather cheap camera film. Now came Kodak paper, sharp, defined, in focus, the colours bright and true and clear for the first time.

Later, alone, I went for a long walk in the countryside outside Oxford to think about David's absurd suggestion. It was cold, and wet, and windy: I had never before seen the trees as glorious and angry as God made them. I was very annoyed to be in love. Marriage was the last thing I wanted. But that was the moment when I realised that if I turned away and kept all the things I had valued until that moment, my dreams of a glittering career, my freedom, my independence, I'd lose the very taste of life. The very slightly brighter colours.

I find it hard, now, to imagine how different my life would have been. None of this would have happened for a start. Perhaps we could blame David for it all. It was always rather comforting when he took responsibility for things. I never thought I wanted an authoritative male around, but there is a lot to be said for it. How odd it is, though, that when I talk of him I almost seem to do so with resentment. Is that what it is, this feeling? Bitterness? Perhaps I use anger to keep myself going. Perhaps I haven't forgiven him for leaving us. It wouldn't have turned out the way it did if he had still been here.

The other day was different, naturally. The third of May, I mean. That ominous afternoon a few months ago which found itself, so incongruously, in the middle of an idyllic English bank holiday weekend. The weather was better for one thing. But it had that same unforgettable quality, the images photographed on the mind, the details picked out and lingering in the memory, as if one were part of a Merchant Ivory production. I still remember shots – forgive the pun – from the Fair. The thick china teacups, which Diana mysteriously produces every year from a bygone age of Mothers' Unions in the Church Hall, slopping with luke-warm, milky tea. The tiny beads of sweat on Hugh's forehead as we met to give out the prizes. The paper plates laid with little home-made butterfly cakes, their soft cream-coloured butter-icing glistening in the heat. The tent flapping sluggishly as we queued for our tea. The dark gobbets of blood dried and clotting on the wall. I can still see it all in front of me as if it had been there a few minutes ago, rather than fifteen weeks.

But the days and weeks afterwards are already a blur, a child's painting over which someone has split a glass of water, so the images are slowly but resolutely bleeding into each other in a fascinating, puzzling confusion. The deep, draining fear; the sight of Alison's face, shocked to the colour of putty; the awful sense of responsibility, of its all being down to me.

There was another storm last night. I could hear it, as though from a great distance, as I lay here, in a strange bed. I thought at last it's over. The unaccustomed English heat wave has broken. Though the jetsam, of course, to develop rather a silly metaphor, is still there, thrown up on the dirty beach.

It is nearly four months later, but the lawns are still brown, the shrubs withered. The lilacs are long finished now. The first time there was a rough night like last night, all those weeks, almost a lifetime, ago, I wondered whether the lilac blossoms would be pulled from the trees. By yesterday the flowers were forgotten.

Many of the smaller bushes in the garden were staring blindly in the heat, like bunches of dark green paper shrinking in the drought, when I last looked at them.

The last storm must have been at the end of April, apart from that brief torrent of rain last week, on the night of the inquest. Certainly by early May there were all the usual scares about ozone layers and melting icebergs in Antarctica, and the dangerous heat of the sun.

The heat of the sun. As so often happens when my mind throws up a spray of words, I want to swim with it, to go and look it up, to see where the line of poetry takes me. *Cymbeline*. Fear no more the heat of the sun. Apart from the bank holiday weekend I don't think there will now be much more heat to fear. The August bank holiday is always hot; swelteringly, blisteringly so. The last few pale limbs and backs and faces will turn a smart scarlet on the village green. And already, with the year malingering before the autumn, there is almost nothing left but memories, and not just of the dripping heat that Saturday afternoon at the village fete. I can still hear a jug of fresh lemonade, tinkling with ice and one of Prue's little cloth covers weighted down with beads, while we sat idle, as if we could be happy again, into the long shadows of a Sunday evening. The splash of the pool in the late sun, the wood-pigeons cooing across the tennis court, the old wicker chairs in the garden groaning at the unexpected weight of policemen.

Large straw baskets full of early garden raspberries; large straw hats full of laughter and bubbles and curls; short legs scratched by the canes, running through the long grass, and little cheeks stained with juice. The birthday cake, the tearless face, the stillness.

I'm being very foolish: that was years ago.

Two or three more weeks of summer. Just a little longer before we come to dust.

I remember David telling me about the path through the woods when it had gone to dust, brittle and withered, in heat like this many summers ago. He sat me on a tree stump, long before we had children, and conjured up his own five-year-old image, knee socks round his ankles, long grey shorts and muddy knees, scuffing his way through the summer weeks in the spinney behind the churchyard before anything had been built there. Corpses Copses, they called it as teenagers. At that time it was just the woods; the ghosts came later, and not there.

He described the earth to me as he had seen it then, pale and cracked with the drought, full of the deep chasms as if caused by fairies' earthquakes. In my mind's eye I can still see that little boy, dressed like William Brown, watching the ants scurrying over, trying to cross, troop after troop falling down the abyss. Later that day, at teatime, he asked his nanny why the ground was like that and she said, 'Because it's summertime, darling; eat up.'

So at bedtime he asked Prue, who looked it up in an encyclopedia, making both herself and Maurice late for some dinner party or other, and then read to him about evaporation and dehydration and shrinkage and the vast composition of water in most organic matter, and what happens when you remove one of the major components in any given subject, till his mind sang with knowledge and he went to bed hungry and satisfied at the same time, with Prue's expensive scent lingering on his bedclothes, happy to know there'd be another day in the morning.

Prue. She's never passed an exam in her life, nor tried to. A later generation, a slightly lower social class, and how different she would have been. Then she would have been a head mistress, a don, an intellectual pioneer of one kind or another. Possibly even a model or an actress. A hundred years earlier and she might have been the author of an authoritative book of country herbal remedies, or perhaps, if she had been less blissfully content in her domestic circumstances, striding about on the back of a camel or an elephant, crossing some impossible terrain and then writing about it afterwards.

And yet, despite her impeccable manners and flawless cheekbones, she can be quietly, invisibly ruthless. Before I learnt it for myself, the hard way, I would have felt this attitude was not quite nice. Now I know better.

My intention was to 'tell the whole truth' about the third of May. That was why I put pen to paper – or rather, took up one of these horrid mass-produced biros. How arrogant and foolish of me. Did I really think I knew it all? Only God sees the whole truth. The rest of us can merely expose tiny, isolated glimpses. And some glimpses are more dangerous than others.

Now I find the task so repellent I can't seem to stick to it.

As I say, it wasn't the day for it. Though I don't suppose many of us, myself or Prue included – or indeed anyone in the village – usually contemplate anything quite so gruesome at such an early hour on a Saturday morning. On the contrary, I seem to find myself, now, dithering away the time wondering whether the fantails will succeed in mating this year, or how to persuade that rambling rose to climb over the wall outside my study window; how to get more into the school scholarship fund so we can offer realistic bursaries, or whether it is really a fourteen-foot line Hermia delivers to Demetrius when she tells him to kill her as the First Folio has it, or simply a line followed by a half line, as most editors think. Whether to paint the oak panelling in the library a lemon yellow as David once suggested, or to assume he had been pulling my leg. Whether to get Sara's bicycle lights fixed for her or tell her she's old enough to take responsibility for her own safety; whether to organise pony rides for the Fair, whether there'll be any thick-cut marmalade left and have they remembered to put out those ugly brass pots Lady Henly gave me for the bric-à-brac stall, and how, oh how, to keep my desperately severed family intact.

Not, usually, how to blow my brains out. Or anyone else's for that matter.

3

He had always thought of it as a noise. Like a drumming, was how it began. Or like a theme; a tiny, lost little theme of music, developed out of all proportion until it became deafening. Like Ravel's *Bolero* before it was filleted by the sharpened feet of a pair of ice skaters. The first time he'd ever heard the music he was stunned: it described his experience as if it had been written for him.

He had been alone, on the closely clipped lawns of one of the college gardens, Christ's, or Corpus, he thought it was, but he couldn't remember and didn't care. There, Ravel's piece had been played, keeping strangely in tune to a natural storm breaking out among the treetops overhead. The music had started, with the raindrops, almost imperceptibly. Like a small child, tapping on a stick, hundreds of miles away; like the water weeping from the skies overhead. You thought it would never get louder, never be noticeable, never be anything but the softest and gentlest of messages. And yet the sound was creeping up, swelling, growing invisibly like an unborn child, while the rain breathed quicker, running through the trees, chasing the leaves and the wind faster than it had before. The pulse seemed more urgent, the raindrops larger and heavier, more violent in their attack. The water poured; the drumming shouted unceasing in the ear. Music and rain pelted together. You were catapulted towards some dreadful conclusion. The gallop of the drums continued on and on, louder and louder, long after you were sure it had reached the heights, and finally, with a sickening and exhilarating relief, gave a roar of triumph, gasped at its own silence, and died in the air.

And there you were, abandoned and aghast, wondering when it had happened. And how? What had caused the storm to break? At no stage did you give it quarter. There had been no change, no relenting or intake of a pause at all. It had never been anything other than a still small voice. And yet here you sat, surrounded by destruction: sodden leaves and torn branches wrenched like limbs from the trees, strewn about the elegant college gardens, your body wrung out with weariness.

It was like that, the noise in his head. The drumming, the heartbeat, the blood throbbing in his temples, was too loud for him to hear anything else. Once or twice, at the back of his dreams, he thought he heard a child sobbing, whimpering in dull misery somewhere among the old blackberry bushes. That was far worse.

But then he turned his mind away from it, and told himself it was a nightmare, left over from his childhood. What had he learnt at school? 'That was another country.'

4

It was one of those days one spends rushing around, as if preparing for a party, and doesn't realise until suppertime that one hasn't had time to eat. I enjoy events like the Fair, normally. I'm sure, if circumstances had been different, I would have been happy being a very conventional, obvious kind of wife: hosting dinner parties, and drinks-and-canapés in the garden, and organising teams of Alisons or Anna-Maries to do the washing-up the next morning. I've always loved entertaining, and as a teenager could happily have spent my time on nothing else – though it would have driven David potty and wasn't why he married me. And after all, what is the Fair but a great big village party?

Straight after my swim I changed into old gardening clothes and went down to the paddock to see what needed doing. The marquee and various smaller tents had been put up the night before. Sweating neighbours were lugging aluminium poles around, and knocking things into the ground, and making platforms out of scaffolding. I had a luxurious and unaccustomed sense of there being not much for a woman to do, so I went back to the house to make tea for the workers.

The early sun poured through the windows, showing smears of silver where Anna-Marie had washed them badly. I made a mental note to point it out to her sometime, when I could be bothered, and filled the kettle.

I look back on that morning, on our existence before that day, as if on an age of innocence, of simplicity, of a time like childhood when everything was straightforward and honest and easy, though presumably this can't have been entirely true. I sometimes wonder to what extent I was aware at the time of what I was about to lose. Did I know that I stood poised, hesitating at the edge of the cliff? I do remember standing in the middle of the kitchen, quite alone, in an oasis of peace before the storm. Later on the same day, of course, it was very different: the nausea in the pit of the stomach, the sweat on the back of the neck, one's strength draining away – all the clichés, which, when one actually experiences these feelings and then subsequently attempts to describe them, one realises are disappointingly accurate. It really does seem as if one's blood has run cold. Later still, I experienced the wish that the next forty years could rush by and leave me, alone and at peace on my deathbed. But at eight thirty on the morning of the third of May there was none of that. Simply a surreal sense of calm while I waited for the kettle to boil. If the writing was on the wall, I didn't see it or understand it. I was blissfully unaware.

After that I can't remember what I did, or not in exact sequence anyway. Geoff signed me up for a stint on his Human Fruit Machine, and Hugh popped by to check what we were supposed to be doing and when, and Diana came round with my costume sometime after ten. And Prue. Prue called, I can't remember why now. It can't have been to drop her cakes off, because she said she had already been to the church stall. Presumably she was simply on her way back to the Dower House.

She was in a funny mood. She clearly had something on her mind. I'm sure she would have talked to me about it if it had been any other day of the year, but people were coming and going all the time and we wouldn't have had a moment's peace. She said she had to nip into Cambridge, which was odd in itself, on such a busy day, the day of the Fair. What business could she have had which she couldn't have settled a day or two before? Or done by telephone? However, as I say we didn't have the leisure to talk, so she simply said she might be a little late for the Fair but would see me at the barbecue.

And yes, as I said to the police afterwards, she did mention Peter. I can't remember her exact words. She said he'd been seen going into Alison's house, and that we would have to have it out with her. At that point someone else came in wanting something, and whatever might have been said between us went unspoken. Mind you, I don't know what either of us could have said. We'd been over it so many times before, with so many different suggestions, so many attempts at a solution. So she mentioned, as if by way of small talk, that she didn't suppose he would come to the Fair; and I said, as if in reply, that I didn't suppose Alison would mind. I had no way of knowing, then, quite how much she would be made to mind by the end of the day.

Just before she went, Prue asked after Sara. I said nothing. We looked at one another for a moment, before she picked up her handbag and left, presumably for Cambridge. And that was the last I saw of her before it all happened.

Not long after that Sara herself emerged, looking a bit unbrushed and as if she had slept in her leggings. I poured us both a cup of tea, and was looking forward to having a late breakfast with her, but at that moment someone started panicking about the church PA system, so I had to ring Tricia to ask her to track Hugh down and get him to reassure everyone again, then someone popped in asking me for a needle and thread but by the time I'd found it I'd lost the person who wanted it so had to wander around the paddock searching, and while I was doing that someone else discovered that a permanent marker was desperately needed and worked out that I was bound to have one if only I would go home and search through my desk thoroughly, then I realised that there was no loo paper in our outside loo and it would have a queue of wriggling little children outside it all afternoon. And so it went on.

Perhaps it was easier that way. Not having time to spend with Sara, I mean. I often feel I ought to cuddle her, but seldom do, and sometimes end up stroking an arm in an awkward manner, or putting a hand on a shoulder. On days like that Saturday I fleetingly wonder whether it is normal for a fourteen-year-old not to want her mother to touch her. She is nearly as tall as I am. Next year she will tower over me. She didn't venture outside, and I didn't tell her what Prue had told me. I simply found, half an hour later, that I myself felt vulnerable and nervous as I helped the others in the paddock, as if something might happen just behind my back.

Then, before we knew where we were it was gone one o'clock, and all I had time for was to dash home for an instant coffee and an apple, and a quick change into my costume in time to meet Hugh, as arranged, at a quarter to two.

Because it was the first village Fair since 1905 we'd agreed to give it an Edwardian theme. Committee members, at least, were to wear Edwardian costume, and there were special concessions and prizes for anyone else who did too. I assume we arrived at this decision because Hugh had recently acquired his grand-father's frock coat and silk hat and wanted an excuse to wear them. Turn-of-the-century costume wasn't a problem to him, since clerical wear isn't renowned for its rapid fashion turnover, but it was proving a real nuisance to the rest of us.

Still, Diana had enjoyed herself. She'd run up her own creative Lady-of-the-Manor outfit from some old green velvet curtains. I smiled when I saw the brilliant sunshine, and thought how hot she was going to be, spectacular but wilting. For me she had made a far simpler, more comfortable white frock out of a worn sheet. It had a clever bustle, produced in seconds with a few swift knots at the back. The blouse, however, was genuine Edwardian, her great-aunt's, fragile, delicate lawn and lace, which I thought was a shame given the likely nature of the procedings. The whole thing reminded me of pictures in a book of historical fashion plates which my mother gave me when I was a child.

So I threw it all over my head, straightened it out, tied a bit of butter muslin around a school boater of Charles's which I found under the stairs, and put on a pair of old canvas tennis shoes underneath hoping no one would notice. Then I called to Sara. She emerged from the drawing room, where she had been playing something on one finger on the piano. She was still in her leggings. I knew better than to offer her a skirt or straw hat for the occasion.

'Coming?' I said.

'Soon. Don't wait for me.'

'Please come.' She drew breath to protest, then for a couple of seconds we simply looked at each other. She seemed to be assessing the nature of my request. I suddenly longed for a flash of rebellion, the kind of thing her school friends would offer. 'Oh, shut up, Mum,' or a slammed door, or stomping up the stairs. In which case, what could I have done? I could hardly have left her there alone. She must have known, somehow. She nodded wearily, and followed me.

'Get some money from my purse,' I said. 'It's on the kitchen table.'

'How much?'

'How much pocket money do I owe you?'

'Masses.'

'Fine. Take what you want.' We smiled, and it was nearly all right again.

Then, on impulse, I decided to give her the birthday present I had bought for her some weeks earlier. It still wasn't wrapped, and I hadn't even taken it out of its Robert Sayle bag. I had planned to wait till Monday, but instead I realised I wanted to present it to her there and then. So I asked her to wait, took it out of the cupboard, lifted it from its bag, unfolded it and shook it out and held it up against myself while she looked at it, and held my breath for her comments. Sara's taste in clothes changes all the time at the moment, and I had no idea whether she would like it or loathe it. It was a silk and linen jumper, lovely and soft, and perfect for the summer, but in a silvery blue colour which I worried she might think too feminine.

She put her head on one side, then pulled her sweatshirt off, reached out for it, and put it on. 'Thanks,' she said.

Then I did put my arms around her, and hugged her for a moment before she broke away, still smiling, but turning her face from me.

A minute after we'd left the house we bumped into some others on their way to the main stage. By then I had realised that my white cotton gloves were still in my bedroom, so I asked her to join them and go on without me. I didn't mind entrusting her to them. Nor did I mind nearly being late.

But I felt worn, as one does trying to keep one's toddler off the road.

5

Other women were a waste of time. He might initially feel a demand could be met, a need fulfilled. But then, slowly and surely, his shallow satisfaction would begin to turn, like milk left in the sun. Soon he would feel a nausea which, left to itself, became an acute physical pain.

One night had been particularly bad. For some reason he recalled a skimpy piece of clothing more suitable for a child than a woman. It reminded him of something. It made him angry. He loved children: he'd been a child himself once. That was the first of many nights of bitter stomach cramps. So the next time it happened he went out into an indifferent world and got solidly and carefully drunk.

It didn't work. All too soon he would find himself waking, not only with a filthy hangover, but also with a terrible, acute sense of loss. There was a vacuum somewhere. A black hole, just out of sight, ready to suck him in. Something, someone was missing. His head was pressing in on him, waiting to implode. His breath wouldn't come, his eyes were dark.

Then, one day, he found himself in a telephone-box, staring at Brenda in a Bikini, Naughtie Nicole, and a number for the Samaritans. He picked up the telephone. It was like being rescued from the bottom of the sea. It became the first of many such calls.

Everything about their calm unruffled patience and sympathy soothed him. They were detached and caring, carefully listening, suggesting that he might seek help, but very obviously making no attempt to find out who he was or where he was calling from.

After these conversations he would find himself going out

into the world laughing, full of peace and goodwill towards his fellow creatures. How could they condemn or judge him? How dare they suggest he should go to a doctor and talk it over? He knew himself to be a better human being than the passionless commuters who leave their wives and their privately educated children and jump on the 7.32 for Liverpool Street.

And yet, only the day before, he had been with a woman, a girl who had been bothering him for months, and it hadn't happened. Nothing had happened. Not for the first time. She had humiliated him, a sixteen-year-old slip of a girl, had seen him, helpless and naked, unable do anything. And that had enraged him. He had had to find another way to show her he was a man. He had felt better after that. But now he needed to talk about it.

He was careful whenever he rang the Samaritans. He always used a payphone and always withheld the number.

He abandoned his tea and went out into the gay afternoon. Back in his sitting room, in sharp focus and superb colour reproduction, an elegantly manicured and improbably coiffured model testified to the world what immense freedom her new washing powder had given her, flaunting her wonderful body in a minuscule bikini as she swayed across the lawn. But no one was there to see.

6

Paradoxically, I remember the rest of the afternoon with a sharp clarity. Which was just as well as it turned out, because I was able to give the police an exact account of my movements, almost to the minute.

I got to the main stage and its microphone with about two minutes to go. Hugh had the look of the harassed vicar, glancing at his watch and wondering where I had got to. 'Dammit, Harriet,' he said, 'you're cutting it a bit fine.'

'Your microphone's on,' I said, 'and several thousand people have just heard you swear.'

'Rubbish,' he retorted, knowing me of old. 'And dammit's hardly going to shock the assembled parishioners. I can do much better than that, now I've got teenaged children.' Then he frowned suddenly. 'Is it really on?' he said, anxiously tapping it. Then, 'I thought we agreed to meet at a quarter to.'

'I told you to book someone more reliable. James would have been on time.' James Harries was our erstwhile Tory MP, and I had suggested him as the ideal person to open the procedings. But the decision had been taken on an evening when I hadn't been there, and the consensus on the committee was that I would be more suitable, and it was my turn. Which was just as well in the end: James lost his seat two days before the Fair.

Ridiculous, that what happened to David seems to have made me a figure of standing in the community. People feel sorry for me, and that makes them feel guilty. And, oddly, that seems to make them look up to me. That, and the family connection with Willisham House, and the Still Waters Missionary Hospital back home in Phulbari, and perhaps being principal of Langley

House School, and having written a couple of obscure papers on sixteenth-century punctuation, if anyone on the committee, other than Hugh, is aware of that. All these absurd trappings which people register instead of looking beneath the skin. No logic in any of it.

Something, anyway, gives me the right associations of religion and respectability. The missionary worker, home again, to settle her children at school and take over the big house. But home, my real home, is still a long way off. How long, oh Lord, how long?

In some ways they understood us better in Phulbari. They didn't mistake misfortune for courage. They didn't dismiss David as 'such a brave man' as people in Willisham do. They thought he had gone there for the money, because our simple, swept house out there – which, if it had been in Stratford East, would have been demolished as an unspeakable slum dwelling – was so very much smarter than their own red mud huts. And besides they know in Phulbari, that you don't have to be brave to die.

But people over here have the arrogance, the stupidity, to judge David good and strong because he suffered against his will. The victim-as-hero. But David was no hero. Not in that way, at least. He was simply a doctor, doing his duty, and he got unlucky. People in Willisham behave as though he agreed to it. As if he had welcomed death with a smile and shaken him by the hand. As if he had not held on to the three of us and pleaded to God, like a little boy, to be allowed to stay. He was brave and good, oh, he was. But not for the reasons they think.

In the same way, they watch a child go through a dreadful ordeal and then call her courageous. She wasn't courageous at all. She was barely seven years old.

7

In the small cluttered room that served for an office, the counsellor on duty picked up the receiver. The 'Samaritan' was alone today. Normally they worked in pairs, but the colleague who should have been there had a sick child and had not had time to find a replacement.

He announced himself. The Samaritan knew all about him. There had been several calls before, and those who had taken them had alerted the rest. They had described him and discussed him, and received their own counselling on how to cope with him after the receiver was put down and the voice quiet, while the images it had conjured still lingered in the air. They knew he had problems, and they knew his problems might be dangerous. But they also knew he was unlikely to hurt them personally. And they did their best to stop him harming himself. Or anyone else.

The call, therefore, did not come altogether as a surprise. But it was no less a shock. The counsellor had, after all, had suspicions. It seemed too fantastic to believe, but it was possible. A sickening sense of familiarity. Recognisable characteristics. A horribly similar taste of fear in the mouth.

Now they had spoken together it was a certainty. Even the voice was unmistakable.

He was on the telephone for some time, or so it seemed to his listener. But the Samaritan was patient, and listened with great attention. He hadn't spoken to this one before, but he felt an instant connection between them as he talked. At first, he spent some moments trying to work out whether the voice was male or female. It was disconcerting, and reminded him of something. Something which made him feel irritated, and small, but he couldn't remember what it was.

Usually he talked about his childhood. About her. What she had meant, and how pure it had been, with both of them so young, like Romeo and Juliet. And how he had had to leave, and then they had stolen her away. Sometimes he went further back, and talked about what they had shared as children. But this time he couldn't. For some reason, he couldn't tell this one about his past.

So he talked about the day before, and the sixteen year old who had tried to make him look small, and the way he had turned the tables on her and taken her by force, to show her who was boss. He sorted her out there and then, describing it over the telephone. That's right: that was the way it had been.

And then he talked about the future, his hopes, his ambition.

He would watch, he would wait, he would be there. One day, if he waited long enough, he would find her again. He had to, to find himself. It would be the same as it had been once. And she would laugh into the sunshine. He didn't mind telling the Samaritans any of this. None of them knew him – not by name anyway – and they certainly didn't know her. So he described exactly how it would be. He spread out his dreams.

When he had finished he waited for some response. Some kind of reaction was customary. None came. He felt awkward for a moment, disconcerted, embarrassed to be the first to end the conversation. The way this one had listened was different. He couldn't put his finger on it, but he felt uneasy. Suddenly, without saying goodbye, he put the receiver back on its holder.

He stared for a moment at the big fat telephone directory in front of him, with its vaguely pleasing watercolour of the prettiness of the Backs decorating the front cover. He reflected, out of the corner of his mind, that one of the punts in the foreground might have contained an acquaintance of hers. He continued to gaze absently at the blobs of leaves in the evocative, watery, painted sunlight. Then the sound of a crowded pub on a street corner somewhere stumbled across his concentration, and he looked up through the dirty window of the telephone box. He was surprised to find himself in the grip of a momentary agony. He wished it were all over. He wished, acutely, that there were some way out.

He shook himself out of such nonsense, and kicked open the door of the kiosk.

After the receiver had been put down in the office of the Cambridge Samaritans there was an eerie silence in the room. The pedantic click of the electric clock seemed to be marking the time till some hidden explosion went off. The hand which had put the telephone down was white and tense. And when the other line startled itself awake, biting angrily into the silence, it was allowed to ring and ring. Whatever desperate misery it signalled went unheeded. The Samaritan had already enough ministering to do.

A few minutes later there was a sound, erratic and violent, of vomiting into the basin in the corner of the room.

8 ∫

I think I would have done anything to have avoided my duty that day. What I saw as my duty, anyway. Nevertheless on the dot of two I made all the right noises and smiled the right smiles and told a joke or two, and the Fair was open. I was then immediately whisked away to do my stint on the church stall. Dick, our local vet, and a member, as I am, of the Parochial Church Council, had got there before me and was treating a few stragglers to his rather limited but very rhythmic guitar-playing, while his friend whose name I can never remember was playing a pair of tom-tom drums as if his life depended on it. Tricia, Hugh's wife, was bravely leading the singing and rather too much clapping and tambourine-shaking. Tricia sings rather well, as it happens, but you wouldn't always know it from the combined sounds of the church band. It was then, some ten or fifteen minutes after the Fair had started, as Sara listened to their chunk-chunk and spiritual fa-la-lah-ing, that she realised she'd promised to play her flute and asked for my keys so she could go home and get it.

I did try to tell her, tried to warn her somehow, but couldn't see how to do it. What should I have said? Don't go home without me? You're fourteen, but I don't want you wandering off, two hundred yards in broad daylight, on your own, just in case? In case what? There were things I was terrified of as a teenager, though I hadn't been through what she had. But there was nothing I could say. Nothing that wouldn't make her nightmares burgeon and her fears worse.

I gave her the keys.

I was on duty with a couple of others, and our job was to smile a lot and hand out literature about the church, but of course everyone in the village knows about St Saviour's already so it was more a question of making sure people had the free cup of tea we were offering and a slice of flapjack. Sara took nearly twenty-five minutes, though how she managed to do that just walking across the paddock and through the garden to pick up a flute I have no idea. Again, if they had wanted to know such a detail I could have told the police exactly how long she had been. But if they had asked me why I had timed her so precisely I would have had nothing to say.

I didn't notice then, and only realised afterwards, that she had shed her new jumper by the time she came back. It was a very warm day. Presumably she left it at home when she got her flute. By the time she was back in the music group, and had been joined by three school friends brandishing a clarinet, soprano sax and viola, the church band was all sounding rather good.

My stint was due to finish at three. At a quarter to Geoff came and asked me if he could borrow the basher from our croquet set to knock something into the ground as someone had mislaid the proper hammer. So I told him to get the back door key from Sara and I explained how to get into the outside storeroom, the 'apple shed'. Stupidly, I didn't tell him to be sure to pull the door to – hard – behind him when he finished, and, as came out later during the investigations, he probably failed to do this. He returned my set of keys to me about ten minutes later.

I had agreed to do an hour on the church stall followed by half an hour on Geoff's Human Fruit Machine, so a couple of minutes before three I went and took my place in the middle booth of the machine. I was on duty with Hugh and his daughter, Katy. Geoff's game, which he invented himself, involves three people sitting in three open booths in such a way that they can't see each other, each holding a carrier bag containing an apple, a miniature bottle of spirits, and a banana, which tends to look very bruised by the end of the afternoon. Punters pay 20 pence a go, or 50 pence for three, then pull the huge arm on the side of the machine, which little children have to be lifted up to reach. This rings a bell, and the three of us each then take an item out of our carrier bags. If all three produce the three apples or three bananas the child wins 50 pence back. Three bottles constitute the jackpot of a pound.

It should be a flawless system, as random as a mechanical fruit machine. But Geoff's design hadn't bargained on the human sympathy factor, an invisible telepathy which began to build up among the three of us. Without anything being explicitly agreed, each time a pretty little girl in a summer frock and curls and ribbons took a turn we all spontaneously produced our little bottles. The jackpots were rolling over and over again. The game was losing money hand over fist. Geoff was getting increasingly alarmed, telling us to stop cheating, even thinking of sacking one of us, until he thought to remind Hugh that we were hoping to put some of the proceeds of the Fair towards the church roof. After that he didn't pull the bottle out again, not once.

By three thirty, when my turn ended, I was flagging. It wasn't tiring in itself, but it was boring, and I thought I ought to wander around and see how the other activities were going.

As I came out of my booth I bumped into Diana. In retrospect it's lucky I did, though I have a theory that none of this makes much difference in the long run. She suggested a cream tea in the big marquee, and I readily agreed. The queue was very long. The heat was sweltering by then, people were thirsty, and crowds had turned up from Cambridge and some of the other villages. The publicity had been good.

'This is going to be more successful than we had begun to imagine,' I remarked.

Diana agreed. 'But it's going to take ages to get a cup of tea. It would have been quicker to nip back to your kitchen. You grab a table, over there, and I'll queue.'

So that was what we did. I found a table for two outside the marquee, fully in the sun but there were no others, and sat down to wait while Diana queued. I hung my bag on my chair, put my hat on the table to show that it was 'saved', and looped my strip of butter muslin on the other chair. I watched the queue edge forwards, counting the number of people in it, and tried to judge how long Diana would be. It was moving almost unbelievably slowly. I made a mental note for the debriefing committee meeting, that next year we would need two or three more people serving in the large marquee.

I was very grateful for that tea. I couldn't eat much of the scones and cream, but could have drunk several cups of tea if they'd been on offer.

Diana looked around with satisfaction.

'Going brilliantly.'

'It is,' I agreed.

'Should net thousands. You all right?'

'Fine. Hot. They should have these tables in the shade.'

As Diana and I sat having tea together, I was content to let her inexhaustible commentary wash over me. I was aware that, as committee members, we shouldn't sit there too long. We were on duty, and soon we ought to circulate and help. But we were both drooping with the heat, Diana quite red with it, and I felt exhausted and, by then, slightly queasy. It was tempting to stay there as long as we could, fanning ourselves with our Edwardian sunhats. Eventually, just before half past four, I suggested we should see if there was anything which needed doing.

We went together and watched the children spinning in gigantic teacups, and visited Karen who was selling helium balloons, and admired the hackney pony who was pulling the smartly painted trap, and when we got to the plant stall, at what must have been about twenty to five, Tony told us he was desperate and very stressed because he'd been let down by his helper and no one, not even Tony Blair he said, could do everything all at once, advise about bizzie lizzies, count change, and make sure nothing got pinched. I offered to help till five, so Diana left me there, collecting up little plastic pots of plumbago and runner beans and sweet pea and wondering whether to buy some myself and pop them under the table with my name on. In the end I never got around to it.

At five o'clock, having helped all I could, I went to join John and Pat on the book stall, where I stayed till the end of the Fair. I took one break of less than five minutes, when I told Pat I was going to nip to the loo. I said I'd use the Portaloo rather than going home because it would be quicker, but in fact when I got there there was a queue there as well, so I didn't bother.

'You were quick, dear,' she said, and we continued with our work.

I found it soothing being with them. They didn't make small

talk, or ask me anything, or make any demands. The stall was busy so we concentrated on the work in hand. We were occupied for the whole hour simply taking money and giving change. Just after six, when the Fair was officially over, we began the task of putting all the remaining books back into boxes, and at half past the stall was taken down and packed away.

So, as it happened, I was able to account for my time between two minutes to two and six thirty pretty accurately. I expect all other committee members were able to do the same. Hugh was the only one, I think, who had spent a substantial chunk of the afternoon unwitnessed and unseen.

I had agreed to host a barbecue for all the workers that evening, so I sought Hugh out just after half past six and asked if he would come and help me.

'I could do with someone lighting the fire, if you can spare the time.'

'How fortunate. I could do with an excuse not to dismantle scaffolding and load lorries,' he grunted, depositing a heavy box full of metal joints.

He had changed out of his frock coat and dog collar and into a scruffy tracksuit, so he must have been back home to the vicarage. That, no doubt, was where his missing hour had gone. He had probably been in his study finishing off his sermon. This was a trick which David's father had perfected, and passed on to him: if you show your face at events and join in whole-heartedly while you are there, people will think you have been taking part all afternoon.

As it turned out, of course, by then it had happened. But only one person on the committee knew about it at that stage. Or have I got that right? Graeme is on the committee after all. I'm not sure about Graeme, to be honest. All I can be certain of is the other one. Most of the rest of us were fully occupied with making the Fair go well.

Hugh and I went back to the house. On the way back we passed my bicycle, abandoned in the wrong place by the back gate and unlocked, so I pushed it back to the kitchen yard, took out the newspapers and wood and the meat which Geoff had brought over earlier, and poured us both a drink and went and sat by the barbecue which Charles had built out of bricks for the kind of parties he likes to give for his friends.

'Blimey,' Hugh said, tasting the level of gin.

'Yes,' I said. He looked at me for a moment, and I knew he wouldn't miss much.

9

There was a pause in the call box for a moment, after he had opened the door, while he waited in the assorted sounds and smells of a Cambridge summer evening. Taxi cabs drifted round the square, or moored lightly at the kerb. A gaggle of leather-clad teenagers kicked their way between the deserted stalls, heralded by an empty Pepsi Cola can, which rattled its way in front them. The sweet, soft smell of abandoned oranges and tomatoes struggled with the background stink of urine which reeked its way up the wrought-iron staircase leading from the underground gentlemen's convenience. The staircase recalled the lost civilisation of Victorian England: the stench seemed somehow, illogically, modern.

He left the Market Place and headed for King's Parade, then past the Senate House and down the little lane that ran along Caius College. The Clematis Montana rioted over the wall with generous abandon, breathing its quiet scent into the evening air.

It was late when he prepared to open his shared front door. He made very little noise as he opened the gate. His feet were soft on the ground. His key had nothing to jangle against as he pulled it out of his pocket.

But he didn't go unheard. As he put his key in the lock there was a rustle on the ground a few feet away. He stopped. It stopped. He waited for a full minute. Then he moved very slowly towards it. The sound breathed again. He bent down and saw, buried in last autumn's fall of sweet wrappers and crisp papers and other dead vegetation which breezed in from the road, a frightened, fluttering young starling, its stunted tail and underformed wings not yet equipping it for escape.

He pondered. If he left it where it was its chances were small. The neighbourhood had other predators as well as those who twitched net curtains. A cat would be merciless. Driven by some overwhelming instinct of destruction which she could neither control nor comprehend, she would toy with this terrified creature until its wits were gone. He had seen them, tossing a helpless animal to its death and snatching it back again.

Gently he took the bird in his hands and cradled its shivering frame until he had opened the door and set it down, still in the dark, on his kitchen table.

He talked to it softly and meaninglessly. He cooed, and clicked his tongue, and kept up a gentle chatter while he tried to find the things he needed. He searched blindly under his sink, in the margarine tub which served as a first aid box, for a pipette. The table, with the bird on it, stood in the middle of the compact, tidy room. As he went over to the fridge he continued to chat to it softly as it crouched, petrified, on the polished surface. The squeak of the door, the harsh light from the fridge as it invaded the darkened room, startled the bird and it shifted nervously away from him on the table, slipping helplessly. The frightened eyes never left him as he poured a little milk into a saucer, crumbled in some bread, and finally opened a bottle of beer from under the sink and added two or three drops.

He put some clean rags on his knee and gradually coaxed and persuaded his new guest to enjoy this overpowering hospitality. Half an hour later the bird was settled for the night, tucked up in the rags, at the bottom of a covered cardboard box. He took a last protective look inside the box, went out and softly closed the door.

The room was almost quiet. The fridge hummed. From the street an occasional vehicle mumbled past or group of youths shouted to each other. From the bedroom came faint sounds of drawers opening, and a wardrobe door being clicked shut. The bed creaked distantly through the wall.

At the bottom of the box the young starling cowered, shaking, until fear sent it into a fitful, agonised sleep.

By the time the police came it was early evening and the garden was full of people. I say 'the police', but I mean Graeme, of course.

Children were jumping in and out of the pool, adults were relaxing on the lawn, and the rock band which had been booked to play all night was thumping the ground when Graeme came and found me.

Because of the heat, Graeme had taken his policeman's helmet off and had it under his arm, while sweat glistened on his forehead and made thin strands of hair stick to his head. He looked vulnerable without it on. Robbed of his usual muscle, shorn of his Nazarite's strength. Shorter. I remember when the children used to wait anxiously to try his predecessor's helmet on, till they got used to him and took it from his hands as soon as he entered the house. Then they would run around the garden arresting each other. Sara did so once with no other clothes on at all: we were sitting on the terrace having tea with Prue and Maurice one Saturday afternoon when PC Brookes called about something or other. Suddenly a tiny naked figure in a huge helmet appeared from nowhere and marched us all off into the library to be put into prison.

Writing my account now, as I am several months after the event, I have tried to work out exactly what I felt when Graeme came to ask me if he could have the use of a room in the house, so he could talk to Alison. I think, looking back, I'm remembering myself more fearful than I was at the time. There were moments over that weekend when I was terrified, but being honest I don't think that was one of them. I feel scared now, knowing the significance of Graeme's words, imagining how my life would be if he'd never said them. In reality, of course, it wouldn't have made any difference at all. The act was already committed. A man lay dead. Or sat dead, strictly speaking. But I wish I could wind the skein of time back to the few seconds before Graeme opened his mouth, and plead with him, ask him not to tell anyone, beg him to go away and leave us all alone. And then what? How would we avoid the inevitable spring of tragedy, as Anouilh put it, uncoiling and pulling all our lives with it. I can't see how, at any point over the last ten years or so, I could have pre-empted what occurred. It must have been possible at some stage, and it feels as if the day of the Fair is the day I should have lived my life differently, but it's difficult to see how.

I do believe that David could have avoided it. If he had still been with us it wouldn't have happened. I don't know what he would have done, but he would have thought of something, and easily. If he were here now, he would say, 'Harriet,' – I can hear him saying it: tolerant, kind, but incredulous that I could have been so blind – 'Harriet, why didn't you . . .' What? Why didn't I what, David? Why didn't I leave it up to you? That's what you'd say, isn't it? If you were here. Why didn't I let you sort it out?

Because you weren't here, my love. Because you did what you had promised not to do. You left me alone, with two young children, one of whom – no, both of whom, for companionship's sake – had been right down into the Valley of the Shadow of Death. Yes, I know I'm exaggerating, but that's what it feels like at that age.

I offered Graeme the drawing room. I didn't ask any questions – naturally – and had no desire for any answers. Instead, I asked whether he would like some tea, briefly wondering whether something stronger would be more appropriate, but not offering it. I was already feeling fuddled after my drink with Hugh on an empty stomach. The whole experience was rather surreal. Graeme's being in uniform surprised me a little. I suppose I would have expected him to be off-duty for the Fair, though there is a sense, presumably, in which a village policeman is always on duty. He had his radio on, which occasionally burst into unintelligible babble as they tend to do, and he spoke into it while I waited for an answer.

I gazed out of the window and found myself wondering, irrelevantly, whether Hugh was coping with my barbecue. Would the sausages all be burnt? They were Geoff's own sausages, all meat and fresh herbs. Would I get to eat anything that evening? Would Alison? Would either of us care? Even as I thought of it I heard my own stomach rumble and felt embarrassed, as if it proved I wasn't taking the police seriously. I turned back to the room, trying not to look at Graeme as he talked to his radio, and noticed a bird on the pattern of David's parents' Persian carpet which, even after living at Willisham all this time, I'd never noticed before. Why was I thinking of the house, this evening, as if it were theirs again, not mine?

'Thank you, a tray of tea would be a help.' I stared at Graeme for a moment before registering that he was talking to me.

I went into the kitchen, and, as I laid the tea and milk on a tray, tried to concentrate on how many cups would be needed. I opted for three. Prue always used to make a habit of putting out a couple more than she needed, on the grounds that more people would turn up – which, in those days when she lived at the house, they always seemed to do. Other than that, I tried to keep my mind blank. I knew we were on the verge of something, of course I did: policemen do not make a habit of borrowing rooms in houses for no reason. But I told myself it was nothing to do with me, and that I was not to get involved.

Which was easier said than done. I timed it badly. As I was walking to the drawing room with the tea the doorbell rang, and Graeme opened it to admit a cuddly young woman PC in a clean white shirt, shepherding in Alison herself. I can't recall now what Alison's face looked like, but the effort of remembering seems to conjure up in my mind an air of defiance about her. Presumably she had often had to come to Peter's defence – at parent-teacher evenings for instance – and had learnt to prepare herself for the onslaught. I gave them a rather embarrassed smile, and the little PC smiled back. Her face lit up, and she reminded me oddly of Harriet Smith in *Emma*, plump, pretty and blonde. And far too young.

I was holding the tray. I hesitated for a moment, then preceded them awkwardly into the drawing room, put the tray down, and dithered between abandoning it, and staying to pour the tea. I longed to leave, to be spared the awkwardness and the sight of pain, to know nothing about any of it. But something made me linger and pour, and I doubt whether it was just good manners.

'It looks as if your fête went well,' the Harriet Smith girl said brightly, following Alison into the room. I put milk into the tea, then turned to her and realised she was looking at me for an answer.

'Oh. Yes, it does seem to have done,' I agreed. 'So far.' We could hear shouts and laughter across the lawn. Prue's beautiful carriage clock on the mantelpiece ticked steadily, reassuringly, as if nothing were wrong.

I felt cold, despite the warm air outside. I put two sugars in Alison's cup without asking her, and couldn't help wondering what on earth she was expecting the police to tell her. She would surely anticipate something to do with her troublesome son. She had the last nineteen-odd years to go on. But what? Drugs? Theft? Whatever it was, it could not, in any way, have prepared her for what was to come.

'It's Peter, isn't it?' she said abruptly.

'Your son? Yes, Miss Midland, I'm afraid it is. Would you like to sit down?'

I tried to hand Miss Smith the next cup of tea so I could leave, but she declined it, and then so did Graeme, who was still standing between me and the door. I looked at them, not knowing whether to put it down or take it with me, and found that the PC was expecting me to take a seat too. She doesn't come from Willisham, so inevitably she didn't know any of us. 'Do sit down,' she said, indicating my own chairs. 'We have some rather distressing news for Miss Midland. I gather you are an old family friend?' I knew it wasn't right, and that I shouldn't be there. But to leave would have been to make a point, to contradict the PC's innocent assumption. I sat down.

Alison didn't look at me. 'Alison,' Graeme said, 'did you know Peter visited you today?'

'Yes. I told him I'd see him later if he wanted.'

'You must have been pleased to see him,' he said, as if to encourage her.

'No, I wasn't actually,' she said unexpectedly. 'He's not supposed to turn up like that.'

'Not supposed to?'

'That's right. We agreed.'

'Why?'

Alison gave nothing away. She didn't even glance my way. I kept my eyes on Graeme. I now acutely wished the PC hadn't asked me to stay. It wouldn't help either of us. Graeme had joined the village after David's father died, shortly before we came home – but that didn't mean much in a place as small as Willisham. I was sure he knew more than we had told him.

'He doesn't care for the village,' Alison continued. 'He's got a lovely flat in Cambridge, a good part-time job, and a place at college next year, and I take him meals every week.'

Graeme nodded. 'He didn't have any worries? Losing his job, or paying for college?'

'Not yet. But he will have if he keeps messing about. He's been jolly lucky, and it's thanks to what this family's done for him.' She must have meant us. I hadn't seen our responsibility in quite that light. But I suppose she was right.

She cut Graeme short. 'Why don't you tell me what he's done? I've got to know sooner or later.'

There was a tiny moment's pause. Nothing Graeme, or the other PC, or anything anyone else said could have prepared Alison for the crash, given her an air cushion against the future. I thought I was ready for anything the police might throw at us, but when the sentence finally came it was like a rock heaved into a loch, crumpling up the mountains and the sky.

As a child, once, I was kicked by a seaside donkey. I had turned away, and his little hoof caught me in the small of my back and knocked all the breath out of me. I can still remember the panic as I thought I was drowning, unable to heave anything into my lungs, staring at the blue summer sky and wondering how long I had to live. It can only have been a split second before I caught my breath again, but I can feel the panic even now.

Graeme's words were as astonishing, as shocking, gave me the same feeling of having lost control. I can still shut my eyes and see Alison's face staring at him, stripped naked of emotion. When I had heard comparable news a few years earlier I had at least known it was coming.

In those few words he passed a verdict on our village, his own community, which cut us off from the harmonious life we'd had before. He put fear between friends and neighbours, doubt where there had been trust, malicious suspicion where there had been harmless gossip.

'Alison,' he said gently. 'Peter's dead.' She stared at him. The air was heavy and close. The guests in the garden were suddenly, eerily, silent. 'I'm afraid he killed himself.'

There was a clatter and a dull thud, as a cup fell to the floor, and tea spread and seeped into the lovely old Persian carpet. I looked down, thinking the cup was Alison's.

It was mine.

It wasn't until this summer that I really saw what Alison was made of. I suppose it's to be expected. Tragedy famously brings out our essence, what we consist of at rock bottom, so they say. I've certainly noticed that misfortune brings out the worst in me.

Alison had always struck me as a victim: a sweet, good person, but rather passive. Now, however, I can't think why I ever thought this. After all, nineteen years ago there was no need to have a baby one didn't want. Most teenagers, in Alison's position, would have solved their problems far more simply. Her parents, and possibly Peter's father too, if he knew anything about it, were putting the usual pressure on her to get rid of her baby in the most convenient way. It takes courage, at seventeen or eighteen, to swim against the stream.

Being brutally honest, as I'm now trying to be, I have to admit that somewhere, deep in my heart, I blamed her for what happened to Sara. I suppose she must have been responsible in some way, if only for choosing Peter's father, and giving Peter his genes. At least she did her son the favour of bringing him up without his father's example, but I wonder whether even a bad father does as much damage as an absent one. I'm sorry, David, that wasn't meant to be directed at you. You aren't absent, my love. Far from it. You're present in every decision I take, in everything I do for the children, in their very faces and smiles and tears. In the woods and gardens which you ran in as a child, in the river and the whispering willows, in the strike of the clock and the churchyard shadows – even in the graveyard where, unlike your St Joseph forbears, your bones don't lie and presumably never will. You were here in everything we did, in every moment of this grindingly awful summer. You protest? Not your fault? Perhaps not, but I wish it had been.

Sitting in my own drawing room, in the late afternoon that Saturday at the beginning of the summer, I glanced at Alison's face and saw the first wave of the hideously familiar reaction. Donne is wrong. We are islands. God help me, when I sat there and saw her expression I thanked Him that it wasn't mine. I couldn't have taken any more. Then I imagined the Almighty thundering His response: you can take any amount more, if I choose to throw it at you – and of course, as always, He is right.

After an almost interminable silence, presumably only a few seconds, I got up and went and sat by her on the sofa. I wondered whether to put an arm around her, but I got the impression she wouldn't welcome it. She didn't look at me, or Graeme or his colleague, she didn't even seem to see the tea she was staring at, which she hadn't touched. I got the disquieting, almost obscene impression that her first reaction had been one of relief. Not that she didn't love Peter. Of course I don't mean she was relieved he was dead. But as if she had been expecting him to have done something awful, and he hadn't. That's all. She hadn't taken in, yet, that what had happened to him this time was infinitely irreversible. All too soon she would bitterly regret that first, instantaneous reaction of gratitude that at least he hadn't gone and done anything else.

There is a sense in which Peter always had everything. Not in the way that a poor-little-rich-kid has everything, expensive bikes, Nike trainers and unlimited visits to McDonald's. But he had a mother who loved him unconditionally and was dedicated to the best for him, and influential, well-connected friends who did what they could to help her achieve it.

The first time I met him, ironically, was at my own wedding, though I only know this from photographs, not from my own memory. He was a little baby of three weeks old, with thick black hair despite his mother's pretty blonde bob. He was beautifully turned out, more beautifully than his mother, while she carried all the things I never bothered with for my babies: a changing mat in a matching bag, sterilised bottles and dummies and playrings and rattles, and a spare Babygro in case he soiled the first one. I, meanwhile, in the same photographs, drink champagne and laugh with David and eventually share his great-grandfather's sword to cut open the glistening three-tiered cake.

Was Alison wondering, that day, why she wasn't getting married herself? Did she ever want to be married, I wonder? I have no idea. I've known her nearly twenty years and I still don't know.

There can't have been a month which went by – until we went abroad, of course – when I didn't see Peter thrive and grow. Though again, as at my wedding, I didn't take as much notice of him as I could have done. I certainly had no premonition of the effect he would have on our lives. Alison pushed him around the village in his gleaming, fashionable buggy and bright, freshly laundered baby clothes from Mothercare, and I saw her as a fairly ordinary teenaged single mum, though one who was doing a much better job than most.

She must have started working for David's parents shortly after that. The Bridges were pushing seventy, and Prue and Maurice had been saying for ages that it was time they took a break. I had no real experience, outside books, of nannies who span the generations or gardeners and odd-job men who stay for life, and asked David where the Bridges would live if they retired. He laughed. 'Where they do now, of course. Did you think my parents would put them out on to the streets?' This attitude was completely new to me, and I found it thrilling. I was now a member of a class whose habits, expectations and responsibilities went back hundreds of years.

At that time Alison and Peter were living in cramped conditions, in her parents' house at the other end of the village. Prue and Maurice owned a row of three cottages, of which the Bridges' was one. Alison's plans of going to college had been abandoned because of Peter. She was earning a bit of money waitressing in Cambridge, but it meant leaving Peter with her mother, which she didn't like doing. She is independent, is Alison. She preferred, when she could, to do cleaning and ironing for people in the village, so she could take Peter with her. And Prue, with all the kindness and compassion and *noblesse oblige* which characterised the St Josephs, thought she could kill two birds with one stone: the cottage could be put to good use giving Alison and Peter a home, and she could give Mrs Bridges her well-deserved retirement at the same time.

So that was when they moved in. When Peter was still a baby. Extraordinarily, until May of this year I'd never set foot in the cottage, although it now belongs to me. Alison undoubtedly transformed the inside. No doubt the St Josephs equipped it with a new cooker and fridge and kitchen units, but it was Alison herself who sewed the Laura Ashley curtains and chose matching sheets and duvet covers and carpets which co-ordinated with the walls.

We considered all the legal channels last year, Prue and I, intending to ask for the cottage back. Not that we resented Alison, or blamed her, but we wanted to sever the links. But how could we? We couldn't make her leave Willisham, nor would we have wanted to. All her friends, her family, her support network and the only church she knows are here. She would have stayed on in the village, even if not on the estate. Perhaps that would have been better. But we both thought that, this way, we had some say in what happened. We could bargain, negotiate, decide who visited our own property. It was a mistake, I see that now, but we reached an agreement, which Alison claimed to be very happy with. Prue continued to employ her to work at the Dower House, while I, for one reason and another, have had a string of various different cleaners since we came back. Now I have Anna-Marie.

Alison shows no sign of moving house now. I haven't had the heart to ask her to go, not now Peter's dead. I couldn't do it myself, stay on in a house where Charles had shot himself, sit in front of the telly in the chair which was his last resting place. Though of course, having said that, we did the equivalent thing. We came back to Willisham after all, back to the place where it all happened before, despite the fact that we all said we would have been quite happy to have stayed in that other, little, much-loved house, on the hillside, in the shadow of Still Waters Hospital, and the towering peak of Anapurna, a few miles above the plains of Pokhara, where we said goodbye to David.

So, virtually from the first, Peter could be said to have had all he needed. A bright, well-kept home, a parent all to himself, and, thanks to Prue's efforts on Alison's behalf, a place, when he was three and a half, in the nursery department of Willisham Primary.

I first became aware of him at about that time. I had Charles by then. I'd never been particularly fond of babies or young children so I'd not noticed them, but once you have your own you do start to be more aware. I must be careful not to reconstruct Peter's early behaviour and imagine, with hindsight, other things which I learnt about him afterwards. The temptation is to look back on his childhood and think there was always something wrong. But there wasn't, in those first days. There really wasn't. Or not visible to me, at any rate. David, I'm sure, always knew. Perhaps Maurice did as well. Perhaps that's why the St Josephs did so much for him, to try to compensate, to help Alison in a task which was always doomed.

Charles and I would go over to the house, and David too at the weekends, and Charles would play with his Granny and sit on her knee and thread buttons with coloured thread and learn nursery rhymes. And when he got old enough, when he was two or three or four, he started, sometimes, to play with Peter. The tension which was later so evident didn't seem to be present at all then.

Meanwhile Peter flourished, after a fashion, at the village primary. It's not a bad school. If the village were further from the centre of Cambridge, the middle-class families would probably all send their children there too. It does have a smattering of dons' children, but of course St Faith's and King's and St John's – and Langley House – are easily accessible from Willisham, so most of them send their children there.

I've sometimes wondered whether Peter's father was an academic. He could have been: a junior fellow, who didn't want his wife to know about his bit of nookey on the side. If so, he could have had the decency to pick on an undergraduate, not a schoolgirl. But somehow I think he must have been a student himself. I don't know why, but that's how I imagine him. A first or second year, some Hooray Henry reading Anthropology at Downing and going beagling with the Trinity Foot on a Saturday afternoon. He probably met Alison in a pub somewhere and tumbled her without a second thought later that evening, while she fell head over heels in love with him and has remembered him ever since, every morning for years as she watched his image over a bowl of Coco Pops.

He may have no idea about Peter's existence, and is now forty and bald and a bit of a city chap but not seriously rich, just enough to keep his mortgage ticking over and send his son to a minor public school and his daughter to some not-quite-first-rank independent day school. In which case the first fruits of his loins got the best education too.

As his time at Willisham Primary drew towards its end, David's father asked Alison about Peter's future schooling. It was obvious to Maurice that Peter was reasonably intelligent, and would eventually benefit from a decent university education. I don't suppose Alison had thought about it much. But Maurice had links with Christ's Hospital, and mentioned it to Alison, and presumably told her what an opportunity it would be. He went to considerable trouble for her, I know that: Peter was nominated, and all he had to do was pass the entrance exam.

Later that same year Maurice must have doubted his own wisdom. It wouldn't have been too late to have contacted the school and told them. But I can understand why he didn't. In his situation I probably wouldn't have done anything either. Under British law Peter was innocent – until proved, et cetera, the burden of proof being with the prosecution. This spirit of justice goes deep into the British soul. And Maurice was profoundly, quintessentially, British. He always saw the best in everybody. Unlike David who, despite his own goodness, perhaps because of it, was always cynical about anyone's motives, and his own most of all. But Maurice could always see mitigating circumstances for everybody. He would have believed that, if only Peter could be given a chance, be given the privileges that Maurice's own children and grandchildren would have, he would turn out all right in the end.

Possibly, without even realising it, he had also wanted to remove Peter from Willisham all along. Perhaps he had sensed the danger well in advance, even subconsciously. After all, the Cambridge state schools are excellent and there was no reason for him not to have got into the best.

In any event, Maurice decided not to prejudice the boy's chances. Peter went off to public school in the autumn of that year. Events were forgotten, if not quite forgiven.

Perhaps, if he had been punished instead, he wouldn't be the only person who would still have been alive today.

12

The party had to go on.

From where we sat, in the drawing room, we could hear the shrieks of teenagers across the lawn and the delighted whoops of children, flagging but not yet in bed, and the underlying hum of adult conversation. The rhythmic shudder of the pop group, from the further field, vibrated through our feet. Luckily almost everyone in the village had been involved in the Fair, so we didn't anticipate protests to the local police from disturbed senior citizens. Meanwhile, the local police sat opposite us, on the pouffe, his hands politely folded in his lap.

I wasn't quite sure what was supposed to happen next. It began to dawn on me that Alison couldn't be expected to go home, not if Peter had shot himself. Perhaps Hugh and Tricia would have her to stay. But then, why should they? Hugh frequently tells us, rightly, that the work of the church is to be done by the whole church, not just the vicar alone, and we shouldn't leave him to do all the visiting of the sick and feeding of the poor. Or, presumably, the caring of neighbours whose children have killed themselves. Besides, they had an elderly missionary couple staying with them for the weekend of the Fair, and their modern, box-like utilitarian four-bedroomed vicarage was full enough of their three teenaged children at the best of times. It is not the largest house in the village.

I took a deep breath. 'Would you like to stay here tonight?' I asked her, praying that she would decline.

'No, thank you,' Alison said, shaking her head slightly and not even looking at me.

'I think that would be a good idea,' Graeme said, and the PC added, 'Yes.'

'Either that,' Graeme continued, 'or go and stay with your family.'

Alison turned to look at them. 'I'd rather go home. My home.'

He paused for a moment, before saying, 'You can't right now. Your house has been cordoned off. My colleagues have been looking at a few things, and I'm not sure that they've quite finished.' I wondered whether this was true, or whether he was sparing her the sight of her ruined front room. 'We'll be out as quickly as we can.'

Suddenly, without warning, Alison said, 'Are you sure it's Peter? I mean, are you sure he's – is he in hospital, or what?'

Graeme said very gently, 'The man we found is dead. There's no hope of him being revived, if that's what you're asking. There'll have to be a formal identification, and we'll be asking you to do that, when you're ready. But there doesn't seem much doubt that it was Peter. You let him in this morning, didn't you?'

'I told him he wasn't supposed to come. But I thought it would be easier this way. If I let him stay, and then talked to him about it later. I was wrong, wasn't I?'

I ought to have wanted to cradle her, to put my hand on hers, to wipe away her tears, anything to absorb some of the pain. I didn't touch her.

Besides, there were no tears.

'But why . . . ?' she went on. 'I don't understand. It's not the sort of thing . . .' She stopped. Are there people for whom this is their 'sort of thing'? I suppose there are. I had a schoolfriend who often used to threaten it, though as far as I know she never did it. She never even struck me as particularly unhappy. She simply used to talk about throwing herself under a bus.

I asked Graeme what would need to be done about the identification of the body. 'It's on its way to the mortuary now,' he replied. 'Alison ought to go as soon as she feels strong enough. If you can't face it tonight,' he continued gently, looking at her, 'we might be able to postpone it till tomorrow.'

'I'd rather go now. I wouldn't sleep otherwise.' I was surprised at her certainty.

So it was arranged. Graeme rang the mortuary, was told the body was on its way, and that they would be ready for Alison in an hour or so. Everyone – Graeme, the little PC, even Alison herself – seemed to assume that I would be going with her. And that was that. It was bizarre, after all that we had been through, that I should accompany Alison to identify Peter's corpse. I simply found myself doing what others wanted of me. I thought I'd trained myself not to do that any more, to be more 'assertive', but in times of stress old habits die hard. I suppose that I, too, was in considerable shock, and not thinking about what I was doing – far less, what I wanted to do.

Meanwhile I tried to collect my thoughts. The barbecue. Sara. The weekend. The guest room for Alison. Sara was the most important, the barbecue the simplest. I decided to go and find Hugh. There was no good reason why I should have expected him to accept the responsibility, as he had to preach several times the next day. But Hugh is like a brother, and I knew I could turn to him.

I found him easily. He had handed the cooking over to several other men who were clearly enjoying the primitive ritual, and he was sitting chatting to Maude, a white-haired lady from the congregation.

We strolled away from the noisy revellers. Suddenly, I didn't know what to say. I have confided in Hugh at some of the lowest points in my life, and there isn't much left about me that he doesn't know. I took a breath, and then shut my mouth again, like something in a petshop tank. Finally I said, 'Could you keep an eye on your goddaughter?'

He frowned, puzzled. 'Yes,' he said, as if to imply, Of course. 'What – now? Are you going out? She's here somewhere.' He looked around for her face.

'Yes, I suppose I am. This is ridiculous. I don't know whether I'm supposed to tell you.'

'Tell me what?'

'Exactly.'

'Harriet,' he steered me over towards the bench on the other side of the lawn, before realising that a couple of people were already on it. We stopped, half-way there, and turned our backs on the crowds by the barbecue and looked towards the house. 'Now then, what? Is it Charles? Prue? Has something happened?'

'Not to me. Nevertheless,' I said. 'I wouldn't mind your familiar old shoulder to cry on.'

'Well, as you know it's always available to you. But perhaps not quite here, and now.'

'Fine. Peter Midland spent the day at Alison's house. He's in her front room. The police have just told her he's shot himself.'

Hugh said nothing for a moment, gazing over to the room where Peter's mother sat. Then he said, 'Badly?'

'What d'you mean, badly?'

'Has he hurt himself badly?'

'Yes and no,' I said. 'He's dead.'

'Shit.' Suddenly he put his arm around me.

'I thought you said not here.'

'So I did.' He dropped his arm, and turned back to look at the hundred or so people who were expecting me to feed them. They seemed to be getting on quite well without me. Then we both saw Sara, fighting playfully with her schoolfriend the clarinettist, whose mother had said she could stay till ten.

'What did you say you wanted? For me to look after Sara? Or should I be coping with the barbecue and this lot?'

'Sara,' I said. 'Please.'

'And you're taking care of Alison?'

'That's the general idea. The police are with her now, but they wanted a familiar face with her when she identifies the body.'

'Wouldn't it be better for you to stay here, and someone else to go with her?'

'Yes, I suppose it would. But it's sort of happened this way, now. Besides,' I thought for a moment. 'What would I say? What reason would I give for wanting to stay with Sara?'

'You wouldn't need to give a reason.'

'Hugo, think for a minute. Engage your superb theological and intellectual equipment and address it to the matter in hand. A neighbour's son has died. I've been asked to be with her. What compelling prior engagement could I possibly refer to which would have a greater claim to my time?'

'Right. OK. If you're sure. Do you want Tricia to do anything?'

'Yes. We'll need to clean up Alison's house. Maybe after church tomorrow?' I wondered whether I could ask him to put Alison up that evening, and hesitated.

'What?' he asked.

'Nothing.' It really wasn't fair on them. They tended to get little enough privacy as it was, and I knew they would make one of the children sleep on the sitting-room sofa if I asked. And how would that look, that I couldn't even spare one of my eleven bedrooms for Alison, so that Hugh and Tricia had to squeeze her in somehow?

As I turned to go, Hugh called me back. 'Hey,' he said, and smiled the old smile from our schooldays, that I don't seem to see so often now. For a moment I thought he was going to give me a hug after all, but then thought better of it as we were in the middle of the lawn in full view of half the village. 'He would be proud of you, you know.'

'Who?' I said.

'You know who,' he said.

Though, funnily enough, I wasn't sure that I did. After all, Hugh is my vicar. He could have meant God.

As I left him, in the middle of the lawn, gazing after me as I went back to the house, I felt relieved. I had committed Sara to the care of friends. They would look after her. I knew I couldn't have left her alone.

Which was quite illogical of course. There was nobody dangerous around.

13

As I walked back to the house I was longing for Alison to stay somewhere else. I couldn't bear the thought of her under my roof, and I couldn't believe she would want to be there. How long would she stay? Could I find someone else at church to put her up?

All this made me feel guilty, perhaps rightly so. I reacted by resolving to make her room as welcoming as I possibly could. I keep a spare bed made up – or rather, Anna-Marie does. She insists on ironing sheets and turning beds down, and doing all sorts of things that I wouldn't bother with, but for once I was glad she did.

I had a few minutes before we were due to leave for the mortuary, so I went almost surreptitiously into the lilac garden to collect some flowers for Alison's dressing table. I felt absurd, embarrassed to be in my own garden in case anyone saw me picking flowers at such a time. But there wasn't much I could do to make up to Alison for losing the most important person in her life; the least I could manage was to be a good hostess.

It was when I was there that I saw the door to the apple shed. The back of our house, beyond the kitchen, sprawls in a delightful tangle around a yard, with buildings, connected to each other, on three and a half sides. Doors open any old how on to the courtyard, which still boasts a mounting block and horse trough. One room is the laundry, another the wood shed, yet another is a lovely old-fashioned cool vegetable larder. The biggest, and most secure of the storerooms, with a Yale lock on the door, is called the apple shed. It isn't at all like an apple shed. It has housed boats and garden games and all sorts of things in its time, and still contains our largest freezer, and its name comes from the fact that, on shallow shelves along the outer, coolest wall, we store apples when we get organised enough to pick them. It has another, inner room, lockable too, where we keep ammunition and shooting belts, ear defenders and shotguns.

I stood still for several minutes, staring at the outer door to the apple shed, wondering what to do. It stood two inches ajar, instead of being closed.

I would have to tell the police, of course. Though not in front of Alison. I tried to remember what Graeme had said about Peter's death. My mind was a blur, a whirl of details and half-remembered, half-imagined images. Should I go and look inside the apple shed or fetch Graeme first? I didn't know whether there would be fingerprints everywhere: mine, and Sara's, and Charles's – even David's and Maurice's, perhaps Alison's and Peter's from long, long ago. I tried to work out who else might have been in there recently. Bob Bridges would have been in the previous week, and of course Geoff earlier in the day, to get the croquet basher. Would the police be able to tell whether Geoff had been the last person in there? If popular television programmes on forensic science are to be believed, the police can work out more now from one speck of dust than Sherlock Holmes ever could from a roomful of evidence and Conan Doyle's wildest flights of fancy.

But perhaps the handle of the shed was not the kind of surface which took fingerprints.

I went over to it and pushed the door open with the stalks of the lilac I was holding. Everything seemed as it should be. I decided to leave it and have a good look later.

I found it difficult to work out what was the next thing I was supposed to be doing. I looked down at the flowers I was still holding for Alison's bedroom. 'Now that the lilacs are in bloom' . . . I realised, sharply, how exquisitely pretty they were, and buried my nose deep into the petals to drink in the smell.

I had offered to drive Alison into Cambridge, to the mortuary, but in the end it seemed simpler to go in the police car. We sat silent, side by side, on the passenger seats in the back. The dusk was gathering under the roadside trees in Trumpington as we drove along, the street lamps not yet lit, the trees beginning to darken their waving shapes against the sky. In other circumstances the evening would have had the heady, relaxed and luxurious feel of a day which has really been hotter than an early English summer's day has the right to be; as if one has been spoilt, rather, and knows it. Perhaps this was how most of the village, enjoying themselves in our garden, were feeling now. It occurred to me that I could have asked Diana to oversee the party. She would have enjoyed that. She had offered to have the party in her garden, after all, but the committee had considered mine more suitable.

The mortuary is in Addenbrookes Hospital. I must have been inside that hospital dozens, perhaps hundreds of times, picking David up after work or visiting him, occasionally taking the children in, but it had never occurred to me that it contained a mortuary. It seemed, at first, to have the sweet odour of disposable nappies, though that can't have been what it was. But as soon as we were properly inside we realised what smell it was trying to hide.

The worst thing about the evening was the waiting. Why they took us there before they were ready for us, I can't imagine. They showed us into a little room, and brought us polystyrene drinks which could have been tea or coffee, or even, with a stretch of the imagination, hot chocolate. A clock grinned at us relentlessly from the wall. It moved painfully slowly, deliberately so, as if it were determined never to relieve Alison and me of each other's company.

What can one say, after all, to a woman one suddenly barely knows? Alison and I have been acquainted for half our lives. For years she knew where we kept the coffee and what we wore in bed and what colour our loo paper was. But she doesn't understand what happened to Sara all those years ago or what I lost three summers ago in a narrow bed in Nepal. Why should she?

I saw her glance up at the time, and could see, registered in the fear on her face, a wretched thought. It was one that I recognised. The movement she made, to speak, or get up, or ask permission for something as she has done all her life, was barely discernible. But at that moment, for the only time in all our lives together, I knew exactly what she was thinking. She was thinking if they don't let me go soon I'll have missed Peter by the time I get home. I can remember, you see. I can still feel the spasm of pain when, yet again, one finds one has made a pot of tea for two. And even that phase has its own thin comfort, and is over far too soon. Alison and I have so much in common, and yet nothing after all.

I looked at the table, with its yellow Formica and chipped edges. It reminded me of something, another room somewhere. 'Isn't that . . . ?' I started, but then never finished my sentence. I watched a brown puddle spread along the surface, and realised she had been shaking as she picked up her drink. She looked at me half expectantly, waiting for me to continue speaking, but I didn't.

I didn't want to sympathise with her. I did not want to remember what it was like. The beating, tyrannical sun, the whirr of the crickets, and the far-too-brief goodbye. It wasn't like this, but it was too familiar, and I asked myself why on earth I'd come. I could have asked Diana or Tricia to be with her instead, or left it up to the police to look after her. I smiled at her too brightly, and asked if she were all right.

She nodded. 'It hasn't happened, has it? I can't believe it. I know it has, but it can't have done.'

There was nothing I could say. I thought it good that she would see him. The process would be more brutal but quicker, like being in labour when it starts to get serious: the pain far more acute but the ordeal over sooner.

At last they showed us into a viewing room. It was divided by a thick pane of glass the full width of the room. On the other side a corpse – presumably – was covered with a green sheet. The PC touched Alison on her shoulder and asked her if she was ready. She nodded, and eventually a lab technician in white theatre overalls appeared on the other side of the screen and removed the sheet from just the face. He did it carefully, gingerly, as if he didn't want to uncover anything by mistake. There was another covering resting on the eyebrows, giving the impression that he had a very low forehead. As perhaps he has now, I thought to myself.

It was Peter.

Alison looked at the woman PC, and nodded almost imperceptibly.

And that was it. No tears, no hysterics, nothing.

14 ∫

His face was just as I had seen it last, but greyer, as if shocked at his own death.

The man in the white overalls covered him up again. The policewoman began to usher us out. For a split second, she put her hand on the small of Alison's back, protectively, kindly. I noticed it almost subconciously. How like a pack of animals we are, I thought. It was a gesture the young police constable would never have dared towards a superior. Alison's status had already been lowered to that of the bereaved: she had lost the dominant male to protect her interests. Like me.

On our way out, my mind doodling, trying to forget why I was there, I saw Colin. Bustling in, bristling with papers. Dear old Colin, frayed and busy and blessedly healthy, as he has always been. He didn't notice me, and I thought to let him go. But as he actually brushed past me I spoke his name.

He turned, rather wildly, as if affronted, and stared at me. Then his brow cleared.

'Harriet, you daft old bean,' he bellowed. 'What the blazes are you doing in this hellhole?' He kissed me on both cheeks, ignoring Alison and the woman PC as if they were invisible, which perhaps, to him, they were. 'A drink. Come on. Coffee, or that poisonous stuff they have here under the name of tea, or some gin if only I had some in this Godforsaken place and it weren't against the regs and likely to be confiscated by Matron after Lights Out. I want to hear all your news. You're looking great.' He narrowed his eyes as he looked at me. 'No, you're not actually. You look like bloody death, but of course that constitutes positive animation here.'

'Colin, I'm with someone,' I said, turning and indicating Alison.

'Oh, yes.' He glared at Alison. 'Oh, well, if you're busy. Another time, eh?'

'I'm fine,' Alison said. 'Please don't feel you must come with me.'

There then ensued one of those silly arguments, each of us insisting on what she thought the other wanted. Alison that she was perfectly all right, the PC that I wasn't needed if I wanted to see my old friend, almost forbidding me space in the police car, and Colin gaily promising a cab and an apology for disturbing my evening. I was too tired, somewhere deep inside, to care any longer what I did. A Saturday night at the morgue was not how I had intended rounding off the day of the Fair. But Colin's presence was swathed in comfortable memories, and Sara was safe with Hugh.

As the others left he asked me why I was there.

'Nothing grim, I hope?'

'Not for me,' I assured him. 'My neighbour's son.'

'Thank God for that. I couldn't bear it if you had to go through that again. Hitched up again yet?'

Suddenly I realised how glad I was to see him, as if I'd travelled back in time, and, instead of slapping his face, I laughed.

'Come on then,' he continued. 'Coffee. I've been chopping up these ruddy cadavers all day. Going on holiday on Monday, and I've been trying to make it easy for the new girl. Start on that emergency that's just come in, Charlie. And let me know when she's ready.' He steered me away. 'Yours the suicide, Harriet? Neighbour the mousy girl with you? Next time, be a sport and tell her to persuade her son to put his brains on the ceiling on a Monday morning, not when we're trying to knock off for the weekend. Sorry. Mustn't be flippant. It's this place. The chemicals addle the brain.'

He showed me into his tiny office and we perched, drinking grey instant coffee, and remembering the evenings the four of us had spent when we had tiny children and Colin and David were still barely more than housemen. The very taste of the coffee seemed the same as it had been then, when we sat in Colin and Helen's tiny poky kitchen in the centre of Cambridge, where Helen used to type envelopes and eventually write multi-purpose articles for the *Cambridge Evening News*, paying for the mortgage while the

twins were still in nappies. As I looked at Colin's lined and busy
face I was glad, with a light-headed kind of happiness. They still,
at any rate, had all the joy they had had then. They had each other,
and their bright children, and their world of work and success and
doing well.

And he was still a very attractive man. I almost remembered, in
the pit of my stomach, the feeling I had had for him once; when
David and I had been married for a few years, and I suppose I was
bored with being taken for granted, and Colin had told me all sorts
of nonsense and why hadn't he found me first. The usual thing.

Colin glanced at his watch. 'I must go,' I said.

'Funny thing,' Colin said. 'These suicides. Got a colleague
writing a paper at the moment. How you can tell a suicide from
a murder. Putting it crudely. What the hell are you standing
up for?'

'I need to go, Colin. Sara's at home. And about two hundred
guests.'

'Oh, for goodness' sake. They'll wait, if they're hungry enough.
I'll get you a cab in a minute. Sit down. I haven't finished my
coffee. What was I saying?'

I sat down again.

'This chap who's just been brought in. This would make a good
plot for a novel. I'll write it up one day, when I've got a moment.
He shot himself, right?'

'Colin . . .'

'OK, you've got to go. Wait five minutes, and I'll drive you. Have
you ever seen a PM?'

'No. And I don't want to start now.'

'What, doctor's wife and you've never seen a dead body?'

'I didn't say I'd never seen a dead body.'

'Right. Never seen 'em chopped up. You wouldn't be squeamish though, not after that leper colony in Bongobongo.' Colin's
hair-raising insensitivity still has the ability to make me shudder.
I thought he knew what we'd been through, or some of it at any
rate. Though he was right: I'm not squeamish. Duncan cannot
come out on's grave. 'Come with me, and I'll tell you about this
theory. You want to be careful, though: never show an interest in
dead bodies. You get struck off the Cambridge dinner party circuit
quicker than if you committed adultery with the Junior Proctor.'

The quickest way home seemed to be to follow him into the PM room. As we passed before the dead gaze of a naked, disembowelled old man, gazing blindly at the ceiling above us, I thought how shortlived it all is: hopes, fears, love and romance, it all comes down to this in the end. A fine and private place.

We passed Charlie, in the white overalls, drawing out the innards of a shrivelled old woman. As he pulled her tongue out of her mouth and through the cut in her throat, I noticed her eyes were closed, as if to the pain. 'OK, mate,' Colin said, 'you push off home and I'll finish off.'

Colin took over. He did indeed work quickly and easily. His eccentricity and insensitivity fell off him like an ill-fitting coat that he had put on by mistake. He sliced through the ribcage like an expert butcher, tossing it to one side where it rested, forgotten, against its previous mistress's thigh. He removed the organs, vast mutant giblets, and broke his concentration for a moment to show me some huge red and black speckled sack.

'See that? All that muck. Soot. Black. Filthy. That's what living in a town does for you. Even a pretty little town like Cambridge.'

Then he went back to the carcass, pulling something out which looked as if it were a string of used teabags tied together like garlic, till I saw it was nothing but a huge long sausage. This he washed in the basin, like a housewife rinsing out a dirty dishcloth, then he heaved it out of the water again and slapped it on the chopping board. While he worked he seemed to have forgotten me. It wasn't until he had mutilated his piece of work so much that it was no longer a tortured body but a huge plateful of tissues for his mind to savour, that he looked up again.

'Look,' he said to me, pointing out a red bag. 'Bladder full.' I watched him slit it open and empty it down the sink. It had indeed been full. For a moment the room stank of ammonia, and my mind went straight to years of nappy buckets and simultaneously to a buried teenaged memory of insanitary French loos. It seemed outrageous now, this final humiliation of the dead. He put the empty bag back with the rest of the body.

It was fascinating watching him work. Just as he was finishing, and pulling off his gloves, he looked up at someone who had just come in. 'You with the new one? What did forensic say about him?' He turned to me. 'Coroner's Officer,' he explained.

'Evening,' the newcomer replied. 'Shot himself.'

'Charming. What else? Best friend of Harriet's here, he was,' Colin said, nodding towards me. The Coroner's Officer looked scandalised.

'That true?'

'No,' I said. 'It isn't.'

'What'd they say?' Colin repeated.

'If this lady is acquainted with him . . .'

'She isn't,' Colin said crossly. 'It was a joke. Or not much, anyway.'

'Doctor Wesley, the correct procedure . . .'

'I know what the bloody procedure is. I was working here when you were in nappies. Just read me the notes will you?'

He looked at me uncertainly, opened the file he was carrying, and quoted unhappily, ' "The deposit of shot on the hands and clothes is consistent with a side-by-side twelve-bore being fired in very close proximity to the deceased. The lead shot recovered from the immediate surroundings of the incident is not inconsistent with the weapon which was discovered with the deceased; confirmation necessary with shot and wad to be recovered from carcass. The angle of the shot does not contra-indicate the deceased having pulled the trigger. Therefore the possibility of the wound being self-inflicted should not be ruled out." '

'See what you mean,' Colin conceded, throwing his gloves in the disposal bin and ushering me out. 'Thanks.'

'He shot himself,' the officer repeated, as we left the room.

We reached Colin's little office. 'Little Mr Smarty Pants,' he said, as he sat down heavily in the chair at his desk. 'Surrounded by morons, I am. Anyway, that's what I was telling you,' he said, swivelling in his chair. 'Do you remember Sophie?' Sophie? Who on earth was Sophie? ''Course you do. Gorgeous thing. Tits like, oh I don't know. Cruise missiles. Worked with David, years ago.'

'What was she, a nurse or what?'

'Nurse? She's a professor, you twit. Anyway, your neighbour's son made me think of her latest theory. She's good at the kind of ideas which look great on telly. The last thing she demonstrated, on one of these BBC things, was the notion that you feel more pain if you're told you're going to feel pain. You know. That's why it hurts women when they're in labour, because they've been told it's going to hurt.'

'That—' I said.

'Is bollocks,' he completed. 'I know, but she proved it very prettily for the cameras, anyway.'

'I've heard a doctor expounding this theory to me, claiming that ethnic women without a culture of labour "pains" feel nothing. No, he didn't call them ethnic, he said native. "Native" women!' I said, remembering my irritation. 'Who did he think he was? Livingstone? I tried to tell him I've seen women in labour in Phulbari . . .'

'Screaming blue murder. I'm sure you have. Look, don't blame me: it's not my theory. Old Sophie will change her tune the minute she starts breeding the little blighters herself, and finds herself bawling away on the maternity unit chewing lead and gas-and-air rather than doing soundbites for Auntie Beeb. Anyway, her latest theory is to do with what happens to your body just before you blow your brains out. Or go hopping off the Empire State, or whatever your individual taste happens to be. Just before you jump, you feel a certain apprehension, right? Where's my ruddy jacket?'

'You've got it on, Colin.'

'Oh, so I have. Where are my car keys, then? They should be in the pocket.'

'I don't know.'

'Find them in a minute. Where was I? Oh, yes. Now suppose you're pushed. Or someone else shoots you. This theory doesn't work, by the way, if you know you're going to be pushed or shot. But suppose somebody shoots or pushes or stabs you without warning. Or whatever. Though perhaps it wouldn't work with the Empire State example, because you'd have time to realise you were dying. As you hurtle towards the ground, right? Basically, Sophie's idea is that you can tell, or rather the pathologist can tell, whether you knew you were going to die. If you anticipated it, the body will be pumped full of adrenaline. If not, nothing. Mind you, there's no adrenaline by the time we look at the chappie anyway, because it's so volatile it's disappeared by then, but don't spoil the plot. The long and the short, with this bloke who's come in, which is what made me think of it, is that with Sophie's new theory she can tell whether he topped himself or it was just a very clever set up. That your handbag?'

'Um . . .' I was trying to follow the twists and turns of his dialogue. I picked up my handbag. 'Can we go?'

Just as we were leaving, a lab assistant passed us wheeling the most recent arrival in on a trolley. I was shocked. Not because his head was pulled back in a silent scream of protest, nor because what remained of the back of his head had been blown away. But because he was naked. I was ashamed, somehow, to see him so vulnerable. His ankles were tied submissively together, and labelled rather pessimistically, as if he might get lost. It almost seemed unfair, to subject to him to all this. I wanted to look away, but found myself staring. This was the man who had driven us into exile. This was the boy we had tried to love and help.

'It's all right, Harriet. He can't get up and bite you. You look worse than he does.'

'Colin, I must get back.'

'We're going, we're going. I know, all these dead bodies are giving you the willies. Happens to the most intelligent of people. Pass out, some of them.'

Twenty minutes later we were in his car and threading through the quiet evening streets of the city. The sky was dark, and the pavements were lit up by the yellow street lamps, the shuttered lights from the restaurants, and the bright laughter of under-graduates walking home to their rooms from the cinemas or the theatres, or other colleges.

'If adrenaline is so volatile,' I said, 'how can the pathologist detect it anyway?'

'What?' he said, swerving to miss a cyclist. He wound his window down. 'If you'd seen the injuries I'd seen,' he yelled, 'you'd wear a bloody helmet. Daft kids,' he muttered, winding it up again. 'That's the trouble. She's having a hell of a job verifying it. Sexy idea: difficult to prove. The point is the pathologist takes a bit of this and that at the scene of crime. Plain tube blood sample, that sort of thing. Test for alcohol and what have you. All you need is to bung a bit of serum in the freezer, dead easy, and you're away. But you have to do it pretty sharpish while the adrenaline's there, and these forensic wallahs tend not to. Until Sophie's proved her theory, they're not likely to, and it's impossible for her to prove it until they have. There we are. If life were easy it wouldn't be fun. But she may be on to a good thing with this one. Your neighbour's son. Imagine the scene. Or rather the telly programme. *Science with Sophie*, prime time. Now, the police have looked at all the obvious stuff. Angle of the shot, sites of election.'

'What?'

'Oh, you know. Where he shot himself. Forehead, chin, temple, heart – all suicide. Nape of the neck or back of head – murder. Easy. Agatha Christie stuff. Police have looked at all that and decided he's done himself in. And of course he has. I mean, I can't see a chap like that letting someone put a twelve-bore up his nose for the fun of it. Besides, the Boys in Blue never get it wrong, curse them. Though mind you, it's odd that he didn't do it at home. His mother's place, wasn't it? Her front room will be a pretty sight. That doesn't fit, you see.'

'What doesn't?'

'Away from home. If you were going to kill yourself, where would you do it?' I hesitated, being quite ignorant on the subject. Having had children at the time, it had been a luxury I couldn't afford. 'I tell you, you'd do it in your own place. They all do. So we've got enough to be suspicious about. No suicide note, wrong location. Let's suppose for a moment we decide it's suspicious. We propose a thesis: he didn't know, was asleep, stuffed full of coke, something like that. All right, all right, it doesn't sound very credible, but for the sake of Sophie's paper. Give her a chance. Along comes genius pathologist – in well-cut white suit and perfect makeup – looks at tube of serum conveniently frozen for her, no adrenaline, thinks, "Fishy", Bob's your uncle. Beautiful heroine solves crime which had baffled the police. In fact no one else had realised it was a crime. Clever girl, Sophie.'

I wanted to ask him something else, but as he negotiated the roundabout I simply said, 'Sorry to take you out of your way.'

'You aren't. Oh, see what you mean. No, we've split up.'

I was so stunned, I couldn't think what to say for a moment. 'What? What do you mean, split up?'

'Yup. Shame, really.'

'You and Helen?'

''Fraid so.' I couldn't believe it. I felt it was the last straw. Suicide, theft, mutilated bodies, theories about adrenaline – and murder – had all been manageable, somehow. This was too much.

'Why, Colin?'

'Oh, you know. Start to lose the buzz. Things get stale. Perhaps you and David didn't have time.'

Oh, Colin, we tackled that one long ago. You were the one who made us face it. It was just another growing pain which seems so easy now, and was so agonising at the time.

Somebody banged on the car window. It was the same cyclist, who had caught up with us. She looked frighteningly young, but she must have been an undergraduate. Colin wound the window down again. 'Trying to kill yourself?'

'I didn't hear what you said back there.'

'Wear a helmet, ducky. We drivers are lethal.'

'Oh, is that all?'

'All? It'll save your life one day. Lights. Cheerio.' As he drove on, he said, 'My fault.'

'What d'you mean? You didn't hit her.'

'Helen?'

'The cyclist.'

Suddenly, despite ourselves, we both started to laugh. I remembered what had made him so attractive.

'I meant the marriage. I'm the Big Baddy.'

I turned to look at him. 'Not Sophie?'

He took his eyes off the road, and returned my look. 'You always were a bit too perceptive for comfort. The one with the tits out to here.'

I thought of Colin's children, who used to adore him reading to them at bedtime, and helping them with their homework. The girls who must now be leggy intellectual teenagers applying to Oxbridge colleges from the Perse. The boy who admired Colin more than all the heroes in his bookshelves. And of course Helen, the gutsy, brilliant Helen, who went through much more than Colin did to get him his place in medicine, and lost her chance of a fellowship at Newhall because of her dedication to his career. Who is now in her forties, beyond academic success, and probably beyond that off-beat beauty which made her all the rage once. Is any of it Colin's fault? I don't know. It seemed such a waste, because Colin is so brilliant and we were so fond of them both.

'Point is, Harriet,' he said, turning left into Trumpington. 'The point is, she wants to marry me.'

'Oh?' He seemed to expect me to say something more. 'And?'

'Oh, I don't know. I miss the kids.' I said nothing. There was nothing to say. 'That's all. I miss the kids.'

'Don't you see them?'

'Every other weekend. Not when I come home at the end of the day, or want to laugh over a bacon butty at eleven o'clock at night, or fancy watching Mr Bean with someone who doesn't care what he'd look like cut up on a table.'

In the end I broke a long silence. 'Do you miss Helen?'

I heard him sigh again in the darkness beside me.

'I don't know. Sometimes. Not much. But I don't really know any more.'

When he dropped me off at Willisham House it was nearly ten o'clock. There would still be plenty of people lingering on at the barbecue. Just before we turned into the drive, I said, 'Is Sophie putting this theory into practice?'

'Trying to. She's working with the forensic pathologists to get the samples. I paged her to tell her about your chap, so she can have a look at him. She's probably there already. He's a text-book case; too good to be true, almost. Could prove her whole thesis. I'll get her paper for you when it comes out. Mind you, you know medical publications. It'll take months, if not years.'

As I sat there in the darkness I wondered what I could do. But I don't think there was anything. My links with Peter had been severed long ago. If I learnt only one thing from David, it was the value of saying nothing.

He obviously wasn't going to get out of the car to open the door for me. As I turned in my seat to say goodbye, he kissed me on the lips.

I smiled at last. 'Goodbye, Colin.'

'Goodbye. I'll ring you.' I lingered for a second, before getting out. Then he seemed to remember that he had the stunning Sophie and all her attributes waiting for him at home. 'Don't worry: if it's a cunning murder, Soph will spot it a mile off.' He winked.

I watched as he turned the car and drove off, and stayed watching the same spot for quite a while afterwards.

15

Sunday dawned beautiful. The sunlight skipped on my bed; the leaves shivered in the morning breeze. Lovely May, I thought, and sat up. I couldn't think what day it was or what I was supposed to be doing. Five to seven, my clock said. For an awful moment I thought it was Sara's birthday.

Then I remembered.

I got out of bed and felt leaden, as if enveloped by a dark, heavy blanket. The sunlight continued to shake itself into my bedspread. The day was quite delightful.

Silence seeped from Sara's room as I walked past.

When I was doing my 'gap' year in Paris the father of the family I was living with killed himself. We weren't in Paris at the time, but in their holiday cottage in Brittany. He walked out into the dark night and didn't come back. I can remember sitting round all evening playing cards with his family: he had five children, all of them intelligent and beautiful and fun in their different ways, the youngest fifteen and the oldest twenty-eight, and the girl my age was away at university in Italy. It got later and later, we still didn't eat dinner, and I couldn't understand why anyone was worried. I didn't know. They did. Then we heard the sound of the car, and went outside to greet his wife who had been out looking for him.

I remember her getting out of the car. '*Ça va?*' I asked in my still rather schooly French: I'd only been there a fortnight.

'*Non, ma petite. Mon mari est mort.*'

Now that I think about it, she must have told me before any of her children, though presumably they were there to overhear. This strikes me as extraordinary now. After all she didn't particularly like me, and after that night I think she actually hated me. Soon bereavement put a wall about them all, and they closed ranks and resented me. Except perhaps Yves, the quiet one, the eldest, who was half in love with me. He remained kind, though he was part of this family with a suddenly different identity; the family which had changed from the rich, happy, talented and delightful Pointillards, and had overnight become *les pauvres*. The family of orphans who now went out to dinner without me.

What makes me think of the incident so many years later is the remembered radiant brilliance of the next day. Madame sent me back to Paris. Understandably. She had too much on her mind to think of my arrival, late at night, alone and only eighteen, at their huge and deserted old house in St Cloud, set on its own on the hillside; she wasn't to know that for weeks afterwards, even in the daytime, I would see her husband gliding silent and unsmiling towards me through the glass doors. So Yves was asked to drive me to the station to catch the train for the capital. It must have been one of the most spectacularly beautiful days either of us had seen. We both had the same, unspoken thought together. We had both seen the still grey form of his father, after he had been dragged out of the water that they had all loved and sailed in, and then dressed and laid on an upstairs bed with a bunch of heather in his hands. At least, I presume Yves had seen him. I had crept up in a quiet moment to steal a view; I wanted to touch him to see if he were really as cold as Falstaff was reported to be, but I was afraid. Of what? I think, of Madame coming in and finding me; as if, by touching him, I would have been stealing something.

'*Il est beau*,' I said, of the sky and the sea and the sun, shining almost like an insult at us. My use of the language remained uninspired. Nevertheless, we understood each other perfectly.

'*Oui*,' Yves replied sadly. '*Il est magnifique*.'

The day after Peter's death was very similar.

I ran across the lawn, barefoot and in my towelling dressing gown, and the clean dew stuck little pieces of cut grass on to the soles of my feet. As a superstitious concession to the events of the day before I went into the little changing hut to put on a swimsuit. Normally, during the day, I keep a large towel by the water's edge in case guests arrive unexpectedly – then, if I hear voices crossing the lawn from the house and coming round by the tennis court, I have plenty of time to drape myself. In the early morning I don't need to; alone, I never wear anything. But I did that day.

As I sat on the edge of the pool with my toes in the water I tried to feel soothed by the plump, insistent call of the wood-pigeons. They had nested one summer outside the room I had in my second year at Lady Margaret Hall, and the call, since then, has always comforted me and brought back that hazy, careless summer, sitting in boathouses in Eights Week drinking Pimm's and wearing floaty dresses and straw hats and worrying about exams. Whenever I go to Oxford now there seems to be none of that any more. Not even the worrying about exams. Now the students look miserable in tatty jeans and worry about the next fifty years.

One of the neighbouring cats regarded me defiantly from a herbaceous border, then dug a careful hole in it. I was surprised. I had always thought cats very fastidious and private animals. He seemed at last to become embarrassed as I gazed at him and eventually turned away from me, sniffed at his own deposit, examining it without disdain, then covered it with earth as if to say, You can have your garden back again; there was no need for all the fuss.

I dived. The clean blue pattern of sunlight, as I broke the surface of the water, danced on the bottom of the pool like huge illuminated chicken wire. I try to keep the chlorine level low: I love to open my eyes in the water and come up into the sun. For a moment it was almost as if the water could wash away Alison's coming loneliness, and the messy death of the day before, and all the past and future grief, just as it washes away the sound of the distant traffic every morning when I dive in. That, and all the perfumes of Arabia. I swam the length of the pool under water, not wanting to surface.

I came up, spurted the water and mild chemicals out of my nose and eyes, and recovered my blurred vision. And for a moment I saw a young girl running, like the past, over the long shadows on the early morning lawn.

It was a nightmare. When the gods wish to destroy us, they give us our heart's desire. I seemed to see someone, free and happy, running across the May sunshine. I saw a lifetime's beliefs begin to crumble. A dreadful wickedness had been done. A man had been killed. But there was no judgement, there was no Nemesis. There was only this: happiness and freedom running across the bright dew.

'Hello Mummy,' she said. 'I heard the splash of the water from my bedroom, so I thought I'd come and join you.'

16

It was later that morning that I reported the missing gun to the police. That is, I told Graeme at the morning service.

Alison, Sara and I went to church together. Hugh had explained to Sara, in my absence the night before, the essence of what had happened. I have no doubt he had toned it down. Something non-committal and anodyne. 'An accident.' Luckily it hadn't formed part of our awkward, halting breakfast conversation. I noticed that Sara was much more natural with Alison than I was. She is remarkably mature in her ability to cope with others' pain.

I escorted both of them to a pew at the front, and as I watched Alison kneel on the uncomfortable hassock to say her prayers I thought of Prue. She too had knelt there, after Maurice's death, in the place where Maurice's family had derived comfort for generations, still in the family pew with the St Joseph name on it. In a spirit of rather belated egalitarianism I asked Hugh to have the family name unscrewed from the pew, and I took it home as a memento, but out of habit nobody else sits there, so in practice it is still the St Joseph pew.

When Prue knelt there in the first wave of shock after Maurice died the rest of us were still abroad. It had all been so sudden we didn't hear until it was too late. So she knelt alone. And, she told me afterwards, for the first time in her life she found herself angry with the jangling banality of the Alternative Services Book and Tricia's jolly band of bean pod shakers. She believes in the Church of England being accessible to the masses, in theory she approves of the modernising. But when she knelt, in her hour of need, in the Church of her childhood she longed for Cranmer's finely sprung prose and Wesley's deep chordal harmony, and she found that the mediocrity of late twentienth-century jingoism left her hungry and bereft.

I wondered if this was how Alison felt now. I doubted it somehow. Alison never went to church with her parents when she was a child, and had no experience of a school chapel resounding with the *Book of Common Prayer*. The usual Sunday morning service, with familiar toddlers running round and children charging in from Sunday School rather too loudly before the adults had quite finished, was probably exactly what she wanted.

Prue was normally there in the pew before us, but she wasn't that day. It was unlike her to be late for church. But I didn't have time to worry about Prue. I settled Sara and Alison, then went to the back of the church again to look for Graeme. I knew he'd be there, provided he wasn't on duty. He's a member of the Parochial Church Council and a regular church-goer, and never misses church if he can help it. Then I saw the back of his head, sitting as he was with Penny and little Tim, who was waiting to go into Sunday School.

'Can I speak to you?' I whispered, as the first hymn started up. He got up and came outside without a word. 'I'm sorry,' I said as we went out into the sunshine. 'This could probably have waited till the end of the service, but I wasn't sure.'

Then I told him about the loss. 'It's one of Maurice's old twelve-bores. Or perhaps it was David's. It's kept in the apple shed, a sort of storeroom off the kitchen yard. I think you've inspected the guns there before. Next to the laundry. We keep odd things there, spades, and flower pots, and leaky gumboots, and the freezer. And the shotguns. The more valuable and dangerous ones, Maurice's collection, are kept in the safe under the stairs. But the air rifle and a couple of shotguns live in a gun room inside the shed. Both doors usually locked, of course. But one of the twelve-bores isn't there any more.'

He nodded. 'We'd better go and have a look. D'you mind?'

We set off for the house. The strains of hearty singing followed us down the empty road.

'When did you miss it? This will save us a bit of time, if it was what he used. Cambridge CID will be tracing it now.' He looked sideways at mc as we walked along. 'The licence is up to date, isn't it,' he asked, frowning to remember. 'Renewed about eighteen months ago?' I nodded. 'Well you never know,' he continued. 'It's amazing what slips through the net. I'll have to take a look at the licence, if you don't mind. In fact,' he said as we neared the house, 'if you can fish out the paperwork for all the firearms in the house, I'd better cast an eye over the lot.'

As we went through the gateway into the back yard, I took him to the apple shed, which was still unlocked from the day before. I hadn't yet plucked up the courage to tell him the room hadn't been secure. I had been to look round the room early that morning, planning to tell about it him at church. 'The guns are kept in that inner room through there. The keys live here, unless we're away.' I showed him the little wooden box, hidden behind some overalls above the apple shelves, where the keys to the gun room are kept. 'I'll let you look around while I go and find those licences.'

They didn't take me long to find. I knew exactly where they were in my filing cabinet, but when I came back downstairs to go into the yard and show them to Graeme, I found he'd already let himself into the kitchen and was talking on his mobile phone, presumably to the Cambridge Police.

'When did you say you first missed it?' he asked me as soon as he'd finished.

'The door was ajar last night. I wasn't particularly surprised. Sara had been back for her flute, although she wouldn't have gone to the apple shed. But then Geoff borrowed my keys to get something from the croquet set. I didn't think to tell him to make sure the room was locked again. Because of the Yale lock, it didn't occur to me to make a point of it: it's natural to pull it shut behind when you leave anyway. But of course, anyone who didn't know there were guns in here wouldn't have any reason to think it matters. It just looks like an old storeroom for garden games, so presumably Geoff didn't attatch any importance to it. I meant to see if there was anything missing when we got back from the mortuary, because I'd already noticed the door was ajar, but in the event it was much later than I'd expected, and dark, and to be honest I just forgot.' I stopped. 'Besides,' I continued, trying to be ruthlessly honest, 'I was quite shaken. We've known the family a long time.'

'Of course, Harriet. You've been marvellous. To Alison, I mean.'

'No, I haven't.' I thought of her, abandoned at the morning service. I shouldn't have left her with Sara, but I couldn't be everywhere at once. 'Anyway,' I went on, 'I went outside to take some bread out of the freezer this morning and remembered. I checked the cupboard, and found the gun missing.' I handed him the file with the papers in it. 'I could have rung you straight away, but I thought it would be easier with Alison out of the way.'

'Understandable,' he said, looking at the papers. He started reading through the file. I was fairly confident it was all in order. I had found the regulations quite complicated, on taking over, though Prue had tried to explain it all to me. But Maurice had always dealt with the guns before, and Prue hadn't adjusted to the fact that the law is much tighter now.

After going through most of the file he looked up, and went rather red. 'Harriet, I don't think that room will do, you know. With the keys kept by it, and everything. Hungerford was bad enough, but since Dunblane you just can't do that. I hope Cambridge Police don't cause a fuss.'

'Right. I'm sorry, I've been keeping it much as Prue and Maurice did.' Cambridge Police could confiscate the whole lot as far as I was concerned. Though Charles would mind. 'Would you like some coffee?'

'Please. To be honest, I think you'd be better dismantling the shotguns and putting them in the safe too. I know it's a nuisance, but it's not as if you use them all the time. You'd better tell me when those guns were last used.'

I started to organise the coffee. 'Charles had the air rifle out when he was home, a couple of weeks ago.'

'What for?'

'Cats. He wasn't shooting at them,' I added quickly. 'The fantails are nesting. The cats are real pests. I can't bear it, the way they creep up on the doo'cot whenever the birds are sitting. Charles said if he released a little bang over their heads they might push off for the rest of the day. I told him he was daft, but he said it might keep them off long enough for the babies to hatch. I'm sure he would have locked the guns up properly again afterwards.'

'Can't you turn a hose on them?'

'The cats? They see me going to the garden tap. Believe me, I've tried everything, those high-frequency electronic devices, the lot. They're too cunning for all of it. But they don't see Charles loading an air rifle.'

'And when was this?'

'The eggs were laid about two and a half weeks ago. Charles was here on the Sunday. So it must have been the weekend before last. The twentieth of April.'

'And what about the shotgun? Does he ever shoot anything with that?'

'Sometimes. Occasionally he goes on a shooting weekend with friends. He shot a duck last year in the garden, and we had it on New Year's Eve. But it's not used much here. We're too fond of watching the birds on the lawn. And there's all the business of plucking them. It's hardly worth it in the end. If we take a bird to Geoff we might as well buy one off him. You said you wanted coffee?'

'Thank you. Crikey. What's this rifle certificate for? That Charles' as well?'

'No. That was Maurice's. I don't suppose he used it much. I've told Charles he can have it eventually. He's got a school friend with a place in Scotland. Quite a bit of stalking on it. But that's one of the ones in the safe. Lethal. Bullets travel three miles, apparently. Not that I've tried. Have you seen all you need in the gun room?'

'Yes, thanks. CID'll come and snoop around. Fingerprints and everything. Keep it locked up, for goodness' sake. And the shotgun is definitely stolen?'

'No. It's definitely *missing*.' Suddenly, for no apparent reason, I wished I could simply talk to him as a friend. Coming with him straight from church, seeing him in the clothes I saw him in at the weekend, off-duty, I wanted to tell him all the things we'd coped with over the years, things which would seem irrelevant, which had no apparent bearing on his line of questioning. I had to remind myself how unfair this would be. On Graeme himself. He was doing a job of work and, as the good policeman and Christian that he was, would do it conscientiously and well.

'When did you say you last used it, exactly?'

I poured the beans into my little grinding machine and pressed it down. It makes such a fearful noise we could neither speak nor think for a moment. 'Hang on,' I shouted at him. The noise ceased as quickly as it had started. The pungent dark smell began to fill the kitchen. 'Sorry about that. What did you ask me? When was it last used? Well, yesterday of course.'

'What?' Graeme dropped the file on to the kitchen table, and half stood up in his excitement. 'Why on earth didn't you say so? When?'

'Well, I mean when it killed Peter. That's all.'

'Oh, I see.' He sat down again slowly. 'I see what you mean. OK, when was it last used before that?'

I filled the coffee maker. 'Just after Easter I think. Charles took Sara on a clay-pigeon shoot with some friends.'

'Sara?' He raised his eyebrows.

'Why do you look like that?'

'Unusual for a girl to handle a gun, that's all.'

'Nonsense. Prue's a crack shot.'

'Prue's unusual.'

'So is Sara.'

'Fair enough.' The machine gurgled and spat. For years I made coffee in a jug, but Charles gave me the filter machine for Christmas. I don't think the coffee tastes quite as good, but it keeps it hot. 'Has anything else been missed?'

'Are you implying Sara missed her clay pigeons?'

For a moment he hesitated, puzzled, Then he smiled. As he did so, I realised how tense we had both become. I sat down opposite him, and tried to smile as well. Graeme is fond of Sara. 'I wouldn't dream of suggesting it. I expect she's a crack shot too. I meant has anything else gone missing? As well as the gun.'

'No.'

'Any signs of break in?'

'No.'

'Left the house unlocked for any period?'

'Oh, all the time.'

'Pardon?'

'I never lock up. I mean unless I'm going to be out all day. The apple shed's kept locked, because of the guns. The doors are locked at night if Sara's at home; and I lock up when I go into Cambridge, but not if I'm around in Willisham, shopping or something.'

'Oh Harriet!' He shook his head.

'The front door's sometimes locked nowadays. But most people come to the back of the house anyway, and try the kitchen door. Well it's such a bore if you're out, and someone just wants to sit down and wait for a few minutes. If everything's locked up, they can't make themselves a cup of tea or anything.'

'Then, strictly speaking, it could have gone any time over the last fortnight?'

'It's no good looking at me like that, Graeme. It's not against the law to leave your house open.'

'It's a damn nuisance for the police. And it's an offence to leave guns insecure. Doesn't all this invalidate your insurance policy?'

'No, it doesn't actually. I looked into that.'

'Deliberate negligence. That's worse. Did you lock up yesterday afternoon?'

'During the Fair? Yes. Yes, I did. I was quite careful yesterday: I knew there would be a lot of strangers around.' I thought for a moment, trying to recall it all accurately. 'Sara and I left the house together. I had checked the front door and the windows. There might have been the odd window which had been pulled shut and not locked, but the house hasn't been disturbed so I'm sure no one's climbed in. After we left I realised I'd gone out without my gloves – for my Edwardian costume – so Sara went on while I came back for them. I unlocked the back door to go back in, but I know I locked it again afterwards. But this is all irrelevant, because the gun was in the apple shed.'

'Which was locked?'

'Yes. As I say, it's always kept locked. We have the small freezer here in the kitchen, so we don't go in the apple shed often, and we lock it and unlock it every time. It really couldn't have been taken any time in the last fortnight.'

'Thank goodness for that. So it seems pretty clear. It must

have been taken after Geoff came and left the shed unlocked. And presumably anyone could have lifted it.'

'Well, anyone who wasn't involved in the Fair. Who knew where we keep our guns. And where the key's kept. That rules most people out.'

Graeme nodded. 'Except one, of course.'

I thought about this for a while, but said nothing. The coffee was ready. I poured Graeme's, making it just as he likes it, milky, with half a spoonful of sugar. 'Thank you.' He took a sip. 'That's great. Presumably Peter knew where to find the keys?'

'Almost certainly. He knew the house well as a child, and not much has been changed. I'm sure he knew where the guns were kept, because he and Charles got into terrible trouble about them one day. Maurice said if he caught them playing with them again he'd spank them both. After that he taught Charles to shoot properly. Peter remained fascinated with them. A few months later he stole the air rifle and hid it behind the shed down at the pool. He wasn't allowed in the apple shed after that. That was when Maurice put the new lock on.'

'And was he spanked?'

'I doubt it. Charles would have been.'

'Well, that does seem to be an obvious explanation. We'll have a good look for his prints. It sounds as if it would be the first place he'd come for a gun.'

'I would have thought so, yes.'

'And it might explain why he chose to kill himself away from his own flat. We'll check that it's the same gun, and return it to you as soon as it's finished with. You've got a message on your machine, by the way,' he said, indicating the little flashing red light with a nod of his head.

'Yes,' I said. I had noticed it the minute I walked in. I had felt instinctively uneasy about it, but I hadn't quite worked out why. Perhaps it was because it was Sunday: I'm not used to being rung up on a Sunday morning, because most of my friends know I'll be in church. I wondered whether it was from my mother; perhaps she had heard the news about Peter somehow, and linked him with us and the village, and wanted to gossip under the pretence of asking whether we were all right. But no: she hates answerphones and never leaves messages. Why would she ring me while I was at church, unless specifically in order to avoid me? I didn't want to listen to it in front of Graeme, but as soon as he mentioned it I felt it might be odd not to.

I pressed the 'Play' button.

'Harriet, darling . . .'

It was Prue. What should I do now? She would have heard the news, and would know how shaken we all were – as she would be herself. She might refer to the past, Maurice's death while we were out of the country, David's own suffering, deeply private things which I never wanted anyone outside the family to hear ever again. Everything had been stirred up, for Prue as well as me. In the muddy water in which we were all stumbling about, she might say anything. What should I do? Stop the machine, before Prue announced all our family secrets in Graeme's hearing?

The voice continued. 'In case you're wondering where I am . . .' I pressed.

'Only Prue,' I said unnecessarily. 'She's away for the day. I'm always forgetting to clear this thing.' I kept my back turned towards Graeme for a moment. I had realised, too late, that I had pressed the wrong button, the one which wipes the message immediately. I cursed silently. There was nothing I could do now. I took a deep breath before turning back to Graeme.

'How's it all going?' I said. 'The investigation?'

'Interesting. Very interesting. Dreadful for Alison of course,' he added as an afterthought, guiltily. 'Obviously suicide, but we just have to clear up why and how. This'll sort out the how.'

I thought of the usual petty theft, minor traffic offences and rather sordid domestic nastiness that policing in Willisham must usually entail. For the first time in our acquaintance I wondered why Graeme and Penny had settled in the backwater of a small village, comparatively early in Graeme's career. Knowing him as I did, I assumed he simply didn't care much about promotion. It was a lovely place for children to grow up in; it suited Penny well. For all I knew, Graeme was in the police simply to try to make the world a better place to live in. It's as good a way as any other.

'How on earth will she cope?' I found myself asking, and then shivered involuntarily. 'I can't imagine anything worse.'

'I wonder why he did it.' Graeme stood up and took his mug into the scullery.

'You're sure he did?'

'It's pretty clear. House locked up. No sign of forced entry. Neighbours swear no one else was there except Peter himself. And forensic confirmed it. Not to put too fine a point on it, the trajectory of the blood on the walls, angle of the shot, that sort of thing. You'd be surprised: if there's anything out of line they pick it up in five minutes.'

I stared at my coffee. It was strong and lukewarm and sludgy at the bottom of the mug.

'There was one odd thing, though,' Graeme mused. 'A phone call. A nine nine nine call. At four forty-eight, to Cambridge police station. The caller said he'd heard a shot from the middle cottage at the bottom of the lane, and could we investigate. That was what took me there.'

'What's strange about that?'

'It struck the detective superintendent as odd. Why didn't he call the local station? Why didn't he give his name and address? Why did he hear the shot when the neighbours didn't? Come to think of it, why didn't he comment on it to the neighbours the moment he heard it, and ask if he could use their phone?'

I thought of a number of reasons why: that he didn't think of ringing the police till later, when he'd been walking for a while. That he was too embarrassed, or frightened, to disturb the neighbours. Even that he had killed Peter. But I couldn't be bothered to say so. Peter lay dismembered on a mortuary table. It hardly seemed to matter who had made the telephone call. It wouldn't bring back the dead.

We heard a car on the drive outside. 'That'll be Cambridge CID,' Graeme explained, 'come to look at the gun cupboard.' We got up to go and greet them. We walked towards the front door.

'Was it a man's voice?' I asked suddenly.

'Yes. Why?'

'I just wondered.'

17

Three quarters of an hour later, as soon as Tricia was free from church, she and I went down to Alison's cottage to clean up. She had arranged for another family in the church to give Alison lunch and look after her for the day.

The task was unpleasant, as I had known it would be. I had asked Graeme about it, and he said he supposed it might be possible to get the council to clear up, but he wasn't really sure. Certainly they wouldn't do anything over the weekend, and it hardly seemed fair on Alison to leave it like that.

Since I had got back from the mortuary the night before I had imagined the pervading smell of a corpse everywhere: when I opened the fridge for a bottle of milk, or went into the airing cupboard to get a towel for Alison. When I walked into her house that Sunday with Tricia I wanted to hold a handkerchief up to my face. Tricia didn't seem to notice it. She certainly didn't react. Perhaps, being a nurse, she is used to it.

Alison has done the house very prettily. It was spotlessly clean, except the room which Peter had been in. She has decorated it in a rather feminine way, but quite tastefully. It contrasts favourably with her parents' house at the other end of the village, where everything has a rather gilt-edged exaggeration, with thick, bright, wall-to-wall carpets, shiny, unused ashtrays, and a clean, flickering fire under plastic flames. Alison's house is much more Habitat.

There was one detail, though, which didn't seem quite right. Inside the hall there was one of those paintings which you can buy in department stores, mounted in a highly decorated frame which looks rather like tin foil. I wondered whether her parents had given it to her. Somehow, I didn't think Alison would have hung it just to please them, but I could have been wrong.

The colours in the painting were all slightly brighter than they should have been. It was a picture of a glade in autumn, with the leaves a gaudy orange and scarlet, and the sky an uncomfortable strident blue. There was a horrid absence in that picture: as if it were a glade on a slightly different planet. Another Earth, but an empty one. Looking down the silent avenue, there was no sense of a human family just out of sight having a picnic, no evidence that any living being had ever seen that glade at all. I stared at it, oddly fascinated by the glaring lack of taste and unpleasant emptiness of it.

There was a similar gaudy vacancy in her sitting room. I thought I had prepared myself for the shock of it. I stood in the doorway while Tricia walked on in past me, trying to control my nausea. The scene was revolting, and yet utterly absorbing, presumably like watching a public hanging or execution of some kind. I couldn't believe the blood was real.

Peter's chair – the chair one assumed had been Peter's, for the afternoon – was still facing the telly. Beside it, on a highly varnished occasional table, were several half-dried, sticky rings from a number of beer cans, and some crumbs from a packet of crisps. Presumably the police had removed the empty cans and the packet.

I thought of Colin, and his mistress's research into adrenaline and its presence in a man who has plucked up courage to shoot himself. I supposed it must be interesting, from an academic point of view, that she would be able to confirm – or deny – the police's findings. I tried to speak my thoughts out loud to Tricia, but I couldn't find it in me to phrase the words. The police could sort it out for themselves. And would, whatever we thought. Besides, whatever conclusion they came to, it wouldn't help Peter, or indeed Alison any more.

And there in the back window, sure enough, was the yellow Formica table which matched the table in the mortuary waiting room. Tricia reached through the net curtains and opened the windows while I filled a bucket in the kitchen with hot water and disinfectant. We were both equipped with rubber gloves. It wouldn't take us long. But we should have brought a step ladder for the top of the walls. We would have to stand on the yellow table.

'We didn't see much of Peter recently,' Tricia said, as we started work.

'No,' I agreed.

'I never took to him much, actually. I suppose he was just shy.'

'I don't think he was shy,' I said carefully. 'Bitter, perhaps, or angry. Perhaps simply unhappy. But I'm not sure that he was ever shy.'

'You knew him as a child, didn't you?'

'Yes. We knew him well. David's parents put Alison in this cottage when he was quite young. Prue took her on to work at the house, and thought she needed somewhere for herself and Peter instead of living with her parents at the other end of the village. So Peter had the run of the grounds as a child. He and Charles and Sara grew up playing together much of the time. We were living in Cambridge then, and Prue arranged for Alison to come in and work for us once a week.'

'Doing what?'

'Oh, you know. Dusting and Hoovering.'

'Just like me,' said Tricia, smiling. 'The charlady.'

'Not like you at all. You're not a real charlady.'

'I most certainly am. I'm very professional.'

'I'm sure you are. But popping into Diana's once or twice a week to push a broom around doesn't entitle you to class yourself as a charlady. Charladies have headscarves and rollers and varicose veins.' I tried to smile. I was determined to continue with my task somehow, and small talk was the only weapon to hand.

'Then Alison isn't a charlady either.'

'No, she isn't really. Not by that definition. I'm not sure what Alison is.'

I sponged the top of the chair gently. The liquid which ran out of my sponge reminded me of the Sheti River: pale brown, and full of white, creamy bubbles. But the water in my bucket was dirty and thin, while the Sheti always seemed sparkling and bouncing and gay. Though it, too, has connections with death. Those dying in the Hindu faith are thrown into the

Sheti, sent on their way with fire and flowers and rich dissonant singing.

Tricia was wobbling precariously on top of the Formica table, which she'd moved so she could reach the top of the wall. 'But wasn't it a long way for Alison to come? Pass me that J-cloth can you? All the way into Cambridge?'

'Not really. She used to come in on Saturdays, on the bus. I think she liked bringing Peter somewhere where he could play with other children.'

Tricia climbed down from the table and rinsed her J-cloth in the sullied water of the Sheti in my red bucket. The water, as I continued to sponge, was coming out more grey than brown now. I started on the wall.

'What was he like?'

I scrubbed a bit harder. 'Do you think it matters if this wallpaper gets wet?'

'I don't think you've got any choice. Presumably it'll dry out again. It may go yellow, I suppose.'

'I think we're going to need to replace it. What was he like? Not quite what you'd expect of Alison, somehow. He was quite clever, in some ways. I don't think life was all that kind to him.'

'Go on.'

'Maurice always said we shouldn't blame him for things, that a boy without a father has problems enough.'

'Humph. Very nice and Politically Thingy, but there are plenty of fatherless sons who manage to become charming, civilised human beings.'

'Are there? I hope so, for Charles's sake. But it always sounded reasonable to me when Maurice said it.'

I had got the wall clean, but it had gone very sad and soggy. I hoped it would dry out properly. I climbed down from the chair I was on, and went to get a clean bucket of disinfectant. The armchair would need another going over with fresh water. I wondered whether it should have been dry-cleaned. I started on it again anyway.

'I think Peter respected Maurice. He didn't let on so I'm not sure, but it was a feeling I had. Perhaps Maurice was the only person who really understood him. Peter seemed almost to resent things, or people, just because they were happy, or healthy, or simply right. And yet in a funny kind of way he wanted them to be like that. Somehow Maurice sensed that. But even Maurice didn't predict what happened.'

'What do you mean?'

'Well, presumably Hugh has told you.'

'No?'

'Oh.' My face went hot. I fingered my sponge awkwardly, and realised I must be blushing, for the first time in years. 'I'm sorry, I assumed he would have done. I had no idea.' I dropped my sponge in the bucket and sat down. The room closed in on me, and I shut my eyes and willed myself not to faint. 'I'm sorry, Tricia.' I was breathing heavily, but was determined to continue. 'It's not been easy. Then seeing this house, like this . . .'

'Harriet, I'm so sorry, I should have realised. You shouldn't have come. It doesn't mean much to me, because of my time on a ward. Do you want to lie down? Or have a glass of water?' First I shook my head, then I nodded, and she went into the kitchen to put the kettle on and get a drink of water. By the time she had made a couple of mugs of tea I had pulled myself together.

'I wish I knew how to make life easier for Alison,' I said rather feebly, as I took the tea. 'She'll never get over it.'

'You're doing what you can.'

'It's not enough, and it never will be.'

'I get the impression, from Hugh, that Peter wasn't a particularly easy son.'

'I hope you're not thinking what I think you're thinking,' I said.

'What? That in some ways she'll be better off? No. Not that.'

'No,' I said with absolute certainty. 'We're never better off without the people we love. Never.'

I cast my mind over the last three years, the Christmasses without a father, the summer holidays with just the three of us, the birthday on my own, the empty bed, the lonely kitchen, the teenaged son becoming the head of his family and caring for his mother, the daughter without her father's arms around her, and for the first time I fully realised that Alison would never see true happiness again.

Tricia accompanied me back to the house. The job was done. All that was left behind in Alison's front room now were some brown water marks on the wall, and a life sentence of loneliness.

When we got home it was nearly ten to two. And there was Sara, standing on the little slope of lawn which leads from the stone terrace down onto the lawn proper, with a tray in her hands. Hesitating there, not quite motionless, with the mottled shadow from the ivy in the old stone urn dancing over her feet, she almost looked as if she should have been dabbed there by a brush, by Monet or Renoir: her image carried that same wistful promise of endless summers, endless countryside, endless youth. To the side of the lawn, in the dappled shade, there was a tartan rug with the beginnings of a picnic on it.

'Can we tempt you?' I asked Tricia, feeling guilty and glad that we couldn't. She thanked me but said she had to get back to the Vicarage. With any luck the children might have made lunch and looked after the elderly missionaries.

'Hugh's preaching twice tonight, so he probably won't have done anything.'

'Sorry to take you away from him on a Sunday.'

'Don't apologise. It had to be done. It was good of you to think of it.'

'Do you miss it?' Sara asked.

'What, nursing? Not at all. Though we keep having to ask ourselves whether I should go back to it. I don't want to. We've put it off so far, but when the children start at university I don't think I'll have much choice. We can't expect Hugh's parents to pay for everything. But I certainly don't relish all that hard work, looking after everybody.'

'That's a nice charitable thing for a vicar's wife to say,' Sara pointed out.

'Exactly.' They both laughed, and Tricia said goodbye.

So Sara and I had lunch, just the two of us, alone on the lawn together.

I was sorry for Alison, of course I was. But, as I said before, the bell had not tolled for us. The sight of a different Sara altogether, with the liquid sun in her hair and the pink-and-white cherry blossom falling about her, just as it had when she was quite tiny and one thought the memories of childhood were indestructible, cleansed Alison's grief from my mind more effectively than we had cleaned her walls.

I suddenly remembered a night, when Sara was four, when she hadn't wanted to say her prayers.

'Don't you want to talk to God?' I said.

'No.'

'Don't you want to be His friend? You must talk to your friends.'

'No.'

'Don't you want to go to heaven one day, and live with Him?'

'No. I don't want to go to heaven. I want heaven to come here.'

Don't we all? Wouldn't we all rather have heaven here, on familiar territory, on our own terms, than have to be someone else's guest and learn new manners and behave according to God's house rules? I could almost believe it had happened, that afternoon under the cherry tree. That heaven had come down here, on our own, pretty sordid, terms.

I don't know why it is that some of this recent summer has been characterised by sickness and sleeplessness and fever, and some was clear and free. There were whole weeks, later on, when I never slept for more than twenty or thirty minutes without waking up in a cold sweat, and then tossing and turning for a couple of hours before getting a few minutes' sleep again. There were days when I couldn't swallow a mouthful without nausea.

And yet that afternoon I felt none of it. Nor did Sara. We were blissfully, blessedly happy.

She had raided the larder for lunch: some rather unripe, forced tomatoes, a piece of melting Brie, and a bottle of very dry cider. It made me feel pleasantly muggy, in the hot half shade, and I could feel it cool in my stomach after I'd swallowed it. It had a fine, rather thin taste.

'Not bad, this stuff,' I said, and poured myself another glass.

'Good,' she agreed, drinking some too. She was wearing white cotton: a floppy blouse, with the sleeves rolled above the elbow, and a flimsy, full skirt; and bare feet. She had only recently taken to wearing skirts, and still looked slightly strange in them. She sat with her arms resting calmly on her knees, her skirt falling happily about her, between her knees and on the rug around her. She seemed all golden, in the light reflected off the garden: her face, her hair, her limbs.

'Let's go for a swim,' she suggested.

I couldn't be bothered. I thought of the cool blue water, winking in the afternoon sunlight. 'I'll sink, with all this cider in me.'

'Never mind. It'll pickle your body underwater.' Then, quite without warning, 'Do you miss Daddy all the time?'

It was the first time she had spoken of him for months.

The grass, which Bob Bridges keeps clipped very short, was cool and thick underfoot. I won't let him put weedkiller on the lawn, and the unruly clover and some little pink flowers were crawling over it. 'Well,' I said at last. 'Sometimes I don't think of his name, perhaps for hours at a time. Sometimes I think I've gone a whole day without thinking about him. Quite often, if I try really hard, I can think of advantages in living alone. What I can't do is ever make those advantages seem worth having.' I picked a blade of grass and ran it through my fingers. 'I think living with a disability must be similar,' I continued. 'It's like a wheelchair. You adjust. Other people even label it for you. Once, a few weeks ago, I thought I'd forgotten him altogether for a moment, and believed, for that split second, that it didn't hurt so much after all. I really thought the pain had stopped for a tiny, real point in time. And that was worse than anything that had happened before.' I held my hand out to touch hers, then dropped it after all. 'What about you?' I said.

'I miss him all the time.' She looked out over the garden, her face wet. She had gone so long, such tedious, lonely, lonely months without crying that it took me by surprise. I folded her against my shoulder. It felt odd, holding her, after so many weeks of distance.

After a while she wiped her nose on her sleeve. 'Do you mind people labelling it for you?'

'No,' I said. 'I don't care what they do. I just wish he were still here, that's all.'

When we were drying out, on the side of the pool, she said, 'I've been thinking.'

'Goodness.'

'Very funny.'

'Go on then, what? What have you been thinking?'

'I don't want to see Alison. I'm dreading her coming back. I don't know why I told you that. I know we've got to look after her. Sorry. It wasn't what I meant to say.' She picked up a leaf and carefully fished a drowning insect out of the pool. 'What I was going to say was that I want to make tea. A cake, and everything. But I wasn't sure whether Alison would like it. Whether she'd want to see other people or not. Will she be back by tea?' She rolled over again and picked a daisy with her toe, transferring it to her hands and pulling the petals off.

'Why don't you ring her up at Jean's and ask her?'

So Sara arranged tea, nearly eight years to the day after her other tea at Willisham House, and she showed the same extraordinary, unchildlike altruism that she had exhibited for her seventh birthday. As she rang Alison at Jean's house, and found a recipe book and mixed a cake, and organised everyone for that afternoon, I wished that David, at least, could have seen her. I wanted to show him, I wanted some small justification of the way I'd coped on my own.

We sat in the garden, on the terrace because Sara said chairs are more comfortable for adults than sitting on the lawn, drinking Earl Grey which turned a golden shade of amber as the lemon was dropped in it.

And I kept watching Alison, and remembering what she had lost only the day before, and marvelling at her. I wondered if perhaps she would hardly change to the outer eye at all, but gradually, over the years, become greyer and slower and thicker round the waist as she learnt to adapt to the grief. She'd always seemed to me so fragile, so vulnerable, that I hadn't known how she would survive at all. And yet, in those early days, it seemed as though she were absorbing her tragedy effortlessly, as if she'd been made for it. Perhaps she was. Perhaps that's why she never complained about Peter's father. Maybe she expected life to treat her badly, so her lover had done what he was supposed to do. By contrast, the person who seems strong, so healthy and happy and blissfully self-confident, is the one who suffers most when her life falls apart.

Sara had invited all Jean's family over, and when they arrived she took the children all round the garden till they found several ladybirds on a rose bush and then started looking for four-leafed clover. She entered their world completely, like a child herself, as the three of them scoured the lawn for one leaf too many. We ate Sara's cake, which was still warm so the chocolate butter icing melted on the inside. And then Sara chased the children round the trees again, and offered to teach them to play cricket.

And all the time they laughed and shouted and played, I kept seeing a boy of seven, blond and straight and rather serious, and a mercurial four-year-old sister, with even blonder curls in bubbles all over her head, dancing round him. 'Charlie, teach me how to play. Charlie, I'm batting. I've got to bat, all right?' And, though he was pretending to be in charge, it was obvious to us, watching from the terrace, which child always got her own way. Friends used to laugh, and say they were like a happily married couple, with Charles hopelessly in love. He would bowl, field, fetch, and always score in her favour. And if they quarrelled, which wasn't often, but seemed to happen more over things like cricket scores than anything else, Charles would disappear, silent and furious, and refuse to play with her again that day. And she would scream and scream, heartbroken to have annoyed him.

Often Charles would get himself into trouble, twice her size and twice her age, because she'd asked him to do something quite mad. I can remember him thumping David mercilessly for calling Sara a 'nonkin' or a 'whoopsie', or something else he thought derisory. Once, when Charles had only just started at Langley House, long before he went to prep school, he made Sara a Valentine card, and got ragged by all his mates.

Sometimes they would be joined by a sombre, dark-haired boy, older than Charles but no bigger, and far less in command of himself; surly looking, but wanting to be included in one of their games of cricket. So the other two would let him field on the boundary till he complained, no doubt with justice, that it was boring. To which Charles would reply, reasonably if a little unkindly, that no one had asked him to play and he was free to leave any time.

'Mummy, where's a cricket ball? We've been looking in the apple shed—' Sara was back with the children, and an old cricket bat.

'Oh heck,' I panicked. 'Have you disturbed much?' Should we have touched anything? Hadn't the police put a cordon around it? Would Sara have left fingerprints everywhere and moved everything? My alarm spread to the others like fire.

'What's the matter?'

'I didn't touch much.'

'What is it?'

'It's all right,' I pulled myself together. 'It's not your fault, it's all right.' If they hadn't wanted us to go in there, I reasoned, they would have told us again after they'd finished, or sealed it off, or something. They must have taken all the fingerprints they wanted.

But the atmosphere had become strained. I glanced at Alison and she looked guiltily away, as if she were to blame that we couldn't go freely around our own house. Jean referred a question to her, rather too brightly, but she didn't answer.

'See if there's a soft ball in the changing hut,' I said to Sara. 'It would be much more suitable for these children anyway.' It sounded like a reproach.

It was the children who told us about the television programme which at last allowed Alison to give vent to her feelings.

'Harriet!' Jean's daughter Chloe came running back after they'd all been out of sight for a while. 'Harriet, can we watch the *Six o'clock news*? Can we please?'

'Yes, if you want,' I said.

'Oh yes, we were all forgetting,' Jean said.

'Well done,' Simon, Jean's husband, said, taking Chloe on his knee. 'Well done for reminding us.'

So we all went inside, and fiddled about with the video recorder which I can never get the hang of because I hardly ever use it, and watched the second half of a children's programme because we were too early for the news, and checked the recorder was working, and found it wasn't after all, and got Simon to mess about with it again, and in the end we were only just in time for the adverts before the bits that have to fall apart and whizz together again to make the logo had appeared on the screen and rearranged themselves onto a flag. We pressed 'Record', so that Alison would have a memento, if she wanted it.

Fires. Thefts. The opening of a new folk museum. Weather: likely to be one of the hottest Mays on record, say forecasters. 'And finally,' said the carefully coiffured announcer, 'in the Cambridgeshire village of Willisham, a traditional village Fair ended in tragedy yesterday when a young man was found shot in his mother's home. He left no note, and his death came as a shock to those who knew him. We go to Willisham and meet some of the inhabitants.' And then I saw my house, being filmed from the lawn, with a party in full swing.

'When did they do this?' I asked.

'Yesterday evening.' 'Where were you?' 'Alison wasn't there,' everyone started to explain, and then drowned each other out by saying shush.

For there, in the garden, where we had just had tea, were members of the village, telling the TV crew how they had all spent the afternoon at the Fair and how nobody had heard anything, and what a quiet neighbour and clever young man and model citizen Peter was, and how he had kept himself to himself, and perhaps had seemed a bit depressed, now it was put like that.

The children looked at Alison, sitting on our sofa, and Sara got up and left the room. I heard her go into the kitchen, and presumed her excuse would be that she was getting Alison some kind of drink.

And at last, as Alison sat there watching her neighbours say kind words about her son, whom none of them had spoken to for years, the tears began to fall as if a dam had broken.

Meanwhile the camera panned away from the terrace and I glanced at the screen and saw a figure at the back bathroom window, unrecognisable, looking out at the television interview taking place in the garden below. Hugh had presumably tried to keep an eye on her, but she must have escaped and gone to be on her own when she heard the news. I wondered what thoughts that calm exterior, at breakfast, had hidden.

Luckily, no one else in the room noticed the little figure on the screen, because by then they were all giving their attention to Alison.

19

Prue met Maurice and fell in love with him when she was just seventeen. She finished the following year at Wycombe Abbey, went to Switzerland for the winter, did a season in London, and then married him. Aged nineteen.

She is the only person I have ever met who has no insecurity at all, not even deep down in some hidden places accessible only to dreams or intrusive psychotherapy. She spends her life mixing with intellectuals, has no qualifications whatsoever, and yet feels no inferiority and offers no deference or apology to anyone. I expect this is partly due to a ravishing set of features and naturally blonde hair which, at sixty-odd years, still make heads turn the minute her beautifully chiselled bone structure enters a room, and partly the result of being born of a family that was already rich and famous in England when Harold was shot in the eye, and has not been diminished by nearly a millennium of Norman rule. I foolishly assumed, when I first met David's parents, that Maurice had been the one with the money and status, and he had married Prue for her looks. Then I saw a book about her family in the drawing room and realised that Maurice's forbears wouldn't have been fit to tie the thongs of Prue's ancestors' sandals.

Despite my fearful expectations, she never made me feel inferior. She has genuine charm. When she sees you, you become in that instant the one person in all the world she had wanted to see. When you talk to her, she listens as though nothing else has ever been of so much interest to her before. She focuses on people in the way that successful politicians focus on power, and stockbrokers on money, and generals on war. I love her.

In half a decade she lost the two people she cared about more than she cared for the world itself. I thought even Prue would have been crushed by it. But, like Job, she picked herself up and refused to curse God. The only blood ties she has left now are Sara and Charles, her grandchildren, and I know she would die for them, if she had to. And more.

That Monday morning, Sara's birthday, was the May bank holiday. I was looking forward to spending it with her. I had meant to plan something for the two of us together, but we had all been concentrating so hard on the Fair that I hadn't given the day much thought, except to keep it free. As I crossed the garden for my swim I wondered whether Prue would like to spend it with us. She's such good company that Sara and I always enjoy being with her, so I knew I needn't ask Sara first. Her house is so close I decided to nip over after swimming, before breakfast, to invite her to join us as soon as she liked.

The Dower House is a few hundred yards away, in the opposite direction from the row of cottages where Alison lives. It wasn't built as the Dower House, and is a relatively recent, rather incongruous, tiled Victorian cottage which David's grandfather bought for his own mother, Maurice's grandmother. I never thought Prue would adjust to its smaller proportions, but she claims to love it. Last winter, instead of using Willisham House as usual, she had a midseason Hunt Meet at the Dower House, with everybody trampling around her cottage gardens, and inexperienced little ponies, with Thelwell riders, standing and weeing, in her herbaceous borders. I think it was an experiment that didn't quite work, but she maintains it was a great housewarming.

There was no sign of her return of the night before. Her car wasn't out in the drive, and none of the windows were open. It was quite unlike Prue still to be in bed at eight o'clock in the morning, and unusual for her to bother to put her car away in the summer months. I rang the doorbell and waited. I knew already that she wouldn't answer. Nevertheless I rang a couple more times and waited a good five minutes before going to the third flower pot from the end, where she keeps her key. I wondered whether she would have taken it with her. Normally when she goes away, she gives it to us for safe-keeping. But then normally, when she goes away, she confides in us first.

The key was there. I was embarrassed at the thought of using it. Suppose she was having a bath and hadn't heard me? I knew this was impossible, as the house is not large, but I still felt funny putting the key in the lock. Suppose I found a scene similar to the one Graeme had stumbled on in Alison's front room? My imagination went momentarily wild. What if there were a mad shotgun murderer blowing out the brains of everyone living on the estate, one by one, making all the deaths look like suicide? I knew, even as I thought this, that it was an absurd and impossible idea, but I still felt a grip of fear as I turned the heavy iron door handle. As likely, I told myself sharply, that Peter would have come back from the mortuary and be haunting the Dower House with the back of his head gone . . . and then I wished I hadn't entertained the idea, even as a fantasy.

The house was eerily quiet. She must have gone away the day before, to stay with a friend for the night. Presumably that was what the message on my answerphone would have told me, if only I hadn't erased it in my panic and general incompetence with machines. Perhaps she simply felt she needed to get away, after such a gruesome tragedy on our own land. It was unlike her to act on impulse rather than plan sensibly beforehand, but it was conceivable that she had found herself, on Sunday morning, more shocked and upset than she had realised. She had probably explained it all on the message.

How do we know when something is amiss? It isn't a sixth sense, of course it isn't, but rather the other five senses picking up details, too small to be recognised by our consciousness, which register as inappropriate. Prue's house is always meticulously tidy, so it wasn't as though she had rushed out leaving dirty washing-up or all the lights on. But something was wrong. I looked around the kitchen-dining room, which also served as an entrance hall. Everything was in its place. Yet again, I felt annoyance with myself for losing her message, and as I thought about it I glanced at her telephone. It too showed that it had one message on it. I wondered whether to listen to it. I felt uncomfortably nosy. By way of a compromise I decided to listen to the outgoing message she had left for callers: I know she changes it regularly, and when she goes away, even just overnight, she leaves cryptic sentences which are supposed to convey to friends that she isn't around, while giving burglars the impression that the house is full of prop-forwards living there as lodgers left in charge of a string of Rotweillers. In fact these bizarre messages never quite work, and, if anything, tend to imply that her house has been hijacked by an animal-mad gay couple – 'Please leave a message with Henry and Jim who are walking all the dogs'. They wouldn't convince any burglar worth his salt, but they give her friends something to laugh about when they ring.

'Dower House. Please speak after the machine has finished sqwawking at you. Thank you.' That was all. She must have gone out for Sunday lunch, and decided to stay overnight.

I decided to listen to her message, whether it was any of my business or not. After all, if I told the police she was missing they'd listen to it soon enough.

'Prue darling, it's Reg here.' Prue *darling*? Who on earth was Reg? 'I think you should sell now. I could be wrong, but I suspect the stock market may be facing a bit of a patch, and that means high risk portfolios like yours won't be such good news. I still think you're wrong to pay out though. I'm not saying your lovely daughter-in-law is mistaken, but I don't think it's the way to solve problems. However, it is legal and it's possible. You could set up a fund of about fifty, and that should keep him going for a few years. But sell anyway. You must be romping about at your village fair now, being the grand lady. Give me a ring when you get in.'

I felt the hairs go up on the back of my neck. I had no idea who Reg was, and didn't understand a word of his advice. But, apart from anything else, this message meant she hadn't been in since Saturday afternoon. If she had, I felt sure she would have erased this particular advice, which was clearly of a private nature. Besides, Prue would listen to, and wipe, all her messages as a matter of course. I sat down slowly at her kitchen table and tried to think it through. She had been in Willisham on Saturday morning. She had talked of going in to Cambridge. Had she come back from Cambridge? I racked my brains, trying to remember whether I had seen her at the fair. A hat: she had an absurd pink hat she had threatened to wear because she thought it looked Edwardian. Had I seen it on Saturday? I found it hard to believe that I couldn't remember back two days, and such outrageous headgear too, but so much had happened in that time that it seemed like several weeks.

I thought I remembered seeing her at the opening, at two o'clock, milling around beneath us as Hugh and I stood on the platform. I rubbed my eyes and covered my face in my hands, recapturing the sight of the crowd. Yes, I thought I had seen her.

Suddenly someone grabbed me by the shoulders and I jumped up, my heart screaming, head pounding, black in front of my eyes, convinced that Peter's murderer was on the point of killing me too.

But it was only Prue's cat, Tuppence, who had jumped on me from the stairs behind, and now leapt on to the floor and miaowed at me imploringly. 'Oh, you beastly cat,' I panted in my relief, still recovering from the shock. 'Where is Prue, eh?' I picked her up and she purred loudly, clawing at my towelling robe. I went to the fridge to get her some milk, and then realised something else was wrong. I went back to the front door and opened it again. There on the doorstep was a pint of milk. I brought it in, then wondered whether I should have left it there to stop the milkman leaving more. I was oddly confused. I didn't know whether I should touch anything, or leave it all as it was, in case. In case what? In case the police wanted to come and have a look around? But that's ridiculous, I told myself. They won't need to look around: not for a suicide. And Prue's disappearance? I wondered whether that would lead to an enquiry too. But surely not. She would be home by teatime.

One thing I would definitely interfere with was the message. I had memorised the gist of it. Unfortunately Prue's machine was more old fashioned than mine, and a message would only be wiped by a new message coming in over it. I played it again, counting the seconds so I would know how long it lasted, then left it so that the next message would be recorded over the top.

Then I poured Tuppence some milk in a saucer. And left.

When I got home, the first thing I would do would be to ring Prue and speak to her machine about something completely inconsequential for at least forty-five seconds.

20

What's the point? What is the point, I ask myself, of writing it all down? My hand sweats as I do it, and I know it's nothing to do with the heat. Charles and I have just been talking, yet again, about what happened, and it has brought it all back, the fear, the nausea, the breathless sense of panic. I tell myself over and over again that Peter's death was simply the catalyst, that it was already like this, but it's not true. The loss of a human life is so much worse than anything else. Do I mean that? If that is true, why couldn't all this have been prevented?

Because, I suppose, I don't really believe death is the worst thing. I have always felt that some forms of abuse, terror, torture, are very much worse than a quick end. To some extent, I suppose, I could blame Christianity for this view. If we have something else to look forward to, a rapid death can be a mercy.

But the end was only quick for Peter himself. The rest of us go on and on. It was obvious that Alison would suffer. Though in the event we were all astonished by the way she recovered, how she bounced back like a spring, grief-stricken, certainly, but almost as if Peter's death had set her free. As if she could now have the youth and self-fulfilment she'd had to sacrifice in order to be his mother.

And now I look for the umpteenth time for an alternative way out. There must have been one, but I still can't see it.

It was Tuesday before we saw the police again, Monday being the bank holiday. The inquest was due to be opened that day, but Tricia was now looking after Alison so I tried not to think about it.

She had only stayed with us that one night, the Saturday. After she'd had lunch with Jean and Simon, and tea with us, Jean made up a spare bed for her, and said she could put her up till the end of the week. If she still wasn't fit to go home Tricia was going to arrange for someone else in the church to look after her, because Jean was then going away for a few days.

Tricia had arranged to take her to the opening of the inquest, and apart from Graeme, and Peter's doctor who hadn't seen him for several years, no one else from the village was needed.

I planned to have as normal a day as possible. I did, however, drive Sara into school on my way into Langley House. I don't go into the school often. Mostly I leave Jenny, my headmistress, to deal with everything. When Prue bought Langley House she was initially very involved with the day-to-day running of it all, so when she handed it over to me I felt I ought to do the same. But I soon discovered that Jenny seemed more at ease if I didn't interfere too often, so after a while I mostly kept in touch by telephone to make sure everything was going well. But at the beginning of the summer term I started doing a Shakespeare class with the top form, the eleven year olds who had finished their exams to senior school. I had cast them in *Macbeth*, and every Tuesday and Friday went in to encourage them to romp through the lines. Goodness knows why I had chosen such a gloomy play for the summer term, but there we are, I had.

So that day, Tuesday, I dropped Sara off at the Perse School at half past eight, called on the little dry-cleaner's in Newnham to leave Diana's beautiful lacy blouse, and drove on to Langley House. The first few children were just beginning to arrive. My class wasn't until ten and I had intended to welcome the children and then catch up with some administration before then, but on an impulse I went for a walk instead.

It was a beautiful, fresh morning and, apart from parents dropping their children off at the school, there were not many people about. I parked on the gravel sweep outside the heavy old front door, and walked back along the road Sara and I had travelled along together so often when she was a child. The university has built here and there along the road, but by and large the route from the school to our house is almost unchanged.

From time to time I go back to our old house, where we were living when Charles and Sara were attending Langley House. I pop in to deal with the washing machine, or some other minor complaint of the tenants. I used to know the road like the back of my hand, the pavement and the trees and the fences. But that morning was the first time I had walked along it since Sara and I last did it together eight years ago or so. I felt I should have been holding a little child's hand and trying to avoid the cracks on the pavement. I could almost believe that we would be home soon and eating hot buttered toast with cinnamon and sugar.

Sometimes, in those days, we used to cycle together. She would ride her little pink bicycle with stabilisers along the pavement while I rode on the road, she with her huge pink helmet on. Even just a few years ago the road was quiet enough for us to talk to one another as we went along. Now the lorries scream and tear along it, so we could probably no longer have heard a word. The two of us used to chatter all the way like a couple of sparrows, she, rattling non stop, I giving her only half my attention, in the way that adults do.

'Mummy, who was Guy Fawkes?'

'Oh, he blew up parliament, you know.'

'Why?'

'Or rather he tried to. Why? Um. I think because he was a Catholic.'

'Was Joan of Arc a Catholic?'

'Er, yes, I suppose she was.'

'Was Noah a Catholic?'

'No, I don't think so.'

'How come Joan of Arc was a Catholic if Noah wasn't?'

'What?'

'I thought if you're a Catholic you have to marry a Catholic.'

'I think you are supposed to, yes.'

'Then why didn't Joan of Arc marry a Catholic?'

'She didn't marry anybody. She was too busy fighting.'

Then, wide-eyed and very shocked, 'Weren't she and Noah married?'

One day, when she had been riding her bicycle to school for some time, she said, 'When will I be old enough to take myself to school?'

Nothing had happened to us, in those days, to make us worried. There were no roads to cross. It was only a five-minute walk, a few hundred yards. She knew she must never talk to strangers, accept sweets, go near the road, or get in anyone's car. She couldn't possibly get lost. Other parents, I know, would have thought me shockingly careless. Indeed they did. But I knew the statistics, that the abduction of little children is impossibly rare, that by far the biggest danger to them outside the house is cars, above all that abused children are almost always the victims of people they know. Even now, despite everything which has happened to us since, I still think it was a reasonable risk to take. The fact that one ends up being an unfortunate statistic doesn't mean one was irresponsible.

And eight years ago, the staff didn't have the strict instructions which I have implemented, never to let a child out of their care except into the hands of an adult they recognise.

'I think you're old enough to now, if you want.'

'Am I really?'

'I think so. Would you like to?'

'Yes.'

So that day, at half past three, I didn't go to pick her up. I put the kettle on for tea, got out some crumpets and butter and jam, and while I waited for her to arrive, on her own for the first time, I made egg-and-cress sandwiches, her favourite. At twenty to four she still wasn't back, and I put the crumpets on to toast. At ten to four I made a pot of tea, and thought to myself, she's got off her bicycle and she's wandering around that triangular patch of wasteland where all the wildflowers and squirrels are.

I suppose now I would be beside myself if someone else's six-year-old failed to turn up when she should have done. That is, if I ever agreed to another child's taking a risk like that at all.

At four o'clock I thought perhaps it was time I went to find her. I still wasn't anxious, though there was a little knot of worry beginning to harden below my stomach. I got my bicycle out and set off, looking for her all the way. She wasn't there, dawdling along the pavement. She wasn't catching butterflies in No Man's Land. She wasn't sitting down in the sun thinking about life. She wasn't anywhere to be seen. She wasn't even waiting outside the school.

Then I was frightened. What if it were my child who was the next to appear on the front pages? Suppose she'd already been run over and the ambulance had taken her to casualty? Nobody would know to tell me. If she were unconscious, no one would know where she lived. Or suppose she'd been bundled into a boot, and was crying, terrified, in the airless dark before being abused? Other parents would never have done it. Why had I been so stupid?

I ran through the 'Tradesman's Entrance' of the school – the door used by parents and children – into the large, comfortable house. It was quiet and deserted. Even the teachers seemed to have gone home. I saw no one. Not a cleaner, not a caretaker. The side door was open. I passed the row of low, empty pegs, and the old notice asking me not to wear stiletto heels, and I went through the hall and, two at a time, up the wide wooden staircase that had once had chambermaids running up and down it.

And there she was. In her usual place at the upstairs window waiting for my bicycle to appear along the road.

'Hello. Why were you so long?'

Relief washed over me. I leant against the door post to catch my breath. 'Hello, Funnyone. I thought you wanted to come home on your own.'

'Oh. Yes I do. Was that supposed to be today?'

So we set off back home. 'There's crumpets for tea.'

'Goody goody.'

'And egg-and-cress sandwiches.'

After what happened that summer she never came home from school on her own again. I couldn't have let her. Nor would David. Even Charles hardly allowed her out of his sight, but whenever he was home from school would watch her carefully, as if it might all happen again if he so much as took his eyes off her.

But after that summer she wouldn't let him touch her again. Not for a long time. Not till we were out in Phulbari. And even then it was different. There was an invisible barrier between them, as if she felt she had done something wrong.

The wilderness, the No Man's Land, is still there, and I stopped to look at it that Tuesday morning. Once or twice I've taken the children from Langley House there on a nature trip, shuffled, in their blue-gingham smocks, into a haphazard little crocodile. That morning, alone, I stopped for a while, watching the frothing cow parsley and the wild and gaudy narcissi, and the birds fussing about and quarrelling.

The distant traffic roared over Queens' Road, and I realised it would be the first time this spring that I would see the Backs. The nasal peep peep of the pelican crossing ushered me over the road. I prepared myself to be astonished again at the bright carpet of crocuses and aconites which can still cause a catch in the breath. But it had faded already. In front of King's a vast white chestnut stretched between earth and sky. Its lower branches lay along the ground, its top seemed as tall as the chapel. Perhaps it was almost half as old.

As I continued towards the river I heard the soft, gentle barking of the mallards. An elderly couple bicycled past me, he bent and grey-haired, she frumpy and intelligent looking. 'No, no, no,' I heard one of them say, pleasantly and emphatically. They could have been discussing the architecture of the last thousand years, the mating pattern of the wren, the necessity for nuclear power, or even the morning's shopping, though that seemed less likely. The growl of an early lawnmower in Clare Gardens sounded like a drone to the click click of their bicycles going over the bridge. Suddenly two clashing sirens started screaming somewhere in the town; then their noise passed too, whining and moaning, and mingled with the other distant sounds.

I reached the bridge. Always, if I took Sara on my bicycle when I went shopping in Cambridge, to Eadan Lilly or Joshua Taylor or Robert Sayle, we would stop on the top of the bridge. The view compels it. Everybody stops. Even a harassed young fellow or a student late for a lecture will stop for a moment and look over the water. And then Sara would say, 'Please go down fast, really really fast, without pedalling.' It was no good telling her that pedalling would speed us up; freewheeling always seemed so much faster.

The view that day was exquisite. The vista of trees looked as if it were still resting in the eighteenth century; as if Gainsborough had painted them in the background, thrusting elegantly into the sky, and they had refused to move. One, in the distance, was violent dark red and majestic; the others were a dignified green. Birds and clouds wheeled on the painted sky above. The Cam reflected a deep bottle green. Clare Bridge sagged over the water; above its slashed and dappled lattice work the stone ball with the missing segment, hidden out of view the other side, winked at the water traffic. I thought of all the different people who had told me that it was their grandfather who had cut the missing slice out after a drunken bet.

The Clare College lawnmower hummed on. Peter had worked at that garden once, but only for a few weeks. It was a pity. Perhaps, if he'd still been working there, it would have saved his life. There was a gnarled, moss-covered, pollarded willow by the water, but it wasn't weeping; it seemed to be shouting, silently, into the nearby sky. It was very different from the willows on the opposite bank, with their opulent hair trailing into the river.

Several punts were nestling together under Trinity Hall wall. In the rippling water beneath I saw some legs appear slowly in a punt. It was early in the morning to be out punting. Perhaps some had finished exams already. In a few years' time the legs might be Sara's.

It was time to go back. I walked back, down the steep bridge, past the tiny white explosions of hawthorn along the roadside. I brushed the dampness from my cheeks. It was unexpectedly chilly.

The police contacted me at the school. Mr Willcox rang me up towards the end of the morning.

I assumed he must be the parent of a would-be pupil. The school secretary was having her coffee break, so I answered the telephone.

'Langley House School.'

'Hello, is that the headmaster?'

'No, we have a headmistress. I'll go and get her for you.'

I suppose I didn't give him a chance to reply, so I didn't realise, until Jenny took the call and then gave it back to me, that I had been the one he had wanted all along. I apologised for the confusion.

'Not to worry. Detective Sergeant Willcox here. Cambridge CID. We wondered if we could have a word with you, as soon as convenient, please.'

'Of course. I could see you later on today.' I consulted my diary. 'Do you want me to come over to the station?'

'We can visit you at home, if you'd rather. We might need to look around your house a bit more, if you don't object. How long would it take you to get there?'

'I was expecting to finish here at lunchtime. I'm not planning to be in school this afternoon. Any time after about two would be possible. Say, three o'clock. Unless it's more urgent than that?'

'That should be fine. We'll meet you at Willisham House at three.'

Prue has a theory that age has given her many advantages in life. 'Little, grey-haired old ladies can get away with murder,' she announces happily – though she is nearly five foot ten and still blonde without a bottle – as she asks a shop to replace an item whose receipt she lost long ago, or tells a policeman who stops her that she's sure the lights were green a minute ago, or is forgiven any number of things which she says a younger 'and prettier' woman would not get away with. I think she is mistaken. I suspect it's not her age but her title: it is as the policeman writes down Prunella, Lady St Joseph on his little pad that he decides not to press charges. I have one or two friends who use their titles only when they want to book tables at restaurants or get a shop to deliver quickly. It's a passport into a set of values officially dead for years. I have neither Prue's name nor her respectable years – though of course, if David hadn't died before Maurice, I would have been Lady St Joseph myself now. I doubt that it would have made much difference. I don't suppose it would have impressed Mr Willcox much either way.

I did a few errands on the way home. First I called for the blouse at the dry-cleaner's, but it wasn't ready. Then I popped in to Fitzbillies for some fresh bread and a cake, watching the street for prowling traffic wardens as I did so. As I continued on home I wondered how Alison would be spending the rest of the day. It was strange. I could remember my own feelings very clearly, but I couldn't imagine Alison going through the same. I knew she was in mourning, but in my heart I felt nothing. It seemed wrong, as if I were going through some kind of emotional autism. I couldn't picture her grief. I could only picture her sitting, alone in her pretty house for the rest of her life. Her house which belonged to me, after all.

I knew she wouldn't be back in her cottage yet. Nevertheless I imagined her, gazing out of the sitting-room window on to the lane, wondering what to do with her free time now she would no longer need to cook casseroles for one and freeze them and take them on the bus for Peter when she went into town. And then wondering about her old age, thrown back on her brothers and sisters for company, dependent on the family which had seemed quite relieved when she moved out. Picking up a duster in order to keep busy, and wiping her chimneypiece meticulously, beautifully, slowly, over and over again, ten times, twenty times, until she realised what she was doing and put it down to take up some other pointless task.

I imagined her trying to think of the next job; and how long it would take her to decide. Twenty minutes? Half an hour? Perhaps she would do the Hoovering. And she would find the Hoover much heavier than usual, so that it would take her a long time to get it from the broom cupboard to the upstairs bedroom. Then she would wonder if the bedroom needed doing after all; perhaps the downstairs was more urgent? And when she eventually switched it on she would find it much, much noisier than before. So noisy that she could hardly bear it. But she would put up with it; anything rather than the silence.

And so it would go on. All of it taking place in a state of such utter numbness that one is tempted to believe it will one day deaden the agony.

But perhaps it wouldn't take her like that. Perhaps she hadn't yet got around to envisaging the future months, weekends, decades. She did have people to keep her company after all, neighbours who were the same race and skin colour.

I turned into my driveway. It looked as though the police had arrived before me. With any luck they would have looked at everything they wanted in the house and I wouldn't have to show them around. The days were really beginning to be quite hot. I was tired and not feeling particularly well.

As I walked to the front door I glanced at the police car, and realised the two policemen were still in it. They opened the doors and got out, and I apologised for keeping them waiting. I had forgotten to tell them that Anna-Marie would be there.

'There's almost certainly somebody in,' I said. 'You could have had a coffee.'

'We thought we'd wait, thank you.'

But no one was in the house after all. Perhaps Anna-Marie had not come.

I showed Mr Willcox and his sergeant into the drawing room, and then excused myself.

'Do you mind waiting a couple of minutes while I change into something cooler? Do sit down. Or, better still, wander out onto the terrace. I'll be down in a minute, to help in any way I can. Do look around if you need to.'

And I went upstairs to my bedroom, supposedly to change out of my school clothes, but really to breathe on my own for a moment before having to relive the events of that day all over again.

21

Where the Hell was Prue?

That was what I still wanted to know. Not that she was accountable to me. But I needed somebody I could talk to. I hadn't heard from her for three days. It was totally out of character for her to disappear like that, and not even tell anyone where she was.

I went upstairs but instead of going into my bedroom went into the old nursery at the other end of the house. It's always been kept as the nursery. Our children had it whenever they stayed at the house, until Charles was old enough to be given his own room. We keep it as a nursery, for visiting children; it still has the children's pictures up in it, the toy boxes, and the old toy parrot cage hanging from the ceiling. It even still has Sara's teddy, Edward Bear, tired out and needing a few more stitches, sitting on the pillow and waiting.

Nanny's room was next to it, the next one along the corridor. It's just a bedroom now. The two rooms have a communicating door; I suppose Nanny's was once a large dressing room. She used to keep her bedroom door open at night, so she would hear David if he had a bad dream and called out. The light through the open doorway, and the gentle sound of Nanny pottering about, must have been a warm and cosy comfort. I thought of my own bedroom in my parents' house at home, in Farringdon. I felt a longing for their ordinary, middle-class Victorian town house, our ordinary, middle-class existence, and my mother's life as an ordinary, middle-class housewife. I love Willisham House. But I wasn't brought up to run it. A doctor's wife, yes, that I could have managed. If David had been an ordinary doctor.

I used to dream of drowning, as a child. I don't know why: I had never been frightened of water. But for years the dreams haunted me. Never the same, always similar. Trapped somewhere, trying to rescue cherished objects, not knowing if we would escape alive, waves rising over me, unable to scream. Then, after the age of about eight, I had never had them again.

Not, that is, until we went to Phulbari. Then they came back to fill the vacuum left by David. I would wake, horribly alone, and sit up under my mosquito net, sweating and trembling, and gaze into the soft whispering night. I could never see anything. Sometimes I could hear the water buffalo shunting and shifting about outside my bedroom window. There was one we kept tethered in the garden, because she was rather wild. During the monsoon, in the first few weeks of my trying to adjust to life without David, the frogs would be singing and burping all night, no matter what time I woke. And I didn't dare turn and look at the other side of the bed, I so dreaded its terrible empty space. I still slept on my half. I couldn't bear to take up all the room in the middle. I would turn in my sleep for his warmth to lie with, and wake at the awfulness of its absence. Once I found myself crying quietly, and Sara came to see what was the matter. I told her I was simply lonely, and she offered to sleep in the bed with me as I had sometimes done for her. It was kind of her, but it disturbed my sleep more; I lay between waking and sleeping for the rest of the night, not daring to fall asleep fully in case I fell into her arms as if she were indeed David.

I still get the drowning dreams now, very occasionally. I had one a few nights ago. They don't frighten me as they used to; they're just a bore. Even if they did I wouldn't call out for Sara or any one else any more. She couldn't reach me here, even if I did.

I sat for a few minutes in the nursery, that Tuesday the sixth of May, with the police downstairs, and I watched the patterned sunlight on the polished floorboards. The old wooden cot looked at me kindly from the corner of the room. A sunbeam rested on the floor, and the motes of dust danced about as they only seem to in a child's world. I noticed it often when I was little. Then I would creep into the grown-ups' room, when Mummy and Daddy were out, and the little particles would whirl silently up and down in front of the big double bed. I never see it in a grown-up's room now. Not any more. Only on rare occasions, in a nursery, or in some mood or sadness which makes one see momentarily with a child's eyes again, do I see the motes scurrying in the sunbeams now.

Sara and Charles had slept in the Willisham nursery often when we came to stay. In that sense it had been their room. But when we moved into the house two years ago Sara chose a room on the top floor. It had once been Cook's room, so it was bigger than all the other maids' rooms up there. Nevertheless, it was an eccentric choice, with its sloping walls, found up at the top of the narrow flight of stairs which leads to the linen cupboards. I think she took it so that she could see the swimming pool. Only one tiny corner of it, it's true; a triangle of blue tiles glimpsed through the trees if you stand on tiptoe. Maurice had the pool designed that way, out of view of all the family bedrooms, not wanting it to be an eyesore in the garden. I've always assumed Sara chose that view to try to exorcise the memory.

From the nursery, as with the other family bedrooms, you can't see the pool at all. You can see most of the lawn, the huge copper beech and the white-and-pink chestnuts at the end of the garden, the old swing, the top of the green chain-link fence round the tennis court, and the hedge round the croquet lawn. You can also hear voices from the terrace. I could hear Mr Willcox looking round the garden with his colleague, and muttering about this and that. I couldn't hear what was being said. If I'd stepped out onto the balcony I would have done. I could imagine David doing it as a young boy, when he slept in the nursery, hiding under the battlements, eavesdropping on flirting couples at his parents' cocktail parties. Modern parents probably wouldn't allow a nursery with a balcony, with stone pillars which a determined toddler could probably squeeze through. But old-fashioned toddlers probably knew better than to try.

After a few minutes I felt I had gathered enough strength to join them for a cup of tea. I splashed water on my face from the nursery basin, dried it, and then went downstairs, but first I went into the kitchen and considered the cake I had bought from Fitzbillies' cake shop. I had got it to cheer Sara up. It occurred to me that it might serve her interests better if I were to offer some to the police. Nevertheless, I picked up the white cardboard box with its yellow ribbon, and put it safely away in the fridge.

I put the kettle on, and went out to find them. They were hanging around on the terrace, just outside the drawing room.

'Ah, Mrs St Joseph.'

'Good afternoon, Mr Willcox. I'm sorry to have kept you waiting. I got home rather hot and bothered from work and just wanted to freshen up a little. Do sit down.' I don't think I've ever used the phrase 'freshen up' before in my life. What on earth had come over me?

'You run Langley House School, is that right?' he asked politely.

'Not really,' I replied. 'I'm only the principal. The headmistress runs it. She tolerates me very graciously, but I suspect I get in the way.'

'How long have you been the principal?'

'Eighteen months. I found myself helping in a small missionary school when we were abroad, more by accident than by design. I rather caught the bug. My mother-in-law bought the school while we were out of the country, and asked me to take it over when we got back because she didn't feel she had the energy any more. I love being involved with it. People aged five or six can be much nicer than they sometimes are later.'

The sergeant smiled. 'And were the Jesuits right? "Give me a child until he is seven," and all that?'

I thought for a moment. 'You can certainly do quite a lot of damage to someone before the age of seven. Though I'm not sure it was the Jesuits, since you mention it. My late husband said they pinched the idea from Luther. Would you like some tea or coffee?' I stood up again.

'That would be lovely,' he said, following me back into the house. His constable tagged on behind. 'Hard work I should imagine, that age group?'

'Not really. I don't do much proper teaching. I take them on nature trails, and trips to the theatre, and anything I love myself. I sometimes lead a kind of rather chaotic assembly. I try to get to know them all, and I enjoy myself thoroughly. We only have just over a hundred pupils. Some of them are quite bright: two of our parents are Nobel prizewinners. We're in quite a privileged position.' I filled their cups. 'Can I offer you a biscuit? Our church stall prizes itself on its baking. These are some of Saturday's best.'

Mr Wilcox was on a diet and his colleague was giving him moral support, so I helped myself. Then the tall quiet constable weakened and said he might just try one, not enough to spoil his tea when he got home, but they did look good.

'Now then, how can I help? Have you seen what you need to in the apple shed?'

'Well now, I'm afraid we'll have to ask you some rather personal questions. Routine. It's the same for everybody, naturally. As you know our print man's had a look in your room. The firearm is your missing one, by the way. We would have traced it immediately in any case. But we can't find the deceased's prints anywhere in there. I'm afraid we'll have to take your prints, and the prints of other members of your family, so that we know what belongs here and what doesn't.'

'Of course. Surely anyone who's going to pinch anything nowadays wears gloves, don't they? If I were going to take something, I'm sure I'd put gloves on.'

'That's a possibility. But less likely if he intended suicide.'

'Oh yes. Stupid of me.'

'And it was a very hot day.'

'Luckily. It was brilliant for our Fair.'

'You were there too?'

'I should think everybody was. As you've no doubt discovered already.'

'Indeed . . .'

'You're going to have a ghastly job if you're trying to establish alibis. We were all milling about for hours. Do you have to get alibis for a suicide?'

'We just want to rule out various possibilities, at this stage. So it helps to know where people were.'

'Well, I was at the Fair, if that's what you want to know. But we were all mixed up and hopeless; I shouldn't think anyone knows where anybody was at any particular time. I was very obviously there at two o'clock, because I opened the thing. Then I did my turn on the church stall. Then on the fruit machine. The only time I was off duty, as it were, was when I had tea.'

'What time was that?'

'I could work it out, I'm sure. Just after three thirty, till something like four twenty, I should think. That sort of thing.'

'And you were on your own all that time?'

'No, no. I had tea with Diana Ford. She'll probably know the exact times. She's very efficient. And then I helped on the plant stall for about half an hour.'

'With Mrs Ford?'

'No. With Tony Johnson. Diana went on without me.'

'So you were with Mrs Ford before you joined the plant stall?'

'Ye-es,' I said, making sure in my head as I thought about it.

'And then?'

'And then I was on the book stall with Pat and John, Mr and Mrs Williams, until the end of the Fair.'

'All the time?'

'Yes. No,' I said suddenly, and the sergeant looked up. 'No. I left for a few minutes to use the loo, but I didn't use it in the end because there was such a queue.'

'Couldn't you have come home?'

'I could have done: it would have been quicker than queuing, but I couldn't be bothered. Then I came home to get the barbecue going for the workers. That was with Hugh, our vicar. The next thing that happened, more or less, was that Graeme turned up here to speak to Alison. PC McCullough, that is. Funnily enough,' I realised out loud, 'when you break it down, you can work out what you were doing quite accurately. I suppose it's because we were all on rotas.'

Mr Willcox nodded. 'You'd be surprised how much you can pin it down, when people stop to think. They've often noticed far more than they realise. You've done a lot better than some would. At least no one's likely to say they were at home alone all day watching the telly, which will be an all time first. Now, I'm sorry to be personal, but would you mind showing us what you were wearing on Saturday?'

'Of course not.' I went upstairs to get my costume. I wondered where Anna-Marie would have put it. She knows where all my clothes go usually, but where do you hang an Edwardian skirt made out of an old sheet? It certainly wasn't in the drawer where I keep skirts, or in either of my wardrobes. Then I realised she wouldn't have time to take them out of the laundry. I went back downstairs and out into the yard, and saw my skirt and gloves hanging on the line, with the rest of the wash which I had put on late on Sunday night. They must have sat in the washing machine all through Bank Holiday Monday, because I'd forgotten them, and Anna-Marie must have hung them up that morning. So she had been there that day after all.

I went into the laundry room itself, and saw my off-white plimsols sitting on top of the machine still waiting to be washed, though I doubted whether they would ever be more on-white than they were. The skirt on the line was nearly dry, so I unpegged it and took it inside. At first I thought it had a stain on the hem, but when I looked closely I saw it was only a twig.

'Here we are,' I said. 'Not ironed yet, I'm afraid. This is the skirt I wore. What else do you want to see?'

'Ah,' said Mr Willcox. 'Washed. Was there anything else?'

'A blouse, but that's at the dry-cleaner's. I could get it back by tomorrow. Um, apart from that, shoes, gloves, underwear of course. Nothing else. Oh yes, a hat. We were in costume, you see,' I added by way of explanation. I didn't want him to think I always wear a hat and gloves to go out on a Saturday afternoon.

'Perhaps we could take the shoes and the gloves. Presumably they won't have been cleaned yet?'

'The gloves have been. They're white cotton, and were pretty grubby. I was planning to wash the shoes – they're only old tennis shoes – but I haven't got around to it yet. Do you want me to get them?'

'Please. And can you tell us whether your blouse will have been cleaned yet?'

'I've no idea. I know it wasn't ready when I called just now. I could ring them up and ask them. If I can find the telephone number.'

'Please.'

I found the name of the cleaner's in the telephone directory, and Mr Willcox rang them while I fetched my gloves and shoes. When I returned he was still on the telephone, so the constable and I settled into relatively relaxed small talk. He told me he had two sets of identical twins, girls and boys, and I was just about to learn whether the boys could walk and the girls could write, when I suddenly remembered Sara telling me, when she was young, that Peter should have been one of twins only the other one died. I wondered when he had told her this information, and why. Was it true? Nothing Peter said could really be relied upon. What would he have hoped to gain by persuading her of such a story? I tried to imagine a second Peter. By then I had missed the last thing the sergeant told me. It didn't matter. Mr Willcox was back in the room.

'Well I'm afraid that's in the drum already. They confirmed you dropped the garment off shortly after eight o'clock this morning. Does that accord with your recollection?'

'Yes, that would be about right. And you wanted the gloves and shoes?'

'Thank you,' Mr Willcox said, taking them from me. 'And, forgive me asking, were you wearing stockings or tights or what have you?'

'Certainly not. It was far too hot.' It was extraordinary that the underwear I had worn to open the Fair was now the business of the Cambridge police. If I had realised, would I have dressed differently?

'Do you mind if we take these away for a few days?' I must have looked surprised, because he added, by way of explanation, 'For the purposes of elimination. Because of the gun being in your house, and so on. We'll return them as quickly as possible. And of course we'll give you a receipt.' The constable put them in their own picnic bags, see-through and labelled, and bundled them into his arms as if he were collecting for a jumble sale. I worried that the skirt wouldn't dry properly, and might smell musty, but then I told myself I wouldn't often need an Edwardian costume, and I could always wash it again.

Just when I thought they'd finished, Mr Willcox said, 'And your daughter's?'

'My daughter's? My daughter's what?'

'Would it be all right for us to look at the clothes your daughter wore that day?'

'But she's not here.'

'Don't you know what she wore?'

I racked my brains. Leggings. I remembered the leggings.

'If you don't want to give them to us without asking her, we could come back and see her after school.'

'No,' I said, 'I'll get them.' Then I said, more slowly, 'But of course she may want them for the weekend.'

'We can bring them back tomorrow, or the next day at the latest. Will they have been washed?'

'I very much doubt it, but I don't know.'

They weren't. Sara's leggings from the weekend were in the middle of her floor, exactly as she had taken them off on Saturday, half inside-out and with a T-shirt sitting on top of them. I bundled them both up, with the pair of socks which lay nearest to the leggings, and took them down to the waiting policemen.

'Definitely not washed,' I said, handing them over. As they were on their way out, I said, 'Please don't think me rude, but how long are your investigations likely to take? My daughter has exams this term. It's all been rather upsetting.'

'No time at all,' Mr Willcox replied. 'Suicides are usually wrapped up very quickly, although there's sometimes quite a wait for the inquest.'

'But if it's suicide, why the investigations?'

'Routine.' He smiled. 'Don't worry. If there's anything suspicious, we spot it straight away.' I briefly remembered Colin's Sophie, and her sexy research. Was this why the police had called?

They were nearly in their car when I remembered my hat again, and ran after them to ask whether they wanted it. They accepted it gratefully, the more so when I told them the chiffon scarf had definitely not been washed.

22

After the police came to see me that Tuesday afternoon things seemed to settle down somewhat. Alison moved home from Jean's house much quicker than we had expected her to. Others were back at work, or school, after the bank holiday weekend. The inquest had been opened and the PM carried out, so Peter's body could be released to Alison for the funeral, and Hugh took over and helped Alison organise it. It was thought that the final inquest might not be for a couple of months or so.

On the eighth of May, the Thursday, the police called on me again. This time it was the same pleasant, tall constable, and a policewoman I hadn't met before. They were bringing our clothes back. As they handed them over, the sergeant asked me what I could tell him about Peter's character and life, his background and his possible frame of mind.

I considered. 'We knew Peter quite well at one time, or thought we did. But I have no idea how he would react under pressure, or even what pressures he was under.' And I thought of some words of David's. We're all capable of anything. The most astonishing acts of heroism, the most shocking acts of violence. We don't know what our own family, or even we ourselves, may do under certain circumstances. 'I'm sorry. The only honest answer I can give you is that I don't know. I don't know whether Peter was the sort of person who was likely to take his own life.'

On the Wednesday afternoon, the fourteenth, eleven days after the event itself, Margaret Jennings called. I had just got back from hearing a very robust and cheerful Macduff, bouncing through lines which are normally racked with guilt at abandoning his family to their hideous massacre, and I was having my cup of tea in the garden. There had been no rain, and I had taken my shoes off and was wondering whether I could bear to get the sprinkler out for the lawn, when I heard a 'Coo-ee', coming round the side of the house.

'In the garden,' I called back. Most of the village know I can't hear the back doorbell from the terrace. Many people just come straight to the terrace and wander into the house through the drawing room. When people want a swim they simply go on down to the bottom of the garden.

Margaret crept apologetically into view. 'Harriet. So sorry. I'm sure you're wanting a little peace and quiet. You're so busy.'

'Not at the moment,' I said, indicating the teapot.

'I know. You're recovering from a day at work and here I am interrupting you. Your cup of tea. Oh dear. No, no, no *please* don't get up. You've got your shoes off and everything.'

'All right; then nip into the kitchen and get yourself a cup. And stop apologising.'

'Of course. I'm so sorry.'

I was pleased to see Margaret again. I had spotted her briefly on the day of the Fair, of course, in charge of an 'Ideal Home' stall, rather drastically scaled down to manageable proportions and selling drooping houseplants and fluffy bathmats and those knitted things to keep loo rolls warm. But we hadn't talked to each other properly for some time. When she came back from the house she sat opposite me, fidgeting, but refraining from her usual verbal eruptions. I asked her if anything was the matter.

'It's this awful business,' she burst out. 'Poor Alison. So dreadful. I don't know what to do. Or whether to do anything. It's Amanda, you see.'

I waited. I wasn't sure whether I saw or not.

'Oh dear. Well, you probably didn't know about it. We tried to keep it a bit quiet. And when it first started you hadn't been back from India long, from doing your missionary thing. I mean, not India, you know, that other place. Milk, please. That is, if that's all right in Earl Grey, not a sacrilege, some people think it is. Goodness, I mean Amanda was only fourteen, then. A girl, really; a little girl. And we think she was kind of friendly with

Peter. Well, we know she was. A bit soft on him, you know. A bit of a crush. I know he wasn't exactly prepossessing; we didn't think so anyway. But then parents don't always have the same taste, do they? You don't have sugar out here do you? It doesn't matter at all, really, please don't. I didn't think to get it when I was inside. I'm quite all right without, honestly. Good for the figure. Anyway, one shouldn't say anything, I suppose, but I didn't think him much fun for a young girl. Wild eyes, Frank used to say. He said his sister's husband had a look like that, and he turned out funny, used to drink, turn a bit nasty, you know. And too old for her. We thought.'

She stared at her cup. Then she seemed to realise, with a start, that she should have been drinking it. She gulped at it suddenly, her nervous energy almost making her vibrate. She is one of these people who blushes easily and breathes more quickly than the rest of us. Funnily enough, she tends to make me relax because I know I won't have to do anything. Having Margaret to tea is a bit like having a clockwork toy with a self-winding programme. One merely nudges it when it gets stuck. And I don't think well in the heat, despite five years of it.

'Well, it didn't matter to begin with because he didn't show any interest. I mean this was over a year ago, you know; nearly two. He wasn't here much, and when he was, Amanda didn't see him much. But suddenly, when he moved to Cambridge, they started seeing each other. To do him justice, I never thought he was as keen on her as she was on him. I always thought it was a one-way thing. But I was worried, you know. You hear about children nowadays, experimenting, starting relationships, and not taking proper precautions. I know she went to see our doctor. She didn't think I knew, but I did. I don't know if it was about that. I didn't like to ask. She wanted her bit of independence, and we thought it was better to let her have it, than for her to rebel altogether. Perhaps we were wrong.' She stopped, and swallowed, and looked down at her hands. Quite unexpectedly, she started to cry.

I didn't have a handkerchief out in the garden with me. I wondered whether to go and get one, but then she found a tissue up her sleeve.

'She must have found it very difficult,' I said. 'His death.

Especially if she was keen on him. It must have been a big shock. David lost a school friend when he was seventeen, and he never got over it.'

'But it was before that. Ten days before. Oh, Harriet. It was awful.'

'What was? What happened?'

'I thought it was a row. I was quite relieved. Isn't that dreadful of me? I was actually relieved. I thought they'd had a bust up, and it would be better for her. But I didn't know what it was about, honestly I didn't. I assumed he'd got sick of her and told her so and she was just upset about it. And I'm her *mother*. How can I be so insensitive?'

'What do you mean it was ten days before? Before what? Do you mean they had a row ten days before the Fair?'

'She went to see him after school. She'd done it before. Usually with a friend. We said it was all right, as long as she always did her homework. That day she came home later than usual. When she got in she looked a bit funny, a bit tearful, but when I asked her if anything was the matter she said she was fine. She just ran straight up to bed. I still can't believe it.' She began sobbing gently, and blowing her nose on her sodden tissue. It was some time before she could start again. I merely sat, and waited. I could not have trusted myself to speak.

'We hardly saw her for several days. She didn't eat, she lived in her room, she didn't talk to us. Three days later I heard her in her bedroom, crying. I went in but she wouldn't tell me what the matter was. Then I saw her eye. I thought that must have been why she was hiding. A real black eye, purple and yellow, and bloodshot. She said she'd fallen off her bicycle. I said nothing. Then I asked if it was about Peter, and she started screaming, saying she didn't want to talk about him, telling me to leave her alone.

'The next week, her form teacher rang up to say she was very worried about her and was she ill. I said I thought she'd broken up with a kind of boyfriend and was taking it badly. Her teacher said she hadn't done any sport for a week, and kept lying in the sick room with "period pains". Poor little lamb. Perhaps it would have been better if I hadn't interfered.'

'It's usually better to get to the bottom of it,' I said, carefully, saying the most neutral thing I could think of. Why did Margaret think I could give any useful advice on how she should protect her daughter? I was hardly in a position to comment. And it seemed so unfair, so monstrous, that she should feel guilty for being a normal, loving, concerned mother worrying about her child. No other society would condemn a parent for wanting to keep her daughter's innocence.

'I don't know. The trouble was that Jim found out about it. He kept telling me not to bother her, but in the end I went and sat in her room and told her I wasn't going away till she told me about it. She cried and shouted at me a bit more, but in the end it started to come out. How he'd always seemed all right . . .' Margaret stopped for a minute, and blew her nose again. 'You know the Jekyll and Hyde story?' I nodded. 'She said he turned. He turned into a monster.' She was having difficulty continuing.

'When was this?'

'Two days before the Fair.'

'That he did this?'

'No, that she told me. It all happened a week earlier, on the Thursday.'

'What date?'

'Thursday, the week before the Fair. About the twenty-fourth of April. Why?'

'No, no. No matter. Go on.'

'I can't.'

I spoke very quietly. 'Margaret, did he make her have sex? Without her consent?' Margaret shrugged, dabbing her eyes.

'No,' she said. 'No, I don't think so. It was just her first time, that's all. Maybe it went wrong. And they had a row, and he hit her.' I looked at her and said nothing. In the end she weakened, and looked down. 'Perhaps you're right.'

'Say it,' I said. 'He raped her.'

There is a bond between women stronger than class or race or age. I've never been close to Margaret: I find her fussy and irritating. But that afternoon I couldn't understand why I had ever tried to avoid her, or sighed inwardly if she accosted me in the street. I have sometimes mused on the camaraderie shared by men, as they went over the top together at Ypres, or shared unspeakable conditions in trenches, or died for a pointless war. Presumably, there are moments in human history when personality, politics or opinions make no difference. It was the same with us. I longed to cry with Margaret, but I had no tears any more. A deep, seething anger in me dried them all up long ago. But as we sat there, in my garden, over the tea things, with the thought of Amanda and the terrible thing which had been done to her, I wondered what punishment could ever atone for Peter's actions. Had he met his just deserts? Or had he escaped them?

I offered her more tea and she shook her head. We listened for a moment to the sounds of the garden. An aeroplane on a distant journey. The sparrows quarrelling. The Cambridge commuters beginning to come home. The gentle tinkle of Margaret's cup, as she realigned it nervously on the saucer, then put it on the table. A muffled sob, a sniff, a sigh.

'What should I do, Harriet? What do I do now?'

'Love her. Care for her. Spend a lot of time with her. Take her to the doctor and get her checked over. Be wary of too much counselling. Try to help her forget it.'

'So you don't think I should go to the police?'

'The *police*?'

'To report a, you know, rape.'

I was aghast. 'But, Margaret, he's dead.'

'I know. I know, that's it, you see. They've been round, asking questions. Did he know her? Did they spend time together? When did she last see him? Why did she go and see him? How did they spend the afternoon?'

'Margaret, you must get legal advice, straight away. I don't know if she has to answer these questions, but you must refuse, if you possibly can, on her behalf. I don't know if you want my advice, or whether you have decided you know what to do anyway, but I cannot emphasise this strongly enough. You must not tell the police. Amanda has been invaded enough. Peter's dead. It can't do any good. What does it matter whether they get to the bottom of why or how? What matters is Amanda's future. Getting her fit for her GCSEs, and her sixth form, and her life. Tell them they *cannot* speak to her. Get a lawyer to sort it out. And then give them your story, that they had a quarrel, broke up ten days before he died, and she's very upset about it. Get a doctor's certificate, anything.'

'But isn't that obstructing . . .'

'I don't care what it is. The police have one job – to solve crime – which they do well. You have another – to look after your daughter. Your agenda does not fit with the police's agenda. That's their problem.'

'But can't they subpoena me, or something?'

'That's what the lawyer's for. I don't know what they can do. Find out. But do not tell them what he did to her. One humiliation is enough for any child. She can't cope with it all over again, from the police.'

'Goodness. I'm sure you're right. I suppose. Sometimes it is better not to tell everything, isn't it? Sometimes telling the truth can do more harm than good. Perhaps I will have another cup, if it's still hot.'

Suddenly I thought of an argument to clinch it. 'What about Alison?' I said. 'She's lost her son. That's bad enough. But suppose it got out, what had happened that night. Imagine how it would be for her.'

'Gosh!' She put her hand over her mouth. 'Oh, I'm so glad I asked you. I never thought.'

'No. Well, think now, and don't do it.'

'I hope I haven't said too much already.'

'Just don't say any more.' She nodded, and sat on in silence. I started to pile everything onto the tea tray, and offered her the last of the home-made biscuits from the Fair, still on the tray. Then I stood up to carry it all inside. Margaret stood up too. 'How did your stall do, at the Fair?' I asked her.

'Two hundred and thirty-five. Not bad. And eighty-nine pence.'

'Did Amanda come?'

'She couldn't face it. She can't face anyone at the moment.'

'And Jim?'

'Jim?'

'Did he enjoy the Fair?'

'I, er. Oh, Harriet, that's just it. That's why I'm so frightened.' It all came out in a rush. 'That was why I came to see you, I think. I don't know whether I should tell you, anyone, what I

should do. It's much worse, really, than I was letting on.' I stared
at her. What could possibly be worse than her own daughter's
rape? 'I just don't know.'

'What do you mean? What don't you know?'

'Where he was. He never turned up. He was supposed to help
Geoff, and he never turned up. Not at all.'

'Well, I'm not surprised. He's probably beside himself about
poor Amanda. The Fair would be the last thing he'd want. Went
for a drive, I should think.'

'Oh, I hope so. I do so hope so. I hope you're right.'

'Why, what do you think?'

'I've been so worried, Harriet. When it was suicide, it was
all right. But all these stories, you start to think, I just don't
know.'

'What stories? What have you heard?'

'The police, coming round, asking about alibis. They didn't
use the word alibi, but that's what they were doing. Where
had I been, where had Jim been, where were you, had I seen
you, what was Amanda's relationship with the deceased. And
you hear these stories, people live with people for years. You
know, the wife of the Cambridge Rapist, remember, never put
two and two together, never realised she was living with him.
And, you see, when Jim found out, he was so angry, I've never
seen anything like it. He's always had a temper, been protective
of his little girl. But this was different. I began to think, perhaps
I don't know him at all.'

I sat down again. 'Surely, Margaret. You don't think . . .'

'I don't know what to think.'

'When did Peter attack her? Tell me again.'

' "Attack"? Yes I suppose it was, really. I hadn't thought of
it like that. It was ten days before the Fair. Like I said. The
twenty-fourth of April.'

'And when did she tell you?'

'A week later. Thursday. The first of May.'

'And Jim?'

'What do you mean, and Jim?'

'When did he find out? When did you, or Amanda, tell
him?'

'We didn't. But on Friday afternoon he saw her black eye.

Maybe he couldn't take it, and she should have avoided him. Perhaps men can't handle that kind of thing.'

'For goodness' sake, Margaret.' My fear was beginning to make me angry. 'Stop blaming yourself. It was hard enough for you, not to mention Amanda. Jim can cope with a bit of the burden. He probably feels he let her down, failed to protect her, I don't know. What did he do on Friday night?'

She thought for a moment. 'He broke a kitchen chair. He threw a teapot on the floor and broke that too. Full of tea. He threatened various things.'

'Such as?'

'Well, you know. Against Peter.'

'He threatened to go and kill him?'

'Not quite, but that sort of thing. Well, yes: that too. But he didn't mean it. He can't have done. Then he went out, and didn't come back till really late, and slept in the guest room. I think he was very drunk. He didn't get up on Saturday morning, and when I went out to go to the Fair he was still in. Amanda said he went out about half past two. He came back very late that night again. He didn't talk to me till Monday. And then, not really. He hasn't talked to me properly at all. It's not fair, Harriet. I found it hard too. I needed someone to talk to.' She was beginning to whine.

'Don't think like that,' I said. 'Don't even begin to think like that. You need to survive, you need to stay together. You can't afford to fight each other on this. When men get upset they often need time to themselves. It's how they cope. Women cope by sticking together, talking about it. Men don't. They need solitude.'

I hardly knew what I was saying, or whether any of it was true. It was one of those clichés about the sexes, and I couldn't even remember, or care, whether it had been true of David and me. The truth was I could see the implications only too clearly, perhaps more clearly even than Margaret herself, and I felt an icy hand of terror gripping me under my chest. Somehow, I must try to stop her making it worse.

'Margaret, listen to me. I know what you're thinking, and it's wrong. I can't tell you how wrong it is. It must be. Put the idea out of your head right now. Don't say anything to the police.

Tell them nothing. Not what Peter did to Amanda, not about Jim finding out, nothing. Don't tell anyone else, either. You know what this place is like. It'll be around the village in five minutes. Are you listening to me? Jim is innocent. As you say, he must be. But if the police get wind of any of it, it'll all come out. And that means what happened to Amanda too. And they will rape her all over again, believe me. The police will. They won't mean to, they'll mean to be kind, but that's what it'll be like for her. That's their job. They have to find out, they will have to ask her what he did, every last detail of it, over and over again, in court if necessary. If you think Peter humiliated her, believe me, you ain't seen nothing yet.'

Margaret nodded, rather reluctantly, I thought. I didn't know whether she would take any notice. I thought, with horror, of the consequences of her nervous disposition, and the damage it could do. I thought of poor Amanda, trying valiantly to rebuild her self-esteem, and how many years of her fragile dignity she would lose if Margaret so much as hinted any of it to anyone, let alone the police. I could hardly bear to think of it. There was nothing more I could do to warn her, without making it all worse. 'Just ask Jim where he was and he'll have a perfectly good explanation.'

'I have. He wouldn't tell me. Told me to leave him alone.'

'Then leave him alone. Trust him, and leave him alone. You're wrong. I know it. Believe me.'

The days grew hotter and sweeter and more beautiful. The laburnum came out on the trees, dripping vivid yellow over fences and in gardens in garish waterfalls. Lupins and hollyhocks stretched themselves up in proud front gardens. Along the lanes, hawthorn blossom spattered the hedges. Birds grew busy, mating and building and laying, feeding and scolding, watching anxiously the first flights of the year.

And still there was no Prue.

23 ∫

A patch of sunlight lights up the bark of an old tree just outside my window. A thrush sits completely and utterly still, on that same bare bark. He, or she, has been there for nearly an hour. From time to time he turns his head about. That's all. He seems to have no immediate needs or desires. He just looks.

The weather has ceased to be spectacular. Or perhaps I've ceased to feel it. At any rate today it seems merely warm and thick. The aeroplanes continue to growl overhead, the midges to bite, the earwigs to get into everything, and there's been no more rain. But the sun seems to have relented of its burning and scorching and has faded into a lazy mugginess.

No. The sun never relents. I should have learnt that in Phulbari.

In the end I was miles away, down by the river. It was the fourteenth of June, three years ago. I had sat by his bedside for days, knowing it was hopeless. I longed to pray for a miracle, and sometimes I did, even though we knew God would not make him well. Sometimes I sat by him, almost praying to David himself, blasphemously, that he would hear me, inside his head, and respond, and sit up and shake it all off and stay with us. God knows, he would have if he could, even though I wonder whether, at the very end, deep down, there was a kind of relief at knowing the struggle was over. Perhaps that's unfair. David always had that deeply old-fashioned sense of family, and duty. Just like Maurice, despite the superficial differences between them.

We had known for nearly a fortnight. In theory we should

have known for longer, but we never thought it would happen. David had gone trekking in mid April, way up country where there were no communications. He had gone with two medical students who had come on placement to Phulbari, to see the work he was doing, and they were visiting strings of tiny villages, taking medicines and health education programmes. He was worried, but not unduly so, when the incident happened. They had all had their rabies jabs before going out, and should have been adequately protected. The precautions they had taken had been exemplary.

But it was a bad bite. It had happened without warning, as he was squatting down on the ground inside a mud hut, attending to a sick child. He heard shouts outside, but he took little notice and before he knew it the dog had run in and leapt at the child. David didn't even have time to think about it: he threw himself in front of her, and saved her life. But, in doing so, he took the brunt of the poor dog's savagery. He put his arms up to protect his face, but he was badly bitten on the fingers of one of his hands, and nicked on one ear. The dog was caught and killed almost immediately. Typically, David washed and dressed his wound without a word and went back to attending to the little girl.

Whenever I think, now, of the terrible cost of what happened eight years ago, and blame Peter, as I have so many times and so unfairly, for our trip to Phulbari, and think of the years in front of me without David, I remind myself of that nameless tribal girl, and tell myself that there is a Nepali teenager now, perhaps Sara's age, who would not be alive today if we hadn't gone abroad. I try to picture her face, and almost wish I had a photograph of her, or knew her so I could write to her. But it is better as it is.

It wasn't until he had finished attending to her that he considered his own life. The rabies injection which all three of them had taken before travelling offered seventy- or eighty-per cent protection. He even momentarily contemplated taking no booster at all. They had intended to travel for another couple of weeks, and they would now have to turn round again. The medical students, however, were emphatic. David had received a serious bite, and he must get proper attention. Indeed, David would quickly have come to that conclusion himself: to be bitten on the face or hands, badly, as he had been, is far more dangerous than a nip to the ankles. So they packed up that afternoon and started back. The nearest communications centre was a day's walk away, but the radio was down. There was nothing for it but to walk all the way back to Phulbari.

When they arrived home again four days later, two weeks earlier than expected, I wasn't particularly surprised. Such changes of plan happen all the time in Nepal. David started a two-week course of rather unpleasant injections to the stomach, and Sara and Charles included in their daily prayers the request that Daddy would be all right. We were concerned, but not unduly so. David thought he had almost certainly caught it in time. Doctors do not get ill. And we were surrounded by so many, more obvious, illnesses that we didn't consider ourselves to be in much danger, by comparison.

We were wrong.

I think David realised a couple of days before he told me. It was several weeks after the bite, and we thought he was in the clear. But the anxiety, the restlessness, the 'fluey symptoms,' the aching limbs and sense of weakness, the tell-tale signs must have been there for forty-eight hours or so before he plucked up courage to face the facts. The first thing I noticed was that he kept pouring himself glasses of water, and then not drinking them.

One morning, as Sara was getting ready to go to school, David got up from the breakfast table and went to the water container in the corner of the kitchen: we kept cooled, boiled water in a large plastic drum with a tap. He picked up a glass, moved his hand towards the tap, then changed his mind again. He turned, and caught my eye. I dropped my gaze, then turned to hurry Sara up, although she had plenty of time.

'Will you walk with me?' she asked.

'Not today,' I said. It was the first time I had ever refused her. I told her to take herself to school, and after what seemed an interminable few minutes, waved her off. Then I turned and looked at David. We both said nothing for a long time. I could feel the tears wanting to come, and David opened his arms to embrace me. I crossed the room, and he simply held me. I heard, and felt, him swallowing. At last he spoke.

'What is it, your favourite play?' he asked me.

I gave a tiny shrug. '*Romeo and Juliet*? No, *Antony and Cleopatra*, probably. Why?' I tried to move my face, but he took my cheek and pressed it against his chest.

'That's it. Antony. Marc Antony. "I am dying, Egypt. Dying."'

I clung on to him, hard. '"And there is nothing left remarkable . . ."' I couldn't finish the quote.

He did it for me. '"Beneath the visiting moon."'

We told Sara as soon as she came home. Someone had already set off in the mission jeep for Pokhara, to ring Charles at school. We guessed that David probably had a week of sanity left, more if we were lucky. That night, after several hours of crying and hugging and praying, we sent Sara to bed, and I saw a grown man frightened as I have never seen a man frightened before, and never want to again.

He told me to promise that I wouldn't nurse him at the end. I said I couldn't promise such a thing.

'Harriet,' he said. His eyes were red and watery, but he wasn't crying. He was, however, shaking slightly. He didn't often call me by my name like that, and it hurt to know how much I loved him. 'Harriet, I've seen it. I've seen a woman die of this. It is not a pretty sight. Listen to me. In ten days from now, if I'm still alive, I will be mad. D'you understand? Mad, and very dangerous. I will not be me, not David. I shall be a lunatic, with a raging and lethal disease. It'll be like some tacky, B-movie vampire horror. If I bite you, you'll die too, and the children will then be orphans. You once promised to obey me. I am now ordering you not to nurse me when that happens. Do I have your word that you will keep your vow, and obey me?'

What could I do then, but bow my head, and let the tears fall?

'Daddy.' Sara stood in the doorway in her nightdress.

I saw David run his fingers past the corner of his eye before he answered her. 'Yes?'

'Is there any hope?'

'Oh, yes, darling. There is a very certain hope. That's why we're out here. There's a glorious hope ahead of me.'

'Don't be stupid, you know what I mean. Is there any hope that you won't die?'

David took a deep breath, and thought about her question for a long time. In the end he simply said, 'No. No, Sara, there is no hope of that. I had hoped it was simply coincidence, that I just had a virus, but I'm pretty sure it's more than that now. If that's what you're asking, I'm afraid there is no hope at all. Better we spend the next few days enjoying each other and saying goodbye, than that we pray for something which isn't going to happen.'

'But does everyone die who gets rabies?'

'I believe there is one reported case of a survival, though I'd have to look it up. But he ended up like a cabbage. Please, don't pray for that.'

And then Sara ran into his arms, and sobbed her heart out again, and this time David sobbed too.

He did look it up. His text books confirmed what he'd thought. More recently, since we came back to Willisham, I read about rabies in a new medical encyclopedia which came out last year, and the prognosis has changed. If David caught the disease now, and could somehow have been flown straight from Phulbari to one particular centre in America and put in intensive care for six weeks and goodness knows what else, he just might have pulled through. Three people in the world have done so. The only ones ever to have recovered from rabies in medical history. But when he caught it, three years ago, fatality was a hundred per cent.

Two days later Charles was there, and David's creeping fear, a sure sign of the disease, momentarily abated at his arrival. During the first supper we had after Charles's arrival, I would hardly have known David was ill. We had been laughing and joking, and behaving more or less normally, and were beginning to think nothing was wrong, that we had a pleasant excuse for having Charles over mid-term for no reason, until, unthinking, David picked up his glass, brought it half-way to his lips, then hurled it across the room as if someone had jerked a string. It happened quite without warning. There was a deathly silence. The children stared, shocked. Charles glared at his father, as if he'd done something outrageous. Sara looked at the puddle of water and broken glass on the bare floor. David cleared his throat. He wiped his hand over his face.

'Sorry,' he said. 'I'm so sorry.'

It was truly pitiful. It reminded me of Sara, apologising for what had happened to her five years before. She got down from the table, climbed into his lap and tried to comfort him.

'We forgive you Daddy. It's all right.'

The next day, as we sat together after breakfast, he asked the children whether they'd like to hear about the journey ahead of him. 'What we know about it, which isn't much. Do you remember, when we were planning our trip here, how we got atlases out, and photographs of Nepal, and kept imagining what it would be like? Pass me that Bible, will you please, Charles?'

I left the room. I went into our small bare sitting room in my large bare feet and looked out of the back door towards the vast and impersonal mountains. Anapurna looked down at me with a wonderful haughty scorn. Look at me, she seemed to say. You'll all die in that dreadful heat, while I still have snow in my hair. It was some comfort to me that she didn't care. That there was something in the world, at any rate, which would stay unmoved and indifferent at the demise of David St Joseph.

It wasn't long before the monsoon, and the air was heavy and bright. Thick, hot and stifling, and almost shining in the morning heat. Somebody's little fat black pig had got into our garden, and I watched him snuffling about, turning over leaves and looking for this and that. I couldn't be bothered to shoo him away. Or her. I remember now, it was a she; her little slate grey nipples nearly scraping the ground as she rummaged about and stole titbits from our garden. I stood by the open door, while the ants ran up to my feet, and considered, and then ran around them, and the sow regarded me warily from one eye, and Anapurna glared down on me and said don't worry about me, I'm beautiful; I don't care at all.

I went back into the kitchen at last, the plain, bare room which led off into the sitting room on one side, with its threadbare carpet on the beaten floor, and our bedroom on the other, with its mosquito net hanging up above the simple bed. Sara sat at the table listening to the book of Revelation, with her eyes wide open and her lips a little apart, while Charles stood, as I had done, by the open window with his back to them, torn between child and man, with the tears streaming down his face and his cheeks like a little boy's.

Crying over little things was never encouraged in either of the children, but it has always been a rule in our family that if you really have something to weep over you can wail and bawl. If we hadn't known it before we would have learnt it, and painfully, through Sara: when you hate the world you must sometimes tell it so. King David complained in the Psalms, and our children were taught to as well. Charles knew he was free to cry. But I could tell that it hurt for a young man of his age to act, as he thought, like a child.

His father had less than a week after that. But God was merciful, and David didn't go mad. He sank into a coma, and went peacefully.

And I was far away. I always wanted to be with him at the end. Just as he wanted to be with our children at the beginning, and was. But perhaps, deep down, I wanted to avoid it too. I told myself I had an urgent letter to post. There were no telephones in Phulbari, so all we had was radio communication to Kathmandu or Pokhara, and then telephone messages on from there. Maurice and Prue hadn't yet arrived, although they were on their way. There had been a delay in contacting them because they weren't in Willisham when we first tried to get in touch. I had a letter for my parents, and David had written a page to them in his own handwriting a day or two earlier, and I wanted to post it. I suppose I could have sent one of the girls with it. But Shanti and Maili both hated long walks, and the younger girl would have spent all the afternoon dawdling through the bazaar. Besides, I was sick to death of the house, and the awful waiting, and David had been asleep for nearly two days. For an afternoon I thought, unlike him, I could escape the tyranny of the deathbed.

Though of course it was he who did.

If Gerald, David's colleague at the hospital, had told me this was the end I would never have gone. But Gerald was busy with other patients. A hospital can scarcely afford, after all, to lose one of its doctors to his death and the other to his colleague's bedside all in one day. Though Gerald would have been with David too, if he'd known. But in the end David was alone, and Gerald was with other, living patients, who perhaps needed him even more.

No doubt one could get to the post office at the other side of the village in a fairly short time, walking quickly. But no one in Nepal ever does walk quickly. There's too much walking to do. It's taken at a steady pace which can be kept up for days and weeks, with a load as big as a piano sometimes, through the hills and mountains and wet and sweaty monsoon forests. They know. They earn their living at it, half the men in the land. They set off and walk all day, from seven in the morning till seven at night, stopping by the track for glass upon glass of sweet, milky tea. Though now you can spend a man's daily wage, or two days of a woman's wage, on a can of Coca-Cola served alongside the tea at the little hillside huts. Once, new to the country, I was very thirsty and bought two cans, and was stared at as if I were insane. Realising how much I had spent, I gave the boy the price of another. He, and a dozen friends, followed me for an hour asking me for more.

Then they stop, these men, these porters, for a plateful of rice, barely flavoured with a dollop of curry like red hot sandpaper. And they carry on their backs a basket of wood the size and weight of another man. So they set the pace of walking, and the pace is slow.

I can't even remember what I thought about. For all I know I spent hours walking there. I walked my mind into a state of numbness, and found myself, on the way back, by the Sheti river with its foaming pale brown water dancing madly over the rocks and beating them into the powder which gives the river its colour and its name. Sheti: White. The other river, the Kali, is Black: clear, and clean, and dark. And I stared at its livid movement, like terrible, savage laughter, and watched the gaudy butterflies exhibiting themselves in the air. I sat for a long time, while the dry grass prickled my bare legs beneath my worn cotton shorts.

I never wore proper Eastern clothes, being of the opinion that Europeans look rather silly in a sari. Even in Nepal, where the clothes are simple and cotton, I would have looked sallow and unhealthy if I had tried to wear the traditional dress which looks so appropriate on the robust Nepali women. Other missionaries had saris, or lungis, while the older ones still sometimes wore sensible, neat cotton frocks and A-line skirts, with white ankle socks and open sandals in the daytime, and occasionally, for something special in the evening if it wasn't too hot, nylon tights, brought with great care and trouble by friends visiting from home, along with shampoo and razor blades and lots of batteries.

When I first went out, I wore T-shirts with no bra, because it was hot hot hot, and I felt so free out there. And tatty old khaki shorts. An Englishwoman in her seventies, a marvellous doctor of the old school who had been there almost since the border opened, told me in her forthright way that it wasn't suitable dress for the work we were doing.

'I bring up children and I run a school. These are the most suitable clothes I have,' I argued mildly.

'Nonsense. It doesn't breed respect among the women. Nor, I shouldn't wonder, the children.'

Which I, in my turn, thought nonsense, but didn't say so. If they couldn't respect us for the way we behaved, I thought our clothes would hardly do the trick. Besides, the Nepali women still found us so strange they wouldn't know what we ought to wear. So I persisted in my braless state.

I admired that woman enormously. That week in the prayer meeting she prayed for our 'dear sister coming to terms with our funny ways', then never mentioned it again.

And yet it turned out she was right. I gradually came to realise that a loose T-shirt and shorts were not appropriate. It was not fair on the Nepali women after all. Then I started to wear the long, baggy shalwer-kemise which had begun to come in from Pakistan. I wear them still, on hot summer evenings, alone in the garden.

So why was it that I was wearing shorts on that afternoon, the fourteenth of June three years ago? What was I thinking of, when I got dressed? I don't know. But I know I was, because I felt the dry grass on my bare legs, and I can still feel it now.

Nobody runs in Nepal. Charles, back from Eton after his first term and full of frightful English heartiness, once went jogging up towards the Tibetan camp in a daft and enthusiastic attempt to keep fit. Several people asked him where the fire was, and one old man tried to exorcise him. He didn't go jogging again. So when I saw a boy run towards me I did, in truth, know what had happened, and turned my face away to gaze on the comforting danger of the Sheti. How did I know, I wonder, that it was already too late? There must have been something in his look or his manner: something to tell me that my pleading hope could end. Downstream of me a porter was crossing a tiny, rickety rope bridge with a bed on his back, way above the charging torrent. The rope swayed and creaked and wobbled, and I wondered idly if this unknown and, to me, totally insignificant little man would meet David and go in with him together.

'Memsahib, memsahib! *Namaste*, memsahib!' Because I refused to turn and look at him, he darted round to my other side and started again. But when he saw my face he fell silent. He knew I knew, and he knew I didn't want to.

Funnily enough, that boy in his youth and ignorance knew all he needed to about me. He neither spoke nor left me, but sat idly a yard or so away from me, throwing stones into the Sheti; and pointing out, from time to time, an unusual bird or a friend of his.

He sat for a while. Then he got up and said goodbye. He didn't give me his news, for which much thanks, wherever you may be. He gave me a little longer on this earth without David dead. I never learnt his name. And when I saw him again in the street, he would smile and greet me with a '*Namaste*', and the tears which abandoned me that afternoon would always come to me then.

I wonder now if he got into trouble for not bringing me back. I have no idea who sent him. Perhaps it was Gerald, or Charles. Whoever it was, he probably told the boy he'd get paid if he brought me home within the hour.

I went through the motions, I suppose, of what everybody goes through. The boring and urgent insistence that it couldn't really have happened. The desperate, energetic attempt to persuade myself, and incidentally God, that of course it couldn't be true – like so many people's motions of prayer: if I can only convince myself, God will be persuaded by the by. The desire to call the boy back, and make him tell me he was mistaken, as if that could somehow turn back the tide of death.

I did get up eventually. I had two orphans to comfort. But I walked back as slowly as if every bone in my body were bruised or broken. Every step seemed to cause me pain. And when at last I saw our little house, our dear little house where we'd all been so happy, I seemed to hear somebody wailing, and I think it must have been me.

Sara stood on the step looking out for me, and I wondered how long she had waited. When she saw me she ran towards me. 'Don't worry Mummy. We'll look after you. Daddy told us to and we will.'

I tried to say, 'Did he wake up then?' but nothing seemed to come. I knew he couldn't have done. He must have told her several days earlier. So I went into the kitchen, and Charles stood up and towered over me and said, 'You can cry, Mother, if you want to.'

And when I went in and saw him, my first feeling was one of intolerable resentment that this lump of nothing, this thing, this dead piece of yellow flesh, should have been flung there in David's place. Then I thought, he's breathing, I can see it; and I watched his chest move up and down. Then I sat down on his bed and took his hand, as I had done so many times before, and it was cold, quite cold, cold as any stone.

And then I cried.

24

My life has become a useless weight around my neck. I suppose, at forty-one, I'm barely half way there, but I would do anything to be rid of it, if I could.

I certainly would have done almost anything to have David back, in those early weeks. Called up spirits, resorted to a medium, sold my soul like Faust; if I hadn't read my Marlowe and Goethe I'd be there with him now, I'm sure.

And sometimes I think – I'm convinced, I really believe – that David is here again. I sit here, in this confined space, writing down what happened since May, and I suddenly hear him breathing behind me, feel the warmth of his body in the room. And I turn with a silent shout of joy on my face and there is nothing, nothing, nothing. And then I believe there is no eternal life after all, and David has rotted away, and I will never see him again. And then I could commit any crime.

Then I know God has put me here as a slow torture, or, as He would call it, a test, because I have two children to look after and I mustn't leave them alone.

Though, God Himself knows, I'm not much use to them any more.

It was funny how all four of us knew, within a very short time and without needing to tell one another, that our days in Phulbari were going to be the happiest of our lives. In such a beautiful country it was impossible to remember what had happened to us in Willisham. Beneath such breathless, unfathomable skies, such equally impossible mountains, our petty problems became like the domestic concerns of ants.

A few months after we arrived the children were invited on a week's holiday in the mountains and David had to go to Delhi for a conference; I decided to go for a few days' trekking alone. It was ridiculously dangerous, I nearly killed myself several times, and David was furious with me on his return. Not that one ever minds that kind of anger much: being told off for not looking after oneself. I found myself covered in leeches for two days, crawling with them at every step, half a dozen latching on to me at the merest brush with a leaf in the jungle. My socks and underwear were soaked in my own blood where they had dropped off, and there were sores all over my legs where I had pulled or scraped them away, standing mid-current in fast, cold mountain streams. A year later I would never have been so idiotic, but I was new to the country and hungry for adventure.

As I walked the homeward stretch, I was stopped by an abrupt and miraculous view at the top of a wide, wide valley, stretching down and away, gasping into the evening. I stared, speechless, for what could have been half an hour. There are no spectacular views in Britain after that. I love England dearly, but everything is drab and small and flat when you come home. And I thought, it's true: the fields of the earth clap their hands. The mountains shout together. The psalmist was not absurdly fanciful.

Things unimaginable here are possible over there. It wasn't so much that Sara's hurt was healed, as that it was simply forgotten, left behind in the England we adored but didn't miss at all.

So when David submitted to the rapid effects of the disease, with nothing he or anyone else could prescribe for himself, and then sank into his final, peaceful sleep, we did cope with our loss better out there than we would have done under the oppressive small sky of Europe. When we talked about it that night with Sara, when Charles arrived and all four of us tried to face the last enemy united, I really thought I might one day be able to bear it; that we honestly could bring ourselves to go on, if only we could stay out in the open under the heady vastness of the soaring Asian heavens, just out of earshot of the shouts of the bazaar.

It wasn't that we missed him less. If anything, we probably missed him more, surrounded by all that beauty that he loved so much, than in the cold confines of an English home. Perhaps it was that somehow, in the weeks afterwards, as I walked alone in the foothills among the gnarled and twisted, ancient banyan trees, I almost felt that they, the trees themselves, had seen it all before; as if the all pervading animism of thousands of years had informed the very air; as if the wide and stretching mountains could draw our loss towards them in their great absorbing embrace, knowing better than I did that if I forgot it I would forget my very self. Which of course is what they wanted, what the religion of those powerful mountains was telling me to do.

I even wondered if I was beginning to understand, at last, after four and a half years in the country, the strange and magical beliefs which our small, smiling neighbours mixed like potent drinks. I've always prided myself on a rigorous intellectual training, an objectivity, an abhorrence of hocus pocus and vagueness particularly over matters of the soul. But suddenly I longed for the mists of Buddhism, or the confusion and chaos of animism. It seemed that the wail and whoop of a Hindu funeral dancing down to the Sheti river might have carried my acutely chiselled loneliness along with it and tossed it into the fawn-coloured, foaming white water, along with David's charred corpse.

But of course we didn't burn him, and we didn't throw him into the river. He had a Christian funeral. We gathered around, in our sunny cotton frocks, trying to be as cool as possible in the awful heat, as if that would somehow help. Prue and Maurice wore painfully proper western suits. Many of the local people joined us: David had been very much loved. Various people sang and prayed; Charles and Sara read the readings David had chosen. Charles's was from Revelation, and Sara's from the Song of Songs, for me. The Song of Songs, Solomon's Song, oh David I love you so, just thinking of it. My beloved is like a deer, bounding over the mountains. He was, he was once.

Then Gerald spoke. I have no idea what he said. He committed the dust to the dust, and his ashes to indifferent ashes.

For weeks and months afterwards I wandered through the village at night, or up to the rice terraces by day, longing for some kind of blur, some amnesia, even just a bit of muddle to ease my mind. But Christianity, the gift we had brought with us like a hard little kernel of reality into that vast great land of dreams, is bright and uncompromising. The God of Abraham, Isaac and Jacob, of Paul of Tarsus and Erasmus and Isaac Newton, insists on a ruthless clarity; He won't allow a romantic fog around life, as if it were a sentimental fuzzy-edged wedding photograph. There's comfort in Christianity, of course: the only comfort, in the end, if it is true. But it's the comfort of facts, hard and cruel, not what I wanted at all. David's in a far better place: I believe it. But David's also gone. I was alone. The children needed me. This was the truth, and I didn't want it. Perhaps another religion would have offered me some anaesthetic, some intoxication, even some contact with the dead. But our God is Job's God. He scorns all this. He allows pain. Let it hurt, He says unkindly: you'll survive. And so we did.

Prue and Maurice had tried to persuade us to come home there and then, but I couldn't bear it. I needed time to say goodbye to David out there. It didn't make much sense to stay: Charles was boarding in England, and it was nearly time for Sara to start secondary school. I tried to lose myself in my work out there – I loved running that little school. So I don't know when I would have come back if we hadn't received news of Maurice's stroke. I couldn't believe anything more could happen to us. Maurice was younger than my parents, and healthier, and we had had enough misfortune: God knows we didn't need any more.

We packed our few possessions in an afternoon, and climbed into the hospital jeep which would drive us for two or three days to Delhi for the aeroplane back to Heathrow. Kathmandu was closer, of course, but our visas were due for renewal and we thought it would be quicker, in the end, to cross the border than risk getting stuck at the airport.

The children didn't begrudge their father final possession of the land we'd all loved so well. But as the jeep stopped to cool the radiator ten miles from the Indian border, and I turned back to gaze on the bright and extraordinary hillsides we were leaving, I felt a burst of anger and resentment against him. It's all right for you, I thought crossly, singing in glory now. But we'll never see this beautiful country again. In that instant, unbearably, I knew that I'd never be back. I don't go in for premonitions, but I was pretty sure of it, as I still am now. Even more so. And I longed to turn and run, all the way back to Phulbari, ten days' journey on foot. To arrive panting and sit down in the dust next to our little house where we'd all been so happy; our luxurious westernised house with the bare swept floors and the pictureless walls. To arrive to the warm pungent smell of the goat and the buffalo tethered in our tiny garden, to arrive and refuse to leave. I would run all the way, shout every step of the road and shout when there wasn't a road, halloo my pain to the reverberate hills, and make the babbling gossip of the air cry out.

The jeep hooted its horn. Sara, excited despite herself at the thought of England again, called 'Mummy!' I turned and smiled briskly, felt my cheeks cold as I faced the soft breeze, and I climbed into the jeep.

Within a week Prue and I were comforting one another, two widows together.

She told me she would be moving into the Dower House, and Willisham House was mine. Poor David, he loved it so. I never would have been foolish enough to stay if it hadn't been for that.

25

We drifted towards mid May. The days grew longer, the insects multiplied, the flowers became more varied, rabbits grew careless and could often be seen out in the fields in the early evenings.

It was the seventeenth before I heard from her. A postcard, from France.

It was a Saturday. I was due at Diana's for dinner. Diana had called that morning, ostensibly to remind me that I was having dinner with them that evening, but I suspect more to tell me of the police visit half an hour earlier. They had asked her all about her whereabouts on the day of the Fair, what time we'd had tea together, what she did after she left me. She was adamant that she was a 'suspect' – despite the fact that officially there weren't any suspects – and clearly thrilled to bits that she had been questioned. She tried to play down her excitement, and play up a sense of drama, but it was obvious that it was all a game to her. She didn't know Alison well, had scarcely known Peter, and had all the confidence of the British landed classes who have never been the wrong side of the police as far back as family memory goes. I could understand her attitude. I thought of capping her story by telling her they had removed some of my clothing for examination, but managed to restrain myself.

When I had collected her blouse the week before, I learnt that the police had visited the dry-cleaners, too. The proprietor, a Polish immigrant, was far less amused than Diana had been. Mr Willcox (presumably it was Mr Willcox) had wanted to check whether I had really left my blouse when I said I did, just after eight on the Tuesday morning. When she confirmed this, he then wanted to know whether it showed signs of having been washed before I took it in. She told me, most indignantly, that she had put him straight. I tried to imagine the delicate conversation: I couldn't imagine she would tell the police that her client's garment smelt of having been worn on a hot afternoon, and showed signs of grubbiness under the armpits. But she informed me, with all the pride of one who cares for clothes almost with a reverence, that such a beautiful piece of lace and *broderie anglaise* would fall to bits at the very mention of a washing machine.

It was another week before I understood why Willcox had bothered.

The day of Diana's dinner party had been yet another beautiful day. I had to go out to the shops to get something, and I decided to take a stroll to the end of the village. I don't often go for a walk that way: the obvious walk to take from the house is down the lane, past the cottages, towards the Roman road, the way riders usually go.

The midday heat was beginning to wane, the light no longer so harsh that it hurt the eyes. The whitened glare now filtered into a softer, yellow colour.

In the butcher's, at the corner of the lane, Andrew, Geoff's father, was packing up for the weekend. I've always thought his shop almost too picturesque, with its thatched roof, plaster and wattle exterior, and ornate italic writing advertising itself as a 'Traditional Family Butcher'. He was getting rid of the last few items which wouldn't keep till Monday. On his marble counter in the window I could see meat pies, back bacon wrapped in greaseproof paper, and home-made pork-and-apple sausages, all labelled at their Saturday afternoon bargain prices. There was even porterhouse steak for £5.10 a pound instead of £8.50: Andrew still, resolutely and for all I know illegally, refuses to advertise anything in kilos. I wondered who would buy it. Perhaps Diana would have done, if she hadn't been having a dinner party. It wasn't the sort of thing Alison or her family would enjoy, and it would be far too expensive for the vicarage. Presumably our London commuters, the Warrens in the Old Vicarage, or the Hunter Smiths at Brick House, usually bought steak at full price instead of waiting for Saturday afternoon bargains. I suppose I might have bought it, if I hadn't been going to Diana's.

I smiled at Andrew and Geoff, and they waved back. I could see Margaret in the shop, going for one of the bargains. I hurried on before she could see me and catch me to ask my advice again.

Further down the road, the baker had run out of almost everything. All that was left on his shelves were two characterless see-through bags of flabby-looking white sliced, some unwanted jam tarts, and half a tray of anonymous turnovers. As usual he was preparing to shut up shop early, hoping to get home for his Saturday tea soon after five o'clock.

When the children were small his predecessor used to deliver the bread to the house. The granary bread in those days was unbearably delicious, and he only had it on Tuesdays, Thursdays and Saturdays. It was the same baker that supplied Fitzbillies, but somehow it tasted even better in Willisham. We used to love visiting the house on those days of the week. We would sit around the kitchen at teatime, waiting for the baker's boy to come and knock on the back door, then as soon as he'd gone Sara and Charles would pounce on the loaves, which were always still warm. We'd sit at the old pine table, round the big brown teapot, while the butter dripped over the nutty, squidgey bread and onto our fingers. It was too fresh to cut; it broke off in chunks. When David was with us we often got through a whole loaf within minutes of the boy coming. Prue said it was a disgusting sight. She didn't believe in eating in the kitchen anyway, having never been brought up to it. But David told her she was missing a treat, so when she had grandchildren she broke the habit of generations.

Over the road from the baker, the old greengrocer was displaying everything from eggs and Cheddar to fresh coriander and kumquats. The health food shop next to it was selling exactly the same, but unpreserved, muddy, and twice the price.

People were still popping into shops, buying this and that at the last minute for Sunday lunch.

A middle-aged jogger passed me, panting and sweating his desire to be young again into the afternoon air. A short distance away, down a street off the main road, a pneumatic drill was shattering the peace of the lengthening afternoon. A panda car passed, entering the village, obviously not hurrying, the young

PC in the passenger seat chatting amiably to his colleague. I didn't recognise either of them.

I was near the open countryside. Everything was covered with a light film of growth, misty with the fresh young green characteristic of the still early summer. Gorse bushes spiked the landscape with a harsh mustard yellow and dark green. The birds were changing their tune to one more appropriate to dusk. Back in the village, kettles were being put on, children called in for tea. Everywhere, under the cheerful smile of the May sunshine, the dirty white of the hawthorn frothed and bubbled on the hedges, flecking the hedgerows like a Constable painting.

And there at last were the fields. One an undulating stretch of red brown earth spattered with white, like tiny stones carelessly sown on the ground. Another yellow brown, with a faint unshaven growth of early corn, nestling, suggestive and green, in the furrows. Then, sudden and loud, the bright, unashamed glare of rape.

I must go home, I thought, and have my bath.

And there, waiting for me, was a cheery blue-and-brown postcard of the flat Breton scenery. The first post had been and gone long before I had left the house. It must have come in an odd second post. She said she was having a lovely time, and would bring us back some cheese. I suppose, if you don't know Prue, that doesn't sound particularly strange. I almost expected her to sign off, 'Wish you were here.' I had the odd impression she was expecting someone to be reading the card over my shoulder.

Well, if that's what she had in mind, I thought, I'd better respect it.

I pinned it up on the kitchen notice board as if that was what we did with all our postcards.

Then I ran my bath.

26 ∫

I was due at Diana's at eight. She had invited an eligible don
from St Catherine's for my benefit. You know: rich, intelligent,
divorced. That sort of thing. She means well, but I wish she
wouldn't. No, that's not true. I don't wish she wouldn't at all:
I don't care one way or the other. I'm just not interested, that's
all. Diana thinks it's some sort of religious prudery. Not a bit of
it. But I was adored once, too.

He was a crashing bore and thought the world of himself, and
suddenly over the cheese he turned to me and said in a very loud
voice, 'What's all this about this local lad you've bumped orf?'

I couldn't think what he meant for a moment. Then I found
myself, stupidly, going rather prickly at the back of my neck.

'Courtney, what on earth are you talking about?' Diana
demanded.

Courtney said, 'You know, it's been in all the papers. Made to
look like suicide. Not at all. Suspicious circumstances, all that.'

'Don't be an ass,' Diana replied.

'What papers?' Gareth demanded. 'Hasn't been in *The Times*.'

'No, well, I don't mean those kind of papers. But I'm sure
it was in the *Cambridge Evening News*. Or one of those freebies
you clear up the cat sick with. And of course, I'm reading
between the lines. But then that's what historians do.' He
laughed unpleasantly.

So of course we then had to go on and hazard who had done
it. There was an improbable guest there called Leone, with big
hair and most unconvincing teeth. She claimed to be 'something
in rags', and was wearing most of them to prove it. I assumed
rather unkindly that by 'something' she meant nothing. I would

never have expected to find her at Diana's dinner table. Her husband seemed to be a barrister and was quite good looking in an iron-grey way. He was presumably the attraction. They had 'come up from town'.

Leone said it must have been the bloke's mother. Believe it or not, it was the most interesting thing she said all night. I thought of pointing out that his mother was elsewhere at the time, but it really didn't seem worth it as nobody listened to anything Leone said, least of all the good-looking barrister.

So then Mr Leone said perhaps it was a member of a gang. This opinion held sway for a while. Within five minutes we knew what the murderer looked like and where he came from. Soon we had a fair opinion about his relationship to Peter, what had driven his sister onto the streets, and why he no longer lived with his brothers in Sicily. The only things we didn't have were motive and method.

Gareth said, 'Has anyone been to one of these dinner parties where you all dress up as murder victims? Or suspects. Or smart members of a houseparty or a boat or something. My children had a craze for it. It didn't seem to catch on at High Table.'

Before anyone had time to answer this, Courtney said, 'It's obviously a member of the village.'

'It can't be that obvious,' Diana said, 'or the police would have made an arrest.'

'Nonsense. Lack of evidence. Don't want to risk a verdict of "not guilty".' So saying, he leered at me as if he had imparted an incredibly important piece of information which I couldn't possibly have known.

'All right,' somebody said. 'Why someone in the village?'

'Obvious,' he said again, and leant so close towards me that I could have spat grape pips down his collar one by one. Pity Diana had provided seedless. 'Inside information. You know. Known to the victim. Rings the doorbell. Victim lets him in . . .'

'And conveniently sits down and opens his mouth for the guy to put a side-by-side twelve-bore in,' someone else objected.

'Funnily enough,' Gareth said to Diana, 'didn't Reg ring up from somewhere . . .'

'No,' Diana said quickly and very firmly down the table to him.

'Oh, sorry,' Gareth said quietly. Then I saw him mouth the word, 'Forgot.' Diana looked like a headmistress who'd just sucked a lemon.

'All right,' said Courtney. 'I'll tell you how it happened. Someone who knows him. Or rather, someone he knows, and knows quite well. Someone he rather likes: no sign of any struggle, no protest at all. Presumably a girl, probably attractive. Unless he's gay, of course. But if so, the press would have got hold of it: too good a story not to be picked up. Beginning to sound like a pretty girl who was brought up in the village. How old are your daughers, Gareth?'

'Ha ha,' replied Gareth. 'They're too lazy and stupid to have pulled it off.'

'You can't blame them for that,' Diana objected. 'They're only following the paternal example.'

'Now, why would she do it?' Courtney went on, ignoring the interruptions. 'Probably sex: jealousy, or anger, or insecurity. That means it shouldn't be hard to find her. Look into the victim's past, she'd be found in five minutes. Might have to look some way back, of course. But the evidence is bound to be there somewhere. *However* . . .' At this point he made a dramatic pause. 'Perhaps she was right. Women don't often kill. They usually have a very good reason. No doubt she did. There was some reason why she couldn't go to the police. Perhaps she was ashamed. Perhaps he'd humiliated her. Or blackmail? Perhaps she's engaged to somebody rich and famous. So, should we keep quiet and let her get away with it? Don't forget, she's young and beautiful. He's dead anyway, so nothing can help him now. I'll think you'll find, members of the jury, that a verdict of "not guilty" would be both compassionate and convenient.'

Leone shrieked with delight. Gareth clapped slowly. 'Very good, old man. Have some more plonk. Not bad this one.'

'Well?' Courtney turned to me.

'Well, what?'

'What do you think?' he persisted.

'I think you should write short stories,' I said, and meant it. Extraordinarily, he had a gift of which he was unaware: he was perceptive, in a crude kind of way. 'And I think it's not a game. Or a joke, or a television programme.' I was speaking quietly, but my hands under the table were trembling violently, and my face felt as if it had gone rather red. 'It's a mother who's lost her child, a man who's lost the rest of his life. I'm sorry.' I stopped. 'Diana, I'm sorry. It's just we've known them a long time.'

'You're right. Harriet. You're absolutely right.'

'My dear girl,' said Courtney, patting my arm, as if I were nineteen and he thirty, 'you really mustn't get upset.'

I turned away from him, not trusting myself to say anything, and helped myself to more Perrier while Courtney had yet another glass of Gareth's college plonk, which, I could smell from where I was sitting, was very good claret. Gareth turned to the guest on the other side of me, and smoothly changed the subject.

'Well, Paul, you poor old thing, how are you looking forward to being the bride's father?'

'Don't let your girls do it, Gareth,' Paul laughed. 'I've had to double my private patients in order to pay for it. Let them live in sin.'

'I don't care what they live in,' Gareth replied. 'Your Selina was here in Willisham the other week, wasn't she? I'm sure I saw her at that ghastly Fair that we all have to go to.'

'Yes, she came home for twenty-four hours to make one or two arrangements. She was hoping to see the vicar, to ask if she can have a harp playing in the church while they sign up, and photographs in the churchyard, and that sort of thing. She's got some chum who plays Mozart in Harrods, you know. I think she thought it would look a bit classier than a second-rate organist or a trendy boogey-band. Mary's helping her to sort most of it out, aren't you darling? But the vicar did better than you, Gareth. He gave the whole fête a miss.'

'He can't have done,' Diana objected. 'He introduced Harriet at the beginning and was helping with the barbecue at the end.'

'And scooted off in the middle,' Paul said. 'We saw him creep off, actually, and assumed he was coming back. But Selina had to leave before four to get back to town by the evening, so she didn't see him to talk to. Don't blame him. Quite clever for the vicar to skip the church fête. Wish I could do that with half my hospital functions. Probably scraping up a sermon for the morrow.'

'Saturday is Hugh's only day off,' I said defensively, 'and he doesn't "scrape up" sermons at the last minute.' I don't know why I was doing it: he doesn't need me to stand up for him, and I had already been too embarrassingly earnest once that evening. But I went on, 'It's the day he spends with his family. And the Fair has no official connection with the church, so it's good of him to come at all. I'm sure he'll fit in with whatever Selina wants. It'll be lovely, Mary. Hugh does that kind of thing very well.' I rose. 'Diana, will you excuse me? I need to be up early in the morning. Please don't let me break anything up.'

Courtney made a half-hearted offer to walk me home and I replied with a whole-hearted refusal. I thought on balance I'd rather be mugged by anything Willisham had to offer than walked home by Courtney. Strange how one can be so careful for someone else and so careless for oneself. Charles is the same. Whenever he's home he finds some excuse to accompany her. Always.

When I got home from Diana's dinner party I didn't go into the house straight away, but went out into the garden and sat on the bench at the edge of the shrubbery listening to all the sounds of the night air. Soon there would be frogs and toads all over the lawn, but much smaller and quieter than they were out in Phulbari. It used to distress me when we first arrived. I used to think we wouldn't be able to step out of the house during the monsoon without killing frogs at every step. I imagined David being called out to attend to some illness, and having to tread on dozens of frogs as he walked to his patient's bedside. After all, you could hardly let a fellow human die, because you didn't want to hurt a frog. We aren't Buddhists. We don't believe in preserving every living thing, always, regardless of right or wrong. Doing the right thing is sometimes a messy and unpleasant business.

Though in fact, as I learnt very quickly, they almost never did. Get killed, I mean. It sounded as though the ground was thick with them, a living carpet of croaking amphibians, but I only once stepped on a frog all the time I was out there.

I leant back in my bench and regarded the night-time sky. The light from over Cambridge glowed yellow against the blue-black horizon. Despite the garish light pollution from the city, the stars multiplied even as I looked at them.

Where is Peter's soul now, I thought; thrown with such violence out through the back of his head. I could see Alison's bedside light still shining from the cottage window which had been old Nanny's retirement cottage before Alison had it. Does she muse, all the time, on what has become of him? Does she dream of the time when she might see him again? I wondered if she blamed herself. Perhaps she'd be right to. I stared through the mist towards her window. After all, he was only dead because he was the kind of boy he was.

And then I went on to consider whether the police were any nearer finding their solution. Whether they had ruled out Peter's own suicide. And if that were the case, whether they had their prime suspect now. If they were to make an arrest, the village would have a field day of news and chatter. And if it were the arrest I sometimes feared and half anticipated, Willisham would have plenty of gossip for a long time to come.

At last, meditating on these and other excitements, I pulled myself up from my bench and went somewhat wearily up to bed. Her bedroom light twinkled through the drops of moisture in the night air, and then went out. She would probably sleep better than I, after all.

When I got inside, there was a message on my answerphone. I contemplated leaving it till the morning, but then pressed the 'Play' button anyway. I was too tired to deal with it, but I could find out whom it was from.

It was Colin. He didn't give his name, but I recognised his voice.

'Harriet. Promised to tell you about Sophie's research. Funny thing. No blasted adrenaline in the body at all. Not a trace. Jolly annoying for her paper. Suppose she didn't get the sample frozen quickly enough. Either that, or she's barking up the wrong tree.'

Then, as an afterthought, he added, 'Or your friend was done in, of course.'

27

It was Friday the twenty-third when Mr Willcox came to visit me again. It was late in the afternoon. The shadows slanted across the lawn. It was still very hot. Hugh and I were sitting in the garden having tea, and we had moved to be in the shade. This is the more extraordinary as Hugh is a man with one physical vanity and one only: his suntan. He says he likes people to think he can afford holidays abroad. Goodness knows why. His family has never been further abroad than Devon since he's been ordained. I tell him that the smart people, those who own villas in Tuscany, wear a sunblock all day and sit under a wide-brimmed hat. He doesn't listen. He ignores the dermatologists. He takes no notice of the more compelling argument that the loudest herald of middle age is wearing the fashions of one's youth. He's got it into his head that a suntan makes him look fit, so he fries himself religiously on an annual basis.

Anyway, this is somewhat beside the point. I mention it simply to illustrate what a very hot day it was. Even Hugh was so uncomfortable by five o'clock that Friday afternoon that he agreed to sit in the shade.

He had come, ostensibly, to ask my advice about a difficult meeting he would be having the following week over the church building. I told him I thought most English churches ought to be given to the National Trust or English Heritage: then the Church could get on with her real work, instead of patching up roofs for tourists.

'It costs millions of pounds every year to keep Westminster Abbey alive,' I bleated. 'Millions. And who has to find the millions? The tourist board? Not a bit of it. The Abbey itself. Think of what that money could do in terms of missionary work. And we spend it on a piece of architectural history. It's a disgrace. Give it away, Hugh. After all, they've given away your gorgeous Georgian house, which would have given you so much pleasure and been a darn sight more use than that horrid little red box of a vicarage you're stuck in now. So why should you look after their beastly church building? Give it away; it only gives you headaches. Then we can meet somewhere sensible.'

'Like where?'

I looked around. 'Here? In the garden.'

'Fine. Now can I have some serious advice, please, Harriet?'

'Never been more serious in my life.'

'This is Willisham, Harriet. Not Phulbari or even Cambridge University Faculty of Social and Ecological Correctness, if there is such an institution, which I sincerely hope not. People still like a little bit of tradition.'

'They don't need to come to church for it. They can go to that ghastly Tudor pub for some tradition, then come on to church for the real thing.'

'But tradition may be the reason some people come. And then they hear the real thing when they get there.'

'Or don't hear it. Because they adopt traditional patterns of not listening in church.'

'Look, I agree with you. I don't want to be caretaker to an inefficient and expensive building, however beautiful it is. And ours isn't, 'specially. I don't think it's the work of the real Church either. But we have inherited a small corner of history, and it's not that easy to shed it. Come on Harriet, you've done it yourself. You were given David's inheritance, and found you couldn't give it away. You said you ought never to come back, and you did. You said the memories were far too painful for her in Willisham, but here you are. If you weren't in possession of one of the loveliest houses in England you'd be miles away by now, perhaps even back in Phulbari. But you couldn't turn your back on a place that was full of David's childhood, and hers. And her grandfather's, and great-grandfather's. And Charles's. Well, the church is full of memories too. We're not the first disciples, and we're not the first generation of missionaries out in Phulbari, meeting in a room. Whether you like it or not the Church of England is part of the same history that provided your beautiful lawns. Good grief, Harriet, I know we don't need to have the buildings in order to preach the Gospel. And you don't need an elegant country house in order to raise your children. Perhaps it is a distraction. No doubt we could do the job much better without it. But you couldn't ignore your heritage, and I don't think I can either. So tell me what I should say to the PCC about my refusal to fund-raise.'

I had no answer. It was all true. Were Hugh and I both wrong to be enslaved to the bricks and mortar? Why had we left the country we had all loved, and come back thousands of miles just for a house? Did it have a spirit of its own, like Howard's End? Was the memory of David which haunted the house and garden, reminding me of him as a prep-school boy in shorts and a sports jacket and knee socks, not a benign spirit at all but a malign ghost trying to wreck our lives? Or am I simply *nouvelle* upper class, caring more about my recently acquired estate – worse than the fool in *A Handful of Dust* who at least had possessed it for generations – than about the family I claim to love?

I clung to Hugh's direct question instead. 'I don't know. Stick to your guns. I couldn't bear a huge placard, with a giant red thermometer on it, stuck outside the porch saying only another half million to go.' I looked across the lawn at the sparrows dipping into the old bird bath, the bird bath which had been there since it was taller than David. 'It was her decision, you know. To come back. I suggested we didn't, but she loves it too.' It was at that moment that I knew I must tell him. As much because he was my vicar as my oldest friend.

'Oh Harriet, I know that. Goodness, I wasn't accusing you.'

'But you're right. I shouldn't have given the children a choice. It wasn't fair on them. We should have moved. We didn't need to come back.'

'It was a reasonable decision.'

I shook my head. 'Hugh,' I began, and looked up to see that we had been joined by the detective sergeant. He must have appeared silently round the side of the house, and was half apologetic, surprised to find us there.

'I'm sorry to let myself in . . .'

'Not at all, Mr Willcox. You were right to.' I got up to welcome him.

'I rang the bell several times, but there was no reply.'

'Quite right. Just walk in. It's what everybody else does. We can't hear the doorbell from the garden. I've sometimes wondered whether to have the telephone changed so I won't be able to hear that either.' I was speaking fast, with more jollity than I felt. He didn't smile. 'You can help us solve a little ecclesiastical problem,' I continued, pouring him a cup of tea without asking. 'Should we sell up, leasehold, freehold, or hang on to an architectural millstone, having Fairs every summer till the company of the faithful drops dead under the weight of its own home-made cakes?'

He looked at me quizzically, and thanked me for the tea.

'You see,' I continued relentlessly, 'in about fourteen seventy some rich, anonymous wool merchant put up a church building, we suspect more as a witness to his profit margin than to his Lord and Saviour. Medieval corporate hospitality, I suppose. It's not a beautiful building, but it is big and old, and Hugh is legally responsible for it. Unfortunately.'

'Well,' Mr Willcox said politely, 'I'm not much of a believer myself. At least, not what you'd call practising. My children are at a church school.'

'It's a nice comfortable road,' I said quietly, passing him the milk, 'with plenty of other people on it.'

'Harriet, I think perhaps the sergeant takes sugar.' There we were, Hugh and I, back in our school days, when he was my older brother's friend, and I had to look up to him. And he would see me heading for trouble and tactfully steer me back on course.

'No, no,' Mr Willcox said. 'This is fine: no sugar. I just wonder if I could ask you one or two questions? We're rather keen to interview your mother-in-law. We'd be grateful if you could tell us her whereabouts, please. Would that be possible?'

'No,' I said too quickly. 'No, I'm so sorry, it wouldn't.'

'Why?'

'I don't know where she is. I haven't seen her for, oh, two or three weeks. She's on holiday. She's very independent. She doesn't live with us, you know.'

'I gather she was expected to help at the Fair?'

I could have denied it, of course. I didn't know who or what his source was, but I would presumably be expected to know more about Prue's movements than anyone else: if I said she hadn't been expected at all perhaps he would believe me. But the trouble was I really didn't know why she hadn't been home or where she was. It was odd. More than odd. To those of us who knew Prue, it was extraordinary. Something was wrong, but because I didn't know what, I didn't know how to cover it up.

28

Besides, I'm lousy at lying, can't remember when I last did it, and never get away with it anyway. I doubt if I could lie to save my life. And why should I? I honestly didn't know where Prue was. I had no reason to suppose she needed me to lie. Mr Willcox wasn't to know that she wouldn't dream of going away without telling her family where she is, that it was completely out of character for her not to keep in touch, that not a day has gone by since we got back from Nepal when we haven't spoken to each other. Until the fourth of May, that is.

'I don't know,' I said truthfully. 'I don't know where she is.' Then I remembered the postcard still pinned to the kitchen board. 'She was in France, I do know that much,' I added, and offered to get the card.

It was cool when I went back inside the house, and my eyes had to adjust to the light. As I pulled the drawing pin out of the cork of the kitchen board I tried to remember the feeling which had made me keep it. Because the picture was beautiful. Summer and wildflowers on a hillside and a family picnic. Prue would know that I'd love it. And because something about it was so strange. What had she been trying to tell me? Had she calculated on the police asking where she was?

I went back into the garden, handed it to Mr Willcox and said I didn't need it back. Then I changed my mind. 'On second thoughts, when you've finished with it, I think perhaps I will keep it after all.'

'Of course. Is she alone, do you know?'

Again I was caught off-balance. 'I'm sorry. I can't tell you any more than you'll find on the postcard. I could go to the

Dower House and look through her things, if you really think it's necessary. I have keys to her house. But I'd much rather not.'

Willcox nodded.

I said, 'Perhaps you could tell me why you want to know?'

He chose to ignore the question. Hugh was staring out over the lawn as if he were taking no notice at all. Willcox referred to his notes. 'Does the name Reg Butler mean anything to you?'

'Yes,' I said slowly. 'Yes, it does.' After hearing the message on Prue's answerphone that morning of the May bank holiday I had racked my brains and remembered a jolly man in his late fifties or early sixties, his face like a wrinkly apple, the broken veins, the cheerful laughter. I had met him at the Dower House the previous winter, when he had been there for supper. He was a widower, with grown-up children, slightly younger than Prue herself. A romance? Surely not. But then, why not? They were both free and single.

I had also remembered something else about Reg, which I was not going to tell Mr Willcox. Perhaps I should have done. The information would be available to him anyway, and it might have been a good bit of counter-bluff to offer it. But on the other hand it might be suspicious that the thought had even crossed my mind.

'Is she with Reg?' I asked.

'Had that thought occurred to you?'

'I simply wondered why you mentioned him.'

Hugh turned to look at us. Suddenly, my mind went back more than twenty years, and I recalled a fallen tree trunk in a clearing in a wood, birds singing, sunlight filtering through the trees. How old was I then? Seventeen? My brother and I had been on a weekend houseparty together once, in Hampshire. I went for a walk before breakfast on the Sunday morning, and came across Hugh sitting astride a tree stump with a tatty black leather-bound zip-up Bible open in front of him on the soggy bark. The kind of Bible which those keen, muscular young Christians tended to have. It gave the impression it was a book which was read, regularly, rather than kept on a shelf with the complete works of William Shakespeare.

I sat beside him, and he read me the psalm he was reading, and David's anger and bitterness and deep faith seemed to fill the wood. That was the first time I realised the Bible wasn't simply poetry, a requirement of an Oxford English degree, a fine example of seventeenth-century prose: that Hugh expected the voice of a long dead tribal chieftain to change his life.

Did I say David? Am I getting hopelessly confused? No: I do mean David. King David. He had been through it all too – the doubt, the frustration, the fury at an omnipotent God.

Hugh is a good vicar. The weight of pastoral cares and parish duties and the compromise of everyday life have all blunted his edge a little, but he's still a good vicar.

'Sergeant,' he said. 'Lady St Joseph is quite an independent woman. She's very fit for a woman of her age, comfortably off, energetic, and free of responsibilities for the first time for nearly half a century. She's also mildly eccentric. If she's decided on a spontaneous holiday with a friend who also finds himself in a similar position, it's not particularly surprising.'

'Quite,' Mr Willcox replied. 'I just wondered whether Mrs St Joseph was at all surprised at her mother-in-law's disappearance?'

I considered.

'Yes,' I said. 'I was. She was going to help on one of the stalls at the Fair, and she's normally very reliable.' Then I simply shrugged. 'There we are.'

'And would you be surprised to hear that she had been spotted at Miss Midland's house during the afternoon of the Fair?'

'Surprised? I'd be astonished. What on earth would she be doing there? She'd known Alison would be out. Someone must have made that up. Or rather, made a mistake. They must have seen someone who looked like her.'

'It was Mr Bridges who thought he'd seen her. Miss Midland's neighbour. Would he make a mistake, d'you think?'

'No,' I said reluctantly. 'No he wouldn't. He knows Prue well, and he's very reliable. I still find it odd, though. Is he sure?'

'Funnily enough, he did say, when we questioned him again, that he might have imagined it. He had seemed sure, the first time.' The sergeant put down his empty cup on the tea tray, and I thought he was about to stand up. As soon as he's gone I will talk to Hugh about all of this, I determined. Then he seemed to change his mind. This time he didn't refer to his notebook. 'I wonder,' he said, looking straight at me, 'if you want to tell me anything about your daughter and the deceased.' I looked down at my cup and watched it swimming on my lap. Slowly I lifted it to my lips and took a sip. It was nearly cold. I put the cup back in the saucer, and then felt the teapot. It, too, was luke warm.

'Would you like more tea?'

'No, thank you,' he replied, waiting expectantly.

'Hugh?'

He hesitated a moment, as if wondering whether I needed the excuse to get up and go inside for reinforcements, but he shook his head anyway. 'But thanks all the same.'

I looked out over the lawn, over the garden where the three children had played cowboys and indians, or Thunderbirds, or, Peter's preference, ravaging Vikings. 'Peter Midland,' I said, 'used to play here. We've known his mother for many years. He and my children were friends, of sorts. Alison worked for my parents-in-law, here in Willisham, when they still lived in this house. On Saturdays she came into Cambridge and cleaned for us. My mother-in-law paid for her to come, as a Christmas present to us one year, and somehow it never ran out. Naturally, when Peter was small Alison brought him too, so he could play with our children while she worked. Later, my father-in-law did a great deal to try to help him. Got him a place at Christ's Hospital, encouraged him to do well. My husband's family were rather . . . Well, I suppose you'd call them old fashioned. They believed in what you might call aristocratic patronage. They also thought Peter was at a great disadvantage in life, having no father.' I stopped. I had said enough, surely. I made myself breathe deeply.

'What happened to his father?'

'I've no idea. Presumably Alison could tell you. If she wants to.'

'And was there any more recent connection between Mr Midland and your daughter?'

'What do you mean?'

'He lived near by. They were childhood friends. One would have expected them to see each other.'

'We went abroad for five years. I'm talking about when she was six years old. They wouldn't have anything in common any more.'

'So, you were not under the impression that he was trying to see her.' I said nothing for a moment, and he continued, 'Had they met up, in the last few months, say?'

'No.'

'Not at all?'

'As far as I know my daughter hasn't spoken to him since she was seven. Until recently we didn't even know he was living in Cambridge.'

'And could we check that with her?'

'I'd much rather you didn't.'

He looked at me sharply. 'Why?'

'Sergeant,' Hugh cut in, 'forgive me interrupting, but I have a vested interest. Sara is my goddaughter. She's not had an easy few years. She moved to a very different culture. Then her father died, which is enough to knock any child sideways. Then her grandfather. Now a childhood friend does away with himself in an extremely gruesome manner in the nextdoor house. Obviously a death like this is unpleasant to anyone who knew Peter, even if the acquaintance was slight. Sara once knew him well. And it is the exam term. Give the poor child a break. Please.'

The garden door banged. Sara's bicycle clattered into the path. She dropped her bag on the gravel. 'Hello,' I called over the lawn to her. She glanced our way. 'Cake here, if you want.' She barely nodded, and went into the house.

I turned back to Mr Willcox. He proceeded in a quieter tone. 'We found amongst the deceased's possessions a number of things relating to your daughter,' he said, slightly awkwardly. 'Do you have any explanation as to why he would have had them?'

'Such as?'

'Photographs of this house.'

'That's not surprising,' I said, relieved. 'It's an historic house, and he virtually lived in the grounds.'

'A picture of your daughter as a little girl.'

'How did you know it was her?'

'Identified by Miss Midland. A clip from the local paper about her winning a scholarship to her present school. And so on.'

I was very conscious of the heat, even though the sun was

now quite low. My clothes felt sticky, and my hand shook as I reached out to tidy the tea tray. I changed my mind, and left things as they were.

'Mr Willcox,' I said, wondering whether I sounded rather like Margaret. 'I'm sure you found nothing there to indicate she was in contact with him.'

He nodded. 'That's true,' he conceded. 'He could have been harbouring a fantasy. Do you think that's likely, after all this time?'

'I'm not a psychologist.' I paused for a moment, weighing up the pros and cons of saying more. 'However, I do know my daughter would be very distressed if you asked her about it.'

'Why?'

That question I did not answer.

'Did you find anything else of interest?' Hugh asked, as if we were discussing the cricket score.

'Yes. Yes we did.'

'Oh?' The sergeant said nothing. 'What?' I don't know whether it was because of his professional position, or simply due to his great charm and impeccable manners, but Hugh made it sound very inoffensive, as if he had a right to know.

Mr Willcox shrugged. 'Oh, this and that. Clothing. Videos. A diary. And a baby bird, dead in a box. We think he was trying to care for it.'

I heard Hugh ask him, 'What exactly is it you want?'

'Ah. What do we want? Some reason for his action perhaps? Why he would have wanted to take his own life. Some instability in his nature?'

'I can help there,' I admitted, finally. 'Anyone who knew Peter as a child can tell you he was never stable. He could never have been described as a peaceful or an easy boy. Though, to be honest, I think it was mostly because he was unhappy. Unhappy, and very insecure.'

'Enough to kill himself?'

'As I said, I'm not a psychologist.'

'But what do you think?'

'What do I think? Do I have to tell you what I think?'

'It would be a help.'

'Then, I don't think so, no. But I really don't know.'

*   *   *

He went before Sara reappeared for tea and a swim. I was glad. I walked with him to the gate at the side of the garden, and watched him get in his car.

Now that I had placed him, I knew exactly who Reg Butler was. I was sure Willcox did as well. The evening he was at Prue's was the night parliament had passed the new handgun bill. Reg, who had voted Conservative for decades, was incandescent with rage.

'I've been a law-abiding man all my life,' he had said, quietly but very angrily. Thinking back, I realised I had liked him rather a lot. It was none of my business, but I thought, if Prue and Reg are striking up a long-term friendship, I wouldn't find it hard to come to terms with him. 'It's a bloody disgrace, this lousy law. It won't save a single life. It's a sentimental sop to a bereaved town, because they can't catch the man who did it. I understand it perfectly. They're angry with Thomas Hamilton, but he's not there, so they don't know what to do with their rage. Perfectly normal response. We all want revenge. Nothing wrong with that. Bunging him in prison would have made us all feel better. But they can't do that, so they're taking it out on the rest of us.'

I remembered the conversation as I watched Willcox turn on his engine. And now I wanted to tell Hugh. I suddenly wanted to tell him very badly. I hate secrets, and not being able to talk to Sara about what had happened to Peter was making me wretched. Willcox's tasteful dark blue Sierra swept down the drive. I would have to find a time to talk to Hugh when he was alone, when Sara was at school.

After all I didn't want her to know that her grandmother had disappeared, the day Peter was shot, with a friend who was the secretary of his local handgun association and could have got her a gun at the drop of a hat, if she had wanted such a thing.

29

There was a time when I thought I loved Willisham House so much it hurt. That very first time David showed me around, before we were even engaged, I felt as if I'd fallen in love twice. I could understand Lizzy Bennet, seeing Pemberley glimpsed through the trees of its enormous park, realising the attractions of its surly master for the first time.

Willisham is less grand, but far more friendly than I imagine Pemberley to have been, with its sixteenth-century weathered stone and sunny corners, and hidden paths in the garden. I keep a postcard of the south side of the house on my desk as I write, and it seems to smile at me.

We often dreamt of our return to Willisham when we were in Phulbari – though we were never homesick. We talked of the pony Sara would have, and the tennis we'd play again, and what it would be like having Maurice and Prue round the corner in the Dower House, which they had generously offered to move into whenever we decided it was right to come back. We thought of tea on the lawn again, and messing about on the river, and the village events, and the bakery we all remembered, and having Hugh five minutes away in the vicarage.

And in the end what was it? The reunion of two widows who had both lost what they most treasured. And a sordid tragedy spilling out into the front room of one of the cottages on the estate, on a sunny Saturday afternoon which was supposed to herald the beginning of summer.

None of it made sense. As I stared at the back of Willcox's car and watched him drive away, I tried to work out the pieces which didn't fit. Peter was killed by a twelve-bore shotgun. One of ours. Taken from Willisham House just before he died. How did Reg come into the picture?

I stood for a long time gazing at the drive after Willcox had gone. The dust from his wheels settled. Children called from the lane. I wondered whether they were coming to my house for a swim. I leant against the low brick wall which holds my garden gate, and closed my eyes. I asked myself, irrelevantly, how my father came to get ulcers. Nick Cowden, my GP, would surely give me something to settle my stomach. But I didn't want to ask him.

It was nothing to do with me. I told myself that whatever Prue got up to was none of my business. But I knew it was. Her disappearance was connected with Peter's death, though I couldn't for the life of me see what the connection was.

I could, presumably, try to get hold of Reg Butler. On the other hand, if the police couldn't trace him what chance did I have? I shivered slightly, and tried to pull myself together. Reg was one of the most respectable people imaginable. Church warden, QC, all that sort of thing. But then, I reminded myself rather bitterly, so was Prue: magistrate, lady of the manor. Come to that, so am I.

I threw back my head and stared at the aggressively blue sky. Prue would turn up again. She was bound to.

After Willcox had gone I walked back across the lawn to where Sara and Hugh sat chatting. I was conscious of a burden on my shoulders, the failure, the fact that I had let her down at some level which was so profound I couldn't even understand it, and she was unaware of it.

'Ma, tell Hugh he's got to go for a swim.'

'Hugh?'

'Yup?'

'You've got to go for a swim.'

'Fair enough,' Hugh said, and sat there doing nothing. Sara had changed into a swimsuit and covered herself up, despite the heat, with a long towelling dressing gown which she pulled tightly around herself.

'Why are you being so boring?' she complained.

'Because I'm a fat, dull, balding clergyman sinking rapidly into middle age.'

She picked some grass and threw it over him. Then she turned to me. 'What did the policeman want?'

'Oh,' I replied, slightly flummoxed. I looked at Hugh guiltily, then averted my eyes. 'I think he wanted Granny.'

'Why?'

'Routine investigations,' Hugh stepped in quickly.

'Where is she?' Sara asked, looking straight at me.

'I don't know.'

For a while all three of us sat in silence, edging round a topic which none of us knew how to broach. Sara knows Hugh knows. She came to terms with it. But there are others – her headmistress, the school nurse and doctor, and our GP – who have been told without her knowledge or permission. I hate having secrets from my own daughter. I despise myself for breaking her confidence. And I never thought I'd do it. I considered it long and hard, and wished, oh how I wished, David were here for me to ask. Perhaps I shouldn't have told any of them. But I was anxious about her health, the pains she gets which she tries to hide from me, her eating, or rather her lack of it. She lost over a stone last year. I wanted the doctors to know. Perhaps it was just selfish, simply that I wanted to share the responsibility, to know I wasn't the only one keeping an eye on her. There was no point her knowing I had betrayed her.

'Are you worried?' she asked me.

I may have kept things from her. But I have never lied to her. Nor, as it happened, did I ever lie to the police. That's something which David might have done differently. He would never have tried to solve Sara's troubles in the way I had, but I believe he might have lied, through his teeth if necessary. It probably would have been a better way of handling it.

I realised I could have got around the question somehow, in the way that politicians do when cornered by persistent media presenters: 'Prue isn't the kind of person one worries about', or, 'She's very good at taking care of herself'. But I didn't want to deceive Sara; there were barriers enough between us already, goodness knows.

'Yes,' I said. 'I am worried. I suppose she'll be back soon, though.'

She thought for a moment, then got up without saying anything to either of us. We watched her walking across the lawn towards the pool. As she moved she swung, like a model, but unconsciously. I'd never noticed it before. It amazed me.

'She's a lovely girl,' Hugh said. Because I'd been thinking of her figure, I assumed at first that was what he meant. I frowned.

'What d'you mean?'

'Harriet, don't worry so much. She's fine.'

'Yes, Hugh. But if Tricia died, wouldn't you worry about your three?'

I held his eye for a moment across the tea things. I don't often think of the physical aspect of losing David, but at that moment I felt a sudden lurch: I could have married Hugh, twenty years ago, and I would live in that hideous vicarage with Hugh's children not David's, and I would be going to bed with him tonight. For a second or two, as I gazed at him, the thoughts which went through my mind were lurid.

I looked away. I was tired.

'Did you want to talk to me about something, earlier on?' he said. I realised his face was red and glistening, and he didn't look his best.

'Yes. But not now. Not with Sara here.'

30

To some extent the village of Willisham began to absorb Peter's death into its routine. I don't mean that callously. I believe a community can deaden some of the harshness of bereavement by sharing it. Alison didn't have to cope alone. By talking about Peter's death, Willisham made it easier for her to mourn. The loss was still as great, the emptiness as real. But she could spread it about and know it was there as she walked around the village, because others knew it was there too. Part of our problem, those years ago, was enduring a secret pain.

Hugh arranged for the funeral service to be held three weeks after Peter's death. I wondered whether I should offer the house for refreshments afterwards, but Hugh said the church hall would be fine. It wasn't hard for him to read between the lines. As it happened, the weather was still good so we took two of the church-hall tables out into the vicarage garden. A dozen of us in the church had agreed to bring plates of sandwiches and cakes.

I was relieved that the event could take place. I thought it would focus Peter's life, and death, for Alison. In an odd way I wondered whether it would be the first time she'd ever been the centre of attention. After all, she'd never had a wedding day. I also believed it was bound to help her, become the fresh start upon which to build the rest of her life.

I'm not sure that it really worked. Hugh took the service sensitively, and the church was full – presumably for Alison, rather than Peter, as some people there barely knew him – but afterwards Alison herself seemed to fade into the background and watch the occasion as if it had been someone else's party.

And of course she still had the continuing investigations, the inquest, hanging over her.

I found myself on the corner of Hugh's garden having a glass of wine with Graeme, who asked me how Alison was.

'I find it hard to tell,' I replied. 'She's coping brilliantly, but I don't know what that means under the surface. She doesn't seem to have got upset, cried, been angry, anything. I don't know how to read that. Does it mean she's fine, or is that worse than weeping all day? I don't know.'

'Some people react that way. I've seen it before.'

'What I can't bear is the way other people judge it. "You ought to cry." "You ought not to be on your own, in your own home."'

I looked out over Hugh and Tricia's unmown, messy lawn. That was something, at least, which I'd been spared. At least nobody had judged me. 'Presumably it'll be easier for her after the inquest, when she can put it all behind her,' I continued. 'Do we know when that's likely to be?'

'Nothing to do with me, really. It takes a while to gather all the facts, get the paperwork in order. It usually takes two or three months, I think.'

'Why?' I was appalled at the idea of it shadowing the village for the rest of the summer.

'Oh, you know.'

'No. I don't.'

Graeme shrugged. 'Motive, that sort of thing. Harriet, I can't really talk about it.' He picked up the old tennis ball that his son, like a dog, had dropped at his feet. Penny hadn't brought Timmo to the service because she hadn't thought it would be suitable for him, but they had joined us for the refreshments afterwards to give Alison her support.

'But I do think you could have told me what had happened,' Graeme said suddenly. He didn't look at me. For a moment I said nothing, not trusting myself to comment. At last I cleared my throat slightly.

'What do you mean?' I said.

'What you all went through eight years ago.'

I breathed out very slowly. I thought the secret had been kept so well. And now Peter's stupid, wasteful, violent death threatened to destroy everything we had built so carefully, just as it threatened Amanda's privacy too. 'I see. So Willcox knew all along.' I thought of the conversation in my garden, and wondered what clever game he thought he'd been playing with me. 'Why should we have told you, Graeme? We told nobody, except Hugh. He's her godfather. Poor kid. It was hard enough us knowing. She could hardly face her own father. What happened to a victim's anonymity? Why the hell should anyone else know about it?'

'Hey, Harriet, don't be angry with me.'

'Why not? Why shouldn't I be angry with everyone? Why should I have told you? Or anyone? The police have no rights to her privacy, none at all. They did nothing about it then, so why on earth should I bring it up again now? Nobody asked me about it. It was a long time ago, and a little child tried to put a terrible nightmare behind her. But I don't suppose she'll ever be allowed to. She was nothing to do with Peter any more, we were scrupulously careful to avoid him as much as we could, but because of this business, she'll have to go through the whole thing all over again. And then she'll never get over it. I'm sick of it, the whole thing. It's as if Willisham will always be tainted for us. I don't know how you know about it, but if the police know anyway, I don't see why we have to tell them all over again.'

'I'm sorry,' Graeme said very gently. I looked away. I had never had an argument with Graeme before, and perhaps I had said far too much. But even as I thought these things to myself, another part of me wondered whether this outburst was what had been needed.

'All right, I'll tell you how I know. I don't see why you shouldn't be in the picture. Do you remember a policeman called Fred Little?' I shook my head. 'Oldish chap. One of the few in the Cambridge Station who's been there more than five years, hasn't been moved on. He was away for the bank holiday weekend. So he wasn't around when Peter shot himself. But when he came back after his break and heard the talk about the case, he said he remembered you. There was nothing on computer, because no charges were pressed at the time, but he remembered, that's all. Look, I honestly don't know much about it. Peter's death is obviously suicide. But, because of your links with him in the past, the family connection, and particularly because it was your gun, they have to investigate, that's all. It's routine, it really is. They have to do their job.'

'I know. I do know that really.' I had no quarrel with the police. I admire them, by and large. 'I know it's their job. It's just a pretty foul job, sometimes.'

'Tell me about it,' he said. 'Look, they had to check your movements for the afternoon, and a few forensic details, to put you absolutely in the clear. That's all. From what little I do know, your alibi was watertight, and, more to the point, your clothes must have been completely clean. Otherwise, you'd know about it by now.'

'What do you mean, clean?'

'Not to put too fine a point on it, if you'd killed Peter there would have been shotgun deposit all over your clothes. As well as your prints all over the gun. If there were any of that, you wouldn't be sitting here now.'

I sighed. Was that all? 'That's stupid. How do they know I was wearing what I said I was?' Not that it mattered much, but presumably I could have produced anything, and claimed it was what I had worn that day.

'They will have checked quite carefully. Asked around. Got descriptions from other people as to what you wore for the Fair. Look, I can only tell you this because I don't actually know anything. But someone would have noticed, if there was any discrepancy. Don't worry, they won't need to bother you again. Apart from anything else, I do know that Cambridge CID know when he died, almost to the minute, and you were not there.'

'What do you mean?'

'I mean they know you were elsewhere because you were seen to be elsewhere. By several people.'

Despite everything, I found myself curious. 'I'm amazed, actually. I thought my alibi was shambolic.'

'Yes, well there you are. Listen, I really shouldn't talk to you about any of this.'

'So why are you?'

He finished off his wine. 'I don't know. You weren't treated well, were you?' I said nothing. He continued, 'You have a right not to go through it all again now. I just wanted you to know you probably won't any more. I believe they've found pretty convincing reasons for suicide. And I doubt if it was just you being quizzed, either. I'm sure they've checked up on a number of people.'

'Well, I guessed that,' I said. 'There's one member of the Fair Committee they haven't been able to clear, for a start.'

'You see, you know more than I do.' He looked sideways at me. 'Mr Willcox rather took to you. The constable called you, "The nice middle-aged lady with the posh house".'

'Middle-aged? Bloody cheek. In that case so are you.'

'Thought you'd like that.'

'So, because I'm respectable, and live in the posh house, they're going to leave me alone? Is that it?' I thought about my behaviour, and whether I had seemed to the sergeant to be a suspicious candidate. That was when I realised the significance of the trip to the dry-cleaner's. Presumably a decent criminal would not have left incriminating evidence around for three days before taking it to be cleaned. Aloud, I said, 'I've often wondered how much you can tell from personality, and the fact that people do or don't behave like criminals. For instance, my parents were never searched going through customs, they were so obviously respectable. I remember driving through the French-German border with them once, and thinking, no one's ever going to stop us, because my mother's wearing curlers and topping-and-tailing radishes. I thought perhaps one could set up as a drug runner by putting curlers on.'

'I shouldn't try it. We don't take much notice of that sort of thing, since you ask. If there's evidence against somebody, they're usually guilty, whatever their character.'

Luckily, we were prevented from further indiscretions by Penny's arrival. 'It makes me sick,' she said, the moment she joined us. 'At his own funeral, all this gossip. Village life is awful, in some ways, isn't it?'

She started picking old bits of grey fluff off the tennis ball which Timmo had brought to her after his father threw it for him, and which he had then abandoned, in order to play with some older children the other side of the garden.

Penny is much younger than Graeme; a pretty, intelligent girl, who had an extremely well-paid job as a computer programmer in Cambridge, which she had given up the year before. She had been earning twice what Graeme gets, and had offered to continue working after Timmo was born, saying Graeme could be a full-time father. He didn't like the idea. Nor did he like the suggestion that they could get a nanny. So Penny gave up her job without any regrets or rancour, and threw herself instead into running a women's study group for the church. I doubt if she's ever been dissatisfied in her life.

'Don't listen to them,' Graeme said, 'and then they can't tell you anything. Gossip's a two-way process.'

'I don't know where they get half of it,' she continued. 'It's all out now that he was mentally unstable, and this was known about for years. And that he once talked about suicide when he was at boarding school, and Alison and his teachers thought it was just emotional blackmail and did nothing about it. How come we never heard any of this before? And how he kept a kinky diary which shows he was unbalanced. And other things I don't even want to repeat.' I wasn't sure whether her eyes were avoiding mine deliberately. 'Goodness knows where people get all this. How do they know?' she asked Graeme.

'Beats me. I don't know the half of it. That's village life for you.'

'Mind you,' she added, 'I myself would have left a note.' She smiled, softly, and laid her hand on her husband's arm. 'I wouldn't do away with myself without making my loved ones know chapter and verse and everything they'd done to drive me to it.'

'Thanks,' he replied. 'Women usually do. Leave notes.'

'Don't men?' she asked.

'Not always.'

'I knew someone,' I said, 'who killed himself away from home, without leaving a note, when his family were expecting him to take them out.' I thought of the dark shore in Brittany.

'Of course,' Penny said. 'Graeme knew of a woman who took an overdose the day she'd had her hair done and her children were coming to visit. If she did it on purpose, which she may not have done. The coroner thought she had. And Peter can hardly have done it by mistake.' She threw the tennis ball towards the flower beds. 'This grass is looking very brown,' she added suddenly. 'Is there a hosepipe ban yet?'

'No,' I replied. 'I don't suppose Tricia and Hugh have time to bother with watering grass. My lawn looks even worse than this, already. I can't bear to use a sprinkler. I still see water as something which takes a woman an hour to fetch. It goes against the grain to chuck it on the ground.'

'Do you miss Nepal?' she asked me.

'Dreadfully. I'm fond of Willisham, but we were very happy out there. It's a shame we ever had to come back. But it had to end sometime. Even if David had lived, the children had to be educated. But it's quite a change, to go from that kind of life, to tame Saturday afternoons and village fairs. Though of course, this particular Fair wasn't that tame, in the end.'

'I suppose not,' Penny said.

'How do you know whether it was tame?' Graeme asked her. 'Penny wasn't there,' he explained to me.

'What? Not another one who missed it? This is quite a giveaway. It takes a murder enquiry to flush everyone out. We think everyone supports the event with loyal enthusiasm, but in fact when it comes to it we find people skiving off all afternoon.'

'Hang on,' Penny defended herself. 'I didn't miss the whole afternoon. I took Timmo home for a change of nappy. It just happened to be at the wrong time. If you see what I mean.'

I glanced across the lawn. I had just realised what I had said, and wondered if they had spotted it too. I didn't want to think about any of it any more.

We all said nothing for a while. Somebody came round and collected our cups. Timmo appeared from somewhere and ran up to his dad, who picked him up. Penny dug a tissue out of her pocket and wiped his nose.

'Look at this daft kid,' Graeme said. 'D'you think he'll make a copper?'

'Not a chance,' I replied. 'He's far too handsome.'

That conversation, of course, was still a few days before I got Prue's letter. The letter which threatened to change everything, and gave a completely different explanation for what had happened.

31

Unlike all her friends at school, Sara was not at all interested in boys. She never showed any interest in Charles's friends, hates the idea of co-education, swears she will never marry, and always turns off sex scenes on the television, or leaves the room when they're on. None of this would worry me if there hadn't been such an obvious reason for it. I'm not of the opinion that human beings should start pairing off, like budgerigars, every springtime from the onset of puberty. I'm quite happy that Charles will find a suitable girl if he wants one; he doesn't need his mother asking solicitous questions.

But Sara: I couldn't help wondering whether she would ever adjust. It was yet another of those things which would have been much easier to handle if I hadn't been on my own. Oh I know it's easy to moan about the wretchedness of widowhood. Please God don't let me become one of the world's unnecessary martyrs. True Christian martyrs, yes, suffering for the faith; but not a well-off, well-fed martyr in a stately home suffering for lack of an arm to lay a head on in the middle of the night.

David would have reassured me. He would have said, don't worry, she's taking her time, that's all. I used to lie in bed, or stand in the middle of the kitchen looking out over the gardens he knew so well, imagining him saying it. The trouble was I couldn't think what he would have said next. I knew it would have been reassuring, and eminently reasonable, and full of lucid reasons why Sara's state was healthy and normal. But I couldn't hear his voice. Nothing but the same old silence, ringing in my ears.

What is 'normal'? I don't know. There was one question I was asked over and over again by women in Phulbari. As soon as any of them got to know me well enough, they would ask me the same thing. 'Is it true, this thing called "falling in love"? Does it really happen?' (Whereas David would be asked by richer men, with bemused amazement, 'How can you be satisfied by one woman? Don't you get bored?' just as we might have asked them why they don't get bored with rice every day.)

I can remember Prue pouring scorn on the theory that falling in love was invented by the wandering troubadours of the eleventh century. Quite right: the goatherd and shepherd in the Song of Songs, and perhaps even Ovid in his raucous way, had been there long before. But Prue didn't have any historic or literary evidence for her dismissal. She simply said, 'Nonsense! It happens to everybody,' and left it at that. But it doesn't happen to women in Phulbari.

So it can't be 'normal'. One doesn't have to fall in love to be fully human; nor marry in order to be normal. Nevertheless, I do believe that those who stay single will be happier if they've chosen the life, rather than having been frightened into it.

When it first happened she withdrew into herself almost totally. No; not quite when it first happened. Within a few weeks. If it's possible with a child so young, she became almost a recluse. I had mental snapshots of her a week, a year or two, earlier, and I could hardly believe she was the same child. Bouncing on my bed, telling me at seven o'clock she was dressed and ready for the day. She was always very quick; Charles was the slow and steady one. Then I'd say, 'Have you cleaned your teeth, Sausage?' and she would clap her hand to her mouth in mock horror, and shrug her shoulders; her eyes would shine and she would giggle at the terribly funny side of life, at the wonderful joke of having forgotten her teeth.

She peopled our world with an entire imaginary cast, making a telephone call to some dragon called Hepsi, at the age of three, to tell him what she'd done on her first day at nursery school; refusing to sit in that chair at table, because Lop Ears was there already, only we couldn't see him; whispering to an invisible Mungo at bedtime, telling him secrets the rest of us were not allowed to hear. And her imagination wasn't always crazy;

sometimes it seemed to smack of a reality that the rest of us had never noticed.

'I can't remember what Jesus looks like,' she said to me once.

'I don't think any of us knows,' I said distractedly.

'Yes but I can't remember. I mean, from before I got here, before I was born.'

She was always the leader. If she were in a group of children, even older ones, she would always eventually be found directing everything they did, having the ideas, organising the project. Not being noisy or bossy; simply being listened to.

She was also a performer. We took the children to the pantomime at the Arts Theatre when Sara was barely walking, and hadn't yet learnt to talk. We were sitting at the front of the stalls, and when the dame invited the children up to the front Charles volunteered, and was chosen to go up on the stage. Unseen by the usherette, Sara followed him up the steps and turned to the audience, and suddenly saw the vast crowds of empty faces. Her first reaction was stillness, and utter silence. She was uncertain. Before her was an unknown, many-headed monster that could have gobbled her up. Then she realised one or two were laughing at her, and she began to play.

She had a dummy in the pocket of her trousers. I used to keep one, to Prue's horror, to help the children sleep: it saved them sucking their thumbs. Sara looked at her huge, sympathetic audience, ready to laugh at her, or with her. So she took the dummy out of her pocket and put it in her mouth the wrong way round, with her teeth gripping the ring and the teat sticking out. And then she began to dance. She swung from leg to leg like a drunkard, fell on her bottom, spat her dummy out towards the audience, then simply sat there blowing raspberries. The audience was beside itself. The fat man next to us was shaking helplessly. The usherette at the end of the row was in tears. Our sides were aching. Charles was looking embarrassed and rather proud at the same time, glancing at us occasionally to see if he should do anything. David gave him a barely perceptible shake of the head. The unfortunate dame was in a state of exasperation and near panic.

'Well, little chap,' he said very loudly to Sara, both their sexual identities being now quite confused. 'I think we'll send you back to your mummy and daddy now,' and he looked piteously and pointedly out into the hooting audience. David was all for letting her stay there and watching them fight it out. But some organising woman in the front row came to the rescue of the upstaged old pro, and lifted Sara back down to us. She smiled a happy and triumphant smile. Her performance had been a success.

She lost that side of her nature in an afternoon. She started to speak so quietly that we could barely hear her. She stopped joking and laughing. And she was always frightened in the company of men. She never told me her fear, but if there were men around she would come and sit by me, or try to leave, particularly if we were in a confined space, a room. David found increasingly that she shrank from his touch. When he put her to bed, and sat down on her bedside to pray with her or read her a story, she would burrow into the bedclothes away from his embrace. He would come out of her bedroom looking old and tired, and the sight of his face made me want to cry. He simply didn't know what to do. He had used up all his instinctive, confident fathering. He had simply run out of ideas. He knew she didn't want to talk about it. And his reaction, as a man, to the little girl he loved, was to want to hide her in his arms and fold her to him, and this he wasn't allowed to do.

She became worse and worse that year, the summer of her seventh birthday. Her teachers, to our surprise, had previously held her up as a model pupil. She had always been so mischievous we had assumed it would be the same at school. Not a bit of it. From her very first day, at the age of four and a half, she settled down to study seriously, and wouldn't look up from her desk, even when playtime had been called, until she had finished her work and she was satisfied with it. But after that summer we sometimes wondered if she'd ever work again. Her work became scrappy, untidy, sparse, and almost stupid.

I have a photograph of her taken at about that time, and, even though I know it well, it still shocks me every time I see it afresh. She looks as if she has a very bad case of chicken pox. Almost as though someone has painted her face all over with a red pen, to get her off school. Everywhere on her cheeks, forehead, chin, are bleeding, weeping spots. As far as I can remember, she scratched her face all the time. Her skin still shows the scars, if you look closely.

We'd had to tell her teacher, of course. One day I went to pick Sara up, and she was the last to leave. Coming home alone was now out of the question. While I waited for her to put on her coat and shoes, I wandered into her classroom, and there at her desk was Sara's teacher, a girl in her early twenties. She looked up at me, and in the light from the window she looked as though she had been crying. 'She was such a beautiful child,' she said quietly, as if she would never be beautiful again, 'and so bright.' Her gentle face sagged slightly, and then, in language which I found utterly shocking in a teacher, especially one so gentle and young, she said, 'I hope they kill that bastard. I'm sorry, Mrs St Joseph, but I hope they kill him.' At that point Sara came in, saw her favourite teacher in tears, and took no notice of her at all. It was then that I realised that suffering sometimes does more than simply hurt its victim: it can also harden and twist and make the victim ugly. I took Sara home.

Early in the next year, in January, we left England. Then, she genuinely seemed able to leave it behind her. I think it was partly because, in Phulbari, there were very few boys around. At her new, tiny, unpretentious school the few westerners, other missionaries' children, were mostly younger than she. And the Nepali boys didn't seem to pose a threat at all. They are not a threatening race. In all the time we were there I seldom saw an aggressive or brutal act. The women are not under a constant offensive, as they seem to be here. Oh, they're expected to plough the fields and reap the rice and carry heavy loads and bear all the woes and responsibilities of living with nothing to spare. But they're not expected to bare their breasts in a newspaper, which is then dropped open on the tube or blown along dirty pavements. In Dehli perhaps: in Phulbari never. They are downtrodden in many ways, but they also have a certain kind of dignity that Western women lack. They may have to share their husband with another wife, if he is well off. But they are never expected to share themselves with a string of boys and men, one after another, some of whom they barely know, as all Sara's school friends will be expected to do, at some party or other, before they're even in the sixth form. And Sara found, in their company, she could begin to grow, and heal, and, against all the odds, start to become a woman.

She didn't regain her vibrant spring of fun and irresponsibility, her offbeat naughtiness. That only started to come back much more recently. But she did seem to be losing her fear. The psychologists and psychiatrists and psychotherapists had all told us we should make her talk about it. But it seemed to us, as mere parents, that Sara had been abused enough.

When we came back to this country again I began to understand that, in the safety of Phulbari, she hadn't needed any defences. Back here, she began to build them again. Perhaps it was in response to so much death. Daddy, then Grandfather, and both of them so much loved.

She started at the Perse School, in the Lower Fourth, that September. After a while, when she got used to it, she liked it. She seemed to be finding her feet again, and I almost began to hope that perhaps this was the Sara we might have known if it had never happened. She was at times quite stunningly beautiful, when the light seemed to catch her eyes and a fit of laughter was on her. Always she was pretty, apart from her poor skin left over from the bad scarring.

Then the other moods would strike. She would stop eating, or eat nonstop, surreptitiously, when I wasn't watching. Her hair became greasy and dull, her face grey and pimply and depressing to look at. Sometimes she didn't wash at all, sometimes she washed obsessively. It was extraordinary that the same girl could be both so beautiful and so plain. She would retreat into her room and seem unable to speak to anyone. And a pattern would begin to emerge. When she was at school, amongst her peers, in a classroom of girls, she was the life and soul of the party. They looked up to her. She was bright and fun.

But at church, or around the village, where there were men or boys, she became quiet, went home, read a book. If Charles brought friends home she would drift to the wall, and sometimes end up in her bedroom, even in bed, silent and immobile. Charles sensed this, and stopped having friends over. I wonder if she was simply frightened of being attractive. Like a shy, nocturnal animal thrown into broad daylight.

Often she talked about going abroad again. Back to Phulbari. Back home, as she called it. They understand such things, these dark spirits, in some ways much better than we do.

In 1952, when the borders were opened to the west for the first time in two hundred and fifty years, two women doctors set off from Delhi on foot to reach Pokhara, carrying their medical equipment with them, to found the first hospital and bring the first Gospel the country had ever known. They didn't ask for gratitude, but they did ask for a piece of land; and there was one corner of Pokhara cheaper than all the rest. No one wanted it. No one could use it. It was owned by the evil spirits. These two brave women, perhaps breathing the fresh wind of western scepticism as much as the combating power of Christianity, encamped on the haunted land and set up the hospital. It was called the Shining Hospital, because the sun burnished the corrugated-iron roofs, which could be seen from a long way off. And within a few years, or so the western doctors were told, the evil spirits had gone.

But not given up. One night a tribesman came down to our house in Phulbari from the hills. He had converted to Christianity, which was hard enough, though not as hard as it had been for others in the past. And he was terrified. All the angry members of his tribe were persecuting him. At first we didn't understand. David's Nepali was not yet that good, mine wasn't much better, and he spoke his own language anyway. We thought members of his family were angry with him. Human beings. But these were persecutors he couldn't escape. They would kill him. Or so he said.

We prayed with him and gave him a meal and he slept in our house for the night. In the morning we told him we would continue to pray for him, and he set off for home seeming reassured. He was never allowed to reach his village on the hillside. He had been right. That afternoon he was found dead at the bottom of a ravine. No human being had been near him.

They seem to be more aware of spiritual things over there; just as we may be more aware of other things. They don't see H_2O in a glass of water. We don't see the spirits on a piece of wasteland.

Sara was amongst people who understood her, in some ways. She went to their church one day, not the missionary prayer meeting but the little hut on the mountainside where they beat their skin drums and sang songs about Christ to the old tunes of the hills. It's ironic: the old national religions of Hinduism and Buddhism and pantheism are based on tolerance. Their gods aren't jealous at all, and can easily move over and make room for one more, unlike ours. But the Hindu government, under the influence of westernisation which sees tolerance almost as a god in itself, had, until 1990, put men in prison if they changed religion. Two years for converting to Christianity, six for causing someone else to convert. Nepali Christians can still face awesome family pressure, and lose their inheritance.

Someone asked Sara if she had anything she wanted them to pray for. She wasn't brilliant at the language either, but she told them what she could. They prayed with her. She didn't explain the crime and they would never have understood it if she had, but they could understand the fear.

Sara's problem, as it happens, wasn't spooky. She wasn't being pursued by evil spirits. Not as far as I could see, anyway, with my limited western vision. She had simply been attacked and was very frightened. God heals in very commonplace ways. After that funny little two-hour loving cluster of Christianity hanging tenaciously on the side of a mountain, Sara knew she was healed. Time, years of flinty loving, the wide deep sky and the freedom of tens of thousands of miles had shaken the tyrant off.

She hadn't got over it. We had accepted that, in a way, she would never do that. But she had genuinely learnt to live with it. She couldn't have her childhood back. But she could live as if she hadn't lost it.

What we would never have predicted was that he would want to do it again.

32

It was nearly half-term. Charles was coming home, and, for the first time for ages, bringing a friend. He was called Tom. His parents live and work in South Africa so it was hardly worth his while to go home for a week, and Charles invited him to Willisham.

I had struggled for days with the feeling of exhaustion and nausea which kept trying to lay me low. I contemplated going to the surgery, or talking to Nick about it. I wondered whether to ask him for Temazepam, or Valium, or something harmless just to take my mind off things. If David had still been alive he could have prescribed something. But then, if David were alive I wouldn't have needed it. I would have had someone to lie with at night instead of staring at the ceiling. And what explanation could I have given Nick? So I put up with it instead, with the aching, the heaviness, the inability to eat, the headaches and palpitations.

Then, that Saturday after Peter's funeral, Prue's letter arrived. A French postmark, and Prue's handwriting. The moment I saw it, I felt ill. I fumbled to stuff it quickly into my pocket so that Sara wouldn't catch sight of it, even though she wasn't even out of bed when the post came. I have never in my life behaved like this, like a guilty person, frightened of everything. Why should Sara not see a letter from her own grandmother? I had no idea what was in it. Nevertheless I knew she mustn't be aware it had come. I went up to my bedroom, opened my jewellery drawer, and rummaged around looking for a suitable place to hide it. Would Sara ever search my private drawer? Surely not. But the police might. Or even a burglar. In the end I went downstairs again and put it in the safe. Even the police wouldn't get inside that without the key from me.

I still had no idea what the letter said. It might have been perfectly innocent.

When I came home again that Saturday morning, after shopping for the weekend, I felt awful. I longed to lie down, but couldn't because of Charles and Tom coming. Sara's unexpected enthusiasm helped me: she never referred to it, but she was clearly longing to see her brother again. So I pushed myself on, too tired to be excited, but determined to give his new friend a warm welcome. I set about peeling potatoes.

It reminded me of the early years, when we were first married and used to have roast Sunday lunches, almost as a joke. Look at us; aren't we very 'married', as it were. But after the children were born it became more chaotic, and we had salads and pâtés and cheeses. And of course in Phulbari it was rice and red hot chillies. If we'd moved into the house together we would have done it properly, and had the dining table full every Sunday. Dinner parties and gleaming silver and the white linen napkins starched and ironed by Anna-Marie every week. Perhaps we really would have settled down into an English country house way of life.

I slept badly again that night. I kept drifting off into disturbed and fitful dreams. I would see the boys arriving, and then smell burnt lunch, and find the kitchen full of black smoke. Or else Tom turned out to be a vegetarian, and we sat in embarrassment round the huge joint of beef I'd got. Finally Charles turned up to lunch with Peter Midland, and Sara went white and screamed, and Peter turned round and the back of his head was missing, and I woke sweating. I shook the blankets off my bed and turned on my bedside light to read till my eyes ached; but I'd no sooner turned back to sleep again than I woke up too cold.

Much as I longed to, I couldn't stay in bed the next morning. My body ached with insomnia, but Charles had said they'd be on the nine thirty from King's Cross – they had been to a party in London the night before, and spent the night in Tom's parents' flat in Kensington – and they wanted to be met at Cambridge Station.

*   *   *

He was charming.

When I say that, I don't mean what we English normally mean by charming: dark and smooth and perfectly horrid. I mean he was quiet and softly spoken and rather gave the impression of being shy, though I'm not sure that he was. And he looked like a young man who would hold his convictions in the face of a storm, and be utterly dependable.

I saw Sara through the window as I parked the car. She had watched us arrive, but she was nowhere to be seen by the time we were in the hall.

'Come and sit in the garden,' I said to them both as soon as we were inside. 'I'll put the coffee on, and look after you as soon as I've picked some fruit.'

'We'll pick it,' Tom said immediately. 'What do you need?'

Charles protested, saying he wanted to take his things up to his room, so Tom asked me to show him what to do and where to go. And at that point Sara appeared, so I asked her to show him, and watched them carry their china pudding basins down to the end of the lawn, beyond the tennis court, towards the swimming pool, where they could pick blackberries, far away from the house. The Willisham blackberries are huge, sweet, cultivated. They always fruit early and for a very long time. This year they were out by June; I haven't seen them for some weeks, but they're bound to be still going.

When the coffee was ready I called Charles, then took the tray out to the table on the terrace, and went to the bottom of the garden to tell Sara and Tom to come. I reached the long grass, near the blackberry patch, and watched them for a while before they saw me. They were both completely absorbed in their task, silent, concentrated, fixed on the bramble bushes. I remembered her with Charles, before, doing the same task. Whenever they remembered, in the summer, they would run down to the bottom of the garden with bowls and big wicker baskets, and sunhats to keep off the sun; Sara's wide-brimmed and of straw, and Charles with a sou'wester-shaped cotton hat. Then they would fill their faces and hands and mouths, and sometimes even put a few in the bowls and baskets. And Charles would help Sara over the brambles, and she would crawl where he couldn't reach, and usually they would forget to bring their

hats back and always they brought back thorns in their hands
and legs. They learnt to wear shoes for that task, they were so
sick of having the splinters pulled. If we couldn't find them for
a meal it was always worth wandering down beyond the apple
trees and the pool, to see if there were two fair heads bobbing
amongst the brambles, and four bare legs getting scratched and
pulled about. Sara always gave the pool a wide berth; she had
been told never to go nearer than six feet away from the edge
till she could swim five lengths, even if Charles were with her.
Despite her overflowing, everlasting contrariness, she always
knew when something was seriously forbidden.

As I watched, Tom caught his hand on a thorn, and said ouch,
and sucked it. Sara turned to look at him, and he looked up, and
they smiled at each other, and their concentration on the task
was broken. Then they sensed me looking at them, and began
to untangle themselves and come towards me.

They had picked enough some minutes before, but Tom had
suggested they should collect more for the freezer rather than
leave them for the birds. Sara considered this ungenerous; I said
it was a kind thought and a jolly good idea.

He wasn't vegetarian, and loved beef, and hadn't had a real
Sunday lunch for ages – 'I mean a family Sunday lunch, not just
the big roast; we get all the roast meats we can eat in College.
But I do miss having a family.'

'Are you a scholar?' Sara said, impressed. 'Seriously brainy, or
what? I thought you and Charles were Oppidans together, in the
same house.'

'No fear,' Charles replied. 'That's why he finds it such a
relief to be amongst non-intellectuals, and not to have to make
pretentious conversation over lunch.'

'Well,' Tom conceded, 'it's certainly good to be in such
a relaxed atmosphere, and have the freedom to talk about
nothing.'

'D'you mean the freedom not to talk?' Charles said. 'I haven't
noticed much of that. You don't know us well enough, or Mother
anyway, to sit in front of her and not talk.'

'No, I didn't mean that. I mean what I said: the freedom to
talk about nothing. To talk small talk, like we are now. Rather

than feeling one's always got to talk about politics or medieval literature. Or even the latest James Bond movie. I love College, but it's good to get out and relax sometimes.'

'I've never met anyone interesting who could talk about politics,' Sara observed. 'It's so boring.'

'Isn't it,' Tom agreed.

'Isn't that typical of a Colleger,' Charles complained. 'Any subject he doesn't know about is written off. Then he needn't display his ignorance.'

'Do you find medieval literature dull?' I asked, ignoring Charles.

'Not at all. I love it. No doubt a lot of it is extremely dull, but most of what we bother to read today is wonderful, because it's the best.'

'Such as? What are your favourites?'

'Villon. Langland. The Gawain poet. Chaucer of course.'

Sara jumped up. 'Come on, let's play dead hen.' Then she added, to my complete astonishment, ' "Where are the snows of yesteryear?" '

'You know Villon?' he replied excitedly, jumping up to join her. 'What on earth's "dead hen"?'

'Daddy coined the phrase. "That game where you knock a thing like a dead hen over a net." Shuttlecock. Come on, Charles.'

' "Where are they?" ' Tom recited, belatedly, as the two of them disappeared through the French windows.

'Well, that's my friend stolen from me,' Charles said. 'They told me it would be like this, if I had a younger sister.'

And I could tell that he was as pleased as I was. It would never have occurred to me that Sara knew any Villon.

Tom's stay was delightful. I felt as easy with him as if I'd known him for years. He seemed very old for his age. I was glad. Illogically, it made me feel that he would be careful with people, wouldn't mess a girl about, would understand. Or perhaps he is simply gentle by nature.

That first day, the Sunday, we sat outside till evening. The boys had intended to go to the cinema. You know how it is in summer. You think it's just gone teatime, then you look at your watch and realise that little children should have been in bed hours ago and it's nearly nine o'clock. The three of them had yet another last swim, then they helped put the tea things away, then they sat in the garden saying they hadn't got time for a drink.

Eventually they said they would go out for a walk. Charles roused himself, and kicked Tom lightly on the shin, and told him to get a move on, and they got up and turned to go. Then Tom turned back, and looked at Sara, and hesitated. I dropped my gaze, feeling an intruder. Then I gathered up the glasses and tray and went into the house, having seen him smile shyly and say nothing. When I looked out of the kitchen window a minute later there was no one in the garden, and I imagined poor Charles, who had lost out yet again, being the one tagging along listening to Tom talking to Sara.

As I loaded the dishwasher I had that glowing, clever feeling one has after giving a good party: the garden littered with food and dead glasses, the plates cleared away, a delicious and slightly tipsy exhaustion in the air. That was almost how I felt, as if dozens of people had been feasting in the garden and had gone away satisfied.

Then I remembered I hadn't been feeling well. My limbs had forgotten to ache for the day, and my temperature seemed to have dropped. I went back into the garden and the tiredness began to flow back over me. I wondered what time they would get in. Youth is cruel, and has no remorse, I thought to myself irrelevantly.

I wandered slowly down to the bottom of the garden. I felt slightly dizzy. The blackberry days. It came on me with a shock that the last time Sara had gone there alone, to pick blackberries, had probably been her birthday. I mean *that* birthday, eight years ago. She had often been to the pool to swim of course. No ghost lurked there for her, as far as I knew. But she'd never used the changing hut again. Of that I was sure.

She had been avoiding the swimming pool that May day eight years ago, just as she had been told to do. I shivered in the evening air, and turned to go back to the house. Then I made myself turn around, and go back, and walk to the pool again. The surface of the water trembled slightly in the evening breeze. I experienced an absurd feeling of being watched, as the light darkened around the trees. In the end I forced myself to go all the way down to the changing hut, and walk behind it, and show myself that there was nothing there. What did I expect, after all? Did I expect some primitive ghost to haunt my swimming pool and reproach me?

As I looked at the brown and parched deadness behind the hut I fancied I saw an uncanny indentation in the earth, as if someone had lain there, behind the hut. I turned away in disgust and walked back to the house. I decided to lock up early, just leaving the back door open for them, and go to bed straight away.

Before I did, I went and retrieved Prue's letter from the safe. Leaving it unlocked, I went into the dining room and opened her letter with a knife. Inside was another envelope, unsealed, and addressed simply, 'For the Police'.

The note to me was brief. 'Harriet dearest, You will know what to do with this, I think. Read it first. Prue.'

I didn't need to read it. Not yet, anyway. Now, I knew what Prue was doing; I knew it all.

Still shaking, I put it all back in the envelope, and went back to the safe. I locked the door securely, and, for the first time, took the key up to bed with me.

When I got to bed, I cried and cried.

33

Sara's previous birthday tea at Willisham House had been on a Saturday. Saturday the fifth of May. She was going to be seven. It was another unnaturally hot summer.

She was very excited about the day, and had been talking about it for weeks. She didn't want a party at home, with other children. She liked her school friends, but she saw them every day. She wanted a party at Granny and Grandfather's house, at her favourite house in all the world, at Willisham. With her grandparents there, and Charles, and Mummy and Daddy. And anyone else? Yes, she wanted to invite Charles's schoolfriend Jamie. Charles was horrified. He said Jamie would think this wet. We told Charles he couldn't reasonably prevent Sara from inviting anyone she wanted. Jamie was perfectly at liberty to refuse, if he didn't want to come. We also pointed out to Charles that it wasn't his responsibility if Jamie thought his sister wet.

Jamie said thank you, and he would be delighted to be there.

The boys had morning school, and David was working till lunch, so it was decided that I would take Sara over to Willisham in the morning, buy all the food she thought we needed for the tea, and then run back in the car into Cambridge in the afternoon for the others.

We had a long shopping list, Sara and I. Prue had ordered a cake from the baker's, and extra bread, but all the other things we were going to choose when we got to the shops. And of course half the fun of the party was getting it ready beforehand. We left Prue reading up on cup cakes in the kitchen, and set off together to denude Willisham. Cup cakes were supposed to be

Prue's thing. Almost her only thing. That and hard-boiled eggs. And a sort of shortbread that fell to bits when one looked at it. She planned to wait for Sara to come back from the shopping expedition to help her with the cake mixture. She probably genuinely needed the help. She is not a great cook, even now, my mother-in-law. Most of her life she had other people to cook for her.

We went to the butcher's first, for some ham for the sandwiches. 'It's my party today,' Sarah explained to Andrew. 'I'm seven.'

'Well now,' said Andrew, slicing the ham. 'Geoff was thirteen last week. He took us all to the pictures, to see *Return of the Something or Other*.'

'I'm giving a tea party. The ham's for the sandwiches. Children don't like ham sandwiches, but adults do. Ham sandwiches with mustard. They're horrible, but adults think they're nice. I chose the ham for them.'

And so she did the round of the village, explaining to everyone what she was buying and why. Cucumber. Eggs. Apples for Grandfather, the sweet green ones, because those were the ones he liked. Balloons and streamers, and those squeaky things you blow. She particularly wanted these for Charles and Jamie because, she said, boys like to make a noise. But the little post office in Willisham was low on its stocks, and we could only get one. 'Never mind,' said the assistant. 'You can have that because you're the birthday girl.' She was shocked. 'But Jamie's the guest,' she said.

At last we ended up at the baker's. We collected the bread – still hot, as it should be, and in its paper bag. We chose far more cream and jam doughnuts and iced buns and chocolate slices than we could eat. Then we asked for the cake. It was in a large cardboard box, tied up with ribbon. The shopkeeper asked if we'd like to see it but Sara said, no, it was a surprise, and it mustn't be looked at yet. Granny had ordered it, so we didn't know what it looked like.

Then we went back to the house, laid the treasure out in the kitchen, and Sara set about helping Prue.

By the time I left, after a light and early lunch, the party was nearly ready. Alison was helping, of course. Prue wouldn't dream of having a party, even a child's tea party, without domestic help.

The table was laid in the dining room with names for everybody. 'I've done one for Peter,' Sara said, 'in case he wants to come. Is Peter here today, Alison?'

'He's somewhere about,' Alison said. We had got used to Peter as rather a fixture, even though he was too old, now, to need to accompany Alison while she worked. He sometimes used the pool, or kicked around the grounds, so we were never surprised when he turned up in unexpected places. I don't think Sara really wanted him at her party, but she thought, with Charles and Jamie coming, it would be rather rude to exclude him. I wanted to say don't worry, you needn't invite him if you don't want to. But in all honesty I thought her instinct for courtesy was right.

The dining room looked lovely. The balloons were blown up, the cakes set out, and the birthday cake itself, at Sara's insistence, still firmly in its box.

I gave her a hug and said I'd be back in an hour or so. And soon after I left, I gather, she went down to the blackberry patch to pick some for her party. I very much doubt if there were any so early, even in that hot summer, even those thick, rich, cultivated blackberries. But she wouldn't have realised that. And perhaps she intended to pick flowers as well. She often did bring flowers from the garden to decorate the house. She may have wanted some for the table. Having seen Prue do it for dinner parties, she would have considered it appropriate. I never asked her afterwards. Obviously. There was never an opportunity for so trivial a question. And yet perhaps I should have done. Perhaps we should have walked that journey together, safely, over and over again after the event. Perhaps I should have done many things.

Still, even now, I can shut my eyes and see her skipping through her childhood and the sunlight down to the bottom of the garden. Some rather ribald nursery rhyme comes to mind. It can't be a nursery rhyme. It must be an old folk song that was meant to be sung with a laugh and a mug of ale and a happy wench on the knee, but it plagues me like a toothache. '. . . went out the maid, That home a maid Never . . .' What is it? Never returned again? I don't think I've got it right, but it makes my blood run cold nonetheless.

We got back at twenty to four. It had taken us much longer than we expected to round everybody up. First Jamie wasn't ready. Then Charles. Then we had to wait ages for David for at the hospital. Then Jamie said please could we call on his parents' house because he had a birthday present for Sara. As soon as he got it into the car, he peeled some of the wrapper off so we could see it. It was a huge rag doll, with petticoats and knickerbockers and a bonnet and buttons, and everything came off like real clothes.

'Jamie, she'll absolutely love it,' I said. 'What a wonderful present.'

'My mother chose it,' Jamie said with sheepish honesty, as if I couldn't possibly have guessed.

'I think it's dead soppy,' said Charles.

'Real men don't find things soppy,' said David.

We went into the house with cries and shouts and halloos. Prue came to meet us, and said tea was all ready.

'Where's the birthday girl?' said David. 'Hello! Sallyoo!'

'I think she must still be out in the garden,' said Prue.

'I'll go,' I said, and went.

She wasn't hard to find. She was underneath the chestnut tree in the middle of the lawn, standing quite still with her pretty party dress on. She was looking towards the house, and I realised afterwards that she was trembling slightly. I thought nothing of it at the time. Or perhaps I thought she'd been in the hot sun, and now was chilly here in the shade. Or perhaps I thought she might be excited about her party. Or perhaps I never thought. Perhaps I never thought enough at all about looking after her. Why am I being idiotic? We've been over this a hundred times. That way madness lies.

'Come on, Flopsy,' I said. 'Your guests are here.'

She looked up at me and nodded.

'You all right?' She nodded again. I thought for a moment that she was trying to look behind her, but was frightened of something. In that absurdly beautiful sunshine, I nearly asked her if she'd seen a ghost at the bottom of the garden.

'Come on then.' She turned back to me, and held her hand out towards mine.

'Do you want me to carry you? Come on. Gosh what a heavy

lump you are. What have you been doing to your dress? You've got dirt all over it, you silly sausage. And crumpled it. After Sonia specially ironed it for you. She's having a day off today. She'll be back again tonight. She'll want to hear all about your party. Wait until you see what Jamie's got for you. You'll adore it. Look at those pretty lilac blossoms. Would you like to pick some flowers for your party? No? Yes? Right: down you hop. Well you'll have to get down, sweetheart, I can't pick them and carry you. No? All right, then. I know, why don't you pick some of that blossom. You can reach that. Think of all those cherries which won't be able to fruit now.' And she solemnly picked a beautiful sprig of pink blossom, and then hugged herself back to me as if she couldn't bear any space between us.

The thing I found hardest, afterwards, when I remembered that birthday party, was the meticulous care Sara took of her guests. She knew what trouble we'd taken, you see, and she didn't want to spoil it. Prue sat her at the head of the table – because, she said, she was the hostess for the day, and she must make sure her guests had what they needed. And Prue poured the tea, because the pot was too hot and heavy for her, but everything else was hers to offer round. Perhaps I'm sentimental, but I believe that show of manners took as much courage as anything I've ever seen. As much courage, in its own way, as the death her father died in a remote mission hospital. God knows, He demands more from us than we ever knew we had.

The rest of us ate very well. From time to time someone would ask her if she wanted to try something. Mostly she shook her head politely. Once or twice she put something on her plate and took a little nibble of it. We laughed and joked, and said she was too excited, and she'd have to take some of it home to eat tomorrow.

Then Prue said, 'Are you ready for the cake darling?' She nodded, and tried to smile, and mouthed the words, 'Yes please.'

So we drew the curtains and turned out the light, and waited in the darkness, until Prue came back with seven little lighted candles, then we all sang Happy Birthday, and shouted, 'Blow them out and wish. Come on. Blow them out! Come on Sara.'

Then someone turned on the light, and there was a huge gooey chocolate cake with chocolate buttons all over the top, and pink icing, saying 'Happy Birthday dearest Sara,' with the 'dearest' squashed up because there hadn't been quite enough room, and Sara was sitting at the head of the table, quite quiet, and quite still, as white as a sheet, and the tears that would plague her for years afterwards had just begun to fall.

34

She never tasted the cake.

We thought she was tired, and full of her birthday, and had had too much of the sun. She sat on my knee for the rest of tea, eating nothing. And when Jamie gave her the present she looked up at him and said thank you, very quickly. Thank you very much.

Then we thanked Prue and Maurice, and all piled in the car to go back to Cambridge.

Sonia was our au pair. The only one we've ever had. To this day I'm grateful for that wonderful girl. She was the most competent, intelligent, sensitive young woman of her age I have ever known. She went back to Germany to become a doctor, but soon after that she married and gave up work to have children of her own. When we got home from Willisham she was back from her afternoon off, and she offered to give Sara her bath and hear all about the party. We asked Sara if she'd like that and she nodded silently. So I told Sonia she was very tired, and said I would be up in ten minutes to read her a story.

David and I were in the kitchen when Sonia came back down. 'Excuse me, Harriet, David, but I think there is something wrong. Sara is not well. I think something has happened. I saw it in the bath.'

We went upstairs, but Sara had put herself to bed, and was under the bedclothes, not moving, curled up in a tight little ball.

'What's the matter, honey?' David took her in his arms. She said nothing. I don't quite know what she could have said.

Sonia struggled to explain. 'I'm sorry, David, but as the doctor

I think you must see her. Underneath. I mean without the bedclothes. All over, in her private places.' Then she quietly left the bedroom, and went downstairs to talk to Charles. I suppose it was the only thing left to do.

We sat on the bed, and eventually took the bedclothes off and looked at her as gently as we could, and she shivered and shook, and after a long time and, thank God, many tears, she somehow told us what she could. It was Peter of course, near the swimming pool, behind the changing hut, and she had no idea what he'd done. She'd had it all explained to her, but that was with a mummy and a daddy and she couldn't make the connection. It was just as well: we had told her that you don't make love until you've found someone that you want to love and live with all your life.

David went down and explained something to Charles, and then we wrapped Sara up and set off for the police station. As we got her dressed she said to me, 'Please can I take my new rag doll?' It was the only voluntary thing she had said since lunchtime, and the doll stayed with her throughout all that terrible night.

It amazes me now that we went through with it without question. We didn't pause for a moment, that evening, and ask ourselves whether we were doing the right thing. I didn't hesitate by the front door and say, 'David, stop a minute. What does Sara really need at this moment? What would I feel? What would I want?' And I her mother. How could I expect the police to spare her, if I didn't?

Nor did David sit me down, while Sonia got Sara into warm clothes, and say, 'Let's think this through. Let's work out our priorities. What do we care about? Sara herself? Or some wonderful great machine called British Justice? Are we going to do our duty as loyal British citizens? Or are we simply going to be heartbroken, loving parents?'

So we pushed Sara headlong onto some monstrous treadmill, not just that night, but for months afterwards, because for some reason we thought evil must always be dealt with. Whatever the police may have done – and it may have been worse in some ways, more inhuman, than what Peter did – at least they were doing their duty. Which is more than can be said of her own mother and father. Our duty was to our daughter, for goodness' sake.

In the early hours of Sunday morning, when Sara was still being interviewed, the same questions over and over again by different members of the force, a kind, motherly sort of policewoman, with the soft Irish accent of the south, took me on one side. David followed. With nobody else listening, she said to us, 'Let me tell you something. You may not want to take any notice of this now. But let me tell you anyway, because the wee lady's very tired, and you're wanting to do your best. If this had happened to my daughter, now, I wouldn't be going to the police.' She pronounced it, as they do, with the emphasis on the first syllable. I can still hear it. I remember how it made me think of the Irish Garda, in their yellow cars. I suppose she was acting very improperly, from a professional point of view; but as a fellow member of the human race she was being as kind as she knew how.

I had got to the stage where I was too tired to be surprised by anything, but I felt a numb sort of shock at the acceptance of such injustice.

'D'you mean you're telling us to withdraw charges?' I asked her, as much for something to say as to understand what she was telling us.

'No, no,' she said. 'I couldn't do that. You must do what you think is right. After all, as the police, we want your evidence. I'm just telling you what I would do under the circumstances. That's all.'

'Thank you,' said David, and meant it. 'Thank you, but I think we'll have to see this through.' So she smiled politely, and shrugged, and left us alone.

Of course we should have listened to her. Not that we could have at the time. At the time we believed that someone would try to see justice done. Like Sir Robert Moreton in *The Winslow Boy*, we wanted to 'Let Right Be Done'. But at what cost? At what dreadful human cost, Sir Robert?

At last – why did it take us so long? – David put his foot down. He gave his opinion, as a doctor, that they had seen all they were going to see. He withdrew his permission, as a parent, for her to be examined any more. Then we heard it all, and believed half of it too. Protect society. Help the police. Moral duty. David offered to drop charges. So then they promised to do no more than ask her questions for the rest of the night. As if that weren't an invasion too.

And all the time her rag doll was clasped to her side, hearing secrets more terrible than dolls should ever hear, and none of it secret any more.

And all evening Sara had simply shivered, while we had hugged and comforted her at one end and gave the police the other end. As if she really could be divided in two; as if it were possible to hurt the body and love the soul; as if she could be separated from herself. What is extraordinary is that she wasn't more damaged.

We got home at four o'clock. Sonia and Charles were still sitting up for us, in their nightclothes, playing Pelmanism. Of course: it's the Fool in *Lear*. 'Went out the maid, That home a maid . . .' Oh! how does it go on? It will come back to me.

35

It was much later in the year, in November, that we learnt that Peter would not be prosecuted. There was insufficient evidence, because Sara had had a bath.

Someone at that police station could surely have told us almost immediately that it wouldn't come to a conviction. Perhaps the evidence she provided was of some incidental interest. Presumably, an investigating officer's job is always to investigate, regardless of the cost. Otherwise we could have been sent home within half an hour. I suppose that's what the kindly Irishwoman was saying, only we couldn't hear.

But the worst was yet to come. It was meant as a consolation, after we'd been told he wouldn't be prosecuted. Not that I think we minded that particularly. After all, we weren't after revenge. We were trying to do right. Stupidly, we thought we had a duty to report a crime. As if that came above everything else. As if that were more important than our duty to protect our child.

We had no great desire at the time to see Peter punished. Maurice had been like a guardian to him. We never thought in terms of getting back at him. But we did think her ordeal ought to have had some point to it, in terms of prevention, or something. We didn't want to have put her through all that for absolutely nothing.

'You haven't lost much.' Our well-meaning friend was a barrister, and had recently been involved in a similar case. 'He would only have got a few months.'

This I couldn't believe. 'I'm sure you're mistaken,' I said. 'She was barely seven.'

'Promise you, Harriet. Chances are, the judge would have seen his point of view. Underprivileged, without a dad, difficult home background. Very pretty little kid from a posh family, leads him on a bit . . . Good God, Harriet, don't look at me like that: I'm not saying she did. I'm telling you what you would have heard in court. The judge is only human after all.'

I said nothing. The Judge is not only human, at the end of the day. We should have trusted Him, left it up to Him, in the first place.

'For God's sake, imagine the defence. Perky little thing like Sara, probably doesn't know she's flirting, you know. I promise you, I've done several of these over the last few months, and I've seen chaps getting off with warnings and slapped wrists. Believe me, if the judge was feeling particularly tough he might give him a short sharp shock in Borstal. Like I said, a few months. He was underage, Harriet. You know, not responsible for his actions. I'm telling you, you haven't lost anything.'

It seemed to me that we had lost everything. We had allowed her to be abused again, by the police, on the off-chance that Peter would spend a few months in a remedial school. I felt quite helpless. I didn't know how to start trying to understand. I remember feeling the same bewilderment way beyond anger, when I heard of atrocities witnessed by missionaries in other countries, committed by one tribe on another, or hardships imposed by the government on the struggling little Christian Church in Nepal. But even in that I could grasp something. Often those committing the terrors were frightened too, fighting for their own survival. But this? What had anyone to gain by ignoring the wrong done to Sara? Is she really part of the dark, unspeakable threat of womankind which men have to control? I've heard feminists giving such an explanation for the lenient sentences for rape. I refused to believe it.

I complained bitterly to David about it, late one night, as the winter drew in, and we sat opposite each other by the fire. Often, when we were first married, I used to wonder that he didn't sit next to me; that he didn't put his arm around me as affectionate husbands are supposed to, and do in TV soap operas.

'I don't know, Harriet,' he admitted. 'I find it hard too. But I suspect I know why it happens. The simple truth of it is, I don't think we can ever understand.'

'Who? Understand what?'

'Men.' I was about to say something, but he went on. 'To be brutal, I haven't got a clue what Sara's going through. Or you. Though I must say, I can see that her treatment at the police station was pretty unspeakable: being stripped and prodded and stared at by a roomful of strangers. I can understand the horror of that because I'd find it shaming too. But that's all. I don't know what Peter's done to her. I can't really imagine someone getting inside me, and making me hate myself. That's what's happened, isn't it?'

I said nothing.

'Whereas you understood immediately,' he continued. 'You'd sympathise with a woman raped on the other side of the world. I can't. So I don't think the judge has any idea what he's judging. I think, if he's honest, every time a man hears of a rape he thinks he could easily have done it himself. He can't punish it too harshly: he might do it too one day.'

We sat silent while the minutes passed. The old comfortable clock ticked loudly on the mantelpiece. It was well past midnight. The ashes were glowing more grey than red. 'You really mean you can imagine doing it?' I asked him at last.

'Oh yes,' he said immediately. 'Yes indeed. Given the right circumstances. There aren't many crimes I'm not capable of, given the right conditions.'

I thought about this for a long time. 'I can't imagine committing murder,' I said.

'Can't you? Oh, I can. I can imagine it easily.' He looked at me and smiled his old smile. The smile that turned his face from that of a slightly stern, high-principled man to the face of a careless undergraduate.

'How unpleasant.'

'Yes, we are pretty unpleasant, most of us, underneath.'

'Speak for yourself,' I said, trying to sound light-hearted.

'It's called Original Sin.'

I shivered. I remembered, before we were married, David saying the tick of a heavy clock by a wood fire opposite an old friend with a favourite book was one of the happiest scenes to look forward to. At the time I thought it sounded impossibly prosaic and dull. But what wouldn't I give for it now, that old familiar face?

We did suddenly look old. Still in our thirties, we looked middle aged and worn. And the clock went on and on regardless, while Sara lay turning upstairs, with the tears drying on her cheeks.

I have remembered that conversation often since. Is it really true, that a man as good and kind as David clearly was, could commit something as dreadful as a rape? That we are all potential tyrants and bullies, thieves and murderers? How does an ordinary person get to the point where he or she can commit dreadful acts of evil? The same way, I suppose, that equally ordinary people become heroes. Step by step.

'Darling?' he said. He hardly ever called me darling.

'Mmm?'

'It's nearly half past twelve. Come on.'

He held out his hand and pulled me to my feet.

Seven and a half years later, I thought of that conversation with David, and his similarities with Prue. The St Josephs go back several centuries, Prue's family even further. In a strange way, revenge, murder, acts of heroic self-sacrifice to protect the family honour, are still fresh and comparatively recent in their long collective memory.

I thought of the letter Prue wrote to the police, which was still sitting in the safe. My first instinct had been to burn it, but I knew Prue would be angry with me if I did. I had only been able to face reading it through once, but I still felt I knew it almost word for word.

It was, of course, a full and detailed confession to the murder of Peter Midland.

36

And this story – what had happened to Sara all those years ago – was what one solitary PC, Fred Little, too old and content and settled in his ways to seek or need promotion outside Cambridge, had remembered when he got back to work after the May Bank Holiday Monday, and heard his colleagues talking about Peter's suicide. He remembered the connection between our families, and what Peter had done to her, and the fact that we had reported it. He also remembered that it had all come to nothing. And he remembered his own frustration and anger, that Sara's abuser had gone scot free. He felt, acutely, that the system had let Sara down, even though we all knew it was no one's fault. Ironically, it was because he had cared so much all those years ago, that he remembered so clearly now.

This was why the police subsequently visited me, to 'eliminate' me from their enquiries. And that was why I wasn't at all surprised to get Prue's letter.

The next visit was mid June. Eight weeks ago. The new leaves had turned a darker shade of green, blossom had fallen off the trees, the lilac was finished. Walking into Cambridge Market Place from Langley House one afternoon, in the bright midsummer sunshine that spoke of picnics on punts and *Midsummer Night's Dreams* in college gardens, I passed undergraduates in tennis whites, and heard the thwack of a cricket bat as I crossed over the road by St John's. I find it almost unbelievable that I could ever have been as carefree, a mere twenty years ago, as those young people are now.

When I got home from work that day Mr Willcox came to see me for the last time. I offered him a drink, but this time he refused. He launched straight in.

'Mrs St Joseph, I'll get straight to the point. It seems as though you may have been witholding information which might have helped us in our enquiries. You asked us to be sensitive to your daughter.' And none too soon, I thought. 'But we do need you to play fair. It's going to be very difficult if you aren't open with us.'

'Shall we sit down, Mr Willcox?'

'Thank you,' he said, and took the chair I offered.

'I'd be surprised if you can show me information I've witheld which might be relevant to Peter's suicide.'

'All information is relevant to us. You must let us decide what's important.'

'That's impossible,' I objected reasonably. 'Do you want to know what I had for breakfast? What I gave my daughter for her birthday? I might not know what you think important.'

'Well, for instance, we asked you about the relationship between your daughter and the deceased.'

'Yes?'

'You didn't say that he had abused her as a child.'

'You already knew. Graeme McCullough told me. Besides, we went to the police at the time. It was painful to talk about it then, and it is now. It's not the sort of thing any of us would mention unless we had to.'

'Yes, but because you didn't press charges at the time, there was no record of it on the computer. I could have wasted a lot of man hours digging up the old crime sheet.'

'You are completely wrong,' I said, and the deep-seated anger from all those years ago made me feel cold, and very much in control. 'It was you, the police, who wouldn't press charges.' And if you want to play fair, we have a long way to go before we're quits.

'Did he bother her more recently? Was he stalking her, for instance?'

'No.'

'But you did ask PC McCullough's advice about stalking, and the situation in the law, and so on?'

I had wondered whether Graeme would put two and two together. But in the weeks since Peter's death I had assumed, because I hadn't heard anything, that he hadn't made any connection, or that he, or Cambridge CID, hadn't thought it relevant.

The previous winter I had indeed asked Graeme's advice about stalking. I'd also asked him to clarify what one could do about a crime which hadn't yet happened. I didn't mention Peter's name, and there was nothing in our conversation to indicate that it was anything but an academic enquiry. At that time, the stalking law wasn't in place. Even if it had been it probably wouldn't have helped. Oh, Peter may have been mad and confused, but he was also clever, very clever.

'Yes. I did. That was a long time ago. And our daughter was not being stalked.'

'I see. The point is this. Her fingerprints were found all over your gunroom.'

'It is our gunroom. My daughter lives here. I would expect to find her fingerprints around the place. No doubt my son's were there as well. And mine.'

'Of course. But what business would she have in that particular room? Most girls of her age take very little interest in guns. Or of any age.'

'I'm aware that, to one or two unimaginative members of the police force, the fact that my daughter likes shooting will seem suspicious in itself, but fortunately it is not yet against the law for girls to handle shotguns – though I expect that's only a matter of time. Her brother took her for a day's clay-pigeon shooting before the beginning of the summer term. And, as it happens, she was also in the apple shed the day after Peter died, looking for a tennis ball – though I believe you had taken the fingerprints by then. The storeroom which houses our gun cupboard is also a games room. The guns are locked up, but funnily enough, the croquet isn't. You must expect to find evidence of my daughter in her own home.' I stood up, hoping the interview was at an end. I longed to go upstairs, lie down, and go to sleep.

'There was another thing.' Mr Willcox paused, as if waiting for my complete attention. 'On the weapon that was used we found some very distinctive-coloured fibres from a jumper. Silvery blue. We gather that your daughter has been seen wearing a jumper of that colour. In fact, though it wasn't in the clothes of hers you gave us to look at, several people thought she was wearing it on the day Mr Midland died.'

I was cold from head to toe. I knew I needed to sit down

again, but I didn't dare. My mind was bombarded with thoughts, explanations, excuses. Reasons, quite legitimate reasons, why a gun that had been in a house for two generations would have traces on it from the people who lived in the house. That threads from a jumper of Sara's could have got on it anyhow. I had to resist a terrible urge to explain to the sergeant all the things that he was better able to know than I. Through a hectic storm of panic I heard myself saying, 'Surely, Mr Willcox, you're not suggesting . . .' and then I stopped. I didn't want to say any more. Why should I care what he was suggesting?

'I'm not suggesting anything, Mrs St Joseph. But you see why we ought to talk to her. She came back to the house on her own, on the afternoon of his death. She has been in that room recently. You do understand.'

'Yes, I do,' I said sadly. Slowly, I sat down again. 'She is completely innocent, just as she was eight years ago. I can't protect her now, any more than I did then. Have you got a daughter?' He didn't answer. 'Imagine it. Barely seven years old. Try to conjure up what it does to a girl. I know it's hard for men to understand, and I don't blame you for that, but just try for a moment. Imagine her putting her life back together again, painfully slowly, like a broken leg trying to heal, but much harder. She spends as many years mending her life, as she'd had unspoilt years before it happened. And, just as she's getting better, getting stronger, putting it behind her, something happens in a neighbour's house, and the police come round and break her leg all over again. This time she might not heal so easily. This time she may convince herself that she will never be allowed to get better, to forget it, that there is no point being brave because the day she thinks she's got over it, it will all start again. Just imagine, just try. And if you possibly, possibly can, try not to make it worse. Ask someone else the questions instead. Ask me. Ask me anything you like. I don't care what you put me through. But please, if you have any compassion in you, leave my daughter alone.'

'I'm sorry,' he said. He shifted his position, uncomfortably. 'I'm sorry. But I have to know: has your daughter got such a jumper?'

'Yes. I gave it to her for her birthday.'

'When is her birthday?'

'The fifth of May.'

'Oh.' He stopped. 'It can't be that, then.' He seemed puzzled, but almost relieved. 'The gun's been in our possession since the fourth.'

'I'm afraid it can. I gave it to her early. I bought it before Easter,' I added quickly, 'and I thought she might want to use it before her birthday. Before the weather got too hot for it to be useful.'

'And when did your son have the guns out?' If I'd had any humour left in me, I would have been briefly amused that Mr Willcox still couldn't bring himself to say that my daughter had used the guns.

'April. Late April. I can look it up. Before term started, anyway. After Easter. Certainly after I got the jumper. They went to Corry Lodge, the clay-pigeon centre. You needn't take my word for it. You can check with Corry's. They know Charles. And they'd have their names down. They would have checked his licence, everything.'

'And you definitely bought the jumper before then?'

'Yes. A couple of weeks before, I should think.'

'Have you any proof of purchase?'

'I believe I still have the receipt. There'll also be a record of it on my account at Robert Sayle.'

I got up to go, but he detained me. 'Listen,' he said kindly. 'Will she have washed it since the Fair?'

'It hasn't ever been washed. It's supposed to be dry-cleaned, but I thought we could probably risk hand-washing it, or even putting it on a gentle machine wash. But we haven't tried it yet.' I felt a flutter of hope. 'I'm sure you could tell. That it hasn't been cleaned. Don't they have a shop-finish, which comes off the first time something's washed?'

'I believe sometimes they do.'

'D'you want me to get the jumper?'

'I may not need to take it, if you have proof that you bought it earlier. But do me a favour, and don't wash it for the next few days. Why don't you just get me the receipt . . .' he didn't quite seem to finish his sentence.

I went up to my study. On the way up I paused on the landing, and realised I was shaking. It was nothing to do with Mr Willcox. He was a competent, polite policeman trying to do his job. But his colleagues, his predecessors, had abused my child, treated her almost as brutally, as Peter himself had. I looked out of the window across my front drive, towards the village, then sat down at my desk and rested my head in my arms for a moment. What would happen if I went downstairs and told Mr Willcox I'd killed Peter? Would he leave Sara alone? Probably not. I had an unbreakable alibi, after all. Besides, I told myself, guilt must be proved beyond reasonable doubt. They might find enough to make her life a misery, but they couldn't find enough to convict her. Presumably.

Once before I'd reported a crime, at Sara's expense. I wasn't going to make the same mistake again. I'd had enough of the innocent taking punishment for the guilty. I wasn't going to let her suffer all over again, just to 'let right be done'.

Or should I use Prue's letter, as she'd intended me to?

I went into Sara's room, and saw the jumper scrumpled up on the floor on the other side of her bed. I left it there, went back down to Mr Willcox, and gave him the receipt.

'I'll do what I can,' he said. 'This'll enable me to prove to my inspector that she had the jumper before your son took the guns out. Then there'd be a reason, you see, for the fibres to be on it. She needn't even have been wearing the jumper when she went to Corry Lodge. I don't suppose she was?' he asked hopefully.

'No,' I shook my head.

'No matter. She could have been putting the jumper away, in a drawer, and fibres got onto her hands or her other clothes. Anything. All I need to do is show my boss that your daughter had this garment for several weeks before Mr Midland died. That'll prove that she could easily have got fibres on the gun at any time. If he's in doubt we'll come and pick the jumper up, to have a look at it, put it through a forensic test. But this receipt should do it. And we'll give Corry Lodge a ring. I honestly don't think we'll need to bother you again.'

'Thank you,' I replied. 'I appreciate it.'

'I'll give you a receipt for this receipt,' he said.

'Forget it,' I said. 'I was about to throw it away.'

And I showed him the door.

37

By the third Saturday in June the temperatures in London were hotter than they were in Bombay. We had been granted a week of cooler weather, with cloud and occasional drizzle, and then the heat had come back worse than before. Willisham sweltered. Children of friends were ringing up to ask if they could use the pool even though it was the weekend. They normally only come on weekdays when they know that Sara and I are likely to be out, leaving little notes of thanks and home-made cakes and jams in the changing hut for me to find when I take a dip in the evening.

We refused to admit that we were uncomfortable. In any other country we would have been moaning long ago. As it was we met in the greengrocer's and flapped our clothes and said to one another, 'Whew. Another lovely day.' 'Isn't it? Almost too hot.' 'Almost. Don't complain; it might go away.' And with that we sat on in the sun, exhausted, submitting to conditions which would have sent Africans indoors.

On the nineteenth of June, a few days after that hot Saturday when we should all have been in Bombay, I finally left the Samaritans. I can talk about it now. I had told them of my decision two or three weeks before. The director accepted that it was the right thing to do. It was good to agree with him at last. My time with them had not been an unqualified success.

I had joined them six months after we got back. I had some free time while Sara was at school, and I told myself I wanted to help anyone who might be suffering as she had done. The truth of it was that I was still hurting myself. Perhaps it wasn't Sara's pain at all, but mine, which I was trying to expunge. I wonder whether that has been much of the problem, all along. Can I bear the truth of that? Has this all really happened, not because of Sara at all, but because of me? She was so young she barely knew what was going on, but I knew, and felt it all. The guilt, the loss of her childhood, and then watching my children see the lighthouse of their life go out, on a narrow bed in Phulbari. Did I join the Samaritans to lose my own problems by hearing other people's?

I usually did a daytime shift, and felt genuinely useful at first, as useful as one could be with that sort of misery. But I doubt if anything I said to anyone really helped. And when the other calls started it became unbearable.

Despite the disagreement we'd had, the director thanked me warmly for my time and services, and we shook hands and said goodbye amicably enough. We had understood each other. Though we could never have seen eye to eye, we genuinely respected one another's reasons.

The next day, Friday the twentieth of June, I went to see Hugh. I'm not sure that I was honestly asking him to inform me as to the right, Christian thing to do. Many years ago, in that distant clearing in the dappled sunlight, all our problems were so much simpler: then, teenager though he was, he could genuinely tell me what the Bible's advice would be. When the only problem facing me that last time when I asked him what I should do, aged seventeen, was whether I should sleep with the very rich and impressive young man who fell in love with me before David. I took his advice then, but, as with all advice, presumably only because it was what I had wanted all along. He gave me the freedom to believe that my instinctive romantic notions were not absurdly unrealistic or out-dated.

Did I, on this occasion too, really just want a confessor? Someone who could listen without screaming. And indeed, on the more practical level, someone who could listen without having to do something about it. I believe a priest is legally exempt.

Having resigned from the Samaritans, I no longer felt I was betraying the same confidence. And besides, the man is dead.

We had talked about it together, all of us at Samaritans, but we found when it came to taking the calls that it hadn't prepared us enough. I doubt if anything ever could. By and large he was handed over to the men, but this wasn't always possible. Of course, one never really knew if they were genuine. The director still thought it unlikely, though some of the details sounded so convincing. He said that in sixteen years in the Samaritans he had never known claims like that to be truthful. They were likely to be a safety valve, or a show of exhibitionism, distressing though they were. But then, how would one ever know? Another colleague, a retired clinical psychologist, said that Peter sounded genuinely ill and potentially very dangerous.

But it was out of the question to go to the police. We all knew that from the beginning. There was no room for debate on that score. It was simply against the rules. Presumably, if Hitler had gone to the Samaritans – had they existed – in 1935 with his plans for the future of six million Jews, they would still have been unable to break their silence. I can see the point. Once you destroy confidentiality it can never be restored. Nevertheless, on this occasion, I wanted to say that the safety of little children was more important than keeping faith.

And what could the police have done? We didn't know who he was, not at that stage. Even if we had, he had not committed an offence, or not according to the law. Until something had been proved in court, he was, in law, an innocent man, whatever he confessed to over the telephone.

Now I had left the Samaritans I could explain to Hugh, who wasn't involved in any way, the dilemma I had been in. He was a professional priest after all, with professional confidentiality too. He couldn't break silence either. And I wanted so much to tell him. The burden was becoming unbearable. He is a very old friend.

His children were all at home, so he and I decided to go for a walk to avoid being disturbed. They were lounging about in the kitchen, charming and unaffected as ever, with their henna-ed hair and messy homework spattered with butter and tea. The twins, Katy and Pam, are at Comberton School. They admitted that term hadn't quite finished so strictly speaking they should have been at school; but immediately followed this up by saying it would finish in a week or two, and exams were over anyway. Hugh shrugged, and looked helpless, and smiled. Joshua was there too, back from his first year at Durham with a new girlfriend.

So we left them in the kitchen and walked out together, down through the fields to the old Roman road, and wondered which way to turn.

'You can walk all the way into Cambridge on this road,' he said.

'Do you think we'll get that far?'

'That depends how much you've got to tell.'

'Oh, a fair bit.'

We set off in the direction of the city.

'Mr Willcox called on me yesterday afternoon.'

'Mr Willcox?' Hugh had forgotten who he was.

'You know, that friendly detective who is covering Peter's death. The one who discovered you had skipped the Fair for the afternoon.'

'Oh yes. That was rather exciting. No alibi. I liked that policeman.'

'It must be an unpleasant job though. Investigating that kind of thing. At one point he seemed to think he might have found Peter's killer.' Hugh looked at me enquiringly as we walked along.

'His killer? Not suicide then?'

'You know the line they take. They have to "eliminate" all of us from their "enquiries". There's one of us they don't quite seem to have eliminated yet. And, as her godfather, I thought perhaps you ought to know.'

Some people, perhaps without Hugh's training, might have laughed at this, or looked horrified, or simply denied it. He pursued his lips, and sucked in his breath, and raised his eyebrows.

We walked on in silence for a moment or two. We approached a man in his sixties gathering something from the hedgerow into a little plastic bucket.

'Afternoon,' we said.

'A'ernoon,' he replied. We walked on. I wondered what he could possibly be collecting.

'Hugh,' I began again. 'Do you remember, when Graeme came to tell us that Peter had been found, shot dead, at Alison's cottage, on the afternoon of the fair, I asked you to stay and look after Sara?'

'Yes. I remember very clearly. It struck me as unusual at the time, but I assumed you had a good reason for it.'

'I never told you what the reason was. It was quite illogical, because Peter was already dead. He had decided to have another go at Sara. I think he was planning to attack her again on the day he died.'

38 ∫

I had been on Samaritan duty the week before. April the twenty-fifth. Peter telephoned. It was Peter: there was no doubt about it. I had really known it all along. He talked about sex with a child, a girl who had then been taken away from him. The others told me about it. I always knew it had to be Peter. That afternoon, he told me about raping Amanda. The director would have been sceptical, said he was making it up, trying to appear macho. But I knew. I knew what he was capable of.

Then, he told me what he was intending to do. To Sara. 'To' her? With her, on her, what you will. Whenever I've heard those bitter, cruel words of Iago's they always made me shudder.

He went into some detail. We do get occasional unpleasant calls; we call them 'manual relief' calls. One simply hands the receiver straight to the man on duty. But I was the only person there.

It wasn't just manual relief, though. He wasn't dreaming. He was planning. He told me he had been biding his time for months, years, and would continue to. He assured me he would watch and wait. Outside her school, by the church, by our curate's house when she came out of the youth group on a Sunday night as she does now. He knew her timetable. No trouble was too much for him to take. She was the only one he had ever cared about. And one day he would make her his own. That was how he described it to me. As the troubadours themselves saw it. Perhaps that's all courtly love was after all: a violent, arrogant rape.

I have often wondered, since, whether he realised who I was; whether he had recognised my voice, perhaps even subconsciously, and was trying to present his obsession as a chivalrous passion which a parent, five hundred years ago, might sanction and allow. As presumably parents did once, in the days before Willisham House was built, when Willisham Manor stood on the site: allowing men to ravish their fourteen-year-old girl-children, if the contract and land agreements and money were all in order. Peter had always been passionate about history, as a child.

The fear I felt, when I heard his voice at last, was not new. My suspicions had been growing for months. Once or twice, I thought I'd caught a glimpse of him waiting by a bus-stop outside Sara's school, or lurking in a lane in Willisham, but I don't know whether it was really Peter, or my imagination distorted by fear. This was why I told Willcox he had not been stalking her. I don't think he was: I suspect he was too cunning. But my panic infected Sara. She started vomiting, getting high temperatures, going without meals. Her acne was bad again. And the very first time she missed school, I found a little posy by the back door, as if Peter was saying, 'Where have you been? I missed you.'

It is difficult to convey how utterly terrifying it was. But there really was nothing we could do, it seems. We didn't want to report it unnecessarily, because we knew what the effect of further questioning would be on Sara herself. We'd seen it all, years before. She did not need to live through that again. And after I spoke to Graeme about a supposedly theoretical case, I knew what I had suspected all along: with no evidence of his identity, the police could do nothing.

Prue refused to believe this, so she rang a chum at New Scotland Yard. Sir Somebody Something, who, she claimed, 'knew everyone and everything'. She went up to London and lunched him at her club, giving him all the details. But his advice was much the same. You cannot arrest a man without evidence. But, Prue objected, we know who he is. You may, he replied. But we don't: we cannot prove it. She said they'd have all the proof they needed when Sara was raped again. Maybe: but you cannot arrest a man before he commits a crime. Her friend also confirmed what we most dreaded. If we reported it, if the police could pin anything on him, if they could act on any of the evidence, the only way forward was through the courts, and Sara would have to repeat what had happened to her before. She would have to go through it all again, this time in public.

Luckily, Charles missed most of this because he was away at school. He did get some inkling of what was going on, and offered to go and beat the living daylights out of Peter. Said he'd always wanted to, and now was his opportunity. He also said he could bring his school boxing team over for a weekend and they could sort him out without anyone being any the wiser. Somehow, I did not think this would solve the problem. The parents of the school boxing team probably included judges, QCs, and then cabinet ministers. I couldn't see any of them turning a blind eye to such activity, if one of the boys should happen to mention it over breakfast at home. I told Charles we liked the sentiments of his heroics more than we would like the consequences.

Then, towards the end of last year, someone at Samaritans told me about the calls. The caller claimed to have had sex with children, to have committed several rapes. Something alerted me. A sixth sense, a knowledge of the enemy, a deep fear. Sometimes these claims were interspersed with his more ambitious plan: to have his first love again. She was his inspiration, his obsession, the rest were simply rehearsals.

So when I took his call for the first and last time on the twenty-fifth of April, I knew exactly who it was. And I also knew what was about to happen. Soon he was going to go for it. Again, I don't know how I knew. He had stopped planning and speculating, and now he was going to act.

It took me some time to collect my thoughts. It was not yet half past three. Sara was safe in school. The first thing I did was to ring Cambridge police. The line was busy. As I put the telephone down, I asked myself what on earth I was doing. How could they help? As Prue's friend had pointed out, you can't convict a man before he's committed the crime. What did I expect them to do? Give her police protection for the rest of her life? A man who can nurture a sickness for eight years can harbour it for ever.

I rang the Samaritan emergency standby, and left. I waited outside her school for three quarters of an hour, until she came out. She's always later than the others, gossiping and nattering for a long time at the end of the school day. She was surprised to see me, but I said I had finished something early and thought we could go home together. So we did. I told her to leave her bike at school overnight and I would drive her in to school the next morning. And the next, and the next, and so I did until after his death.

That evening, at Willisham, I heard every tiny sound as if it were an army of Peters surrounding the house. Sara asked me, once or twice, what the matter was, but I couldn't bear to tell her.

And I settled in to the living horror of the wait. The haunting presence, or absence, of the man who was going to destroy our lives all over again.

It's a cliché which I had also experienced second-hand, through my work at the Samaritans: that the fear is often worse than the actual attack. A lovely woman, softly spoken, highly articulate and well educated, rang more than once after her husband had beaten her. She wouldn't tell me who he was, but I could spot a senior member of the University from the way she described him. What caused pain was not the physical bruising – he never hurt her enough for it to show, of course – but the breakdown of trust, the fear, the anticipation of the next attack.

And for us, day by day, for the next week, this fear was building, each day worse than the last with anticipation and exhaustion and waiting. At last, Prue said we had to act.

'Act? What do you mean, "act"? Go to the police again, or what?'

That was pointless, she said. She had just spent an hour on the telephone to a psychologist friend of David's. This doctor was convinced that we were not tilting at windmills: Peter was a rapist, quite possibly a murderer, in the making, and Sara was his target.

'Then surely we can get him sectioned?' I pleaded with her, as though it were Prue's own decision.

'Oh, no,' she said. 'That would be too easy. "It's a minefield," as they say. Darling, he can only be sectioned if he's curable. He will be sectioned for his own good, not for ours. Oh, I'm sick of all the terms and definitions and symptoms and syndromes. If it's a psychosis they may be able to do something: if it's a personality disorder they may not. How do we know which it is? And if he's simply a killer and rapist in the making we can't do anything.'

'That's reasonable, Prue,' I argued. 'Otherwise you could lock anybody up on the grounds that they might do something one day. What kind of a police state would that be?'

'Don't you start justifying it. I've had enough of that for the past hour.'

'So what are we going to do?'

'I'm working on it. I'm working on it. Let's talk after the Fair.'

I should have known then, that when Prue starts working on something, she invariably comes up with a hare-brained scheme which only Maurice has ever been capable of defusing.

On the day of the Fair, I remember clearly, I didn't knock on Sara's door on my way down for my swim. On my way back up, dripping from the pool, I opened the door and she lay beneath the bedclothes, her eyes turned to the window which I'd left open the night before. I wanted to pull the window to, and sit on her bed as if she were a little child again. A child again with her childhood gone, her inheritance mislaid, her bouncing years of laughter cut off.

I vividly remembered, when she was younger, sitting on her bed, pulling a dull, sweaty strand of fringe out of her eyes and pushing it into the rest of her hair. She would blink, and shrink from my touch slightly, as if it were vaguely distasteful to her but she couldn't summon the energy to mind.

I used to hate sending her to school on days like that. David was more lenient than I. He would say, Leave her: school isn't the most important thing in the world. Let the poor child have a day at home with a book. But I thought, with meticulous and well-informed folly, that it would only make it harder for her if we treated her as a special case, a fragile creature.

I would perch on her bed eight years ago, as I longed to that Saturday, when she wanted a cuddle and I knew she had to get up and get dressed. If David were there, he would lie down on the bed beside her and hold her it seemed for ever, and let her be as late as she liked. It was one of the few times she let him touch her. Whereas I would hug her for a moment, then tell her it was eight o'clock, time to get up, hurry and dress and go. And she would look past me in the direction of the window, while I smoothed her hair out of her eyes, seeing nothing and shivering.

Sometimes I would sit on the floor with her and try to put an arm around her. Like Elephaz the Temanite, and his friends. And they sat with Job on the ground seven days and seven nights, and no one spoke a word to him, for they saw that his suffering was very great. But for a long time after the incident I found it hard to get close to her. When she most needed me to fold her in my arms, when David's and Charles's caresses were like poison to her, I found it hard to cuddle her with any enthusiasm at all. I did, of course – but perhaps she sensed my revulsion, my hatred of Peter, and therefore, in part, of the person he had possessed.

She had loved the pool as a child. Charles was quite a good swimmer. But Sara was like Maurice, addicted to the water. Every morning, before breakfast, she would be in with Grandfather, getting up at seven to wake him, and running barefoot across the lawn while he followed at a slow jog. We used to dispense with swimming costumes when it was just family, early in the morning. It was half the fun of going in before the world was up. But Sara would be most carefully dressed for the occasion, with her Mickey Mouse swim suit on and her armbands diligently blown up. Later in the day she would invariably forget, and shed her clothes one by one till the garden was strewn like the road to Jerusalem and she found herself swimming again, as she would say, 'by a mistake'.

Those were early days, of course. That was the kind of girl she was. Idiotic and full of fun. Hugh said to me once, long before he came to Willisham, 'Whatever Sara does with her life, she'll make a success of it.'

'Of course,' I said lightly. 'She takes after her mother.' I can't remember whether David was with us then.

'No,' he replied. 'Her father. No thanks to you at all.' Then I think we had a playful fight and he pushed me into the river. No, that can't have been then. Surely it must have been when he was an undergraduate and I was still at school. At some stage we must have learnt to behave like adults.

She didn't have a swim on the morning of the Fair. Nor breakfast. I wanted to take her a tray with a white napkin and my little china teapot with the flowers on it, a hot roll and a vase with sprigs of something or other. I doubt if it would have been appreciated, and besides, I didn't have time. So I gave her her birthday present instead.

It was just before we left for the Fair. 'Would you like me to open it for you?' I was more excited than she was. She looked at the silvery blue silk and linen, and liked it, and put it on.

'So you see,' I told Hugh as we walked on, 'if Willcox does his homework, he'll know that Sara never touched that jumper until the day Peter died. The receipt was dated several weeks earlier, but I kept it put away all that time.' And how did she get fibres onto the gun, unless she touched it the day it was used?

I explained to Hugh, carefully, as if the details were difficult, that if I had told the police more of the truth – that Sara hadn't set eyes on her jumper until the day of the Fair – there was only one conclusion they would have come to.

And that was that Sara had her hands on the gun which killed Peter, just an hour or two before it was fired.

39

And then, on that Sunday morning the day after the Fair, very early, long before we went to church, she appeared like a vision on the lawn, like a dream of her former self. There was no mistaking it. She was the same, but completely different. The same body, the same clothes, the same eyes and face, but she was better. I could see, at fifty paces, that she was better. He was dead. She was free. He'd been killed, and the result wan't remorse and misery, as it's supposed to be, but blessed release. One would have to say it seemed worth it.

'You look good.'

'Mmm.'

'Hugh told you, last night, what had happened?'

'Yes.' She stopped for a moment and looked towards the house. 'Poor Alison.' And there was a moment of real sadness there. Then she took off her towelling dressing gown and waterbombed into the pool like a tomboy of seven years old.

'Dear Alison,' she said again, during a splashy backstroke to the diving board.

I can't remember now how much of this I related to Hugh, as we walked along the Roman Road. Much of it, I think.

Every so often he turned to look at me, but mostly he looked ahead, or at the dried brown verges, or the thin and thirsty hawthorn which ran alongside us. Once we were overtaken by riders cantering along in the heat. We pulled over and greeted them as they thundered past, sweating and panting, and then we resumed our way.

Then I started to tell him the other things. That we keep the keys to Alison's cottage in our kitchen. That all of us, Charles, Sara and I, know where to find them. That Prue told us on Saturday morning that Peter was in Alison's house, alone. That Sara knew this. It must even have crossed her mind that he might try to tail her that afternoon.

Any fool could see the implications.

When I had finished at last I simply looked at him. And he said, 'Is that all?'

'Doesn't it suggest anything to you?' I said.

'Not at all,' he said. 'I should leave it to the police. They very seldom make wrong deductions.'

'But,' I said, and stopped. I felt in need of a great deal of air. I looked at the wide sky over Cambridge, and the martins dipping above us. 'What would happen if the police found out?'

'Found out what?'

'Everything. No I don't mean everything. Just short of everything. Obviously, if they found out everything, they'd know what really happened. But let's suppose, for instance, they discover Sara knew Peter was here that Saturday. Isn't that all they need? And that I gave her the jumper that very day.'

'They've tried all that, Harriet. And found nothing. If there was any damaging evidence, anything which gave them any suspicions at all, the police would have found it by now. They won't have left many stones unturned.' I thought of Sara's fingerprints in the gun room.

'Oh, Hugh,' I said, turning to face him. 'She's fifteen!'

'Yes. And Peter was twelve, nearly thirteen. And she was barely seven. It doesn't mean anything any more. Childhood was invented, like so many sensible things, by the Victorians. It is now over. Let's call it official. Twelve-year-olds become mothers. Ten-year-olds become murderers. Eleven-year-olds are rapists. So Sara is only fifteen. I'm sorry to sound brutal, but so what?' I turned away, and he went on, more gently. 'It was probably Willcox's last duty, before wrapping up the case. Or perhaps, to put it more cynically, you were his last chance of promotion this year. I shouldn't think for a moment he has any genuine suspicions of Sara. He just wanted to be absolutely sure.'

'I sincerely hope you're right.'

'Listen, Harriet, the police are on our side. They may not be if you're sixteen and black and live in Brixton.' Hugh had worked in the East End before coming to Cambridgeshire. 'But here in Willisham we're on the same team.'

'Then should I tell them everything?'

'What do you mean?'

So then I told Hugh. And this time, I told him all I knew.

40

We had walked six miles or more, through the countryside and flat fields and farms around the outskirts of the city, when Hugh said, 'Oh my poor Harriet. You poor, poor thing.'

He put his arms around me for a moment, and gave me a sharp hug. The he said, 'Let's turn around.' But we sat on a bench on a high spot of land for a while and looked out towards Cambridge.

'Why didn't you come and talk about this sooner?' he said.

'What good what it have done? What could you do that I couldn't? I would just have burdened you with something which you might have felt you couldn't even tell Tricia.'

'Oh Harriet, you idiot. What do you think the Church is for? "Where two or three are gathered together in my name, there I will be in the midst of them." Have you no faith in prayer?'

I stared in front of me. That was it. Of course. My legs, my arms and legs, became suddenly heavy. It was the most obvious thing in the world, the simplest thing, and I hadn't thought of it. At last I knew what David would have done. And I knew that I'd failed. Utterly.

Oh, I had prayed, of course. Alone, and without faith. I had never believed that prayer would be enough.

We have friends still in Phulbari, who became Christians, who inherited a life of persecution because of the work we were doing out there. Fathers who haven't seen their children for years because they won't keep quiet about their faith, and their families can't afford to go and see them. Men, and sometimes women, tortured for believing. Languishing in prison, though they are desperately needed to feed their families. All they have is prayer. Their children are at risk, as much as mine was, but prayer has to be enough for them. Why wasn't it enough for me?

Well, I've got plenty of time to learn my lesson now.

I took Hugh's rebuke and said nothing.

At last we got up and turned round for home. 'I presume there wasn't any stage when you could possibly have gone to the police?' he said wearily.

'Oh, Hugh. If you only knew. I thought about it, all the time. I pleaded with the director of the Samaritans to go. I said there are times when silence itself is immoral. He refused point blank. Perhaps he was right. He still thinks Peter made half of it up. But he also said there was nothing to be gained from it. If the police didn't already have leads on him, what we could tell them wouldn't help much. And that was true. It was pure fluke that I knew who it might be: and that was only hunch, only a hideous suspicion, really, because I'd never taken any of the calls. Not until that one and only one on the twenty-fifth of April. And once you break a pledge like that, the Samaritan pledge not to give information to the police, how could you ever restore it? Their duty isn't to the police: their duty is to desperate people. I admire them for knowing where it lies.

'We did try though, Prue and I. Of course we did. I told her. I preferred to break trust, in the end, than face the alternative. I couldn't face it, Hugh. I couldn't cope with it again. Prue went to New Scotland Yard. There was nothing they could do. He hadn't done enough for an injunction. He claimed to have raped other girls. If one set of parents had been prepared to put their daughter through what we put Sara through, they might have got him. But for how long? Three years, for a first offence? Out in one? I'm not convinced it's worth it. I could never advise another parent to make the mistake we made. And anyway, we didn't know who any of them were. We knew, at Samaritans, that we'd never find out. He didn't give much away. It was all pretty vague. I found out who one of them was, when it was far too late, but I'm not sure that her evidence would have done it.

'We hoped he might be able to be helped in a mental hospital. But he'd done nothing to be sectioned: not unless we could prove something. So he would have had to go voluntarily. And I knew him well enough to know that was hopeless. He could be chillingly sane, when he wanted. I wondered whether to go and see him myself; plead with him. But what would that have done? He would simply have become more cunning.

'And Scotland Yard were unequivocal. He hadn't committed an offence. Once it happened they could have locked him up. If she pressed charges. If there was enough evidence to make an arrest. If he were convicted. If, and if again. The chances are the jury would have seen them as acquaintances and assumed it was a "misunderstanding". And who can blame them? You know, Hugh, less that one per cent of rapists are convicted?'

It was all such old ground. I was weary of it. 'It would have been a "first offence", you see. Technically, at any rate. Do you know how little you get for a first offence? Then what? Out of prison again, still obsessed with Sara, and now furious at what she'd done to him. She would be in more danger than ever. I suppose we could have left Willisham, and gone round the world again. She could abandon her dreams of Cambridge. We could leave Charles behind in England to do his studies on his own. We could have split up the family even more than it has been split up already.' I stopped walking. 'Oh Hugh, I'm so sick of it all. The injustice of it. I'm glad it worked out as it did. I'm very sorry for Alison, but it had to work out this way.'

We resumed again, in silence for a while. I felt as if all I wanted was to sit down, in the sun, and never get up again. We came back to the man in the blue overalls. He barely seemed to have moved, and his bucket had little more in it than it had half an hour before.

'Afternoon,' Hugh said alone this time.

'A'ernoon,' he repeated. We walked past. 'Reveren',' he added, seeing Hugh more closely.

'Friend of yours?' I asked him, after we'd moved on.

'Not sure. Think I did a funeral for him last year. His wife.'

I bent to pick a fluffy, blown dandelion, and the acrid milk from the broken stalk stained my fingers. As always, the seeds, which are supposed to tell the time, had mostly shaken off before I could blow it.

'"Fear no more the heat of the sun."'

'What?' said Hugh.

'Nothing. Prevalence of death, that's all. Anyway,' I said at last, 'I'm wondering what I should do now.'

'Is there anything you should do now? Isn't it all over?'

'Isn't there? In the interests of justice?'

'Ah, justice,' Hugh said.

Hugh came back to me, three days after I'd visited him, on the twenty-third of June, to say he'd given my question some thought. I believed him. He wouldn't treat me to an easy answer. I knew he had listened seriously to all I'd said.

'Do nothing, Harriet, for the moment. Will you?'

I didn't reply to begin with, and then I said, 'Go on.'

'See what's said at the inquest. Leave the professionals to sort it out. They're paid to promote justice, and they're pretty good at it. Will you agree to wait till then?'

'If you insist.'

'I do. I'd go further. Whatever conclusion they come to, please trust it. Trust it to be the just one, and leave it at that.' He smiled. 'You never know: they may come to the conclusion it was suicide after all. Then you can stop worrying about justice, and your responsibility, and all the rest of it. Agreed?'

'Maybe.' And I smiled too.

On Midsummer's Day Sara asked if she could go to France with a school friend and her family for most of August, staying in a château in the Cognac region. She was worried that I wouldn't want her to go, that I'd want the three of us to have a summer holiday together. I was overwhelmed with relief at the plan. She was due to come back in time to go to Edinburgh for the Festival, playing chamber music on the Fringe in a quartet from school with her music teacher. I had promised to go with her, and Charles was going to join us, staying in the house of an aunt of David's, near the sea in some smart suburb on the edge of the city. Now, of course, it won't happen. It's the little adjustments that seem so hard to make. Dear God, I hope she copes with it.

Tom came to stay again, after the end of term, and I took the three of them out for dinner in Zorba's, off Bene't Street. I don't know if they sensed something, but Charles and Sara seemed to take responsibility for me, fussing about me together, Charles ordering the wine while Sara said, 'Try the squid, Mummy, it's really nice. Octopus is foul.'

'But squid always tastes the same. And it's only edible if it's just been caught.'

'You're right, Harriet,' Tom said. 'Take no notice of Sara. She doesn't know what she's talking about. She's only going for them because they're flashy. The steaks look good. They do them on charcoal, look, and they smell wicked.'

'Wicked'? I thought. Even his slang is out of date. I liked him even more than I had the first time. Whatever he said about Sara's tastes, there was nothing flashy about him at all. It wasn't until coffee that I discovered he was going up to Balliol in a year's time to read English, hoping to specialise in early Elizabethan drama. I don't know why I hadn't discovered it when he came to stay before. Sara and Charles were reduced to talking to each other and gazing out of the window commenting on passers-by while Tom and I talked of Kyd and Fletcher, Dekker and Middleton.

And I wonder if I will ever see them together again, relaxing in a restaurant or picking blackberries in the sun. It's a pity. I took such pleasure watching the three of them enjoying each other. Why do I say 'it's a pity' with such wretched Anglo Saxon understatement? I want to say it breaks my heart.

It was July. Peter had been dead for two months, and Willisham seemed to be forgetting that it had ever known him. After all, it had said goodbye to him more thoroughly, if less formally, when he went to Christ's Hospital. His death was no longer even any good to natter away the time in the butcher's while Andrew cut minute steaks or Geoff constructed a complicated crown roast. Alison had had her moment of glory; attention had long moved on to something else. The cameras of Anglia news were unlikely to come to her again.

Sara packed excitedly for France. People started to go on holiday. The inquest was fixed for the first week in August.

The only thing which seemed able to keep going was the heat. We no longer pretended it was fun. Old ladies melted under their shopping. Even little children stayed indoors. Dogs slept all day. Horses and ponies flicked flies, and otherwise didn't move. Only Hugh continued to enjoy the weather. He still sunbathed over his commentaries on the Letter to the Romans, which was what he was treating us to on Sunday mornings. I swam.

The inquest finally took place on the fourth of August. The heat was horrid. Our lawns had been scorched to straw long ago. We had only had about five days of rain in as many weeks. Plants had faded and dried up like paper, the leaves too dead to drop off, still and useless on the twigs.

I had to go to give evidence about the gun. We drove into Cambridge in plenty of time, thinking we'd never find any parking. But we found a spot in Silver Street, got to the Cornmarket early, and the policeman on duty said we could go in and sit through the previous case. He opened the door for us, and we saw a family of Sikhs scattered about the room on the large leather chairs. We crept along the wall and sank into the only two vacant seats, which seemed rather conspicuous along the middle of the next wall. A very elegant but not very articulate Sikh woman was giving her testimony. Her husband, it appeared, had attempted to cross Queens' Road at the pelican crossing. The case rested on the little green man. Or red man. That was the point. Had the signal been telling him to go, or only nearly so?

She, the widow, was beautiful and poised and utterly broken. In her poor but firm English she told us, proud and unhappy, about her husband. He was careful, always, when crossing the road. He would press the button and wait. He would wait for the peep peep peep and the little green man. He would never have crossed without permission.

And one had to believe her. One knew without hesitation what kind of a man he was, the man who had won the respect of this remarkable and grief-stricken woman and all her tall and handsome, turbanned sons. He would never have put his feet on a seat in the train, or smoked in the non-smoking compartment. He would never have crossed without the little green man.

And she had suffered enough. We couldn't have subjected her to any more. We couldn't make him guilty for it all; tell her it was all his fault. For her sake, we had to believe her.

Then the young man next to us got up to take her place. He wore ear-rings and green tattooes, and he had a very mild and kind-tempered face, and clean blond hair tied in an elastic band into a pony tail on his neck. He only looked about twenty-one, but he probably had a wife and two children. And I realised, if the widow succeeded in convincing us all that her husband had crossed on the green man, that this man must, at the very least, lose his job. If he had driven, the lights against him, to kill a man on a pelican crossing, he could surely no longer continue to support his family as a driver of tourist coaches. It would do nothing to bring her husband back. How stupid it was to try to prove his guilt. It was with a shock that I realised the man was really dead. Couldn't he just be knocked out, I thought, and rushed off to hospital? Death seems far too harsh for such a small mistake. But then I thought, idiotically, that he would have to have been killed or none of them would be there at the court, and we wouldn't be hearing about it at his inquest. Nothing could bring him back. Couldn't we forget the truth, and let this pleasant driver keep his job? What did it matter after all? Aren't people more important than truth, than justice?

Then Colin was called, as the court pathologist, to give evidence. He must have seen me from the corner of his eye, but he avoided my gaze. Perhaps it's unprofessional to recognise someone at an inquest. He told us that the pedestrian, whose name nobody seemed able to pronounce except the members of his family, had fractured his skull in several places and sustained heavy and multiple haemorrhaging. It doesn't sound as if he did sustain it, I thought to myself. He was indeed quite, quite dead. Then the coroner pronounced him dead too, gave the cause of death in his concise and technical language, and the large and supportive family filed quietly out of the room. I still think of his widow, now, alone with her tall dark sons. Oddly, I can't remember what the verdict was.

Then, after a rustle and a bustle and a settling down again like leaves after a little swirl, Alison was sworn in as a witness and we all started all over again. She was calm, but clearly nervous. I'm never sure of what, in those kind of circumstances. After all, what can she do wrong? Even if she did stumble, what would they do to her? The coroner, with his kind, tired old eyes, would say, 'That's all right, Miss Midland; don't worry. We'll simply start all over again.'

We went through the day. We were told about the Fair. We heard of the stall she was helping with, and I even thought, for a moment, we were going to hear an inventory of what she sold. Then we heard that she was called to my house, and that the police had already been at the scene. Then Alison told us that he had been a happy boy all his life and had no reason to want to dic.

Then I was sworn in. I said I did indeed own the weapon, an AYA 12-bore side-by-side double shotgun; that Geoff may have left the door to the gun room unlocked and this was not how I normally left it; that Peter knew his way round our house and outbuildings and could easily have found the key to the gun cupboard; that I had made a note of its absence on Sunday morning and had informed the police. When I was pressed on the subject of Peter's character, I agreed that he had been an unstable boy as a child, and was quite capable of taking things that were not his own. I hoped Alison would not be upset by this. I even wondered whether she would take it in. Besides, I had no choice: I was on oath.

By contrast, Graeme took the Affirmation. Then he said that the first he knew of Peter's death was a message from Cambridge police station saying they'd received a nine nine nine call. He said he had gone down to Alison's house to investigate, and called Cambridge straight back when he realised it wasn't a hoax. Soon after that he handed the investigation over to Cambridge CID.

Then Colin told us a great deal about the disruption of the tissues, and the bruising around the wound, the fact that the angle of the weapon had been fairly obtuse, so there were a number of jagged exit wounds, though most of the shot had not had time to disperse into a pattern, and so was lodged more or less in a mass. In fact, Colin took far longer than anyone else. He said the deposit of shot on the hands of the deceased was consistent with the deceased's having fired the shot. He estimated death to have taken place about two hours after the previous meal. At last he summed up. I don't know why, but I can still remember it more or less word for word. 'The shot has produced a ragged tear in the soft tissues of the palate and has disrupted bone around the base of the skull and upper cervical vertibrae. There is bruising in the adjacent soft tissues and the wad from the cartridge is embedded beneath the point of entry.' Why did the language remind me of David? Why did I long, at that moment of tedious technical jargon, for his intelligent, ironic eyes to sparkle at me over those desperately earnest procedings, and tell me to stop worrying, and draw my attention to the sunlight and freedom outside?

Alison remained expressionless; Graeme was looking more stupid than I've ever seen him, as if he were half-way between sleep and the afternoon's football score; even Willcox looked as if he were trying hard to concentrate. Only the coroner, with his eyes on his notes, still seemed able to take anything in. 'Death will have ensued rapidly after the shot was fired,' Colin concluded. He never mentioned adrenaline.

Then it was Mr Willcox' turn. He was far more economical than Colin. He described the scene of death as he had found it, said that in his opinion the shot had been fired between fourteen hundred hours, and sixteen thirty hours, the most likely time being approximately fifteen forty-three or thereabouts, because a neighbour had heard 'a car backfiring' at that time. Then he told us that various investigations had led him to believe that the deceased might have been mentally unbalanced.

The most interesting thing about it all to me was that nobody looked directly at anybody. I felt like Medusa. Even Willcox was avoiding me. And Alison looked at no one.

I needn't have worried about hurting her feelings with regard to Peter's character. The police psychiatrist told us she had examined evidence found among Peter's possessions. She said he might be of unsound mind, since they had found a 'diary of a sexual nature' in his room, and he seemed to harbour fantasies, some of which were depressive. In her professional opinion (and what other opinion could we have wanted? She was hardly a personal friend of his), Peter was of a highly volatile nature, and was perfectly capable of taking his own life. She hazarded that he had a personality disorder in the nature of a psychotic obsession, and her experience was that those who suffered from such disorders were frequently violent towards themselves or others, on the slimmest of pretexts which might be impossible to discover posthumously: it was quite likely that we would never know what the catalyst had been.

And finally the Coroner concluded that Peter had died of laceration of the brain, fracture of the skull and brain injury; and that he took his own life while the balance of his mind was disturbed.

In other words, he shot himself. Peter Midland had officially committed suicide.

Nobody was guilty after all.

I treated Alison and Graeme to a modest pub lunch after the inquest. We each had a ploughman's and half a pint in the open courtyard of The Eagle. Alison sipped her lager, and I thought she looked more relaxed than she had done for a long time. It was as if she found it a relief that the coroner had been able to make up his mind. Now she knew what had happened. She knew where she was, as it were.

Graeme took a good swig at his Guinness and said, 'Well done, Alison. You've done brilliantly. You can start living your life again, now.'

'Yes,' said Alison. 'Yes, I suppose I can.'

42 ∫

That evening I went to the vicarage to see Hugh. It's a disconcertingly ugly building, obviously dreamt up by some diocesan board with an ample appreciation of the mediocre, a concern for economics, and no aesthetic values at all. It recommends itself by suggesting that it might be comfortable, can't be expensive to heat, and it certainly isn't embarrassingly luxurious. A glossy holly tree preens itself in the front garden. The nearest building is a BP garage. The church is nowhere in sight.

Tricia has done a brave job on the inside, with a bit of help from better-off members of the congregation, some beautiful furniture and family antiques, and a great deal of good taste. And of course the inhabitants help. At the end of the day, it is the most refreshing house in the village to visit.

Hugh was expecting me. When I arrived he showed me into his purpose-built study, lined wall to wall with books.

'Well?' he asked immediately.

'Well what?' I said.

'How's the gorgeous goddaughter?'

'How on earth should I know? As far as I know, she's in the middle of nowhere, treading grapes to make upmarket booze. I haven't tried to ring her, and she hasn't been in touch yet. She'll probably write soon. She's not coming back until just before she goes to Edinburgh. The twenty-first of August, I think.'

'Ah,' said Hugh, and stood up to rearrange two or three of the commentaries on his bookshelves.

'David used to do that. It's very irritating.'

'What?'

'Mess about with his books while we were talking.'

'Sorry,' Hugh said, and sat down again. 'Well,' he said again. 'I gather it was suicide, after all.'

'Yes,' I said.

'No more talk about going to the police.'

'Does it make a difference?'

'Yes it does,' he said, and suddenly became very serious. He leant forward in his chair and made me look at him. 'Listen Harriet. I want you to listen very carefully. I'm your vicar as well as your friend: and you came to me for advice. You haven't got David to boss you around any more, so you can jolly well listen to me.' He smiled then, but he still meant it. 'There's been enough suffering in your family because of Peter Midland. Now it's over. Let's forget it. Nothing will be gained by raking up old ashes.' He stopped a moment, and decided to try a different tack.

'You've told me in the past that you regretted taking Sara to the police all those years ago. I think you're hard on yourself about it, but there's a lesson to be learnt. Your duty is to look after her, not . . .' He stopped. He took a breath. 'Don't sacrifice her again to some wonderful ideal of justice. Justice has been done. Near enough. Now let's forget it.'

We looked at each other for a long time. Then he stood up. 'Tricia will be home soon. Come on. And no more talk of going to the police.'

'I'll try not to mention it again.'

When we went into the kitchen we found Joshua cooking a large stew, while his girlfriend and Katy sat on the other side of the kitchen chatting to each other, from time to time telling him he was getting it all wrong. Pam, the other twin, was out at the cinema.

'Dad!' said Joshua the moment we walked in the door, in a tone that suggested the US cavalry had arrived. 'Dad, does an Irish stew have pearl barley in it?'

'No idea,' said Hugh. 'What on earth's pearl barley?'

'There you are,' said Joshua triumphantly. 'Nobody's even heard of it.'

'I'm not sure that follows,' said Hugh, unable to neglect justice completely, despite himself, 'just because I haven't. Anyway, I have heard of it. I just don't know what it is.'

'Of course it does,' said Katy.

'Nonsense,' said Joshua.

'Of course it does,' said the girlfriend. She was blonde and small and her hairstyle made her look like a cartoon hedgehog, and I thought she looked great fun.

'Rubbish,' said Joshua.

'For goodness' sake,' said Hugh. 'Does what?'

'Have pearl barley in it,' the girls chorused.

'Irish stew,' the girlfriend continued. 'My granny taught me how to make it, and she's nearly a quarter Irish.'

'Don't be stupid,' said Joshua. 'How can you be *nearly* a quarter Irish? You're either a quarter or an eighth.'

'Unless you're Irish,' said Katy. 'In which case you can be anything. Harriet, does it or doesn't it?'

'My mother said it did, I think. But she wasn't Irish, and she wasn't a very good cook.'

'Harriet, stay for supper,' said Hugh. 'We could do with a diplomat around.'

I needed that evening. It was like water in the desert. Like a momentary escape. For an hour or two I could almost believe there would be no consequences of anyone's actions, that I could stay in that happy, healthy family, with lots of chatter and no questions, and never face the cold at all. Nor the furious winter's wages.

I have a strange land in my mind that I suppose I think of as England: maiden aunts in country cottages in the home counties, serving tea on white linen tablecloths with warm scones and butter and lashings of home-made strawberry jam; where values of cosiness and quietness and propriety are so established they are never questioned; where, if you are ill, you are cared for in a tucked-up, clean and crisp white bed, and people bring you trays. Where nobody ever picks his nose or screams in terror at the evil spirits of the night, or dies on a wooden pallet above an earthen floor.

From time to time I've conjured up this homely place, full of English roses. When I was faint with dysentery, tramping the dusty streets of Kabul, on the way out to Phulbari, in the colourful, noisy evening, saying no to the constant soliciting of the cocaine merchants, or crossing the Khyber Pass in the back of an open lorry, when all the other passengers were equipped either with rifles or chadors. At moments like that, I have tended to think of a world where one can have a long, hot bath, or a cup of English tea, or eggs and bacon for breakfast, dreamt of with unbearable longing from such different shores as the slopes of the Himalayas or the coffee shops of Paris. A world, indeed, of village fairs on Saturday afternoons, when the jackals outside Phulbari are as distant as they could be and nobody ever does violence to another human being.

As I sat at Hugh and Tricia's kitchen table I wanted to believe I could find that safe and easy England, as mythical as King Arthur's, and snuggle up in it for ever.

I've always known it exists more solidly in the imagination than anywhere else. It's an oasis to come home to always, not to live in ever. It's an unreal heaven, dreamt of throughout one's travels, but tired of in an afternoon. At least, I would tire of it in an afternoon. When I realise, or remember, that the maiden aunts with home-made strawberry jam are in fact people, who were once sixteen themselves, longing for lovers in the heat of the night. And then I wonder what terrible and unspeakable boredom lies beyond the polite teatime conversation. And this is the world I thought I had come home to live in now. This is where I was due to measure out my life in coffee spoons.

I felt that Tricia understood what I was going through, as if Hugh had communicated with her invisibly. That she somehow knew and accepted me, without knowing, simply because Hugh was aware of the truth and they were one flesh. It seemed as though the whole family had committed themselves to me, simply because I had told all my fears to Hugh.

It was only an impression, of course: it wasn't true. I know Hugh talks to Tricia all about his work, tells her confidential things about his parishioners which she keeps as secret as he does. But he couldn't have told her this. She would then become an accessory after the fact, I think. What an intolerable burden I had put on him, without even thinking about it.

He walked me home, with William, his old cocker spaniel. A few years ago we would have taken him with us on our walk half-way to Cambridge, and he would have done the journey five or six times, running backwards and forwards around us, hardly panting at all. Now he groaned and shuffled at the thought of going out at all, into the rustling night.

We got to the house and I unlocked the gate. I now secure it properly when I go out. Then I asked him the original question, the one I had wanted advice about two weeks before. 'So you don't think I should talk to the police?' I said.

'No,' he said, emphatically and without hesitation. 'You are not to go to the police.'

But I think he was talking then more as a friend than as a priest.

That was the night of the storm. The only proper one we'd had since April, apart from that other one a few nights ago. It was an immense relief. When we were all tucked up in bed, the rain started. And it seemed to go on and on, unlimited quantities dropping in sheets and floods and torrents in its generosity. I listened to it for half the night, dreaming of the earth soaking it all up.

I thought it was all over. I think we all did. It seemed so final, such a release.

We were wrong of course: it was the only rain we had that month. It made no difference to the gardens at all. The next day they looked just the same, and the warm weather began all over again.

43

That night, as I lay in bed, I read Prue's letter again. I got it out of the safe on my way upstairs to bed. The time had surely come to dispose of it. The police wouldn't look for it now. But I didn't want one of the children coming across it by mistake one day, perhaps years hence, after my death, and then having to live with the thought that they had a murderess for a grandmother. At least, not without any explanation. Not without knowing the ins and outs.

But perhaps, on the other hand, I should keep it so they would always know what kind of a woman she was. So that was why, before I burnt it, I decided to read it again.

To whom it may concern.

I have asked my daughter-in-law to pass this letter on to the police, if necessary. I have no particular desire to be punished for my crime – I feel no guilt about it, so I need no catharsis. However, I certainly don't want anyone else to be locked up for it either. So I have disappeared in the hope that it will blow over and I will 'get away with it', but I am leaving instructions for you to have this letter in the event of an injustice being done to anyone else.

I killed Peter Midland. I did it deliberately, with malice afore-thought as I believe the correct phrase is, and I certainly cannot claim that the balance of my mind was disturbed. No doubt my lawyer will be very cross with me for saying this, but there we are: lawyers are a difficult lot to please. I know, I was mar-ried to one.

I killed him because I feared for my granddaughter. I did not think it was acceptable for her to have to go through that ordeal again, and

I knew the police could do nothing to prevent it if he were determined, or mad, enough. As I believe he was.

One night in early May I rang a friend of my late son's, a Fellow of Downing who specialises in psychiatry or psychology or one of these things; I can never remember the difference. I told him everything we knew about Peter. He confirmed – if confirmation had been necessary – that Peter Midland was an extremely dangerous young man. He was quite likely to abuse my granddaughter again, if he got the chance . . . and possibly worse, if he got jealous enough. My son's friend also said, ironically, that he was likely to damage himself too. I hope you will have concluded that this is what happened, so this letter will not have been necessary.

What could we do? The next day, the day of the village Fair, Peter turned up unexpectedly at his mother's cottage. Because the cottage belongs to us, we had specified, as a condition of his mother's continuing to live in it, that he was not to visit her. This may seem inhuman, but she didn't have to stay in it. And we were very concerned for my granddaughter. Funnily enough, she seemed quite happy with the arrangement.

In a way the situation couldn't have been worse. I sensed immediately that the attack might happen that very day . . . as I believe my daughter-in-law did too, even though we didn't get a chance to talk about it. Neither of us doubted for one moment that it would happen sooner or later.

In another sense, however, it was a Godsend. I hope that doesn't sound blasphemous, when talking of an act of murder. That's what I did, you see. I went to our old gun room – I know where all the keys are kept, of course: nothing's changed much – and took one of my husband's shotguns. I still keep keys to the cottages on the estate, so I simply let myself in.

He was asleep, in his mother's sitting room, having drunk a large quantity of beer. He was snoring rather.

So I shot him. Then I went away, in the hope that the fuss would die down. If you are reading this, it obviously hasn't, otherwise my daughter-in-law would never have given it to you.

I will be back. Quite soon probably. Then I will accept whatever punishment is my due.

Prunella Cawbain St Joseph

44

And the very next day, the day after the inquest, as suddenly as she had disappeared, Prue was there again.

For the first time ever, I missed my swim. I've never done that before, not in the summertime, not when the pool's open and it's warm enough. It's my lifeline sometimes, swimming away my anxiety in the sparkling blue water, easing away the stress behind my neck, washing away my cares. But that morning I couldn't face the pool any more. It's something I love, but I couldn't even bear to swim. For a while I lay in bed. The sun shone through my window, birds chattered, but I wanted to turn on my gas fire and lie there all day. I imagined myself as a eccentric recluse, in my bedroom for the rest of my life. Perhaps I would occasionally make forays into the garden in a bath chair.

Eventually habit prevailed, and I got up and dressed slowly, feeling as if parts of my body were made of blocks of wood. My head, in particular, was a singularly dense, heavy sort of hardwood.

I came down to the kitchen. I suppose I hoped that a cup of tea and some breakfast might help me pull myself together. I noticed the smell of coffee on the stairs, and wondered how it had got there before me. Perhaps Anna-Marie was early – though she always drinks instant.

When I entered the kitchen, the kettle was sputtering on the Aga, the coffee was made, and Prue was pottering about, singing, in the morning sunshine.

I stared at her. I think I was trying to work out whether she'd really been away.

'Darling,' she said. 'I thought of bacon and black pudding and fried eggs, but I wasn't in the mood. So I've bought these funny croissan'y things, with almonds and sugar dusted all over them. They look very jolly, but I'm not sure whether they should be eaten hot or cold.'

Then she stopped, put down what she was holding, opened her arms to me, and we held each other for a long time. Her embrace reminded me of David, but she doesn't feel as strong. For the first time ever, I realised that Prue is frail, and getting old.

At last she let go of me, blew her nose, and turned to look out of the window onto the kitchen garden.

'Well, well,' she said. 'I was going to ask how Sara is, but I see I need to ask about you first. Perhaps I don't even need to ask. Are you as bad as you look?'

'Worse.'

She nodded. 'I'm not surprised. Chin up. You're a very brave girl. I thought David had done well to find you, but I had no idea how well. You seem to have coped quite brilliantly.'

'What on earth do you mean by that? And what did you mean by writing—'

'Breakfast first! It isn't breakfast really, these dotty pastry things, but we're going to eat them anyway. Answer me two things? First, shall I put them in the oven?'

'Um. I suppose so. Why not?'

'Second, how is Sara?'

'Funnily enough, remarkably well. I don't know why, really. I've never seen her so well. Not for years. Prue . . .'

'That's all that matters. Sit down and drink that orange juice. Then I'll pour you some coffee.'

I did as I was told, and we sat down either side of the kitchen table to eat. I drank the juice, accepted the coffee, and tried to eat the almond croissant. After one mouthful I put it down again, and said, 'Prue, where have you been?'

'Oh, this delightful little place in Brittany. Didn't you get my postcards?'

'One postcard.'

'Though I suppose postcards don't tell you much. But what about my telephone message? I left a number where you could contact me.'

'Ah. That. I wiped it by mistake.'

'That was daft. Why did you do that?'

'A policeman was listening over my shoulder. Graeme, as it happens, but still a policeman.'

Prue went very still for a moment. 'Not so daft. How much did he hear?'

'Almost nothing. Unfortunately, that meant I heard almost nothing too.'

She became her breezy self again, in an instant. 'Can't be helped. I'm here now. Doesn't matter.'

'I didn't mean to wipe it. I got muddled with the buttons.'

She clicked her tongue. 'Potty, you are. That's my role. Mothers are supposed to understand machines. Grandmothers aren't.'

'No, well I'm sorry. You can explain now.'

'Oh, I'm not going to explain. So dull. All I said was that I had gone on holiday with an old friend, and here was a number you could ring me on.'

'I don't believe you. If it was as innocent as that, you would have rung me again.'

'All right. I said it was a number you could ring me on if no one was listening. And your telephone line wasn't being tapped, or recorded, or whatever they did to the Prince of Wales. Though it was a very complicated system, with neighbours and everything, because the cottage we were in didn't have a telephone. And then we went touring about.'

'Prue, you're so melodramatic. Why would anyone do that to me? Bug my telephone line?'

She ignored this. 'It seems you didn't use my letter after all.'

'Don't be daft. You can't seriously have expected me to.'

At that, Prue looked genuinely pained. 'Why in heaven's name not? I thought it was rather good. Reg didn't think much of it, but I was quite pleased with myself.'

'I'm sure. But you must have known I couldn't. It was a pack of lies from beginning to end. They would have seen through it in five minutes.'

'It jolly well was not. I did what all the best liars do, and used the minimum of falsehood and the maximum of truth. I think they would have been completely taken in.'

'Prue, listen: in real life, policemen are not like Inspector Slack.

Credit them with some intelligence. It was singularly unconvincing.'

'Most of it was true. I certainly spoke to David's friend at
Downing, and he told me the version Peter himself will have
given you of his revolting fantasies, over your goody-goody
helpline, would be a very sanitised version. If it was suspicious
enough to get the wind up the do-gooders, then the first sources
would be horrifying.'

'Prue, for goodness' sake. Tell me something else,' I was
determined to press my advantage. 'If it had been convincing,
do you really think I could have used it? Let me put that another
way: if it had been from your mother-in-law, would you have
landed her with an unjust life sentence?'

'Unjust?' Prue raised her eyebrows. 'Harriet, I expected more of
you. I thought we were both fighting for the same thing. I assumed
you were capable of putting your children first.'

'Self-sacrifice is one thing. But sacrificing someone else . . .'

'Oh, for shame, Harriet. When you're in battle, you can't afford
such sentimentality. Your colleague's life is worth no more than
your own. Besides,' and suddenly, she became uncharacteristic-
ally grave, 'they're not just your children. They're my grandchildren too.'

I stared at my almond croissant, then pulled a piece off it, but
put it down again without eating it. 'All right, let's go back to the
beginning,' I said. 'Why did you disappear?'

'I thought I'd lie low.'

'Why?'

'Because I'd just been to Alison's house.'

'Ah.' I turned and looked out of the window. After a long time
I turned back again, and Prue and I simply looked at each other.
Finally I broke the silence. 'And?'

'And I saw what had happened.'

'That Peter had shot himself?'

'No.'

'What then?'

'I saw what had really happened.'

I sighed, and took a sip of my coffee. As I aligned my cup back
on its saucer, I said, 'What makes you so sure you understand
the situation better than the police?'

'Darling. I know the people involved.'

The weather has finally quietened down. It's warm, but no longer a heady, extravagant, breathtaking sort of heat. It's now a normal, respectable, decent English summer in the middle of August, when most people are away anyway. The only thing to remind one of the extraordinary weeks that have passed is the dry earth. The two storms, on the fourth and the ninth of August, made little impact: the ground is still rock hard. I imagine the garden parched still, and the fruit trees looking pitifully for me with the hose to come and water them so the fruit can swell and ripen, and not wither on the branches. Bob will do it, Bob'll look after them.

I look out of my window at the now very familiar, rather dirty bit of a tree, where the birds come and visit me, and I remember what the birds looked like on my lawn. Sometimes at night, at about two thirty in the morning, a blackbird calls past the window, in a flash, spitting his sweet song into the night for a moment, and then is gone.

I can't work out that quotation from *Lear*. 'Went out the maid;' that one. Perhaps it isn't *Lear* at all. 'He that hath and a little tiny wit, Must make content . . .' I've been told I'll be able to look it up. I've been told that several times now. There must be a complete Shakespeare somewhere, even here.

I rejected Hugh's advice.

If I listen very carefully I can hear wind in a tree somewhere, very faint, whispering the secret to me that life is still the same. Perhaps the trees in Willisham are whispering to each other that Sara is safe in France, and asked them to pass it all the way back across the countryside, whispering to the waves in the channel, to tell me if I bothered to listen. What a childish, soppy thought.

I had always calculated on Prue. On her being young enough and fit enough to bring Sara and Charles up for me, for me and David. So I felt sick with anxiety when she disappeared. Had I misunderstood her, and her commitment to her family? Plenty of women of her generation don't want to have to start looking after a family all over again by bringing up their grandchildren. We live in selfish times.

But in fact that wasn't it at all.

She says she didn't write and explain to begin with because she thought the police might go through the house with a fine-tooth comb. Nor did she telephone, partly in case someone was here when I picked up the telephone. That was why she rang when she knew we would all be at church. Why she didn't think to ring at 2.00 a.m., as any normal person would, when there was bound to be nobody visiting, I have no idea. That's Prue for you. Though I suppose, if she had done that the day she disappeared Alison would have heard the telephone ring, and might have asked questions. Perhaps Prue was right after all. She does have an uncanny instinct, eccentric as she is.

She also thought it would be easier for me if I knew as little as possible about her whereabouts, so I wouldn't have to lie. What I didn't know, I couldn't tell. Though to be honest, I suspect much of it comes down to Prue's sense of adventure. Part of her, despite all the horror, was loving the drama of the situation.

The irony is that the story might have ended very differently if Prue had got there twenty minutes earlier. She went there with a solution, a peaceful, legal, watertight solution, to make Peter go away and leave us all alone. She was planning to cash all her immediate savings and set up a trust to buy him off, pay him to stay away, in effect. She'd thought it through at length. She wasn't going to give him a capital sum: then he would just blow it and come back. She was going to give him a modest salary – a thousand a month, something like that, if she could afford it – provided he never came within five miles of Sara. If she ever caught sight of him again the deal would be off. Her initial nest-egg, her available shares, would only last three or four years, but she thought it might be enough to buy Sara's peace of mind while we tried to think of something, while Sara grew up, even until the stalking act became law . . . which of course it did, a few months later. She was selling Sara's inheritance, money which might otherwise have paid for Sara's university fees for instance, but she reasoned, rightly, that Sara's freedom now would be far more important to her welfare than higher education later, or skiing trips, or a lavish gap year in Australia.

So she had gone into Cambridge, to the bank, that very morning and withdrawn two thousand in cash to whet his appetite. The whole scheme was so typical of Prue, so very much the kind of thing which Maurice would have seen how to talk her out of before she had even finished explaining it to him. But he wasn't there, and Prue didn't discuss it with anyone except her old friend in the City, Reg, who told her it was a madcap idea but she ought to sell the shares anyway. But by the time he rang her with her financial advice she had gone to see Peter with a cool two grand in her handbag, and rung the doorbell as if to ask him the time.

She was too late. She stood on the doorstep, feeling the money with her fingers as she did so. Because of my own experience, I can't imagine her there without smelling the fear, hearing the heart pumping loudly enough to drown out the sounds of the Fair, feeling the violent shaking of the hand in the handbag. But it won't have been like that at all: Prue has the unshakeable confidence of the aristocracy, the poise of Wycombe Abbey, which we middle-class girls, educated at Girls' Public Day School Trust insititutions, never quite pull off in the same way. And after all she wasn't doing anything wrong. It is surely crime itself, and the fear of detection, which is so terrifying.

Nobody answered the door. She rang again. And again. She suspected Peter was trying to avoid her, though he could never have known it was her. But she estimates it was a good five minutes or more before she looked through the window. There was a gap in the lace curtain, and she saw exactly what Graeme saw an hour or so later. Even through the corner of a net curtain, there is no mistaking a man with a twelve-bore through his face and daylight out the back. The murderer had got there before her.

So then she had to think quickly. She knew Peter hadn't killed himself, and assumed it would be as clear to the police as it was to her. She was eventually amazed to hear of their conclusions. Having been addicted for years to television quasi-documentaries about sophisticated modern policing, she also assumed there would be enough evidence of her visit, just from her ringing the doorbell, for the police to know she had been there. And there was the money. The first thing they would discover, if they were investigating a murder, was that she had been to the bank and withdrawn more money than she had ever taken out in her life before. And if they spoke to Reg before she tipped him off, they might also discover that she had been planning to pay Peter regularly, for nothing. Everything looked like blackmail. An obvious answer to blackmail, if the blackmailer turns the screws, is murder. Prue's mind, fed on a diet of Barbara Vine and Inspector Morse, leapt to all sorts of colourful conclusions.

She looked through the curtain one last time, and then walked smartly out of Alison's neat front garden to go home. She glimpsed a curtain twitching at the Bridges' window, and raised her hand to wave at them. She didn't know whether they had seen her, but if they had they certainly wouldn't think she was trying to cover up. This was her first mistake. The Bridges owe the St Josephs several decades of almost feudal loyalty. If Bob had seen Prue slink away, guiltily – or if she had spoken to him and asked him not to mention it – he would never have told the detective of her visit. As it was, he backed down as soon as he smelt a rat anyway.

As she walked, she wondered whether the murderer had tried to make it look like suicide. Jolly good luck to you too, she thought. And then, like the lousy chess player she is, she tried to consider all possible outcomes. Suppose, she said to herself, the police have no obvious suspect, and think Peter did away with himself. She didn't think this very likely, but on the other hand, Chief Inspector Parker, in the last Dorothy Sayers book she had read, had struck her as being particularly dim. If that was the way the investigations started to go, she didn't want to appear suspicious. In which case, what better than an extravagant holiday, decided on a whim, gadding about having a widow's fling? She had two thousand pounds in her handbag. Reg was virtually retired, and she had confided in him already. She could pick him up and whisk him off to some pretty little foreign farmhouse.

But the case might go very differently. The police might launch a murder enquiry. In which case, Prue wanted to act as decoy. She had no intention of letting them catch the real murderer. So then she would want to look as suspicious as possible. And every one knows that the first thing a guilty person does is run away. What could she do which could be interpreted as extreme innocence on the one hand, or blatant guilt on the other, depending on how she presented it?

It sounds a tall order – and given modern policing methods it was almost insane – but she opted for the dramatic disappearance. That way, she estimated that she could claim, if she wished, that she had taken some money out that morning to go on a spontaneous, romantic holiday with a friend. If the investigations went the other way, however, she would 'confess' that she had murdered him. In which case she had run away simply in order to run away.

Having solved the dilemma with this ridiculously simple plan, she went straight home, picked up her car without even going inside the house, and drove all the way to Reg's weekend cottage in Hertfordshire and told him she was taking him to France for a holiday. She told him everything. He wanted her to behave normally, ring home, tell us where we were, but she wouldn't have any of it. However, he did manage to prevent her ringing the offices of the *Cambridge Evening News* every morning to find out how the investigations were going.

Instead, Reg rang Gareth, the friend who had introduced him to Prue in the first place. He didn't tell Gareth he was with Prue. He simply said he wanted to be kept informed, for private reasons of his own. He also, incidentally, told Gareth not to tell anyone that he, Reg, had been in touch. I don't know what reason he gave. Typically, Gareth nearly let the cat out of the bag at his dinner party. No one else was likely to notice apart from me, and I didn't know what to make of it. After that, Reg thought Gareth might get suspicious, so then he telephoned another friend in the University, and said, more or less truthfully, that he was on holiday with a member of the family and wanted an update of the news on the 'Midland Enquiry' so he could break it to her gently. That was how he kept up to date with the police's progress. And that was why Prue came home the minute the inquest was over. When she was satisfied we were nearly out of danger, and incidentally had consumed more than enough Camembert and cheap red wine, she agreed to come home to England. Reg had known the way it was going to go for some time – his grapevine is very efficient – so they were back and staying at his cottage by the time of the inquest. But she refused to make an appearance in Willisham until everyone was in the clear.

She then asked me why I hadn't asked her to do it? After all, the children didn't really need her any more, and 'life', for a woman in her sixties, isn't so bad a deal. She even said that if she had gone to prison she could quietly have got on with all the reading she's been meaning to do for years – as if prison were a health farm, and she were the kind of person who could ever quietly get on with anything.

I thought her response was singularly unfair. Neither of us had told the other our plans. I like to think this was partly from unselfishness, on my part not wanting to implicate my mother-in-law in such a terrible crime. On hers, not wanting to look generous or give me the opportunity of trying to dissuade her from giving her savings away, as I certainly would have done. But perhaps this altruism was a mistake.

We have left undone those things which we ought to have done. In Prue's case, she feels that she herself should have solved the Peter problem. She wishes she had got there first, taken the initiative, been 'brave enough', as she puts it, to have implemented such a course of action.

But we have also done those things which we ought not to have done. I would give the world, pay any price, do any penance to swap my action for Prue's inaction. I have regretted it oh, so often, so bitterly, so terribly alone and racked as I have been, tormented with guilt in the middle of the night.

Prue believes that she should have done more.

But I. I have no such regrets. My sin was not one of negligence. Prue wishes she had killed him. I know that I should not have.

45

The sentence, of course, is life.

I know, I know: ten or fifteen years isn't much, if that's really all it is. I won't be that different. But Sara will be nearly thirty. Her teenage years, her GCSEs and A-levels, her first ball, her gap year, university – I had always imagined settling her into her rooms at university, as my parents did for me. Her first boyfriend, her first job. Charles's engagement and wedding and first child.

My grandson. By the time parole comes around he might be starting his prep school already. He wouldn't even know me. He might be six, eight years old, playing conkers, grazing his knees. And hardly knowing me at all.

I try to imagine it all. Tom, writing to Sara, tentatively at first, but with growing confidence. Sara being invited, with Charles, to visit his parents in South Africa next Easter. Summer holidays, blossoming romance, Tom and Charles at Oxford and Sara going to visit them at weekends and getting help with her A-level English.

Applying to Oxford herself, though not to my old college, not knowing what to wear for the interview, having no parent to take her out to celebrate her success; Tom staying on to do his D.Phil there so he can be near her; Charles getting his first job; eventually, three years on, Tom coming to visit me and asking, behind bullet-proof glass and in front of a grim-faced warden, whether he can ask my daughter, etc.

It's grotesque, the very idea of it. It's not what will be endured that frightens me, but what will be missed. Where will I be when Sara has blossom in her hair and a long white dress on and the lawns of Willisham are full of music and champagne, and Hugh has to give a speech in David's place, and Charles answers on behalf of the bridesmaids? Do they allow compassionate leave? Where will I be when Sara gives birth to her first baby, without her mother as well as her father because of what Peter did to her years ago. Her son having no granny to take him out to tea or treat him with cakes from Fitzbillies. Instead, being taunted by schoolmates and shunned by their mothers and ostracised in the class room because his grandmother is doing life for murder. What have I done to him? What have I done to them all?

David, I miss you so much, I don't know how I can go through it alone.

I always miss you, all the time. When, earlier in the summer, I was wandering about the garden or taking the children on an expedition, meeting funny parents from Langley House or having dinner with Sara and Charles and their lovely friend Tom. And now I consider the next ten years in prison, having a plate of very lumpy mashed potato and a burnt sausage and baked beans, with a crowd of other women, the noise not unlike the noise of squawking female voices in Hall at LMH – and oddly enough the food not that different either. Lying awake at night, listening to the pipes banging, and doors slamming, and the occasional shout or argument, and still feeling so alone.

All the time there's an ache in my side wanting to find you again. Now there's nothing else to do but to think of you. To wonder if you'll think I did the right thing. I always knew you would have found another solution, but God knows what it would have been. Yes, and I know too now. Too late. I must have known all along, and refused to think of it. I simply never believed prayer would be enough.

I don't really believe it now. Do you remember, when we were in Phulbari a young Australian girl came and asked me for advice. She was travelling around the world, and stopped off with us for a few days. She was terrified of being raped: it was the only thing in life that frightened her. Crossing Asia with a girlfriend and a rucksack had made her worry. Her question was this: if she prayed about it, would God keep her safe?

We couldn't give her the answer she wanted. God never promises us we won't be hurt, you said. You can pray, I said. In fact you must pray. But you might still get raped, or mugged or murdered.

All God promises is the strength to keep faithful. That's all he promised for Sara too. Which meant that all I could do was pray, and pray, and anticipate the torment. Is that really all you could have done, David, if you'd been here? And why do I say all? Perhaps that's everything.

Thinking of you has brought on my headache again; I always feel slightly under the weather now. Perhaps this experience will toughen me up a bit. Life with you was the good bit. Now I have to learn to face the bad.

46 ∫

I knew all along that the hardest part would be going to Graeme. He's always looked up to me, in his affectionate sort of way. How was I going to explain to him what I had done, make him arrest me, ask him to put a friend away for life? Sometimes I woke and sat up in the night, a cold sweat on my forehead, in the midst of the conversation I would have to have with him, trying to justify what I had done, trying to make him see the inevitability of my committing the worst crime there is.

I had no illusions about the field day that the papers would have: ex-missionary, jumped-up middle-class blue-stocking married into the aristocracy, all that sort of bilge. In the short term, this frightened me more than the thought of prison. They would tear away our defences, strip the family bare on the front page of every tabloid in the land, rape Sara's dignity and self-respect over and over again and then discard her a few days later, leaving her in tatters, screwed up in the bin or wrapped around the fish and chips, having humiliated her and destroyed her perhaps even more thoroughly than Peter himself. I didn't know whether they could do this, whether she would have any protection as a victim of sexual abuse, while the case was sub judice, but I knew people would find out somehow, and I feared it beyond reason or logic.

I also anticipated what it would do for the church: the doorstepping of unsophisticated members of the congregation, and then the weaving of wickedly cruel stories out of the most innocent remakrs, an artifical wedge of hatred driven between my family and the village we love, for ever.

Set against this would be the weekly prayer meeting organised by Hugh, specially for me, hardly deserving the dedicated prayers of the faithful. I'm not exactly a persecuted Christian: simply a common murderer awaiting my just deserts. And then, of course, the years and years of appeal, the women's groups, the feminists, claiming that I had been forced to kill Peter because of the patriarchal society around us which ignores the vulnerability of women and the way that we are raped by the system. I, longing to tell them to stop, leave me alone, allow me my guilt and my responsibility for it, and not rob me of my last bit of dignity as a human being, taking the appropriate punishment for my crime.

I talked to Prue about it first of all. Perhaps I should have started with Sara, since it was more her business than anyone else's, but she was in France, and I'm not sure that I could have brought myself to do it. It's interesting that I find Prue easier to talk to than my own parents. I love them, of course I do. But I don't feel close to them. With Prue, I share a faith, and Willisham, and a love of David. Whatever the reason anyway, it was she I talked to first.

Although she told me she knew what had happened, I didn't quite believe it. I didn't know how she would react to my spelling it out. The idea of confessing, making it public, frightened me even more than killing Peter. I thought of my freedom, which I love so much and which I knew would be taken from me the moment I opened my mouth. And I kept thinking of the sickening press coverage, the disillusion of those in the village, the horror in Sara and Charles when they realised what their mother had done. And my oh-so-respectable mother-in-law. Never again will she see me in the same light, the good Christian girl who was such a good choice for her son.

Nevertheless, I had it out with her. I told her exactly what I had done, down to every last detail. And I told her that I couldn't stand the deceit any more, that I was going to go to the police.

All hell broke loose. I always knew Prue to be a forceful character, to have a strong sense of right and wrong, but I had not anticipated her reaction, nor the half of it. As a result of that conversation I sit here, staring at the four walls of the prison I entered voluntarily. I spend the time writing it all up in a lined exercise book as Prue told me to, my only relief being the same little patch of tree and sky through my window, every day.

Prue said Willcox would want to know how I did it, which annoyed me. I said if he hadn't the brains to find out, I didn't see why I should tell him; I had no intention of explaining. If they didn't believe me, that suited me fine. Prue said they would call me obstructive. But I said, I was not obstructive: just very very tired.

Besides, it wasn't a clever murder, whatever the police might think. I didn't plan it at all. How could one plan a murder? The very idea is monstrous. That one could plot the destruction of another human being as if it were a mathematical puzzle.

Just after we were married, David and I went on holiday to Romania. We were taking two boxes of Romanian Bibles, sixty altogether, to the Christians in Romania; to a young baptist minister called Josef Tson. We were told he would be able to distribute them. We found his house at leisure during the daytime, as we were told to, then went away to return at night and ring his bell quickly and slip in unobserved. Not knowing, till he told us, that we would have been spotted within a hundred yards of the house any time of the day or night. His house was under constant surveillance, twenty-four hours a day. He was often in prison. I believe he's still in Romania, still preaching the Gospel, though presumably no longer endangering his freedom.

Before we left England, we had to decide how to take the Bibles over the border from Yugoslavia. We could have had something built into the car, a false boot, or a panel somewhere. They were unlikely to take our car to pieces. But David said no. God could keep us safe if he wanted to. And if he didn't want to, there was little point in making panels in the car.

It was unlike David. He was never one for asking God to do something he could do for himself. I remember him being very angry with a student once for praying for help in an exam, having done little to help himself.

He said this was different. There was no need to display the Bibles on the dashboard and force the customs to arrest us, but we shouldn't sneak into the country, either, as if we were doing something wrong. We were not breaking any official law. But then, the laws concerning Christians were seldom clearly advertised. That was the point. The government moved the goal posts every day. So we put the boxes in the boot, covered one with a blanket and another with a layer of groceries, and asked friends in England to pray us safely through the border. Whether they succeeded in praying Josef Tson safely through our bungled reconnaissance is another matter. For all we know the police may have raided his house the moment we left, and all the treasure stolen. And perhaps that was where it was supposed to be. Perhaps the Romanian police are still reading those Bibles.

The point of this long preamble is that we got in and out of the country all right. And we travelled with a clear conscience because of David's refusal to act like a thief.

Whenever I imagined killing Peter I used to remember that distant holiday. I had no idea how I could ever summon the courage, or how I would go about it. But I realised the only way I ever could, would be the most straightforward one. To go to the house with a shotgun and shoot him like a dangerous dog – like the dog which killed David. To kill him before he ruined any more lives, or any more of my daughter's life. After all, men have to do it in battle, with no personal quarrel with the man in front of them, simply because it's their duty. Whenever I fantasised about doing it, that was how I imagined it.

I had few problems with the justice of my cause. I suspected what he'd done to others like Sara, like Amanda, and I knew how many more wrecked lives I might save by doing what I had to do. Not that this was why I did it. I couldn't kill to save someone else's child. Or could I? Perhaps. But I couldn't go to prison for another woman's daughter when my own needs me so. It wasn't for them I dreamt of killing him. It was solely and simply for Sara. I believed, and perhaps still believe, that I served her better this way, even though she's not with me now for me to test this theory.

You see, I never thought he was making it up, when he'd fantasised about Sara. Sooner or later he would have done it again. If we could have waited a few more months, till the harassment law came into effect, it might have been all right. If Prue had got there before me, and woken him up, and given him the money and sent him away . . . If he had moved from Cambridge . . . If Sara had been older and stronger, if she hadn't been through it all before, if he had been threatening me instead . . . if, if and again if.

Though I doubt it. I still don't think there was any other way out. I knew Peter, you see. He was like a fox. Nothing would have stopped him.

He was a true sadist. Willcox said Peter was trying to care for the bird which was in his room, but I can't believe this. He must have been keeping it in order to pull its wings off. I think he got more kicks from giving pain than from anything else. I've wondered whether he half recognised my voice and wanted me to know what he felt about Sara, because he wanted me to feel the fear.

His method with the Samaritans was impressive. Our evidence would never have been enough to to pick him up, but if anything had come of it, and the involvement of the Samaritans had become public, all our credibility would have been gone. He had us in a cleft stick.

Oh, yes, Peter was clever. Unlike Prue, he would have made a superb chess player, if he had put his mind to it. The awesome thing about him was that something was missing. It was like a colour blindness, which he didn't realise was there: a moral blindness, perhaps. He said he loved Sara, he would conquer her, he would have her, and he seemed to think a twentieth-century girl deserved this kind of machismo, as if he could ravish her and carry her off as dashingly as Paris did Helen.

I had all this in my mind when I dwelt on the idea of killing him. I never thought I would do it, of course. But I used to indulge myself, thinking about it. And that was where I went wrong. I see that now. If you dream of committing a sin, if you gorge yourself with thoughts of how delicious that sin would be, you are well on the way to committing it. In a moment of weakness it will be much harder to resist.

I used to imagine going to his house in Cambridge. Perhaps it would have been easier if I had. Then I would have met him face to face, alive and well, and confronted him with what he'd done to all our lives. Robbed Sara of her childhood, her first tentative teenaged kisses, her tiptoed excitement into love; robbed Charles, perhaps, of the certain faith he had as a child; robbed David of his life, in the end. But I could never have killed him like that: like an act of vengeance out of a Jacobean drama. I could never have gone through with it if it had been genuinely premeditated.

Instead, he landed in my lap, as it were. He turned up, on that day of the Fair, and I knew he was alone in Alison's cottage, while everyone else was at the Fair and nobody would be around. I felt drunk with fear. It was as if I had fallen into a lake and was operating underwater, where different rules of physics apply. Should I cancel my opening of the Fair in order to protect Sara? Should I tell Graeme of the attack which was about to happen? Should I carry a gun around with me in case he appeared unexpectedly? Should I go and see him, and tell him to leave the village? Should I threaten to shoot him if he wouldn't go? Then, if he didn't go, should I indeed shoot him?

And suddenly the urge was there. I could do it. I hardly knew where I was, or what I was doing. But provided I did it there and then, without thinking about it, I knew that now I might do it, pat. Even when I went to the cottage with the shotgun I knew it would either happen or it wouldn't, it would either fall into place, or something would happen to prevent it.

I had prayed about it: of course I had. I'm not completely stupid. Over and over again, specially over the last few months, I had begged God to tell me what to do. Sometimes I got confused, as I did when David was dying, and forgot whether I was talking to God or David. I still do. I forget whether I'm praying, or chatting to a friend I lost once, as if he were still there beside me. But always, on my knees at church, at the end of the morning service, I asked God the same question. I had failed to protect Sara once: what was I to do now?

And always He gave the same answer, the same deafening answer, over the sound of Jill, struggling with Bach or Widor or the syncopated bars of Graham Kendrick on our rather inadequate organ. The same answer that he gave Elijah, over the earthquake, wind and fire. The voice of a still small silence. A thunderous nothing. Go and work it out for yourself.

Why not? David would have said. Why should He speak again, when He's spoken already? He didn't need to speak to Elijah: the old covenant was still valid. He didn't need to speak to me: the old commandment was still there. Thou shalt not kill.

A minute or two after I left the house to go to the Fair with Sara, just before two o'clock, I realised I had left my gloves behind and went back for them. As I walked back to the house, I thought furiously. I kept envisaging Peter only a few hundred yards away. When I got home I picked up the key to Alison's cottage almost without thinking about it. I didn't even know whether I would use it, as I hadn't planned what to do. It was as if I were operating in a daze. I simply collected the key to Peter's death from my own kitchen, and joined Sara again a minute later. I tucked it into my shoe, and forgot about it.

Then I went and opened the Fair and did my turn on the church stall. I felt more sick and sweaty than I've ever been in my life. Though I have experienced far worse since. Night after night, through this terrible, guilt-ridden summer. And all the time I was strangely detatched from myself, working on automatic pilot, almost watching myself, wondering what I was going to do next.

When Diana asked me to join her for tea I thought I'd missed my chance, and the relief was overwhelming. I thanked God over and over again for His intervention, for the fact that He had stopped me in time. Then I saw the size of the queue in the tent, and realised that He hadn't stopped me. I got up rather shakily, leaving my chiffon scarf and bag on a table outside, just out of view of the queue, and walked straight back to the house, a couple of minutes' away. If Diana had got back to our table with our cups of tea before I had finished killing him, before I returned, I would simply have told her I'd wanted the loo, which was quite true. But then I would have lost my alibi.

Funnily enough I didn't tell a single lie throughout the whole enquiry. Though to be fair, that was more sleight of hand than honesty, since I've deceived people from beginning to end.

I went home, and found the gun room door open. I was taken aback, and for a dreadful moment thought someone must have anticipated me. Then I remembered Geoff, and assumed, as the police did after me, that he must have failed to shut the door properly after collecting the basher. Geoff himself can't now remember whether he shut it or not; he feels frightfully guilty and has apologised dozens of times. The poor boy will never leave a door open again, I'm sure.

I unlocked the gun cupboard, took one of the twelve-bores, and locked it up again afterwards. I was going to lock the apple shed properly on my way out, but something stopped me.

It wasn't until I was picking the flowers for Alison's bedroom and saw the door ajar again, as if for the first time, that I realised the significance of it. Geoff did me far more of a favour than he will ever know.

My bicycle was leaning against the wall outside the apple shed. I put a couple of cartridges in the basket, hitched my long skirt up over my left arm, held the shotgun in my right hand, and bicycled precariously down the lane to the cottages. It was not good safety procedure, but it probably gained me several minutes, and made my alibi, which was already quite good enough, almost unbreakable. No one could have left the tea queue, picked up a gun, walked to Alison's cottage and shot a man, and then walked all the way back to the queue again, in less time than it takes to buy a cup of tea. I thought, when I took my skirt off the washing line, that it had bicycle grease on it, which would have given the whole game away. In fact it was only a twig which had got snagged on the hem.

When I got to Alison's cottage there was nobody around. Or so I thought. But as I stood at the porch I saw Bob Bridge's legs, as he sunbathed in his deckchair in the sun in his garden. He must have been almost the only member of the village who was not at the fair. I couldn't see his face but I realised he must be asleep. When I strained to listen I could hear him snoring gently. I wondered whether he would wake when I knocked on the door.

I loaded the gun with both cartridges, took off the safety catch, and knocked. There was no answer. Peter didn't come to the door. For a moment I thought, deliriously lightheaded, that he wasn't in the house after all. I wouldn't be able to kill him. Then I looked through Alison's front window: there was a corner where the net didn't meet the frame. I stared. Peter seemed to be asleep in front of the television. I could kill him without waking him and I wouldn't have to confront him. Indeed, I would never have to confront him again, never talk to him, never take another Samaritan call like the one I had had to listen to, never have to lie awake all night worrying how on earth I was going to protect my daughter from terror and madness. I was to lie awake with far worse fears than any I had experienced before, but I didn't think about them then.

But how was I to get in? It sounds unbelievable, but I had forgotten about the front door key. I was in such a panic it had slipped my mind. But as I walked back to Alison's doorstep from the window I felt it under my toes, tucked into my old canvas tennis shoe. I kicked off both my shoes and left them outside.

Luckily. When the police took them away, there was no forensic link with Peter's death.

I fumbled to pick up the key with my damp and now very grimy cotton gloves, worrying all the time that my gun might go off by mistake. Then I put the key in the door, let myself in, and went into Alison's front room. He was snoring loudly, with his mouth open, and an empty six-pack beside him on the table. I remember being amazed that anyone could drink so much. Then, as gently and speedily as I knew how, I crouched down in front of him, put the muzzle in front of his open mouth, pointing up towards the ceiling, and shot before I could think about what I was doing.

A split second before I pulled, I saw the worst thing I have ever seen in my life. He opened his eyes. I don't know why: I didn't touch him. The muzzle of the gun was an inch away from his lips. I didn't have time to stop my finger, and I didn't have time to think. And yet it seemed to take for ever. He looked at me, realised what was happening, and then he was gone. If I had hesitated for even half a moment none of it would have happened. I couldn't have killed him, and he would never have let me. Not in that way, anyway, in a way which looked like suicide. I suppose I could have threatened him and told him to sit down and open his mouth and reassured him I just wanted to talk to him – and then killed him anyway. But I wouldn't have had the strength of character for this.

I was immediately filled with an almost irresistible urge to pull the second trigger. I was terrified that he would snatch the gun and turn on me, and I wanted to make sure he was dead. But I said to myself, over and over again, Don't, don't do it, don't pull. It's over, it's finished, it's done.

I stared at his open, empty eyes. I couldn't believe what had happened. It seemed to me that I stayed there a long time, trying to take it in. God had given this man a life. Alison, a mere schoolgirl of seventeen, had refused to kill him when she could have done so, legally, before he was born, and had given up more than half her life so he could breathe and eat and love and sleep. He was a creature of infinite value, priceless to his Maker. In less time than it takes to draw a breath, I had blown him away, destroyed him, done such a terrible thing to one of God's children that another lifetime could not make up for it. For the first time in my life I

realised the aptness of the death penalty. Judicial death was the
only answer to what I had just done.

Oddly, I didn't see any of the mess I had made. That came as a
real shock the next day.

I picked up one of his hands gently. It was not like David's.
Peter's hands were warm, as if he were still alive. My hopes
soared wildly: perhaps he was. I looked at his face, and wondered
whether, despite the fact that half his head was missing, he
perhaps wasn't dead at all. I put his right hand on the gun, as
if to steady it, and his left thumb on the trigger. I remembered
that he was left-handed. I also remembered reading somewhere
that this doesn't matter much. Though it will be incriminating,
I thought, when the police are looking for the murderer. Only
someone who knew him would know he was left-handed.

Then I rested my fingers on the cheek of his face. Through my
thin gloves I could feel that his cheek, too, was warm.

When I left the television blared on.

I didn't really know why I put his hands on the gun. I didn't
know why I was doing anything. I must have hoped, at the back of
my mind, that I might get away with it. I must have thought there
was one chance in ten thousand that the police might think it was
suicide.

As I went out of the house I realised that Bob was no longer
there, though his front door was open. I could hear him talking
loudly inside his house. No one replied. He must have been on the
telephone. I assumed he had heard the shot and was ringing the
police. In fact this was not the case at all: his daughter had rung
from New Zealand, and it was the sound of the telephone which
had woken him up. He has an extra loud bell because he and his
wife are so hard of hearing. The call enabled the police to time
Peter's death. For a long time Bob insisted that there had been no
shot at all, but in the end he admitted that he might have heard a
car backfiring while he was talking to his daughter.

I wasn't as frightened as I thought I would be, nor as I had been
before I killed him. Initially I felt a great sense of release. Bob
hadn't seen me. Perhaps he wouldn't know who'd killed Peter.
My bicycle was out of sight of his garden, the other side of Alison's
wall. I slipped my shoes back on, got on my bicycle, left it back at
home, and went back to the Fair, back to my chair in the sun, back

to waiting for my cup of tea. I had been less than fifteen minutes. It might even have been more like ten. It was extraordinary. I had been through the wardrobe, into another country with quite a different timescale, and lived a lifetime there. Murder was part of the other land, a faerie land where battles are fought and a man can be killed in the cause of justice. I had been there for years, surely, and aged beyond recognition, and become quite a different person.

But when I stepped back an age later, through the wardrobe into the sunshine and back to the potted jams, only a few minutes had passed after all. Diana was still queuing, and the people at the next table hardly noticed I'd gone. I looked down at my gloves, expecting to see them red with blood, and they were as white as they had been and shaking. Then, as if for the first time, I realised what I'd done: I shut my eyes, and saw Alison's only child as I had left him.

It was some time afterwards that I made the telephone call. I couldn't have let Alison find him. Not in that condition. I had to make sure the police would get there before she could.

I did it when I was helping Pat and John with their stall. I needed the loo anyway, so I excused myself and went to the Portaloos which had been put there for the Fair. They had queues of twenty or thirty people, sticky children, elderly ladies, so I abandoned the idea and left the paddock to go to the telephone box in the lane which I've hardly ever seen used. Presumably nobody saw me, or the police would have put two and two together.

I rang nine nine nine because I couldn't remember the number of the Willisham Police Station, because I didn't want to waste time on Directory Enquiries, because I knew Graeme wasn't there so my call would have been diverted anyway, and also, I suppose, because I didn't want to run any risk of speaking to him in case he recognised my voice. He wouldn't have mistaken it for a man's voice, as many people do over the telephone when I first start speaking – as Cambridge police station did. He would have known me straight away.

I simply told an anonymous policeman that I had heard a shot coming from Alison's house and I thought they should investigate. That was all. Then I hung up and went back to the stall and told Pat that the loos were too full and I couldn't be bothered to queue. Which was true.

I would have done anything to postpone Alison's discovery. Not just because I wanted the police to get there first. Also because I didn't want her to know, ever. I wanted to put it off as long as I could, just as I did to myself that afternoon, three years and many more thousands of miles away. But I couldn't see how to do that without arousing suspicion, so from then on I just let events take their course.

I doubt if she could ever understand. I could hardly expect her to.

It's quite a gift she has, for not seeing what she doesn't want to see. She never seemed to connect us with the troubles Peter had to go through. She never blamed us, as most doting mothers would have done. I honestly don't think she pointed the finger at us at all: she refused to blame us for going to the police eight years ago. I wonder if it would be possible for her to do the same over this. I'm beginning to realise Alison has quite a knack for kindness and forgiveness, more than I could ever have, as well as for ignoring the ugly side of life.

I hope Sara will understand, and realise it's in no way her fault. She still doesn't know yet. She's camping somewhere now, still in France, and Prue says she can't trace her. I have questioned within myself whether that is deliberate on Prue's part. Once or twice I wondered whether Sara had guessed. A few days after he died she started to ask me how it happened, then went silent and didn't say any more.

I would so love to keep it from her. She is recovering, unbelievably well, and I long to keep it that way. But if she knows what really happened to Peter I sometimes wonder whether all her recovery will go for nothing.

It was Prue's idea that Charles should go to stay with Tom's parents in South Africa, just for a few weeks until the beginning of term. Would Tom's parents be horrified at the company his son is keeping at Eton, if they knew? Perhaps, living where they do, they might be more likely to give me the benefit of the doubt and assume the issue is more complex than it seems. Anyway, Prue said Charles needed to go with Tom and see a spot of wildlife, to observe a few creatures who kill as a matter of course, lionesses who fight to the death for their cubs. 'Then,' she said, 'you'll know where your mother's coming from.'

'I know already,' Charles said rather tartly, but agreed to the trip anyway.

He was angry with me for coming here, and kept asking why I'd left Willisham, allowed myself to come here voluntarily.

'It wasn't exactly voluntary,' I pointed out.

'Yes it was,' he insisted. 'Nobody knew. Why did you have to tell?'

'Apart from anything else,' I said, 'I couldn't bear having such a secret from you.'

I thought I was going to become dangerously emotional, so I turned away. When I looked back I caught Charles looking rather embarrassed. The most valuable lesson I've learnt here so far is to value my family even more. I hope that was what Prue wanted.

As I said, it was she who told me to write this account. The funny thing is that until today I found I was writing it as if the prosecuting counsel were reading every word over my shoulder. Despite the desperate need to confess, I found I still didn't want to say anything incriminating, in case a hostile lawyer got hold of it. It was all true, of course: I couldn't write anything to myself which wasn't. It wasn't the whole truth, that's the trouble.

But I can't be bothered with that any more. It's so wearing, all this deceit. I wouldn't be able to hide anything in court, so what's the point of hiding it now? If that's the kind of thing to distress some smart pin-striped barrister hauled in by Reg trying to help me 'get off', well, I'm sorry, that's all: and I shall just have to hope and trust that this diary never comes to the attention of any such barristers.

At one point Charles said to me, very gently, as though he were talking to a child, 'Mother, please try to explain your urge to go to the police. I can't understand it.'

As I looked at Charles's young, earnestly pleading face, I wanted to explain – but I'm not sure I understand either. At one point I thought I wanted to confess because all the evidence seemed to be pointing to Sara. Though when the verdict was brought in I didn't need to worry about that any more.

One of the worst moments I went through was when Margaret wanted to tell the police about Jim's threat to kill Peter, and his missing the Fair. I don't suppose for a moment that he would have been found guilty. By and large, the British police tend to avoid nailing the wrong man. But that wasn't the point. A wrongful arrest would have put Margaret's family through hell. Jim was innocent, but there might have been quite enough circumstantial evidence to have given them a rough few months. Their daughter had been raped. The last thing they needed was for Jim to be accused of murder. If that had happened, I would have had no choice but to confess.

Even when that danger passed, the longing to confess remained. Murder is wrong, very wrong, and I knew that when I did it. I couldn't live with my conscience, with such a terrible crime unshriven. Justice demands to be satisfied. If I could learn to live comfortably with the memory of this, perhaps I should find myself sharing my life with myriad other evils. It's hardly a good example for those who live around me. I know God can forgive murder, even this murder that I can't wish undone. But I can't see why He should forgive me for sneaking around without taking my punishment just because I haven't the guts to face the music. After all, we tell children to own up, even if it hurts at the time.

Besides, I was on oath.

Funnily enough, I realised at the inquest that I could have avoided the oath. Graeme did. I noticed then that he said the Affirmation instead. I asked him about it afterwards. It struck me as odd at the time, the Christian policeman being the one to refuse to swear by Almighty God, but when he explained it, it made perfect sense. Do not swear by anything in heaven or on earth or under the heavens, but let your yea be yea and your nay be nay. So it wouldn't have made any difference, even if I had sworn 'solemnly', rather than by Almighty God with my hand on the Bible. I would still have had to keep my promise.

I know one can learn to live anywhere, in a nutshell – *on peut s'accoutumer à tout*. I don't know if I've got that right either. But I keep thinking of my lovely Sara, and the day she turns sweet sixteen, and perhaps the day she falls in love, even with Tom, and her wedding day, and her first little baby. And its first few hours and days in the daylight, and its proud father, and all the things I so longed to share with them, the things for which I kept myself alive after David's death. And his first nappies, and his first steps, and his first few words which will never be heard between the mustard-coloured walls of this grim place.

I see Willisham House empty of grandchildren, and the nursery sitting vacant, and no sound of running and laughing and crying down the corridors in the sun, where the motes of dust play in the sunbeams for those with eyes low enough to see. And the blackberries rotting in the sun, with nobody there to pick them. And no one there to make a chocolate cake for the next birthday to come around. Perhaps the next time it would have had blue icing on it, instead of pink. And the old rag doll in the top bunk bed which heard such terrible secrets, with nobody to hug it and pull it about now that the secrets have at last been exorcised.

I try to imagine Prue's going back there, with Sara and Charles, and using the place in my absence, and having Christmas there without me – though somehow I can't envisage this. The Dower House is cosier, with no dreadful memories, and quite big enough for three.

At first, when I talked to Prue, I couldn't help entertaining a tiny flicker of hope that a judge might see my point of view. That he might consider the circumstances to be mitigating, and that the pressure we were under was intolerable. That I might perhaps get five years or so – out in two or three. Prue snorted disdainfully, and repeated this to Reg, who was completely silent for several minutes, and then said, 'No. No, I don't think so. I don't think there would be much chance of that.' I suppose it's fair enough. The circumstances aren't as mitigating as they are for plenty of other murders, with those who've lived with drugs and violence and prostitution and goodness knows what. And the judge we face in court is usually male, after all. As David said, how can a mere man understand the terror of Peter's tyranny?

Prue told Reg straight away. She said he would be discretion itself, and she wanted him to advise me, as I wasn't listening to her. I hope she's right about him. She usually is, about most things.

David, I miss you more every minute. All I seem to want (not all, but it seems that way) is your arms around me, as they were so long ago now that I can't remember how it felt, and your warm back against mine at night, and your awful temper that night when I backed the car into your parents' gateway yet again. D'you know, I haven't done it since you haven't been there to mind? If only you could be cross with me once more! And your kind eyes above your half-moon spectacles, which you would have worn in a few years' time, asking Tom if he could look after her in the manner in which, etc. I want you to look after me, and tell me how to put up with my life sentence, and lecture me on how I should be brave and use the time and read books and talk to people, and how there are plenty of things to be thankful for, and it'll all pass very quickly really.

Much of the time, if I'm honest, I don't want this at all: I don't want consolations, and a sensible silence telling me how to cope. I want the old punishments to come back, when murder was murder and the only answer was hanging. I want to leave it all behind me, leave Sara and Charles and Prue, even Alison too, having done the best I could for them all, and go on to the place where He really will wipe every tear from our eyes. See you again.

He can't be right, Marvell, can he? The grave's a fine and private place, But none, I think, do there embrace. Tell me he's wrong. Tell me he simply put down the first decent rhyme he could think of, to amuse his girlfriend into going to bed with him. I know, I know the correct theological answer: there's no marriage in heaven. Then have we really made love for the last time, you and I? Is there not even that any more? I know heaven must be the best place ever, but, like Sara, I'd rather it came here.

A private place. The grave has nothing fine about it at all. But that's not where David is now. He's in the most public place there ever was and ever will be, where there's no darkness, no secrets any more, and a crowd no one can number. Rather as we'd planned it to be in Willisham one day, with the House always full. It was never meant to be a private place either.

And now at last I'll admit it: I'm really cheating here. I've got my fingers crossed. I wanted to confess in order to make it look to myself, and to God, as if I'd repented of what I'd done, as if I were really sorry. But I'm not. When I think of Sara free, running across Willisham lawn light and happy, her hair soft and beautiful in the sun and the breeze, I'd be sorry not to be there, oh yes. I'd be sorry, in that sense, to be punished for what I did to Peter. But I'm not sorry I killed him. Not at all. I don't wish him alive again, and Sara like a lump of chewing gum in a mental hospital somewhere. I can take the punishment, but I can't repent. I can't wish I'd never done it.

Does this mean I can't be forgiven? I don't think it does, but I've not yet worked out why not. Somehow I know God can still love me, despite this technical theological hitch. David would tell me I'm hopeless for allowing such sloppy thinking. But somehow I know God's still there, in the terrible, thundering silence, when even David's presence seems too long ago to remember. Somehow I know, when I cry myself to sleep, that one day He'll wipe my eyes too.

It's the middle of August. I've been here for ten days, and it seems like as many years.

Epilogue

Springtime in Willisham House. Only a few weeks till Sara is sixteen. Tom and Charles coming for Easter, and I so happy I could cry.

I finished my journal just after the August Bank Holiday, and Sara came home from France three days before the beginning of term. It wasn't long enough for us to be together, but we found time over that term to talk, and be silent, and just be.

Prue said I could come home after I'd finished writing the account. She said I'd done sufficient penance. I believe she underestimated this by several years – if not a lifetime – but I was too tired to argue, and Prue can be overwhelming when she gets the bit between her teeth. Besides, she had Reg and Hugh on her side, not to mention Charles, and most powerfully, though silently, Sara herself.

They all told me I was not to take it any further.

I suppose, from that point of view, Prue's little plan worked very well. She was trying to get me to see other points of view. That there is no such thing as perfect justice on this earth; Sara, for instance, didn't deserve the life sentence of having her mother in prison.

I had become obsessed with my confession. I talked to Prue about it all the time, said I couldn't live with myself, would be no use to my children if I couldn't come clean. To begin with she simply told me I was an idiot, and I was not to do anything. But then she realised it was not as simple as that. I could no longer think clearly, I was like a man in the desert who sees a mirage, or a sex-starved nyphomaniac caught in the grip of an absurd lust. I couldn't rest until I had told someone, everyone, and she could see that sooner or later I could blurt it out anyway.

So she booked the tiniest, most remote country cottage she could find, miles away from any public transport, and drove me there. She bought me plenty of food, exercise books, and biros, and told me I was not allowed out until the whole story was down on paper. For appearances' sake, she went back to Willisham once she was convinced I would do as I was told. Charles visited me a couple of times, but Sara was still in France and knew nothing about it.

I wasn't even allowed outside. She said if I wanted a prison regime I could jolly well have one. The thing I missed most was books. The cottage had half a dozen *Reader's Digests*, and that was about it. The next time she visited me I insisted I should at least have a Bible and complete Shakespeare, and she, entering into the spirit of the enterprise with typical Prue-like enthusiasm, told me I could wait my turn, as someone else had them out of the prison library, and I might be allowed one or the other in a week or two.

I was there for three weeks, and it seemed an eternity. Just when I thought I'd finished, she told me I had to write up the next ten years, as it might happen if I really were to confess, and, though I couldn't put my heart into it, at last that brought reality home to me.

That was when I saw her point, and saw it for myself. Sara, as always, would be the vulnerable one. My confession might destroy her. She still hasn't been told, and Prue says she isn't to be until the time is right. If ever. I said I thought she'd guessed, and Prue said guessing is very different from having it spelt out. If you guess, you can feed yourself little bits of the truth as and when you can take it. If you are told, it happens like an explosion. Surprisingly poetic, for Prue.

She is going to put my journal under lock and key, and might, just might, give it to Sara one day.

A day or two after I got home again, there was a case in the papers of another girl, in Scotland, who was the victim of a stalker. She ran him over with her car and killed him, and had just been acquitted in court, that day. 'There you are,' I said to Prue, though not believing it any more. 'It does pay to be honest and go to the police.'

She told me not to be so bloody ridiculous. This girl had been lunged at with a knife, and, in self-defence, had put her foot down on the accelerator. Rather different from the malice aforethought necessary to leave a polite summer afternoon village Fair with a twelve-bore hidden in your knickers, said Prue. 'Which reminds me,' she went on. 'How did you hide that shotgun?'

'I didn't,' I said, puzzled.

'What do you mean, you didn't?' Prue insisted. 'You had to walk from the house all the way down to the cottages. All right, bike then; whatever you did. You can hardly have tucked a twelve-bore into the cuff of your blouse, like exam notes.'

'I just carried it,' I said. 'Why on earth should I hide it?'

'Because somebody might ask you what you were doing? Because it might be thought eccentric to wander about the village Fair as if you were at a shooting party? Because it's just possible that some bright spark might have put one and one together, and, when asked by the police if he had seen anything unusual, might have scratched his peasant's pate long and hard and eventually said, "Well, you know, it's an odd thing, officer, and I don't suppose for a moment that it's relevant, but I did see Mrs St Joseph wandering about with a loaded shotgun a few minutes before a shot was fired in Alison's house and Peter blasted to Kingdom Come, and it's remotely possible that there might be some connection."'

'Which just shows,' I said, 'that you should have done it. You would have thought all these things through. Prue, I was too frightened to hide anything. If I'd bumped into anyone it would have been a perfect excuse not to go through with it.'

'You are the most useless murderer I have ever come across. If you'd asked me I would have done it. And far more sensible it would have been, too. I haven't got half so much to lose. No children, for one thing.'

'You have grandchildren,' I started.

'Just shut up a minute, will you,' she continued, 'and think of those children. You have some daft idea you might be acquitted, like this other lassie. If so, you need your head examined: you don't stand a chance, my dear, let me tell you. I've sat on the bench for years, and the public hates toffs like us. You would be a jury's most loved target of all the year. And Fleet Street's. But let's just assume, for the sake of argument, that you get an idiotic jury, a blind judge, and the biggest stroke of luck since Crippen nearly got away.

'What do you think the press would do? Say, "This woman has a fifteen-year-old daughter who has suffered enough, so we'll go away quietly and not tell a soul"? Harriet, wake up! Your life sentence wouldn't begin to compare with what she would go through. Being the daughter of a convicted murderer. Who did it because she, Sara, had been raped as a child. Your duty is to your children. It always was and always will be. Mine is to David. He's no longer here to stop you doing foolhardy things, so it's down to me. You promised to obey him, and this is what he would have said: *You are not to go to the police.*'

It was true. It's exactly what David would have said. He wouldn't have let me kill Peter. But nor would he have let me confess to it afterwards. I still wanted to try for a compromise, though. 'Let me tell Graeme,' I said, 'and see whether he wants to take it further.'

'What, and ruin his career and land him in prison too when it all comes out, for being an accessory after the fact and not turning you in? Sometimes, Harriet, I can't believe how stupid an intelligent woman can be. If you must go to the police, at least be a little more sensitive, and unselfish, and go to someone at the top. What are you trying to do? Make it Graeme's guilt and crime, not yours? From the moment he knows, he has an absolute duty to report it. If that conflicts with his duty to you as a friend and fellow member of his church, that's tough. He'd have to report you, and he'd never forgive himself. If he doesn't, he's guilty of a serious crime. Really, darling, how old are you?'

I marvelled yet again at the misfortune which had cast me as Peter's executioner, rather than my mother-in-law. She would have coped with it with ease. I felt the time had almost come to submit. What made a difference was trying to see it from Sara's point of view. Yet again it seems that everything I've done has been from selfish motives. Did she really want Peter dead? Or wouldn't she rather have found the strength to cope with his persecution, to have learnt self-defence and police-approved tactics and fought him off in her own way? I was trying to compensate for David, and that was a sinful thing to do.

I treasure life so much more than I ever did. It isn't that I've stopped missing David, but I've found a contentment I'd never known in my life before. I shall always feel terrible guilt: I'll never be free of that. But, apart from peace of mind, I really do have everything. My children, their health, enough wealth to give them everything they need or want, and David's company to look forward to in heaven. And, here on earth, the most beautiful house in England, full of David's spirit and his memories and his childhood and his ancestors.

Alison has amazed me. I often wondered whether she found what Peter did to Sara almost as hard to come to terms with as we did, and couldn't forgive Peter either. But I now think it more likely that she dealt with it, and forgave him, and there was no unresolved business between them. Otherwise how could she have coped with his death with such bravery and fortitude? What I do now realise is that I always underestimated her. She has far more resources than I have, after all. She has hidden waters running deep, which I will never fathom.

She is also now engaged to be married.

Richard, his name is, and he is a carpenter from Cambridge. She met him at last year's Fair, apparently, and none of us knew. He was very supportive of her afterwards, and she is starting a new life. Hugh is marrying them in midsummer, and the reception will be at Willisham House. I offered to pay for it, as our wedding present to her, and to her everlasting credit she accepted. Not in a manner that suggest I owed her anything, but simply in the way of accepting a gift.

But I'm straying from the point, and I no longer have any desire for detailed, cathartic descriptions. Writing it helped me understand myself far better, as Prue had intended it to. The night after I came home, when Sara and Charles were back and before term started, Hugh and Tricia organised a quiet welcome home for all of us in the vicarage. Diana and Gareth – who don't know what happened, of course, but were told I'd been away 'for a much-needed break' – laid on some champagne, though all I wanted was a cup of tea but I drank the champagne because I was expected to, and Prue was predictable for the first time in her life, and came with Reg. It won't come to anything, I know, but it's fun to see her with him anyway.

And Tom was there. Ostensibly with Charles. But at one point in the evening I went into the kitchen, where the teenagers were, and I saw him holding Sara's hand for a second – I'm sure I did.

I can hear her bike on the gravel. She is home from school. I won't write this diary any more. I shall be busy enough simply living.

I, my family, and my freedom.